HURON COUNTY LIBRARY
3 6492 00461226 0

D1376640

THE DEVIL'S HANDSHAKE

THE DEVIL'S HANDSHAKE

MURRAY DAVIES

MACMILLAN

First published 2002 by Macmillan
an imprint of Pan Macmillan Ltd
Pan Macmillan, 20 New Wharf Road, London N1 9RR
Basingstoke and Oxford
Associated companies throughout the world
www.panmacmillan.com

ISBN 0 333 90843 0

1 3 5 7 9 8 6 4 2

A CIP catalogue record for this book is available from the British Library.

Typeset by SetSystems Ltd, Saffron Walden, Essex
Printed and bound in Great Britain by
Mackays of Chatham plc, Chatham, Kent

Ihr Geist lebt weiter.

(Their spirit lives on)

Acknowledgements

I would like to offer warm thanks to David Harper for sharing his unrivalled knowledge of Obersalzberg in the Nazi era; Frau Ingrid Scharfenberg, daughter of Therese Schuster and current owner of the Hotel zum Türken; the staff of the reading room of the Imperial War Museum, Sir Geoffrey Chandler, Roger Todd and others both in Germany and Britain who prefer to remain anonymous.

Interlude

The train gave a final judder and settled in a hiss of steam. The man called Christian Beck remained seated for a moment, thinking that the station seemed surprisingly large for a small market town. He took a deep breath, as if nerving himself for what was to come, then lifted his valise down from the luggage rack, feeling the scar tissue pull against his chest. He inspected the platform with quick, almost furtive glances. His fellow passengers, most of them in army or air force uniform in this, the fourth year of the war, were tumbling out into the arms of smiling, waving wives, girlfriends and mothers. The surging wave broke up into tight, hugging knots. Then slowly, arms woven around one another, heads close, sharing secrets of reunion, they drifted out of the station.

Beck was alone – but then, Beck had no one to meet him.

He transferred his walking stick to his right hand and limped to the buffet, where a handful of soldiers, their kitbags and rifles piled in the corner, were chewing on bread rolls and drinking from chipped mugs. A plump mother in black, her eyes leaking tears, was fussing over her teenage son in his new uniform. He swatted away her hands, embarrassed at her attentions in front of the seasoned veterans. *Walls Have Ears* warned one poster, while another urged people to eat less bread. Beck bought a pressed-meat roll and a hot mug of what passed for coffee from a jolly woman volunteer. Through the window, he watched the returning servicemen and their welcoming families climb onto a ramshackle old bus. Others had already set off arm in arm in an untidy crocodile towards the town.

Beck chewed as slowly as possible, delaying the moment when he would have to go out into the dismal March afternoon. Finally, he finished the roll and pulled a face at the last cold dregs of the coffee.

He could not put it off any longer. Time to go out into the rain. Time to go – where?

The scenery was spectacular, he'd been told, but sheets of rain hid the hills, tattered wraiths of white cloud fleeing beneath the threatening sky. Beck found it intensely depressing. Across the road, two rivers met, their translucent green waters tumbling in a white-flecked torrent. An ancient steam tractor clanked past a tired farm horse, its wet flanks steaming as it hauled a cart heavy with timber. A stooped man, his head hidden under a potato sack, walked beside the horse's head.

In the station yard, a sergeant in a leather jerkin was tunelessly humming a popular song as he fastened the tailgate on his lorry.

Beck hailed him. 'Do you know of an inn, or a small hotel, that's open around here, sergeant?'

'You'll be lucky, sir. The small ones have been closed for the duration and the posh ones are full of top brass, if you understand.'

'Oh.' Beck shifted his weight onto his walking stick.

The sergeant caught sight of Beck's insignia and his face split into a grin. 'My kid brother's in your mob, sir. He went through Tobruk and Alamein without a scratch but now we've not heard from him for a month or so.'

'He'll be fine. You'd have been notified if anything had happened to him.' Beck turned away, wondering what to do next.

The sergeant nipped the end off his cigarette and put the butt in his top pocket. 'There is one place still open,' he said slowly. 'But whether they'll take you . . .'

'Why?'

'It's not bad, if that's what you're thinking. I'll give you a lift there.'

Beck climbed awkwardly into the cab and pulled his damp greatcoat around him. The ghostly reflection of his face, etched with tears of rain, looked back at him from the side window. The lorry was reluctant to start. On the third attempt, with a crash of gears that made Beck wince, they pulled out of the station yard. The solitary wiper swished ineffectually and Beck hoped the sergeant could see more through the windscreen than he could. They drove past a huddle of women waiting outside a food shop. The glistening roofs of the town rose above them on the left; on the right, they passed two sentries standing to attention outside a guardhouse on a river bridge leading to a mountain road. A military policeman, metal gorget on his chest, gave them the once-over.

The sergeant was explaining how proud he was of his younger brother. Beck recognized that he was seeking reassurance.

'It takes ages to find out if someone's been taken prisoner.'

'Yeh. I hope so, sir. Here we are. Hope you get a room.'

Beck studied the Red Ox with interest. The old coaching inn sat peacefully behind its timeless ochre walls. Red, white and black bunting streamed from its windows and a friendly plume of smoke rose over the uneven roof. Warmth, shelter and companionship beckoned. He pushed open the heavy door and found himself in a long flagstone passageway.

'Hello,' he called.

Voices could be heard from the first door on his right. He entered a small, cosy bar with a vaulted ceiling. Antlers were mounted on the wood-panelled walls and a green-tiled stove radiated heat. Three old men, in caps and gaiters, raised their beer mugs in greeting. Beck was about to speak to them when a tall, willowy woman in a white apron appeared. She looked flustered.

'Can I help you?'

'Do you have a room free?'

'A room?' She put her hand to her blonde hair, tied tightly back.

'For a week, ten days – no longer.'

'Um.' The woman turned away, a faint blush infusing her cheeks.

Beck played his strongest card. 'I'm on convalescent leave. The doctors told me mountain air'll be good for my chest. I was recommended . . .' He smiled into her eyes. Unusual amber eyes. Troubled eyes.

'I'll . . . I'll see.' The woman, in her late twenties, spun round and almost ran through a door at the side of the bar.

He followed her slowly. At the doorway he heard a man's gruff voice. 'Give him a room.'

The woman: 'But it's not easy. There's rationing . . . and things.'

'Don't be stupid. He has money to spend, he might as well spend it here.'

Beck became aware that a frail teenage girl with sharp, pinched features was watching him from the passage doorway. He smiled at her but she scuttled away as though she had committed some crime.

The voices were indistinct now. By her tone the woman was losing the argument. As he waited, Beck took in the room. Someone had made an effort here despite the wartime privations. The floorboards were highly polished and each table was covered by an embroidered lace cloth. Two silent linnets sat in an elaborate cage in one corner. The white-bristled drinkers, who must have fought in the trenches of the First War, did not conceal their curiosity about the stranger.

'Terrible weather,' observed one.

'Yes.' Beck turned his attention to the small wall-shrine above the locals' table. Two candles burned either side of a signed and bedecked photograph of a man glaring challengingly into the camera.

'Come far?'

The woman returned before Beck could answer him. 'You are welcome to stay here, if you don't mind sharing the little we have.'

'There's a nice drop of beer,' encouraged the old man. 'Best brew in town.'

'What can I say? Thank you.' Beck bowed and the woman blushed again.

A short, thick-necked man in a brown shirt and leather breeches swaggered through the door.

'Captain Christian Beck.' Christian introduced himself. He should have saluted the other's uniform but he could not bring himself to do so.

'My husband, *Herr* Runge,' the woman explained.

'*Heil Hitler*,' said Runge.

PART ONE

1

Monday. Bloody Monday.

The damp, dark January morning matched Robin Lusty's mood of frustration and depression. In one way he was glad to be back in the office, pleased that the empty weekend, spent aimlessly mooching around his digs in Chalk Farm, was over. No more being forced to listen to the endless drone of his landlady's wireless. He shuddered again at the memory of Sunday dinner with its watery gravy, cabbage boiled brown and gritty rissoles. An utterly boring weekend – not that the coming week offered much better, but at least there were three of them to distract each other as they tried to fill their hours in this garret overlooking Baker Street.

The door opened.

'God! You look rough.'

Annie Cunningham winced. 'An officer is not supposed to say things like that to a lady.'

'Did you get home?'

'I don't generally go to cocktail parties in uniform. Of course I went bloody home.' The effort of being indignant made her head ache all the more. 'There's no milk.'

'Fellow Americans, were they?' He didn't know why he was punishing himself.

'We know how to throw a good party. These were guys from OSS. Oh So Social.'

Lusty felt hurt. When he had suggested she might like to come out with him over the weekend, she had claimed she was busy. Now he knew what she had been busy doing. It reinforced his feeling that Special Operations Executive was altogether too grand for a grammar-school boy like him. Even secretaries like Annie belonged to the socially exclusive First Aid Nursing Yeomanry – or FANY.

Annie was not enjoying a good start to the week either. No amount of make-up could disguise her lack of sleep and her hangover. But, worse, she'd seen the hurt in Lusty's schoolboy eyes when she'd walked in. She felt guilty about turning him down but she wasn't going to break her golden rule of never going out with men she worked with. Not after last time.

As Annie set off to borrow milk, Lusty took up his favourite place by the window. The capital looked like their office – drab and uncared for, as if war had made her slovenly. The parks were unkempt, full of collapsed trenches and the paraphernalia of barrage balloons and anti-aircraft guns, while the south side of Hyde Park was still given over to allotments. Decay lay everywhere. Even in rich areas like Mayfair and Kensington, windows were boarded up, fences broken down and lawns allowed to grow rank and wild. The people, too, looked shabbier. New civilian clothes were a rarity and were worn with an air of apology. Instead, the pavements were a jostle of uniforms. Lusty made out the red pompons of French sailors, probably attached to the Gaullist French Section of Special Operations Executive, who had leased a building around the corner from Bertram Mills's Circus. They rubbed shoulders with Polish officers, Czech pilots, strapping Canadians, Norwegian seamen and cash-heavy American GIs. The Allied Nations!

He ran a finger along the window frame and wondered how often the cleaners remembered to dust this small office tucked away under the eaves. He wondered too if Annie realized how attractive she was, even with a hangover. He suspected that she did. She had the looks of a film starlet, an image reinforced by her New England accent, and the poise of a duchess. She was only twenty-two, three years younger than himself but she made him feel like an ink-specked schoolboy. While most Anglo-American unions were between rich American heiresses and impoverished scions of the titled English families. Annie's parents were different. Her father was American, from a wealthy old Boston family while her mother Emily was the elder daughter of a baron.

Lusty asked himself, what chance had someone like him with Annie?

She returned, carrying two cups.

'I've a treat for you.' She handed him a cup.

He sniffed it unbelievingly. 'Coffee?'

'All the way from Brazil. It's a present from mummy.'

'Good old mummy.'

Annie thought about digging Lusty in the ribs but decided it would be too much effort. Instead she stood by his side, looking down on Baker Street.

'Maroon.'

'Cardiff.'

'Hell!'

It was a game they played to fill the hours, guessing the origins of the different coloured buses drafted into London to maintain some semblance of a transport service.

'Look, there's Cricklemarsh.' Lusty pointed down to where the head of their small department was talking to a fresh-faced teenage boy in naval uniform.

'That's his son, Ken.'

'How do you know?'

Annie handed Lusty the framed photograph on Cricklemarsh's desk. Taken in Oxford just before the war, it showed a family group of a bespectacled, pipe-smoking don, his wife gazing abstractedly into the middle distance and two boys in flannels and open-necked shirts. Now the elder son, Keith, was a prisoner of the Japanese. Worrying about him had pushed the wife's fragile mental health over the brink so she spent most of her time in a private nursing home. The younger boy, Ken, was a sub lieutenant in the Fleet Air Arm. Only Cricklemarsh himself had not changed.

A few minutes later, he shambled into the office, his uniform fitting him like a grain sack.

'Maroon?'

'Cardiff,' chorused Lusty and Annie.

'Oh.' Cricklemarsh appeared crestfallen.

'That was your son, wasn't it?' asked Annie, knowing full well it was.

'Yes, he's just finished his Torpedo Training Course,' said Cricklemarsh proudly. 'He's leaving for Gosport for operational training this afternoon. Now, let's see what the week holds for us.' His face fell as he opened the thin packet of internal mail. 'It seems the French Section's grabbed our idea of draining oil from train axles in occupied France. They claim they thought of it first.'

'Liars.'

'And our suggestion of targeting the heavy-water plant in Norway's been turned down.'

There was a brief silence before Lusty said bitterly, 'They really don't want us, do they?'

'Seems not.' Cricklemarsh took off his glasses and scoured his eye sockets with his knuckles.

'Why don't they just close down Special Projects?'

'Sorry,' said Cricklemarsh, feeling guilty that Lusty was missing the war in this despised backwater.

It wasn't his fault. In the fissured world of wartime British intelligence, Cricklemarsh had been hooked out of Oxford, where he had been enjoying analysing power shifts in Nazi Germany, and foisted on Special Operations Executive's European section by a passing political master. The arrival of the middle-aged don had been met with hostility and suspicion. He had been given an out-of-the-way office and just one assistant – Lusty. Since then they had been sidelined, circumvented, lied to and ignored. Senior officers could not disband Special Projects quite yet but they could let it wither on the vine until the time was right to prune it.

Cricklemarsh found the situation intellectually galling, but Lusty took it personally. He had been mentioned in dispatches for his bravery at Dunkirk. When a flight of Stukas had dived on his men, he had mounted the sole Bren gun on a wrecked lorry and had fired away to the last of the ammunition. He had succeeded in downing one enemy plane but at the cost of two fingers on his left hand. He still had shrapnel in his left leg. After a series of hospitals and a variety of desk jobs, he had been posted to Baker Street. Apart from the fact that he spoke German like a native, he had no idea why.

'Look on the bright side,' encouraged Cricklemarsh. 'You don't pay income tax in SOE.'

'I didn't join up so as not to pay tax.'

The phone rang. Cricklemarsh replaced his round spectacles and picked up the receiver. His raised eyebrows registered his surprise. 'Yes. Yes, fine.' He blinked like a confused owl caught in a torch beam.

'Colonel Purefoy is coming to see us at twelve-thirty,' he explained.

'What! The head of European Section coming *here*? He'll never find his way.'

'I wonder what he wants,' murmured Cricklemarsh.

'I wouldn't trust that man any more than a barrage balloon,' proclaimed Lusty.

'I didn't know barrage balloons were exceptionally untrustworthy,' objected Cricklemarsh mildly. 'In fact, looking at those ones over Regent's Park, they appear positively benign.'

'But why come here?' insisted Lusty. 'Why not summon us – you – to his office?'

'You don't like the colonel, do you?'

'How can I like someone who doesn't even admit I exist? He walked right past me this morning as if I wasn't there.'

'Ah, yes. I think I've solved that one.' Cricklemarsh scratched his nose with his pipe stem. 'I believe he had you mixed up with R. M. Lusty of the Grenadier Guards. Played for Middlesex before the war. Useful slow left arm.'

Annie emitted a peal of laughter, then winced as her head exploded with pain. But Lusty did not find it funny at all.

'The bastards.'

Lusty had a point, thought Cricklemarsh, grinning behind the clouds of smoke billowing from his pipe. Members of SOE were regularly recruited via the Old Pals Act from the better public schools and the older regiments. Lusty, hailing from a county regiment, was definitely the odd man out. So too was Cricklemarsh, for that matter, but no one could ever confuse Cricklemarsh with a professional soldier.

'Oh, dear!' Cricklemarsh had just remembered. 'I've booked a table at Simpson's for lunch with Ken. I won't have time now.'

'Sod's Law,' pronounced Lusty. 'Most weeks we could go out to lunch on Monday, not come back until Wednesday, and no one would even notice.'

'I must collect a silver cigarette case I've bought him. Now we're only going to have time for a beer and a sandwich in the Barley Mow. Will you two join us?'

'I'll just pop in to say hello,' smiled Annie, heading for the door.

'I'm seeing the doctor about a piece of shrapnel that seems to be working its way into my leg instead of out of it,' said Lusty. 'Wish him well. I'll be back in time for Purefoy.'

Cricklemarsh had not been gone five minutes when Annie returned, looking blankly at the clutch of German local newspapers in her hand.

'These came in through Switzerland yesterday and we seem to be on the subscription list. Do you know anything about them?'

'Cricklemarsh had the bright idea of trawling through them to see if we could find any members of U-boat crews who've been away from home for twelve months or more,' replied Lusty. 'Then we put out spoof radio messages congratulating them on the births of their sons.'

'That's evil.'

'Good, isn't it? Mind you, I bet someone else'll nick the idea.'

'The papers have to be passed on by the end of the day.'

'I'll read them before I see the doc. I'm not exactly overworked.'

'Can you really understand these?'

'It may come as a shock to you, *gnädiges Fräulein,* but I'm a quarter German.'

Annie did not miss a beat. 'Really! Which quarter?'

'My mother's side. I spent a lot of my teens in Germany. I'd thought that must be why I was here, except now I know I'm merely a case of mistaken identity.'

Annie wrinkled her nose at the smell of damp uniforms and stale beer. She spotted Cricklemarsh and his son standing over in the far corner of the snug bar. God, the lad was young! A schoolboy who should be opening the batting for his house, not going off to war. He appeared too young even to be in a pub, never mind wearing a naval uniform with pilot's wings.

Cricklemarsh introduced them. 'My son Kenneth – Annette Cunningham.'

'Call me Annie.'

'I'm Ken. W-what c-c-can I get you?'

'Just a lemonade, please.'

'Not the hair of the dog, Annie?'

So Cricklemarsh had noticed her state as well. She had the grace to grin at him. 'Gin and it, then.'

Ken tried fruitlessly to attract the barmaid's attention until Annie saw Cricklemarsh raise a finger behind his son's shoulder. Ken was served next.

'Cigarette?' Ken held out a silver cigarette-case. She smiled to herself at his attempt to seem mature but then the schoolboy in him broke through. 'It's a present from dad. Isn't it smashing.'

'Absolutely. When are you off to Gosport?'

'I've a train at three o'clock. I officially join the naval air station at 0900 hours tomorrow.' He hid nervously behind his pint glass, thinking Annie was the most beautiful woman he had ever met.

'What will you be doing there?'

'ADDLS.'

'Sorry?'

'Assisted dummy deck landings. I'm learning how to land on a carrier. At the moment, it's just a small strip marked out on the runway.'

'What do you fly?'

'Torpedo bombers: Fairey Swordfish.'

'Stringbags!' exclaimed Annie. The Fairey Swordfish had already been obsolete by the outbreak of war – three years after it entered service. It would still be flying in 1945 – the only biplane on either side to see active service throughout the war.

Ken blushed. 'The Swordfish is a lovely solid kite, and they're very hard to shoot down.'

'That's because they're so slow, everyone aims ahead of them,' laughed Annie.

Ken gave her a suspicious look.

'Annie's from an old naval family,' explained Cricklemarsh.

'Forgive me, I thought I caught an American accent.' Ken blushed.

'My father's from Boston but my mother's as English as they come,' said Annie.

Cricklemarsh gave a wry smile, thinking that it was a fair, if understated, description of Annie's mother whose family had owned crumbling Ashfinger Priory since the reign of Henry VIII.

'Annie's a volunteer,' said Cricklemarsh.

'Sorry?'

'I'd just finished school in Switzerland when the war broke out,' she explained. 'I was due to join my parents in Brazil but I didn't want to miss all the fun so I stayed in London. Mummy's really jealous.'

'Why Brazil?' Ken couldn't believe he was chatting to this goddess. He was aware he was getting jealous looks from other officers in the pub.

'Daddy's the American ambassador in Rio.'

'You must have travelled a lot.'

'You could say that.' She smiled. 'I grew up in Boston, came to London when I was ten when daddy joined the embassy here, spent two years in Dublin, then went back to school in New England, returning to England each summer to stay with relations, and ended up in Switzerland.'

'How come you're in Baker Street?'

'Mummy knew some people,' she replied offhandedly. 'But what about you? Are you nervous about the next stage?'

'I'm just glad to have got this far.' Ken blinked, showing indecently long lashes for a boy. 'I flunked my nav exams the first time. I had to work like stink to get through. Maths isn't my strong point.'

'Runs in the family.' Cricklemarsh lifted the corner of a curling cheese sandwich. 'I can barely add up a restaurant bill. But Ken's a stubborn lad. He refused to be beaten.'

'That runs in the family, too,' said Ken quickly.

Annie smiled with polite incomprehension.

'Dad is the most stubborn man I know.'

Annie was surprised. She had never though of Cricklemarsh as anything but placidly malleable. Her surprise must have shown on her face.

'Dad tried to build a tower of playing cards one night but it kept falling down. We left him to it. When we got up next morning, he was still there. But he did it, though, the whole pack. He finished it while having his boiled egg.'

'I'd never tried it before,' confessed Cricklemarsh. 'It was harder than it looked.'

Colonel Purefoy smoothed his left forefinger over his full moustache, every inch a Guards officer. His perfectly tailored uniform had knife-edge creases, his shoes gleamed, and up his arse, according to Lusty, was the broom handle that kept him ramrod straight.

His eyes roved over the two desks, the old radio on the filing cabinet, the worn linoleum, and the camp bed under the damp stain before coming to rest on the opening verses of the Thirty-ninth Psalm pinned above the boarded-up fireplace. *I said, I will take heed to my ways that I offend not with my tongue: I will keep my mouth as it were with a bridle, while the ungodly is in my sight.*

'You're certainly tucked away up here, aren't you,' said Purefoy in an attempt at joviality. 'Everything all right? Feeling you're making a contribution, hmm?'

'Always hoping to do more, sir,' said Lusty with a hint of irony.

'Good.' Purefoy's cold gleam of satisfaction made Lusty feel he had just walked into a trap.

'Tea, sir?' Annie handed Purefoy a chipped mug, with the grace of a concubine offering lapsang souchong to a Ming emperor.

'Ah, yes. Thanks.' Purefoy remained silent until Annie had left, and then nodded towards the door. 'If you would, lieutenant. Don't want any Tom, Dick or Harry wandering in on us in the middle of our chat, do we?' He cleared his throat. 'What I am about to tell you is top secret.'

With that, he glared at Lusty who could not help himself from nodding. Cricklemarsh, however, could have been listening to an undergraduate's paper for all the effect Purefoy's stricture had on him.

'Winston feels SOE is not setting Europe alight – as we are supposed to,' began Purefoy portentously. 'He's let his feelings be known at the highest echelons. Naturally, we are all concerned to dispel such an impression. To that end, all departments within SOE – across Europe and the Middle East – are stepping up their efforts, giving one hundred and ten per cent.'

Staring at Purefoy's satisfied face, Lusty mentally translated that the shit was running down the mountain. It had landed squarely on the colonel's sleek head and now he was about to pour some over them.

'We have a job for you: a very special job, as befits your department.' Purefoy paused for dramatic effect. 'We are giving you the opportunity to change the course of the war – possibly even to end it.'

'Yes?' Cricklemarsh's face puckered in surprise.

'We want you to kill Hitler.'

The hairs on Lusty's neck prickled as the silence expanded.

'Won't killing Hitler turn him into a martyr?' enquired Cricklemarsh finally.

'On the contrary, his death will shorten the war considerably,' said Purefoy stiffly. 'It's only his mystical hold over the German people that welds the country together. They regard him as superhuman. Remove Hitler and the Third Reich will fall apart.'

'Surely, his military blunders make him an asset to us,' argued Cricklemarsh. 'The Sixth Army wouldn't be surrounded at Stalingrad if Hitler had allowed Paulus to retreat. Killing Hitler will canonize him. It'll give birth to the myth that, had he lived, Germany would have eventually been victorious.'

'The tide turned last year at Alamein,' insisted Purefoy, growing impatient with the debate. 'The Germans are in retreat in Africa and facing disaster on the Eastern Front. The sooner Hitler's dead, the better.'

'Shouldn't this be one for the German Section, sir?' enquired Lusty, thinking of its ambitious, empire-building head, Major Rupert Nye.

'X Section has more than enough on its plate at the moment,' said Purefoy, a little too quickly. 'But if you don't fancy the challenge . . .?'

'We'll do it,' murmured Cricklemarsh.

'Good. Now, it must look as though Hitler's been killed by his own people. We can't risk more SS revenge massacres like those after Heydrich's assassination.' Purefoy rubbed his finger along the mantelpiece and looked aghast at the dust. He pressed on. 'Hitler must be killed either in Germany itself or at his command post on the Eastern Front. The Wolf's Lair appears – initially, anyway – to be impenetrable. Hitler lives in a concrete bunker at the innermost heart of Army Headquarters in the East Prussian pine forests surrounded by a complex of barbed-wire fences with check points, patrols and mine fields.'

'He must leave the place sometimes,' said Cricklemarsh.

'In the seventeen months between July 1941 and January 1943, he left the Eastern Front on just three occasions for a total of seven weeks. Each time he spent one or two nights in Berlin en route to his mountain retreat in Bavaria.'

'It's not going to be easy,' mused Cricklemarsh.

'No one said it would be,' replied Purefoy, sharply. 'Hitler's seldom seen in public any more. He refuses to tour the bombed cities or visit the wounded in hospitals. He's paranoid about his safety, and allows only those he knows and trusts near him. He changes travel arrangements at the last minute, often wears a bulletproof vest, and even his military cap is lined with three and a half pounds of steel plate. He claims to have a sixth sense to warn him when he's in danger.'

'Is there a timescale for the operation?'

'The sooner the better. You might find this useful.' Purefoy placed a buff folder on the desk. 'All in absolute secrecy, of course. Don't let any other department know what you're up to, especially Broadway. We don't want SIS getting in on the act, do we?' Suddenly Purefoy seemed ill at ease. 'Right. Well, best of luck. This is your chance. Don't blow it.'

*

'It stinks,' declared Lusty once the colonel had left. 'Nye'll go absolutely potty when he finds out.'

'I must admit I'm surprised we've been given this.' Cricklemarsh busied himself teasing out fresh strands from his tobacco pouch. 'I don't know whether to be flattered or terrified.'

'It's obvious. Purefoy doesn't want us, but we exist, so he gives us a near-impossible operation. If we pull it off, he'll be seen to have used his resources wisely, choosing the right horse for the right course. If we fail, then he'll have been proved right about us in the first place.' Lusty twisted back the hank of hair that hung over his forehead to reveal a crescent-shaped scar. It was a subconscious gesture indicating that he was troubled.

Cricklemarsh knew Lusty was right. Why had *they* been given the operation instead of one of the larger, better-equipped departments? Was it an honour or a further insult?

Well, he had a surprise in store for Purefoy, or whoever was pulling his strings. They were going to make the operation work. He was fed up with being lied to and double-crossed. He'd only agreed to this job because he'd been offered the prospect of taking the war to the Germans. Unfortunately, his sponsor had moved on within a week of Cricklemarsh's arrival, leaving him up in the air to be shot at by every other department in SOE. He had bitten the bullet, always believing that his moment would come. Now it had. Cricklemarsh was under no illusions – this was make or break. If they failed – and the odds were heavily stacked against them – they would not be given a second chance.

He'd make it work, if only for his sons. If the war ended, Ken would not have to risk his life, Keith would return home from captivity, and perhaps even their mother, released from her burden of endless worry, would become well again.

Yes, he'd make the operation work – come hell or high water.

Cricklemarsh opened the buff folder and read the first page aloud. 'Operation Nightshade. A deliberate and continuous effort to try to liquidate Hitler.'

He flicked through the pages and selected at random a proposal for poisoning the drinking water on Hitler's private train, the *Führer-*

zug. The plan depended upon persuading one of six French women cleaners to add two pounds of poison to the 120-gallon water tank supplying the Führer's carriage. This particular poison took a week to work by which time there was no antidote. The document conceded that Hitler drank only bottled water on his train but he was known to be addicted to tea. '"He always drinks it with milk. Since the milk is poured first into the cup it is unlikely the tea's opalescence would be noticed as it came from the teapot."'

Cricklemarsh shook his head in amazement. Not only was there no way of preventing anyone else from drinking the same tea but milk was a well-known antidote to poison.

Another suggestion was to impregnate Hitler's clothing with a tiny amount of anthrax. Or he could be supplied with a poisoned fountain pen. Or his whole train blown up.

'Wherever do they get their ideas from! They're so amateurish,' objected Cricklemarsh.

Lusty scrabbled awkwardly with the two fingers on his left hand to pick up the discarded pages. 'Here's a suggestion that Hitler should be shot. "The operatives should be Austrian or Bavarian prisoners of war with an 'animus' against the Nazis and Hitler in particular. Poles and Czechs are also viewed as suitable candidates." What's an "animus"?'

'In this context it means intention, actuating spirit, hostility. From the Latin *animus*, meaning spirit or soul.'

Annie, loaded with files, pushed through the door. 'These have just arrived for you.'

It was the start of many long days of research, evaluation and elimination.

Where? When? Who? How? Those were the questions, lectured Cricklemarsh. Questions that must be answered if the department was to be successful. Cricklemarsh and Lusty worked late into the evenings, while Annie kept them supplied with files, endless cups of tea, and occasionally treats of cups of Brazilian coffee – courtesy of the State Department's diplomatic bag from Rio de Janeiro via Washington. After work, they went for a drink at the Barley Mow in Dorset Street, or else an indifferent meal at the Travellers Club, now inhabited by refugees from the closed-down London clubs and staffed by frightened Lithuanian waitresses.

Sometimes Annie joined them. She had appointed herself the department's counter-intelligence section, using her excellent connections inside Baker Street, including the director-general's senior secretary who was an old school friend.

'The guys in the German Section still don't have a clue what we're doing,' she confirmed one night. 'It shows Major Nye's not checking the registry or he'd notice what files are being booked out to us.'

'Any idea who's really behind the operation?' asked Lusty.

'My spies tell me Purefoy and the deputy director of operations are very chummy all of a sudden.'

'Brigadier Gilbert! I thought he was still sulking in his tent,' said Lusty. 'Whenever I see him, he looks as if he's sucking a lemon.'

'You can't altogether blame him,' murmured Cricklemarsh. 'He's a professional intelligence officer who was passed over by the new wave of amateur outsiders. In one way, he's got a right to be disappointed.'

'I gather his wife Marjorie's giving him a really hard time for being overlooked,' said Annie.

'It's nice to think that even brigadiers can be henpecked,' grinned Lusty.

'Strange thing, though,' said Annie in her clipped New England way. 'I was at dinner with a couple of guys from our Embassy last night when the subject of assassinating Hitler came up. Almost everyone was firmly against it. Thought we'd lose the moral high ground if we killed him.'

'*Someone* wants him dead,' said Lusty.

But how to kill the Führer? Poisons would be difficult to administer as it was almost impossible to recruit workers with access to Hitler at mealtimes. They might still be looking for someone to suborn in six months' time.

A knife or a hand grenade was discounted. It was most unlikely the assassin would be able to get close enough. He would certainly never walk away alive.

For a while Cricklemarsh favoured planting a time bomb on the aircraft the Führer used between Berlin and the Eastern Front. SOE already had the perfect tool – a sixteen-inch flexible rubber tube filled with plastic explosive and armed at one end with a barometric fuse. A half-turn of a screw made it explode at 5,000 feet, a full turn at 10,000 feet. Once the plane had taken off, the fall in air pressure would do the rest. The difficulty came in finding someone able to pierce the security screen around Hitler's aircraft.*

By elimination, Cricklemarsh came round to the idea of shooting Hitler. One gunman, working alone.

'Not a team?' queried Lusty.

'Three can keep a secret only if two are dead,' replied Cricklemarsh.

Annie flew into the room. 'Quick. The wireless. There's going to be a special announcement . . .'

The opening bars of Beethoven's Fifth Symphony filled the room. An announcer began speaking solemnly in German.

'The struggle in Stalingrad is over. Loyal to their oath down to the last breath, the Sixth Army, under the exemplary leadership of General Field Marshal Paulus, succumbed to the superior force of the enemy and the unfavourable conditions . . .'

Lusty whistled silently.

'. . . Generals, officers, non commissioned officers, and men fought shoulder to shoulder down to the last shot. They died so that Germany might live . . .'

Last September Hitler had announced that Stalingrad was about to fall to German troops. By November, *Wehrmacht* reports had ceased mentioning the battle. The silence caused unease. When, on 16 January, Radio Berlin spoke up at last about the heroically defensive struggle of the German troops against an 'enemy attacking from all sides', the country held its breath.

Today, 3 February, the German people knew the worst. Hitler's

* Ironically, on 13 March 1943, Major General Freiherr Henning von Tresckow, senior operations officer of Army Group Centre and his ADC, Fabian von Schlabrendorff, succeeded in planting a time bomb on Hitler's aircraft as he returned to the Wolf's Lair. The bomb, hidden in a package containing two bottles of Cointreau, failed to explode.

refusal to allow Paulus to retreat had cost the lives of three hundred thousand men.

'Heard the news, colonel?'

'Yes, sir.' Purefoy stood to attention before Brigadier Gilbert's desk.

'The Stalingrad defeat is the greatest single blow in the war for the German people. The shock will force them to reappraise Hitler. The Nazi Party's disliked by most Germans but the Führer's genius has never been disputed – until now.' Gilbert leaned forward, his birdlike head looking as if it was about to snatch at a worm. 'We must be ready to strike while the iron's hot.'

'My people are pressing on as quickly as they can, sir.'

'The mood in Germany is changing. We can't afford to lose one day.' Gilbert rocked backwards, a small man behind a large desk. 'Between ourselves, Winston was grumbling again a few nights ago. In his cups, of course. Usual threats about new brooms and goodness knows what else.'

'I'll impress the urgency upon Cricklemarsh again, sir.'

'Of course, this is your operation – your choice of men. Delegation is the hardest part of command. It's tempting to want to do it all yourself. Keep me informed – but remember, nothing on paper.'

After Purefoy had gone scuttling off to harry Cricklemarsh and his department, Gilbert allowed himself an expansive and luxuriant stretch. He felt good. He'd tell his wife soon, when the moment was right. That would shut her up. In the meantime, an inner secret glow inured him to her nagging and goading.

Robin Lusty came out of the lavatory and looked round the crowded dance floor. He couldn't miss Doreen's platinum blonde hair. She was giggling with two American GIs: doing a number on them, throwing back her head, laughing to show off the white teeth in her wide mouth. A whore's mouth, as she had once described it.

She ignored Lusty and carried on flirting with the GIs. Later, he knew, she would pretend she had not seen him. If he protested, she would be stand-offish for a few days, always washing her hair when he called, before she allowed him to take her out again. This time she had a surprise coming. If Annie worked her magic, he'd be flying out tomorrow. That was why he'd wanted tonight to be something special. Doreen could be a lovely, laughing lady; she could also be a right cow.

Annie and Doreen were as different as two women could be. Annie, slim and elegant, with lustrous chestnut hair, educated at Vassar, at home at a diplomatic cocktail party or the Savoy Grill. Doreen, pert and peroxide, loud and laughing, somersaulting from good time to good time and hoping the bill would never catch up with her. At least *she* would come out on a date with him.

Doreen was still looking right through him. Perhaps she wanted him to get into a quarrel with her American admirers. She liked the Yanks, or rather their money. An American private, first class, earned more than a British lieutenant. Bloody Yanks. Oversexed. Overpaid. Over here.

She would enjoy being fought over. *Dream on.*

'Ready?' he asked, nodding pleasantly to the GIs.

'If you say so.' She assumed a martyred expression. 'Bye-bye, you guys. Have fun.'

As Lusty turned to leave, he caught one of them giving her a conspiratorial wink.

Cricklemarsh had put on a plain army battledress, without rank or other insignia. He glanced at his watch. Through the spyhole he could see Lieutenant Commander Milden RN already seated on a folding chair, facing the door across the bare table. The only other furniture in the room in the requisitioned Northumberland Hotel just behind the War Office was a second folding chair, a blackout screen and a naked light bulb. Milden was staring at some point on the wall above the door, the occasional drumming of the fingers of his right hand betraying his nervousness.

Cricklemarsh said a silent prayer that he had at last found his gunman.

Reports were coming out of Germany that the Führer was mentally exhausted. His doctors were pressing him to leave the Wolf's Lair and take a rest. He would inevitably go to the Berghof, his mountain retreat high above the small Bavarian town of Berchtesgaden.

Where, Cricklemarsh hoped, he might prove vulnerable to a lone sniper.

But first, find the sniper. It was proving a problem – and every day Purefoy was turning the screw ever tighter.

'Milden was wounded when his corvette went down in the Atlantic taking half its crew with it. He almost lost his life freeing two trapped stokers,' Cricklemarsh's contact had said. 'He's currently steering a desk at Plymouth and itching to get back to the war.'

Cricklemarsh swept into the room. His face had become a mask.

'I understand you are keen to get back into the fighting?'

'Yes, sir.' Despite – or because of – the lack of rank badges, Milden addressed Cricklemarsh as a senior officer.

'You want to get to grips with the enemy?'

'Yes, sir.'

'Maybe behind the lines?' Cricklemarsh was affably vague and discursive.

'Absolutely, sir. Can't wait.'

'Warum?' The word crackled across the table: 'Why?' As Cricklemarsh switched into German, his manner became abrupt and businesslike.

For a second Milden was lost, then he recovered. *'Ich möchte viel mehr teilnehmen am Krieg als bisher'* – I'd like to take much more part in the war than I have so far.

That moment's hesitation could cost the man his life, thought Cricklemarsh, but he had collected himself well. *Cool under pressure.* Dark, wavy hair and a square jaw, the sort of gallant *British* looks that would be perfect in Royal Navy propaganda films. Milden would have to do something about disguising that if he was selected.

'How did you learn to speak German?'

'With the Royal Navy, sir. I did a translator's course and then spent time in Bremerhaven and Berlin before the war.'

Milden's German was not bad – a little stilted but that could be made more colloquial. Cricklemarsh decided his candidate had passed the language test and it was worthwhile continuing the interrogation. He did so in German, probing Milden's family background, his naval career, his interests, including competing at Bisley in the inter-services shooting competition in 1939. As they spoke, Cricklemarsh analysed the man's motivation as much as his character. It was not enough that Milden revealed courage and the marksmanship to put a bullet into Hitler. He had to possess a sufficiently cool head to get into a position to fire the shot in the first place.

'. . . And chess.'

'I'd have thought a dashing corvette commander would find chess a rather boring game.'

'Not at all, sir. I'm captain of the Plymouth naval chess club.' It was said with pride and a hint of pomposity.

Cricklemarsh allowed a silence to fall in the room. For some undetectable reason he had gone off Milden as a human being. But as an agent, the man's stock rose in his estimation. Impulsiveness was a character trait that his assassin could not afford. He needed to possess bravery, cunning, a chameleon ability to blend in with the background and the capacity to lie so convincingly that he believed his own words himself.

A few more questions and Cricklemarsh would end this prelminary interview. Before the second one, he'd get MI5 to run security checks and pull out Milden's confidential file.

'How do you feel about the Führer?'

'I'd like to see him rot in hell,' hissed Milden.

'Just Hitler himself or the whole of Germany?'

'The whole stinking lot of them. The only good Hun's a dead one.'

'Even innocent civilians?' asked Cricklemarsh.

'They're the ones who put Hitler in power. They can pay for it.'

'Are you married, lieutenant commander?'

A moment's hesitation. 'No.'

Cricklemarsh thought he had the explanation. 'Have you lost your wife?'

'I've never been married. Been at sea too much, I suppose.'

Cricklemarsh was confused. He had assumed Milden was about to admit his wife had been killed in an air raid. So what else fuelled Milden's hatred? All right-minded people abhorred Nazism and what it stood for, but there was a deeper, darker seam running through this man. Cricklemarsh needed someone who was committed but not a fanatic with a private grudge. That sort were invaluable chaining themselves to machine guns and holding up the advance of battalions but impossible to control in the secret war.

'Are your parents alive?'

'Yes, they've retired to the Cotswolds. Hardly know there's a war on.'

'Lost any close friends?'

'One or two, sir. Everyone does. It goes with war.'

'Yes, it does, I suppose.'

Cricklemarsh was barking up the wrong tree and it perplexed him.

'You really detest the Germans, don't you?' he probed in a reasonable tone.

'They're the scum of the earth. Who else would make a national hero out of someone like Horst Wessel, a pimp and common thief, stabbed to death in a street brawl.'

'You know the SA murdered the man suspected of killing Wessel as soon as they came to power,' said Cricklemarsh. 'No one knows if they got the right man or not but, of course, they were never brought to justice.'

Milden flung himself back in his chair. 'Brownshirt thugs! God, I pray they'll get what's coming to them when the war's over.'

'Had a run in with them yourself?'

Milden's eyes crackled with hate. 'It's easy when it's five against one. And the policeman just walks in the opposite direction.'

'Where was this?'

'Bremerhaven.'

'At the docks?'

'Near enough.'

'Where were your shipmates?'

Milden's eyes dropped. 'I was there by myself. During my language course.' One cheek muscle twitched. 'But I'll have the last laugh. I'll get those bastards if I have to wait a thousand years.'

'Is this true, colonel?'

'Is what true, Rupert?' Purefoy had been dreading this moment.

'Is it true that you're planning an operation in Germany without involving my section?' Nye made little attempt to conceal his anger.

'Executive decision, old boy.' Purefoy could tell Nye it was none of his damned business, demand to know how he dared question a senior officer, or throw him out of the room on his ear. But Rupert Nye was the coming man so he decided to play it lightly.

'What do you mean, "executive decision", colonel?'

Purefoy silently pointed with his right forefinger towards the ceiling. That was a mistake, he realized immediately. Nye would now interrogate his chums on the director's floor above.

'I thought you were too busy, otherwise I would have given the assignment to you.' Purefoy could not resist the jibe. Nye was for ever complaining that his section was snowed under with work and that he needed more staff. In reality, apart from running a few futile wireless games, maintaining contacts with aristocratic German exiles, and sending poison-pen letters to the wives of generals and industrialists, it was hard to know how he passed his time.

In fairness, there was little chance of conducting a successful guerrilla operation in a country where the vast majority of the population were against you. Though anti-Nazi elements did exist among the German working class, SOE could not get through to them. Workers in large towns and cities were too closely monitored by the Gestapo. Also, they were the victims of regular Allied bombing raids. One consequence of bombing – as discovered in the London blitz – was to make those bombed bloody furious with the bomber. The German countryside was little better, filled as it was with homeless evacuees and disciplined groups of *Hitler-Jugend* who had grown up under the Nazi party and its godhead Hitler.

But Nye talked a good operation. And he had his supporters in the building. If Nye gained charge of a successful mission to kill Hitler, his promotion to Purefoy's job would be a formality – as Purefoy well knew.

'At the moment it's all little more than a feasibility study.'

'I still think X Section should have been the one to be tasked.' Nye was not going to let things go. '*We*'re the ones with the expertise and the resources.'

'I agree, Rupert.' Purefoy lowered his voice. 'Between ourselves, I wouldn't rule out your department's future involvement if the project assumes a more concrete form. I'll keep you posted.'

Lusty found Cricklemarsh hiding behind a frosted-glass snob-screen in the corner of the snug bar, deep in thought.

'I'm confirmed on the night flight,' announced Lusty. 'Fingers crossed, I take off at twenty hundred. How did you get on?'

Cricklemarsh waved to the barmaid, ordered two pints of beer, then gave a brief account of his interview with Milden.

'But I thought you *wanted* an agent who was motivated,' objected Lusty.

'There's a difference between being motivated and being merely fanatical. An agent must work with his intelligence rather than his emotions. Pathological hatred is a liability.' Cricklemarsh stopped himself lecturing as he caught sight of Annie at the doorway.

She scythed her way through the crowded bar to hand Lusty a bulky brown envelope and a canvas holdall.

'Your travel orders, passes and bag, sir.' It was amazing how much scorn Annie could imbue that one last syllable with. 'There's a car on its way to take you to Southampton.'

'I was coming back to the office but thanks, anyway. Have a drink?' Lusty was in awe of Annie's ability to achieve things that in theory were impossible – like getting him a seat on a plane to Lisbon. He supposed it helped that her uncle was an admiral.

'Here's to your flight.' Annie toasted him with her gin, standing so close to Lusty that her coat sleeve brushed his uniform. He did not notice. 'You'll need some toothpaste. You can get some at the NAAFI on the Solent.'

'Have you been going through my bag?'

Annie picked a hair off his left shoulder. 'There're reports of increased Focke-Wulf activity over the Bay of Biscay. Take care.'

She reached up and kissed him on the cheek. Then she was gone so quickly that Lusty put his hand to his face, wondering if he had imagined it.

'Shame your naval chap wasn't suitable,' he said, changing the subject. 'What do you think happened to him?'

'He was looking for a boy around the docks and the Nazis gave him a beating.'

'You don't know for sure that he's a brown-hatter!'

'They wouldn't have picked on him if he'd been after a woman. Nazis have it in for homosexuals. They were putting them in concentration camps before the war.'

'So Milden is out?'

'Yes – although not just because of his sexual preferences,' Cricklemarsh was quick to add.

'If revenge isn't a sufficient motive, what else does our man need?'

Cricklemarsh went through the ritual of producing his tobacco pouch and filling his pipe, as two Czech pilots argued loudly nearby in their own language. A thin, blonde girl with a slash of red lipstick stood between them, looking bored.

When at last he spoke, it was as if he was revealing some long-forgotten secret. 'To be able to withstand the strain,' he declared finally. 'The strain of being one person while pretending to be another. The strain of keeping silent; of not correcting the ill-informed. The strain of coping with being vital but being thought a nobody. The strain of remembering addresses and long codes. Most of all, it's the strain of being unable to relax, the permanent uncertainty, even in sleep, when you can sleep.'

'You've done this yourself, haven't you?' whispered Lusty, struck by Cricklemarsh's distant voice and eyes that saw elsewhere. 'Where? When?'

'Back in the Twenties – Russia, Poland, East Prussia. The Russians helped Germany develop their first tanks, you know, in defiance of the Versailles Treaty.'

'Did you enjoy the work?'

Cricklemarsh hid behind his pipe. 'It's an uncomfortable life, a lonely life. And, depending how your colleagues at home look after you, an uncertain one.'

'But London looked after you all right?'

'No, I was betrayed by London.' Cricklemarsh spoke in a matter-of-fact voice but Lusty noticed the fingers that tightened around the bowl of the pipe.

'What happened?'

'I made my own way home. It was all a long time ago.'

Lusty felt as if he was intruding on personal grief. His driver appeared at the doorway.

'Safe journey,' said Cricklemarsh, putting a hand on the other's shoulder. 'You'll find what we need. I know you will.'

Lusty walked out to the waiting car, bolstered by the other's faith and confidence. It was only later when he was left with his own thoughts, cramped in his seat midships in the Catalina flying boat, that he considered the enormity of this task and the odds against him succeeding.

Then he discovered the priceless chocolate that Annie had hidden in his bag and was able to smile again.

2

Beck huddled deeper into his olive-coloured greatcoat and wound his scarf tightly around his neck to keep out the freezing desert night air. He grasped the machine-gun mounting to steady himself as the armoured car bucked over the rock-strewn track. Above him, stars twinkled like brilliant silver jewels against a soft velvet canopy. Their shimmering luminescence made men hold their breath in wonder. He had never seen stars like these until he came to Africa. Now he never wanted to see another one. The crystal-clear night meant another scorching day ahead. It was hard enough waging war in this desolate land but to have to fight when metal was too hot to touch, when flies swarmed over your spoon between plate and mouth and you couldn't breathe for dust, made life sometimes almost unbearable. Beck had been here since the very start. He had tasted both the early elation of hovering on the brink of victory and now the sour inevitability of defeat.

Beck and his driver, Private Schwegg, passed a broken-off pole protruding from a concrete-filled oil drum. A signpost from another battle, another year. A hundred yards off the track the skeleton of a large Matador lorry had sunk axle-deep in the sand – a grim warning to anyone unfortunate enough to get stranded here. The Matador would have once been part of a convoy. Beck and Schwegg were on their own and the desert was a lonely place, especially at night.

They had set out at dusk, heading south from headquarters at Ghaddahia in their SdKfz 222 recce car, known to both sides as Siegfrieds. Under its patina of dust, it bore the squat 'B' of the 21st Panzer Division and the palm tree of the *Deutsche Afrika Korps*. The *Korps*'s commander, Rommel, was withdrawing west to the Gabes Gap where he could hold the line of the Wadi Akarit between the sea and the extensive salt marshes of the Chott-el-Fadjadi. It was Beck's job to scout south towards Wadi Rami and Fortino, to ensure that the British and New Zealanders were not trying to outflank them.

Schwegg pulled out a packet of cigarettes and wordlessly handed Beck two. There was no love lost between them but out here they had to rely on each other. Personal antipathies stayed behind in laager. Beck lit both cigarettes, turning away so as not to impair Schwegg's night vision, and handed one back.

To the right, the barren rock gave way to a sea of fine sand where the wind had created low ridges looking like waves. Beck could understand how aircrews could fly over the desert and believe they were over the Mediterranean.

In the silver starlight, he made out a file of a dozen heavily laden camels being led alongside the course of a shallow wadi. Beck frowned. Something was wrong. Camel trains invariably halted for the night. He decided against investigating. They would be heavily outnumbered and he had to get back to Ghaddahia by dawn. A lone scout car would offer an irresistible target for the Allied fighter-bombers that swept the desert in daylight hours.

'Herr Hauptmann.'

Beck snapped out of his thoughts. Ahead, a tyre track was plainly visible in the drifted sand.

'Slow down.'

This could be the proof he needed that the British were indeed in the area. Or it could be a mine. Both armies used mines extensively and tried to outwit the other in their deployment, setting them so that a man or even a motorbike could pass over safely. Only a worthwhile target, like a tank, a truck or armoured car, would activate the pressure plate. It was an old trick to lay a chain of mines across a track and then roll a tyre through the middle to suggest the way was safe. An old trick, maybe. But old tricks were the best.

Beck was not going to fall for it. 'To the left. Stay on the hard ground. Go easy.'

He stood up, tilting his field cap further back on his head. The car wallowed over the potholes and uneven ledges. A footpath led past dusty scrub towards the remains of a mud hovel. To the right, the sight of a straight line leaped at him.

A straight line!

Nothing in nature is straight. He drummed that into every new draft of recruits.

'Gehen. Gehen. Schnell.'

The world exploded, wrapping him in flame. A giant hand plucked him upwards. The air was sucked from his lungs and then he was tumbling, tumbling.

He next opened his eyes to see two dirty desert boots planted three feet away.

'Nah, then,' said a deep Lancashire voice. 'Let's be 'avin' you.'

An air-raid siren began to wail somewhere in the south of London. People peered skywards and hurried on anxiously. The RAF were bombing Berlin and the *Luftwaffe* was retaliating with deadly pinprick attacks. In the last month alone two raids on London had killed over one hundred.

Cricklemarsh barely noticed the siren. It was more than a week since Lusty had left and not a waking hour went by without Cricklemarsh thinking of the operation. He had been strolling in Regent's Park, deep in thought. He had regarded the beautiful but flimsy Regency houses along its perimeter and not seen them. A loud blast of a car horn reminded Cricklemarsh that he was walking across Marylebone Road. He waved apologetically to the driver and hurried on, his mind instantly slipping back to review the operation.

He was convinced the best cover was the least cover. The assassin had to become a genuine person. But who?

It was almost impossible for the assassin to adopt the role of an ordinary civilian in Germany. Security organizations were everywhere. The Gestapo, SS and SD, together with local Nazi Party officials, kept up a ceaseless surveillance. Neighbours informed on neighbours, friends on friends, even children on their parents. The Nazis had set out to create a society of mistrust and they had succeeded all too well.

There was a theory that if you were going to bluff, then bluff high and use the Gestapo as a cover. Every Gestapo officer carried an individually numbered silver disc. Each disc, actually made from an alloy, had a deliberate flaw. SIS claimed to have cracked the secret of the flaw. It was tempting but, despite their reputation as omnipresent, there were in fact relatively few Gestapo officers, many of whom knew one another. It would be almost impossible to convince genuine Gestapo men that you were one of them.

Cricklemarsh was keen to pare down the risks to an absolute minimum. There was the account of the woman agent parachuted into France who was arrested her very first morning because she looked the wrong way at the kerb. Cricklemarsh suspected the story was apocryphal but one about how a German agent in Egypt had betrayed himself was true. The man had been perfect as an Arab, apart from one small thing. In public lavatories Arab men bent one leg when they urinated. The spy had pissed like a European: a minor detail – but it had cost him his life.

Luck would inevitably play its part but Cricklemarsh was determined that there would be no mindless botch-ups like the one last year when two SOE agents dining in the same restaurant in occupied France were caught in a police documents check because their identity cards, claiming they came from different parts of the country, were in the same handwriting. How could London have been so amateurish!

He had considered having his assassin assume the identity of a foreign worker as cover. There were over three million French, Belgians, Poles, Hungarians, Italians – all the nationalities of occupied Europe – working on German farms and in German armaments factories. Documents could pose a problem. A foreign worker had to carry not just his identity card, police and labour registrations, food and clothing ration coupons, travel permits, housing registration, driver's licence and draft exemption, but also an additional *Fremdenpass* and *Arbeitskarte*.

Anyway, there was a fatal flaw in the idea. An agent posing as a foreign worker could move freely *across* Germany heading for a new job. He would find it impossible to stay for more than one night in any one place.

But a wounded soldier on convalescent leave? Now that had real possibilities.

Lusty closed his notebook and sighed. It was sweltering and airless inside the tent. Sweat dripped into his eyes and ran down his backbone. He allowed time for the German officer to be escorted back to the cage, then rose slowly and made for the exit. The sunlight struck his already aching head like a sledgehammer. He put his hand up to protect his eyes.

The desert was not how Lusty had imagined it. There were no rolling sand dunes, only endless, sunbaked earth, straggly camel thorn, outcrops of ochre shale and shelves of grey rock. It was a different world out here: it was a soldiers' world. Men moved differently, spoke differently from London. They dressed like vagabonds, their clothing ill-matched, stained and patched; their faces lean and tanned almost black. He seemed to be the only one to notice the searing heat or the blinding light.

The desert was a good place for a war, said old hands – there was nothing to destroy. Its emptiness was the perfect playground for generals, but a nightmare for quartermasters who had to supply the armies with the fuel, ammunition and food.

Lusty's arrival at the holding camp for German and Italian prisoners of war near Buerat on the Gulf of Sirte had been greeted with mistrust by the brigade officers. Despite Lusty's pleas to be allowed to conduct his own screening first, the adjutant, Major Barker insisted on registering the steady stream of captives and deserters and sending their names back to base to be collated by the International Red Cross. Only the sparky little intelligence officer McKillican had shown any understanding of Lusty's mission – or the version of it he'd offered. He had even taken him up to the front line to interview prisoners immediately after capture – an expedition that had almost ended in disaster when the Germans attacked through a sandstorm. Instead of interviewing prisoners, Lusty had almost become one.

Lusty flopped down in the shade of an abandoned Panzer Mark III. One of its metal tracks lay unravelled in the dust, and someone had hung their underpants to dry on the barrel of the 37mm gun.

'Any luck?' asked McKillican.

Lusty shook his head. So far he had interviewed over forty captive officers and senior NCOs in his search. None fitted the bill. Or rather, none of those willing to talk had done so.

He flicked his cigarette butt away with his thumb and forefinger. If he looked in one direction he saw a landscape that had not changed in a thousand years. A young Arab boy had appeared from nowhere, beating a dusty donkey with a stick. Behind him, a white bird rose from the reeds lining the irrigation ditch that led towards the sea. If he turned his head he saw everywhere the detritus of modern war: Bren carriers and Bedford trucks each bearing a red jerboa in a circle – the insignia of the 7th Armoured Division – partially camouflaged tents and shelters made out of groundsheets and wooden crates.

'I might have something for you,' said McKillican. 'Some chaps in the Long Range Desert Patrol ambushed a DAK scout car last night. Our lads brought its occupants home with them. Major Barker doesn't know yet they're here.'

'Thanks.'

'Glad to help. I won't be in the desert for ever . . .'

'If you're ever in London, get in touch.' Lusty did not know what he could do to help further McKillican's career but it sounded the right thing to say.

Purefoy's constant visits were wearing Cricklemarsh down like water dripping on a stone. The man's initial friendliness had grown increasingly threadbare each time he called in to demand a progress report. Cricklemarsh could understand his superior's impatience but he was doing all he could. While Lusty was struggling to find a cover in Africa, Cricklemarsh himself was working eighteen hours a day to find the right man to pull the trigger.

Yet he was fighting with one arm tied behind his back.

He was banned from approaching the best recruits, the committed and the talented ones, who went to the French and Yugoslav sections. He could not ask X Section for help. Czechs were *out* after the Heydrich killing. He had trawled secretly through freelances on the Eastern European sections' books but to no avail. He wouldn't trust any of the Bulgars, Hungarians and Romanians he'd met with such a sensitive operation. His own old pals' network had so far failed to find anyone suitable.

'Hitler will be leaving the Wolf's Lair soon. You must have a man ready,' carped Purefoy.

'We're doing our best.'

'I trust your best will be good enough. You don't have much time.'

As soon as Purefoy left, Annie scurried into the room. 'What did he mean?'

Cricklemarsh showed no surprise at Annie's eavesdropping. 'If we don't come up with someone soon, then he'll take the operation away from us.'

'He can't do that.'

'He can – and he will.'

Lusty's first impression was of a tall man with square shoulders and the erect bearing of a Prussian officer. Then he saw the most brilliant black eye he'd seen for years.

'Please sit down. You're lucky to be alive, I'm told.' Lusty smiled. 'Have a cigarette. You'll need it to keep the flies away.'

The German's personal belongings had offered scant clues. A photograph of a smiling girl with *'All my love, Ingrid'* scrawled across it, and a letter from the same Ingrid written last May reporting that she was enjoying helping out in his father's business and everyone was being very kind. She was counting the days to his next leave – and their wedding.

A loving letter from an obviously nice girl. The sort of letter every soldier longed to receive.

'That was a nasty blow to your head. Do you want stronger pain-killers?'

The officer lowered himself stiffly onto the folding chair. He was not as tall as he had first appeared, realized Lusty. In fact, he was about his own build. The man had a stern face, heavy and humourless – but someone loved him. He would likely be a good soldier, too: not the sort to be popular but the men would follow him because they'd trust him to see the job done, properly

'How long have you been in Africa?'

The German gave Lusty a look that said, *Longer than you with your white knees.*

Lusty responded to the unspoken contempt. 'Me, I'm new here. Old to war, though. Lost my fingers in France. Were you there?'

The sun filtering through the khaki canvas cast a dappled light over the trestle table. God, it was hot. Lusty mopped his brow with his handkerchief. The German did not appear to be perspiring.

At last, the man spoke. 'I have given you my name, rank and number. I wish to rejoin my comrades.'

Lusty ignored him. 'Our patrol admired the way you spotted the mine they'd laid.'

The German stared straight ahead.

'Do you wish to see the medical offficer?'

'I wish to rejoin my comrades.'

'I was pleased to be given this job because I could use my German.' Lusty made a final effort to establish a relationship. 'Not to ferret out secrets – we know all we need to know about the DAK – and you must admit the war in Africa is going in only one direction. It's no shame on the Afrika Korps. You've done brilliantly to hold out against such odds. No, I was hoping to improve my German. I'm going to teach the language when the war's over. I studied in Mainz and Hamburg for a time, but I preferred Mainz. The people there are more easygoing. I was also in Cologne for a month. It's a lovely city, especially the old part around the cathedral . . .'

The German's eyes hardened. Lusty had lost him.

'. . . I'm sorry. I sometimes talk too much. I know you want to rejoin your comrades but the medical officer wishes to keep you under observation in case delayed shock sets in. That'll only be a day or two – until he's satisfied you're all right.'

Lusty waited until the German was out of the tent before swearing long and hard.

'How did you get on?' McKillican looked up from the tea he was brewing over a tin of flaming sand soaked in petrol, the blue flames almost invisible in the brilliant sunshine.

'One of those who would die before he'd give you even a "Good morning".'

'Sometimes those turn out to be the most talkative. Push the right button and they'll talk the hind legs off a donkey.'

'Clearly, I didn't press the right button.'

'Pity, because our lad is from the 3rd Motorised Reconnaissance Battalion of 21st Panzer. HQ Intelligence says the division's been broken up. Most of it's gone west to help von Arnim in Tunisia while their tanks and artillery have stayed on our front. Even efficient German clerks'll be hard pressed to cope with that administrative chaos.'

'Hell!'

A breeze rose, carrying for a moment the scent of wild thyme. Then it dropped and again Lusty was assailed by the pervasive odours of sweat, petrol, hot metal and urine.

'His driver's certainly happy to be out of the war. He's chatting away like a good 'un.'

'Can I talk to him?'

'Of course. He's broken his collarbone and he's had twelve stitches in his head but he's still as happy as Larry.'

Camel thorn grew around the medical tent where Schwegg was picking at the Panzer skull on his lapel, at peace with the world.

'Everything OK?' demanded Lusty in German.

'Jawohl, Herr Leutnant.' Schwegg beamed at someone speaking his mother tongue.

'Your captain's concerned about your injuries.'

Schwegg blinked in disbelief. 'He don't care what's happened to me. Bad-tempered sod, begging your pardon, sir. He put me on a charge only yesterday because he reckoned my rifle was dirty. Out here everything's dirty!'

'And was it?'

'You know what it's like, trying to keep anything clean. I had to service the scout car. I didn't have time for everything.' Schwegg's face was a picture of innocent indignation.

Lusty sympathized with the officer. Men like Schwegg were guileless, generally harmless, completely useless and guaranteed to drive sergeant majors and officers to distraction. Schwegg would have two left feet, be full of good intentions never carried out, and be the untidiest man in the company.

'He's had it in for me ever since we lost the Humber,' Schwegg grumbled. 'That car was his pride and joy. He blamed me for cracking its chassis when we went off the road in the Fuka last November. We were being shelled to shit at the time. The British had that road ranged to a metre. It was sheer madness. Just because *he* doesn't care if he lives or dies . . .'

'Why doesn't he care? Was he always like that?'

'Not really,' replied Schwegg, begrudgingly. 'He was never what you'd call a barrel of laughs – but after he lost his whole family and his fiancée in an RAF terror raid on Cologne . . .'

The penny dropped.

'This is amoral.'

'So's war.'

'If Margot ever finds out . . .' McKillican waved his cigarette furiously in front of his face to fend off an interested swarm of black flies.

'Tell her she played her part in shortening the war.'

The sentry stood aside as Lusty approached the tent where the German lay back on a camp bed, hands locked behind his head. He got to his feet, his face impassive.

'We're due a Red Cross inspection any minute. Once the MO's seen to you, you can join your comrades,' Lusty said abruptly and made to go. At the last moment he paused as if remembering something. 'The adjutant gave me some items to return to you.'

Lusty fumbled awkwardly in his breast pocket. A letter and two photographs fluttered to the floor. Both men bent to pick them up.

'That one's mine.' Lusty snatched up a picture of a smiling girl. He glanced at the picture clutched in the other's hand – and paused. A sad smile played over his face. 'They could be sisters.' He offered his photograph. 'Carol was killed in the Coventry bombing. We were going to get married. We had it all planned.' He swore with sudden vehemence. 'War is a bastard.'

'The wrong ones die.' The German spoke for the first time.

'Yes. The wrong ones die.' Lusty looked fondly at the girl. 'Carol didn't even live in Coventry. She just happened to be visiting on the wrong night. My father was killed a month later in the London Blitz. I have only a sister left.'

'I have no one.'

'No one? What happened?'

'They were all killed in the big raid on Cologne on 30 May last year. You called it The Thousand-Bomber Raid. Ingrid posted this letter just twelve hours before they came.' He began talking softly, as if to himself. 'Ingrid was staying with my parents in their apartment in Rheingasse. They thought she would be safer with them but there was a direct hit . . . They were everybody I had in the world.'

'I'm sorry.'

'Afterwards I had a letter from a neighbour down the street. She said that when the sirens started, everyone left their homes and stood outside to see if it was a false alarm. At first there was just the rising moon in the clear sky over Cologne. Then they heard the distant rumble of the aircraft engines; the searchlights came on, their beams describing patterns as they quartered the sky. Guns started firing but they made no difference. The planes drew closer and closer. The first bombs fell some way away, in Bichendorf and Ehrenfeld, then they heard bombs exploding to the north, in Niehl. They thought they might be lucky in the centre . . .'

'Have a cigarette.'

The floodgates had opened.

A sharp downpour brought an influx of wet, laughing men and women crowding into the Barley Mow. The dampness made Cricklemarsh's glasses mist up. As he pulled out a handkerchief to wipe them, he jogged the elbow of the man who had moved next to him. He wiped his glasses vigorously and peered at an officer in the Polish Independent Force. There was a wet patch on the sleeve of a well-cut uniform and a puddle of beer on the floor.

'Oh, dear, did I do that? Milly, a pint please and another whisky.'

'No. Really.'

'It's done. An advantage of my being a regular here.' A thought crossed Cricklemarsh's mind. 'Are you on your way to see anyone nearby?'

The Poles eyes narrowed. 'I'm afraid I couldn't say.'

Cricklemarsh pressed on. 'Sixty Baker Street, perhaps. You came in here to have a stiffener before your interview?'

'Your Sherlock Holmes would be envious . . .'

Cricklemarsh was pleased with himself. 'I haven't seen you before so I know you're not based locally. You are very smartly turned out – or you were until I spilled beer on you. I also know that they are conducting interviews today.' Cricklemarsh produced a card that identified him as a major in the Inter-Services Research Bureau.

'Captain Stefan Brewderski.' The man bowed formally. Average height, average build, brown hair. Everything average. The sort of man who does not stand out in a crowd. *Perfect.*

'Except I have already had my interview. They did not want me.' The Pole's disappointment was palpable.

'Why not?'

He shrugged. 'Ask them. They're your colleagues.'

'Do you mind if I ask you a question?'

Again the shrug. 'It's your country. Your army. Your war. Ask what you want.'

Cricklemarsh ignored the bitterness. 'Do you speak German?'

'Naturally. I was brought up near Danzig on the East Prussian border. I've always spoken German.'

'What did you do before the war?'

'I was a regular officer in charge of army marksmanship.'

Cricklemarsh felt a tingle of excitement. 'You must be a quite a good shot.'

The Pole drew himself up as though he had been insulted. 'I was Polish army champion in 1937 and 1938. In 1939 we had other things to shoot at,' he added dryly.

'How did you manage to get here?'

'I knew the port of Danzig well, so I hid on a Swedish ship, made my way to Norway and linked up with the British army fighting there. I was evacuated alongside them.'

'Why did you go to volunteer today?'

'I'm fed up sitting around on my arse. I want to be doing something.'

'Excuse me, sir,' Millie the barmaid interrupted, holding out a folded piece of paper. 'From that young lady there.'

Across the crowded bar he spotted Annie surrounded by admirers. He opened the note. *'One of Nye's spies is listening right behind you.'*

'Sorry. My secretary's just reminded me of a meeting. Write down your details and where you're based, and I'll be in touch.'

Annie entered their office, looking pleased with herself.

'How did you know I was being overheard?' enquired Cricklemarsh.

'I've seen them out to lunch together. Who were you talking to, anyway?'

'We may have found our man. It's always the way, isn't it? We've slaved through hundreds of records, dozens of interviews and I bump into the right one in the pub.'

'At least it might stop Purefoy going on at you.' There was a rap on the outside door. Annie returned, holding a coded signal. 'It's from Lusty.'

Cricklemarsh smiled at the high points of colour in Annie's cheeks.

Wasn't nature wonderful! Here was a woman who could take her pick from a troopship full of admirers. And she'd fallen for Lusty.

He concentrated on the signal. As Cricklemarsh read, he became more and more elated. 'He's done it. He's found him.'

Annie beamed in pleasure at Lusty's success. 'What now?'

'Now all he has to do is wring him dry.'

Lusty closed his eyes and listened to the buzzing. He began counting. One second, two seconds, three . . . He felt the flies settle on his eyelids, brushing the fine hair on his cheeks and dipping their legs in the beads of sweat on his forehead. More landed. He fought down the overwhelming desire to brush them off. Now they were exploring the dampness at the corner of his mouth, beginning to crawl inside his nostrils; first his right one, then . . .

'Christ! How can you!' McKillican exploded into the tent, waving his arms.

'All about self-control,' grinned Lusty, caught between pride and shame at his antics. He swung his legs over the edge of the camp bed.

'Our holiday's over,' announced McKillican, beating away flies with his hat. 'The battalion's coming out of rest. We're about to catch up with the war for the push into Tunisia.'

'Just watch yourself,' warned Lusty. 'The Yanks got a bloody nose at Kasserine Pass.'

'What'd you expect, putting green troops up against the hairy-arsed Afrika Korps? But at the end of the day it's not going to make any difference,' replied McKillican. 'The Germans'll never gain local air superiority again. Shame you won't be here for the victory parade.'

'What do you mean?' The idea of attaching himself to the Desert Rats had grown in Lusty's mind. Not only had the desert cast its spell over him but he'd be involved in real fighting.

'Your travel orders have just come through. They're in the orderly room.'

Lusty sighed. Back to grey old London, to the dusty files and boredom. He buttoned up his sweat-sodden shirt, rammed his cap on his head and bent out of the tent into the searing heat. A light breeze touched his face as he turned to the sea, sensing rather than smelling the warm tang of salt. On the horizon, fluffy white clouds sat over the blue waters. A fast submarine chaser was sending up a bow wave half a mile off shore. He envied its crew the cool wind.

'If you're sure you've finished with Beck, I'll slip notification of his capture into the next batch to go off to the Red Cross – and pray Major Barker never finds out you saw him first.'

'Thanks for all your help. You must look me up in London.'

Coached by lists of questions from Cricklemarsh, Lusty now knew everything there was to know about Christian Beck and his former life. He came from Cologne. His father had owned three garages, one near the Neumarkt, another on the Hohenstaufenring road and a third near the Hohenzollern bridge – all destroyed in the raid that had wiped out his only relations. He knew Beck had come top of his school class in mathematics, even that Beck's father had bought the Hohenstaufenring garage from a Jew at a knock-down price in 1938. His younger brother Joachim had drowned in the Rhine a month later. The price to pay for his father's greed, his mother had said. What do you think? Lusty had asked. 'I think it was a swimming accident,' Beck had replied.

Lusty even learned that the trams in Cologne were painted blue in an effort to avoid the Gestapo trap of asking suspects the innocent question: 'And what colour *are* the trams in your home town? Ignorance had cost the life of more than one brave undercover agent in France.

'One last favour,' he said to McKillican as they headed towards the orderly room: a camouflaged canvas tent erected over a four-feet-deep depression. 'See if you can get Beck sent to Canada with the next batch of prisoners. I'd hate to see him escape.'

'Why take the risk?' asked McKillican.

'What do you mean?'

'It's easy to have an accident out here. No one officially knows yet that Beck's a prisoner.'

Lusty let McKillican's suggestion sink in. The idea of eliminating Beck neither shocked nor disgusted him. But it was no part of his brief. And he'd come to like the serious German. He wasn't a bundle of laughs but he was a solid, dependable man who would try to do right before he would do wrong.

'No,' decided Lusty. 'Isn't that the sort of thing we're fighting against?'

Brigadier Gilbert had long since stopped caring for his wife Marjorie. He had come to accept that she was a hard and scheming woman but he could not stand the way she constantly accused him of being a failure. In drink, Marjorie turned from merely being bleak and uncharitable into a bitter shrew, carping on how so-and-so was a lieutenant general now, how so-and-so had become a military attaché in Washington. Now, as she approached the end of the second bottle of wine, Marjorie scanned the Dorchester's dining room to find someone who had done better than her husband and spotted Chalky White who had been a young second lieutenant, a mere wart, when Gilbert had already had two pips up. Now the man was a power in the War Office. Meanwhile, what was Gilbert doing? Languishing as deputy director of operations, allowing himself to be leapfrogged by a bunch of civilian amateurs in the uniforms of pilot officers.

'I don't know how you stand for it, Adrian. I really don't.' Gilbert winced at the well-worn litany. In vain, he pointed out that he had, really, not done too badly. He was a lieutenant colonel, and his acting rank of brigadier should be made substantive in the next year or two. In fact, he was doing well.

'Rubbish. How can you believe that? *You* should have been made director-general.' Marjorie sat upright, a thin, angry woman in a plain blue dress, her large black handbag under her chair. '*You* should be on the sixth floor.'

'Marjorie, please,' he hissed. She had a voice that cut through the muted hum of surrounding conversation like a buzz-saw through cardboard. At the next table, a florid businessman and a woman young enough, but too pretty, to be his daughter had fallen silent to listen.

'You're not a man, you're a mouse,' she hissed, taking her anger out on her Charlotte Russe – not even halting her diatribe in front of the black-coated waiter who poured the remnants of their wine. 'Well?'

'Two glasses of port, please. The Grahams '31.'

Gilbert had not been going to tell her – not yet. Not until the time was ripe. But, as always, she was getting under his skin. He waited until the waiter as out of earshot.

'I'm running a rather special operation at the moment.'

'Can't be that special if *you*'re running it.' Her nostrils dilated.

'Assassinating Hitler.'

Marjorie gave him a look of utter disbelief. 'What!'

Gilbert raised a hand to warn her against her habit of indignantly repeating any statement she questioned.

'The directorate's smarting because Winston keeps banging on how we're not setting Europe alight . . .'

'What does he expect if he appoints a bunch of amateurs?'

'So they want to impress him with a *coup de théâtre* . . .'

'And you're doing their dirty work?'

'I've given it to Purefoy. He's passed it on to a former don who's been dumped on us from Oxford.'

'Not Major Nye?'

'Good Lord, no. Purefoy's terrified that Nye's after his job.'

'But it's never going to work with some old professor in charge. Does he have any experience of this sort of operation?'

'I wouldn't have thought so.' Gilbert smiled. It was not a pleasant smile. Both corners of his mouth rose in a clown's leer but his eyes remained fixed and hostile. 'You don't understand, do you? I've made sure that there's no chance he'll pull it off.'

'But why?' Marjorie's mouth fell open.

'I'm not the only one who doesn't like the current gung-ho brand of leadership at Baker Street. A few chaps at Military Intelligence and one or two at Broadway are in despair at the way SOE is being run. It just needs one big balls-up, a national embarrassment, so they can go to War Cabinet and demand a clear-out to get rid of the amateurs. They'll insist that a pair of safe, reliable, experienced hands takes over. These hands, in fact.'

Gilbert held them out over the white linen tablecloth.

'I played Purefoy like a fish.' His right hand cast an imaginary fly. 'Just like a fish.'

'But Adrian, what can I say! That sounds brilliant.'

It had been mid-evening on a quiet Sunday night back in January when Gilbert had summoned Purefoy personally to his office. The curtains were drawn closed and the standard lamps spread a warm glow through the large room. Gilbert had poured whiskies from a decanter on the side desk and the two men stood side by side on the carpet in front of the low fire.

Gilbert cleared his throat. 'Winston is concerned that we are not pulling our weight, not setting Europe ablaze, as he puts it. Any ideas?'

'No, sir. Sorry, I mean, yes, sir.' The sudden revelation knocked Purefoy off balance, as Gilbert had intended. 'We've plenty of operations on the go, all doing their bit to undermine the Nazi occupation of Europe.'

'Yes, yes, I understand all that.' Gilbert turned to play with the fire. 'But it's not really enough, is it? Bit like this fire, really: it's glowing away, giving out some heat, but stand six feet away and you wouldn't know it was lit. It's hardly ablaze, is it?'

'Er, no, sir.' The fire dropped, sending up a crackle of sparks.

'What Winston would appreciate, I gather, is some act that'll catch the public imagination, hit the headlines – something dramatic. He liked the raid on Rommel's headquarters,' coaxed Gilbert. 'Didn't stop talking about it for days, even though it failed.'

'Maybe *we* could do something similar, only rather more successful. Perhaps we could kidnap someone significant. We'd be more subtle: more rapier than club.' Purefoy was pleased with his choice of words.

Gilbert raised an interrogative eyebrow. 'Anyone in mind?'

'Um . . . von Rundstedt, perhaps?'

'I don't think the German Army commander in France is well known enough – and it might appear we were aping the Rommel raid, don't you think?'

'Pétain?'

'Might upset the French, mmm?' Gilbert smiled encouragingly.

Purefoy took a nervous gulp at his whisky. 'Yes, yes, see your point. Have to be a German. Goebbels, Göring, someone like that. Himmler would be a popular choice.'

Gilbert rocked on his heels. 'I was talking to . . . some people last night . . .'

'Of course, if you've any . . .'

Gilbert placed his left forefinger under his nose and raised his right hand.

'Hitler?'

Gilbert took a measured sip and said nothing.

'Kidnap Hitler!' The barefaced audacity took Purefoy's breath away.

'Who said anything about kidnap.'

'Oh! You mean . . . Yes, that *would* set Europe ablaze . . .'

'And go down in history.'

'Would be difficult . . . getting a man in . . . gaining access . . . getting our man out again.' He saw Gilbert scowl. 'Right, we'll do our best.'

'That's the spirit.' Gilbert picked up some loose papers from his walnut desk to signal that the meeting was near its end. 'Who will you give it to?'

'Um . . . um . . .' Purefoy was thinking desperately. 'Might be one for Special Projects, sir. Let's see what that chap Cricklemarsh is made of.'

Gilbert gently sucked his teeth. 'Rather than Nye?'

'Major Nye claims he's snowed under with work. And this is a *special* project . . .'

Gilbert almost laughed aloud in satisfaction. 'Well, if you think so . . .'

'And you're absolutely convinced there's no chance of them pulling it off?' Marjorie asked.

'No chance at all. I sneeze, Purefoy catches cold, Cricklemarsh gets double pneumonia. Purefoy's putting so much pressure on Cricklemarsh that the wheels are bound to come off the operation at the first bump in the road. The funny thing is, the lot of them are too busy fighting like dogs over a bone to realize that the whole project's rotten inside.'

'It'll mean the loss of an agent.'

'We won't lose anyone we can't spare. I barred Cricklemarsh from tapping the usual pool of talent. Security, you know.' He gave a supercilious smile. 'That word covers a multitude of sins, and no one ever queries it. Cricklemarsh did manage to find himself a rather good Pole but I put a stop to that. The man's on his way to Cairo as we speak.'

'You're stampeding him into action before he's ready.' Marjorie glanced over his shoulder to see what had happened to their glasses of port.

'He should have started training up his gunman by now. Mark my words, this operation will shatter like a thin plate-glass window the first time someone taps on it.'

'And you'll be there to pick up the pieces.' For the first time in years, Marjorie looked at her husband with something resembling admiration.

The scenery was stunning but as Ilse Runge had seen it most of her life, she did not give the snow-clad peaks a second glance. Only Obersalzberg gave her a pang of longing. She put down her heavy basket covered in a tea cloth and gazed up the mountain. She could see Hitler's Berghof, Bormann's house nearest to it, and Göring's just above. To the right were the white-painted SS barracks. She regretted that she was no longer allowed to roam the mountain as she had as a child. But the farmers and the local families had been kicked out and the Nazi Party had taken their place. Yet, even if the mountain settlement had changed irrevocably, the sight of it brought back to her a happier time, a lost time of innocence and laughter. When she was a girl, she'd thought the sun was always going to shine, the light would last for ever. Now she retreated into those old times to get away from the present pain and humiliation.

'Ilse.'

Ilse snatched up her basket and came out of her reverie to find Birta Weiss standing in front of her like some broken flower. Her pale face was blotched and her eyes red-rimmed with tears. Her three young daughters clutched the hem of her coat.

'Birta, what's wrong?'

Ilse had known Birta and her husband Sieg since they were all in school together. Ilse was godmother to their youngest daughter, two-year-old Freya, who held out her arms to be lifted up.

'I've had a letter from Sieg . . .'

'Is he all right?'

'He's been taken prisoner by the Russians. He says he's being well treated.'

There was something in Birta's voice that made Ilse temper her reassurances. 'At least you know he's safe. You'll see him again when the war's over.'

Birta burst out crying. She glanced around the small square at the edge of Berchtesgaden before slipping an envelope into Ilse's hand.

'Look closely,' she whispered.

Birta had steamed off the stamp to reveal a square of minuscule writing. Ilse put down Freya and squinted to make out the words.

'They have cut off both my feet. I shall never come home.'

Birta let out an almighty wail, and the children, frightened for their mother, howled, too. A Party official slowed to scowl at the tableau. Ilse met his eye, challenging him to say a word but he recognized her and moved on.

'What I am going to do?' The words came between racked tears.

'Shush.' Ilse put her arms around her friend. She failed to find any words of comfort. 'Shush.'

'He was everything to me. You know, I never even held hands with another boy. My world is finished.' Birta produced a small white handkerchief with a swastika border and began rubbing her eyes.

'Don't be silly. You've still got the girls.' Little Freya had begun poking in the covered basket and Ilse casually moved it to her other side.

'But what's going to happen to us?'

'You'll be all right.' Ilse felt ashamed of such empty sentiments.

Freya was pulling at the cloth over the basket. Ilse quickly bent down. 'I've been baking *Pfeffernüsse* for my father. Would you like one each? Yes?'

The girls nodded solemnly. Ilse felt inside the basket and produced three biscuits.

Birta sobbed, 'I'm going to Aunt Maria in Munich – bombs or no bombs. I can't get work here with the little ones to look after, and if I don't work, I haven't enough money to feed them.'

'You mustn't give up all hope . . .'

'Why not?' the woman replied bitterly.

A picture of Birta and Sieg standing outside the church on their wedding day filled Ilse's mind. It had been a glorious day in May. There had been white and pink blossom and Ilse thought then that she'd never seen anyone quite as happy as Birta seemed that day. She had glowed with such happiness that people came and stood near her to bask in her radiance.

'Think of the girls. You know how proud Sieg was of them.'

Why had she spoken of him as if he was dead?

Because, in Birta's eyes, he already was.

The sharkmouth waggled its wings and plunged into a steep dive. In the leading Curtiss Kittyhawk, Flight Lieutenant Jock Pienaar adjusted the trim wheel as he felt resistance grow in the control stick. Beneath him the white villa and its satellite collection of mud-brick buildings grew by the second. Human specks were running to their anti-aircraft gun positions. He made out the 88mm guns and hoped to get beneath their range before they became awake; then he'd only have 20mm cannon and machine guns to worry about. He planned to catch the tiny settlement of Tarhuna unawares, diving on it out of the sun at noon when the day was at its hottest and men were at their doziest. He ignored the outlines of half-tracks and lorries now visible under their camouflage netting. The briefing officer had been very specific. The white villa and its outbuildings were the target; especially the white villa.

Pienaar glanced back to where the sun glared off the canopy of the newcomer to the Squadron, flying number four. He had done well to hold formation. When you first flew in North Africa, the endless desert – the Bundoo – failed to offer a single sign of life. Just merging shades of sand and dun brown with occasional, darker lines of tracks. Beginners could fly over their own airfields without recognising them, until the sun caught a glint of something, miraculously throwing the barren landscape into relief and making you wonder why you hadn't spotted your home base before.

The first black clouds burst high and to his right. Pienaar turned his head to check there were no Messerschmitts lurking in the sun above and tightened his grip on the control stick as his speed increased. The Kittyhawk was not an easy craft to fly. Pienaar had heard the Mark III was a stable fighting plane but they were stuck with the Mark I – and they were pigs to handle. Some Hurricane pilots flatly refused to transfer to them because so many pilots were lost in training.

His flight were following him down in a steep dive. Two aircraft were carrying 500lb high-explosive bombs, the other two carried incendiaries. You needed a very strong right arm to control the Kittyhawk, especially in the dive. It picked up speed quickly but it had a bad tendency to roll to the right. You could trim against it but that meant that when you pulled out the aircraft rolled violently to the left. Pienaar, like other experienced pilots, had developed the knack of trimming and bracing his right arm against the cockpit wall as the angle of dive increased. It was distracting to keep your left hand on the trimmer when it should be on the throttle but that was the most effective way.

The buildings grew larger in his sights. Men were running for the cover of slit trenches and a car set off, bouncing across the desert. Pienaar saw the flashes of a machine gun on the villa roof. He wouldn't like to be the men behind it. In a few seconds they would be dead.

Steady. Steady, now. He pressed the bomb release. The Kittyhawk bucked free. Pienaar flattened out of the dive and sped across the desert at zero feet. He banked steeply as the explosions went off. released the bomb too early. Through the expanding cloud of dust

He'd and smoke he saw he'd flattened an outbuilding but only scarred the white villa. The rest of the flight would have to bomb blind

His wingman did better. His 250lb firebomb of benzol and rubber splattered the building with hundreds of flaming cowpats. Number three scored a direct hit on the villa with HE. The new man was either very good or lucky. His firebombs plunged onto the remaining outbuildings. Black smoke billowed skywards in a tumbling column visible for miles.

Pienaar and his flight returned with two low strafing runs to deter heroes who fancied trying to rescue anything from the blazing debris, then they climbed in a four-finger formation and headed back east. Ten minutes ago, those buildings had housed the paymaster's office for the remaining section of the 21st Panzer Division – and all their records. Not any more.

3

'It's good of you to pick me up.' Lusty swung his bag into the back of the staff car, parked outside the reception hut at Northolt airfield.

'It was Cricklemarsh's idea,' lied Annie. She smoothed down her skirt and automatically inspected her hair in the driver's mirror. Lusty's suntan suited him. He'd lost that slight flabbiness that came with working in a London office: he was leaner and hungrier somehow. She pulled out onto the Great West Road ahead of a convoy of Bedford three-tonners.

'How is the old man?'

'He's delighted with Beck. Fancy him not having any relatives. You'd have thought everyone would have *someone*.'

'I think there're cousins far removed but they wouldn't recognize each other if they shared a bed. It's sad, really.'

It had been something Beck had mentioned more than once. If he did not have children then his family would die out. He had seen photographs of large family gatherings taken in the early years of the century, but now there was just him. The Great War had taken its toll. Some family members had not married; others had been childless; two had died young. Until, from all of them, like an inverted triangle, there was just Christian Beck left. People had hoped he and Ingrid would reverse the family decline. Now he did not care to speak of the future.

'What's he like, then?'

'A decent bloke.' Yes, that summed Beck up: a decent bloke.

Annie tweaked the lapel of her uniform jacket. Lusty smelled her freshness and her scent. He had not been this close to a woman for God knew how long. On an impulse, he leaned across and planted a gentle kiss under her ear.

Oh, Jesus, why had he done that?

'I'll pretend that didn't happen – sir.' Annie stared straight at the road ahead.

'Annie . . .?' It was almost a plea.

'If I crash this car, it'll be your fault.'

'Dinner with me tonight?' He didn't know where he was finding his courage. It must be his brief time near a real war.

'You'll be disappointed.'

'Why?'

'You want dinner, we'll have dinner. Tomorrow night. But that's all. Is that understood? It's not going to happen.'

I won't let it happen. Damn you, Robin Lusty, you haven't a clue, have you? Haven't a clue what I feel for you. Stupid man.

'Dinner's all I want.'

'Good. Because that's all you're getting.' She knew she sounded harsh and ungracious.

Lusty looked out at the swathes of West London villas spread under the slumbering barrage balloons and wondered why Annie was being so aggressive. She could have just turned him down.

'What else is happening at HQ?' he asked to change the subject.

'We've a problem finding someone to play the part of Beck. Purefoy is nagging Cricklemarsh every day, though I don't know what he hopes to achieve. He's just making thing worse.'

'Why's it so urgent?'

'Hitler's going to leave the Eastern Front before too long, so our gunman should already be training by now.'

'What'll happen if Cricklemarsh can't find anyone suitable?'

'I don't know. He's trying incredibly hard but he still doesn't seem to be able to get anywhere. He thought he'd stumbled upon the perfect choice but the fellow was shipped off to the Middle East.' Annie frowned. 'It's almost as if someone out there doesn't *want* it to work.'

'You really think!'

'I don't know.' Annie sighed. 'I'm probably being fanciful but it's so frustrating, especially with that creep Nye sniffing around. He can't know exactly how far we've come, but he's getting suspicious.'

'You don't think he'll try to hijack the operation?'

'You don't know him very well,' said Annie coldly.

Lusty chose to take it in a different sense. 'No. We don't move in the same circles.'

Annie shot him a disapproving look. She thought about upbraiding him for the perpetual chip on his shoulder, then decided that Nye annoyed her even more.

'Nye's a self-obsessed pig who uses people for his own ends.' Her facial muscles tightened as she remembered those weeks after Paul's capture, when she had lost her bearings and Nye had offered comforting words and false sympathy. Bastard! By the time she had discovered what he was really about, it was too late. She had not forgotten nor forgiven.

'A feast! You've brought me a veritable feast!'

Hugo Guttmann's obvious pleasure and gratitude moved Ilse Runge to kiss the small, white-haired man on both cheeks. Then, as if such effusion was all she had inside her, she sunk down into a chair at the old writing desk.

'It may be a few days before I can come here again. It's getting harder . . .'

A floorboard creaked outside the small windowless office. Her eyes flickered nervously towards the bolted door.

'It's only the building settling,' reassured Guttmann. 'It happens all the time.'

'I'm on edge. I've just met Birta Weiss. Remember, I told you that her husband was trapped with the troops at Stalingrad. She's finally heard from him.' She recounted her conversation, her head bowed. 'Poor Birta,' she concluded. 'I used to envy her her happiness.' She gave a stifled, bitter laugh. 'Maybe I still do.'

'That's enough,' warned Guttmann, gently.

'I'm sorry.'

'Now let's see what you've brought me. Goodness, *Leberwurst*. Compote of black cherries. I don't believe it.' Guttmann's blue eyes twinkled as he capered about like a clockwork toy. 'Tinned goose. Tongue! *enzian*. Ilse, you're a miracle worker.'

'Compliments of the Party.' She smiled, knowing he was putting on an act for her benefit. 'There's enough bread there for four or five days. Father will bring you another loaf if I can't get here.'

'You're wonderful. I will tell you my new joke. In Heaven, Frederick the Great, Napoleon and Hindenburg are talking about war. Frederick says, "If I'd had as many aeroplanes as Göring, the Seven Years' War would have been over in four months." Hindenburg says, "If I'd as many tanks as Hitler, the German army would have swept the British and Americans out of France in March 1918." Napoleon chips in, "If I'd had Dr Goebbels, the French people would never have found out that I lost the campaign in Russia."'

In spite of herself, Ilse smiled. 'Where do you get all these jokes?'

'People used to say there was a secret joke factory in Silesia but the Party closed it down, so I make up my own. I've lots of time.' As Guttmann spoke, he examined Ilse closely. Her eyes burned unnaturally brightly in her drawn face while her fingers picked nervously at a loose thread on a coat button; her hands always had to be busy. 'I'm sorry. It's not fair that I'm putting you and your father in such danger. I should leave this place.'

'Rubbish.' Ilse leapt up to confront him with unblinking, amber eyes that reminded him of an owl's. 'Don't think such silly thoughts. You are our prisoner.'

'I am a very fortunate prisoner.'

Ilse gave a tired smile and felt guilty that she could not tell the old man the truth. Yes, the ever-present threat of discovery was wearing but that was not the reason for her current emotional state. Two days ago she had visited an old woman in a farmhouse near Maria Gern. She had come home in the farm cart and gone straight to bed.

It had been her second visit in eighteen months, as she kept her pledge to herself that she would never carry her husband's child.

'Meissner. Meissner. Where the hell are you?'

Ilse and Guttmann froze.

'My husband!' hissed Ilse.

'What's Runge doing here?'

'I thought he was in Bad Reichenhall on Party business.'

'Meissner.'

The call sounded closer now.

'Quick.'

Ilse smoothed down her dress, slid back the oiled bolt and stepped out into the dark, narrow passage. The louder thump of the printing presses reverberated off the walls. She advanced towards the burly figure emerging in the gloom at the top of the wooden stairs.

'Ilse? What are you doing here? I thought you were ill in bed.'

'I came to visit my father but he's not here.'

'You can get out of bed to see your father but you won't do anything for me.' Runge tried to push past her. 'Move back, will you. I want to get to the office.'

Ilse backed away slowly as he advanced.

'What do you want to see father about?'

'That's my business. Just get out of the way.'

He pushed on past her into the small office, now empty apart from Ilse's unloaded basket.

It was typical of Lusty's father to tell Annie on the phone that he would meet his son for lunch at his club. It conjured a picture of ancient servants, high ceilings, dark oil paintings, pomp, grandeur and tradition. In fact, Abigail's was a drinking club above a hardware shop on the edges of Fitzrovia. The bar had faded carpets and soggy sofas, their backs greasy with generations of hair oil. The back room served badly cooked food whose sole purpose was to mop up the alcohol.

Lusty retained a particular image of his father Basil, a mental snapshot taken during a school holiday of a spare, upright man with crinkly hair. The reality now, he knew, would be different but he was still shocked by the sight of the man rising from the table. His father had become bloated and bleary in the six months since they'd last met. Tiny red and blue veins had spread across his cheeks and his sandy moustache was stained with nicotine. He was dressed in civvies, with a regimental tie. His shoes shone and his trousers had a knife-edge crease, yet his blazer was rucked on the shoulder and the lapels were shiny with age.

'You didn't get a tan like that in this country.'

'No, dad. I've been in North Africa.'

'Thought you were in an office in London.'

'This trip was part of my job. I'm afraid I can't . . . it's hush-hush,' he said finally.

'Surely you can tell your old man.'

'Please . . .'

'Fine. Right.' He tossed off the whisky. At the bar, he slipped in an extra one for himself while his son's pint of beer was being pulled.

It was not going to be an easy lunch, sighed Lusty inwardly. His father was already repeating himself – a sign that he'd been drinking for some while. Lusty politely enquired about his job as production manager of a small munitions works outside Derby.

'The factory's booming. We can't produce enough right now. God, if only it'd been like this in 1929.' He made an impatient gesture that sent his whisky glass skeetering across the table. He grabbed at it.

'It's all in the past, dad.'

'But it's not, is it, Robin? I've been thinking a lot about things. Over a nightcap, that's the time you see clearly. We carry the past with us. If I hadn't gone bust then, I'd have my own business now. Maybe if I hadn't hung on for so long, if I'd accepted the inevitable sooner, I'd have got back on my feet sooner. I paid all my creditors off, you know – paid every last penny.'

'Yes, I know, dad.' Every time they met, they went through the same conversation.

'I failed you.'

'Rubbish, dad.'

Basil Lusty had had what was called a good war in 1914–18. He had finished up a brevet lieutenant colonel with a DSO and an MC. He had then gone into the arms industry, selling armoured cars until he'd decided to go it alone – just before the Depression struck. He had lost everything. His son had been taken out of public school aged fourteen.

Robin Lusty's feelings towards his father were mixed. He was proud of his war record, proud of the way he had paid off all his debts – but then, just as he'd been ready to make a fresh start, he had let things slide. He had begun drinking heavily – and never stopped. There followed a succession of jobs with smaller and smaller arms manufacturers in increasingly obscure countries. While Lusty had seen little of his father when he had been at public school, he saw even less of him subsequently. Teenage holidays were spent with his German grandmother, his *Oma*, in Dresden because his strict Scottish aunts found the presence of a boisterous schoolboy an unwelcome burden. The antipathy was mutual, so he had gravitated towards Germany, spending more and more time with his grandmother there and finally entering Dresden university.

The current war had turned his father into a parody of his former self. The man who had once been awarded the DSO for taking command of a broken county battalion, welding it back into a fighting unit and personally leading it over the top into battle, was now droning on about his Home Guard company.

Lusty tried hard not to pity him.

His father broke off from yet another apology for ruining his son's life to talk about the war. 'We must finish it properly this time by defeating Germany on her own soil. I only pray there won't be the same slaughter as in the last war. This country can't afford to spill the blood of so many of its young men again. I'd worry about you if you hadn't already done your bit.'

But I haven't done my bit, thought Lusty. *Not compared to what you did.*

He'd read the citation for his father's Military Cross. He had single-handedly captured a German machine gun and turned it on the enemy, ensuring that his battalion's attack succeeded. What had Lusty himself done? Shot down a Stuka in a moment of raging madness and lost two fingers doing it

Lusty had trouble finishing the watery shepherd's pie. He left soon afterwards, confused and depressed, and not sure of anything any more.

The gibbet had been built high enough for everyone in the stadium to watch the execution. The condemned man stood meekly on the back of a lorry, a hood over his head, hands tied behind his back, the noose already around his neck. *Sturmbannführer* Jäger of the *Kriminalpolizei* lit a cheroot and wondered, as he always did when he watched an execution, why the man did not struggle. If he was in that same position he'd make life as uncomfortable as possible for the bastards about to kill him. What was there to lose? His dignity? Dignity be damned! Why dignify death? It was a common squalid little thing – as common as a dose of clap.

He wished they'd get a move on.

His superior, *Standartenführer* Esser, was standing on the gibbet, shouting a warning to the five thousand foreign workers, brought from miles around to this athletics ground on the outskirts of Munich, that this should be a lesson to every man who dared to contaminate the racial purity of the German race. Touch a German woman – and we'll hang you. It should have been an awe-inspiring speech but Esser was short and round and looked ridiculous, thought Jäger.

He would have felt sorry for the poor Pole standing on the back of the lorry – if he had not been such in a hurry. After all, what had the Pole done? Shafted a farmer's wife – and got caught. From the little he knew of the case, she had been asking for it. Now she was in a concentration camp and her lover was about to dangle on a rope. He hoped it had been a good fuck.

At last Esser stopped ranting, the lorry lurched forward and the Pole dropped into space. It was not a quick or a clean end; the hangman had botched it. Instead of the man's neck snapping cleanly, the Pole was suffocating to death, twitching obscenely like a worm on a line. Finally, he gave a convulsive jerk and went still.

A collective sigh, like a cloud passing, went through the crowd.

'Get the car, Wulzinger. We've wasted enough time here.'

The man-mountain shot him a warning look. 'Shush, boss. Esser will hear you.'

Jäger did not care. He did not see why he had been expected to attend this execution – just because Esser himself was obsessed with racial purity. Jäger had real criminals to catch: two rapes that he was sure were connected; a black-market shooting, a series of burglaries in

Obermenzing, plus God knew what else that had arrived in his in-tray at *Kripo* headquarters overnight.

Esser approached them. 'A little different from France, eh, *Sturmbannführer*?'

Jäger regarded the tubby little man doing his best to swagger in the black uniform of the SS. 'What about our own soldiers having it off with French women?'

'That's different.'

'That's not what our soldiers' wives think.'

Jäger blew out smoke. Esser tried to stare him down but only succeeded in looking shifty. As always, he felt ill at ease around the sardonic detective with his billhook nose and eyes that seemed to look right into your mind and not like what they found. Jäger was a copper, a thief-taker, a hunter. Esser was a Party appointee. But the Party ruled and Jäger could like it or lump it. Why had he returned from that soft posting of his in France, anyway? Esser certainly wouldn't have.

'I'm sure you have duties to attend to.'

'I'm sure I do.'

In the car driving back to their Ettstraße headquarters, Wulzinger demanded, 'Why do you deliberately rub him up the wrong way? He'll just make life difficult for us.'

'He annoys me.' Jäger lit another cheroot, reflecting that he only had two left to last the week unless he could squeeze some out of a black-market grass who owed him a favour.

'While I remember . . .' Wulzinger fumbled in the inside pocket of his jacket. 'An internal memo came around, listing those who were behind in paying their Party dues. You're top of the list. You owe for four months.'

'Shit.' Jäger inspected the memo. 'I'll say I thought I'd paid in France.'

'Don't let Esser get anything on you. You know you're not his favourite copper.'

'Bollocks.'

'You were bloody mad to come back from France.'

'I've told you, poncing around pretending to capture spies is not my game. Give me honest murderers and thieves any time. The French Milice make our Gestapo look like kindergarten attendants. There's something deeply unpleasant about people who strive to become more brutal than their conquerors.'

Jäger looked out of the window at Munich's shabby suburbs and told himself that part of his explanation was true. He had been posted to Clermont-Ferrand to liaise with the Gestapo and French police tracking down saboteurs and SOE teams dropped by the British. After six months he had returned. He had enjoyed the French weather, French wine, even French food, yet the collaborators unsettled him. He did not enjoy despising those he worked with. But he would have stuck it if it had not been for a letter from his wife Monika hinting that all was not well with their eighteen-year-old daughter Alix who was studying at Munich University. She was worried that Alix was getting involved with the wrong types – anti-social types.

They were about to turn onto the Ludwigsbrücke spanning the Isar river. Ahead the road was blocked by a tram, which had come loose from its overhead power wires as it had swung into the curve. The driver was attempting to reconnect it to the wires with a long pole. Jäger found himself looking at a young woman standing in the middle of the bridge with three little girls. The girls were as pretty as pictures, dressed in their Sunday best with matching red coats with black velvet collars and white lisle socks. Their mother fussed over them, adjusting the collar of the smallest girl, the one with the mass of blonde curls. The woman looked as if she had been crying. She was taking things out of a bag and putting them in each girl's pockets. Now she lifted the children one by one to sit on the parapet. Their little shoes shone, so clean and neat, and Jäger wondered where they had been. To a christening, maybe?

'Come on. Come on.' Wulzinger sounded the horn impatiently.

Jäger continued to watch the mother and her girls who were all huddled together now. She stepped back and for the first time, Jäger noticed that she was as pale as dawn.

He saw also that she had threaded a long, thin rope, like a mountaineering rope, through the buttonholes in the girls' coats.

Fingers of ice crawled up his spine as he glimpsed the awful finality of what was about to happen.

With a clang of its bell, the tram pulled forward. 'About time,' muttered Wulzinger.

The woman was kissing each of her children in turn. She had fed one end of the line through her own coat and was tying a knot.

'Stop the car.' Jäger leapt out while it was still moving, tumbling in the gutter. He picked himself up, running desperately, shouting at the top of his voice.

The woman turned to look at him. Still she did not hurry. Facing him, she levered herself onto the parapet, tucking her legs under her as she swung round. She smiled at her daughters for the last time. Jäger was still twenty feet away as the woman slipped off into space. One by one the girls were snatched away by an invisible hand.

'No. No.'

He dashed across the road, kicking out at a *Wehrmacht* staff car that refused to slow down. Three small red coats and one green one were slowly sinking into the waters of the Isar. Now he understood what she had been putting in their pockets – bricks or stones. The smallest girl was scrabbling frantically, her mouth open in a silent scream.

There was a barge chugging upstream, towing four lighters of coal. The bargeman had seen the bodies in the water. He threw a rope. A good throw. It landed just two metres upstream from the woman.

'Grab it. Grab the rope.'

It brushed against the mother's face but she ignored it. Behind her, sinking in the brown waters, were her daughters. The smallest one, the one with the blonde curls, grasped at the rope. She held it for a second in one tiny hand, then let go.

Jäger clattered down the steps that led down to the island in the middle of the Isar, shouting, swearing. Helpless.

The barge had stopped, its screw churning the water as it drifted astern. The mate lowered a dinghy. He snagged the rope holding the girls with a boat-hook but together they were too heavy for him to pull into his boat. A launch arrived. Together the mate and the launch's crew cut the cord that bound the girls together in death and dragged them on board.

One by one the girls were laid on the quayside. Puddles spread around them. Their little faces were of a whiteness Jäger had never seen before. As though the green hue of the water had seeped into their pores. The mother was the last to be brought ashore.

'Shit! She's still breathing,' exclaimed Wulzinger, as he felt inside her coat pocket for her identity papers. He handed them to Jäger and slammed down onto the woman's chest. Waited. And pressed down again. She coughed. Wulzinger rolled her on her side. She coughed again. River water trickled out of her mouth.

Strangely, her *Kennkarte* was still dry. 'Birta Weiss,' read Jäger.

At the sound of her name, the woman opened her eyes.

The dreadful realization that she was alive swept over her. She tried to turn to see her children but the effort brought on a spasm of coughing. Jäger looked in her eyes and saw the pain there. It seemed beyond measure. She tried to speak but he shook his head to silence her. He took in the three small, huddled corpses and knelt by the woman's side. Then he pulled up her collar so that it covered her neck. There was a muffled shot.

'It's what she wanted,' he said, replacing his Mauser in its holster. 'And what she deserved. For fuck's sake, Wulzinger, it saved the state the bother of a trial.'

Robin Lusty draped his good hand over Annie's, which lay on the white linen tablecloth. He traced her slim fingers and thought how cool her hand was. At the far end of the room, a small orchestra was doing its best to reproduce the big-band sound. This evening was costing him a fortune but Lusty did not care. He raised his eyes to her face, shadowed and softened by the light of their table lamp. Mellowly drunk, he began quoting softly.

> 'Had I the heavens' embroidered cloths,
> Enwrought with golden and silver light,
> The blue and the dim and the dark cloths
> Of night and light and the half-light.
> I would spread the cloths under your feet:

But I, being poor, have only my dreams;
I have spread my dreams under your feet;
Tread softly, because you tread on my dreams.'

Annie, warm, friendly, sexy Annie, smiled sweetly and said: 'That's lovely but I'm still not going to sleep with you.'

Lusty gave her his crooked schoolboy grin.

'I told you I wasn't. Don't look so hurt. Men and women can be friends, you know, without having to sleep together.'

'I don't want to sleep.'

She had known this would happen. She had played down her appearance – very little make-up, as plain a dress as her fashion sense permitted – but Lusty was still acting the puppy dog.

'No.' Annie burst out laughing at his patent disappointment. Her eyes softened. He was so boyish and vulnerable somehow. That was his charm, but Annie could not stand being hurt again. She squeezed his hand. 'I do not have affairs with men I work with.'

'Ah, but if we didn't . . .' Lusty grimaced and doubled up.

'Are you all right?'

'Excuse me, I think I picked up some bug in Africa . . .' He got up and hurried towards the door.

I do not have affairs with men I work with. Left alone, Annie thought again of Paul. She did even not know if he was dead or alive. In one way, she hoped he was dead, and that he had died with dignity. She winced as she remembered Nye. God, she'd been taken in by Nye and his dark good looks. There'd been a certain feline grace about him, a femininity, almost. If she thought in terms of smells, he was a French scent. Expansive but ultimately vacuous. She pursued her line of thought. Cricklemarsh was easy. Tobacco and leather reminiscent of pipes, carpet slippers, kindness, What was Lusty? Something dependable? Wood? Woodsmoke. English apple wood. Maybe a drying breeze, something fresh. She realized she was getting drunk. She was thinking herself into bed with Lusty. Why not? He had leafy eyes. Annie giggled. She was trying to cling to the shreds of her good intentions while a clamorous imp inside told her she was behaving like a boring old cow. Why not? Yes, why shouldn't she?

It was about time . . . And Lusty would not betray her like Nye had done.

He returned and sat down, looking embarrassed. 'Sorry about that . . .'

'You know I said I didn't sleep with men in the office . . .'

'That's what I was about to tell you,' interrupted Lusty. 'I'm not going to be in the office much longer. I'm volunteering for the German job.'

'What!' Something inside her expanded to fill her very being, then contracted until she felt empty and afraid.

'Why?'

'Why what?'

'Why are you doing this?'

'I balanced all, brought all to mind,
The years to come seemed waste of breath,
A waste of breath the years behind
In balance with this life, this death.'

'This new-found desire for suicide is making you very literary.'

'Yeats again. "An Irish Airman Foresees His Death".'

'Yes, I know. I did spend two years in Dublin, remember.'

'Ah, the ambassador's daughter.'

Annie ignored him. 'You're not Irish, you're not an airman. Although you might be foreseeing your death. What's possessed you?'

'You said yourself Cricklemarsh can't find anyone suitable and time's running out. What's wrong with me? I'm bilingual, a good shot, if I say it myself, and I know more about Christian Beck than any man living, apart from Christian Beck himself.'

Annie leaned back in her chair. 'You're serious, aren't you? This isn't just a game.'

'No.' He was surprised that she had for a moment thought it was.

They were silent while the wine waiter filled their glasses.

'Well, that's it,' she announced. 'I'm definitely not sleeping with you now.'

'But you said you weren't going to anyway.' He was confused. One minute she was not going to sleep with him because they worked in the same office, the next she wasn't because he was going away.

'You don't understand, do you?'

'What about a going-away present?'

'No.'

'A welcome-home one?'

'We'll see.'

He beamed but Annie was not going to let him get away with making light of his sacrifice; for sacrifice it was in her eyes. Annie was used to getting her own way. Her mood darkened into one of thwarted truculence.

'No. You can't,' she said, matter-of-factly. 'You can't go.'

'Sorry. There's a war on.'

'Who are you trying to impress? Not me. I'm not impressed by silly gestures.'

'It's not a gesture, Annie. Someone has to do it.'

'But why you?'

'There isn't anyone else.'

She carried on as if she had not heard him. 'Are you trying to get even for something? If you are, you're wrong. Cricklemarsh says revenge is a false motivation. Is it for revenge?'

'No,' he lied.

He had been at university in Dresden in November 1938, staying with his *Oma* and her second husband above their delicatessen. The Nazi newspapers were full of the news that a German diplomat, von Rath, had been shot in the Paris embassy by a demented Polish Jew, Hershel Grynszpan. Two days later von Rath died. It boded ill, said Lusty's Jewish step-grandfather.

Lusty had spent that evening with a girlfriend in the countryside. When he returned to the city centre, the air was electric. Lorries full of cheering Brownshirts waving swastikas and chanting Nazi slogans, hurtled through the night. His tram had been made to inch its way through the crowds on the cobbled streets, its bell constantly clanging.

It was to be known as *Kristallnacht*, Crystal Night, from the broken glass of Jewish shop windows. By the time the Nazis finished their orgy of murder and pillage, ninety-one Jews had been killed and twenty-six thousand rounded up and sent to concentration camps. Seven thousand Jewish businesses and every synagogue in Germany was set alight while firemen stood by, ready to prevent the flames spreading to neighbouring Aryan properties.

Lusty rounded the corner to find a mob of SA thugs smashing the delicatessen's window. He caught a glimpse of his terrified grandfather upstairs. The louts were already through the shattered window, looting bottles and boxes, when he ran up to them.

'Stop! Stop!'

He grabbed one SA man by his collar and hurled him into the street. Someone smashed Lusty over the head so that he fell face forward into the broken glass. A jackboot crunched into his face. Then his grandmother was down among them, screaming and calling them all the names under the sun. They should be ashamed of themselves. Good German boys. What would their mothers think of them? For a second they were at a loss. They had no answer for this spitting lioness who reminded them of their pride. Then someone called out, 'Jew'.

Barely conscious, Lusty heard his grandmother reply, 'I am not a Jew but I would rather be one than be a German tonight.'

Then they were on her. He rose to his hands and knees, blood dripping into his eyes. Through a haze he saw two policemen across the road looking on. He tried to call to them but someone hit him again from behind. When he next opened his eyes, the mob were kicking at a bundle of rags – kicking his *Oma* to death. When they had done, one spat on her body.

Naïvely, Lusty believed in justice. He went to the police station to demand that the murderers should be punished. He was greeted first with incredulity and then with anger. They mocked him as a Jew-lover. A Gestapo officer warned him that if he didn't leave, he'd end up in a concentration camp. When he continued to argue, they threw him down the police station steps, their taunts and jeers echoing in his ears.

He buried his grandmother that same afternoon and that night he hunted down the leader of the local Brownshirts. He had no gun so he took the cheese wire from his grandparents' wrecked shop. He had it around the Nazi's neck before the man was aware, slackening it just long enough to tell the Nazi why he was about to die. Then he pulled so hard the thug's head finished up barely connected to his neck.

The next morning, he took his grandfather, still in shock, back to England. The old man was broken in mind and spirit. His death at the height of the Blitz was the release he had been seeking.

Cricklemarsh did not know whether to be grateful, relieved or dismayed when Lusty volunteered first thing next morning. His first reaction was to say no.

'Why not?' repeated Lusty, his arms spread wide.

Cricklemarsh sighed. 'Are you sure you're not doing this just to help out?'

It was difficult enough to send men you hardly knew on operations where the odds were heavily stacked against them. It was almost impossible to send a friend. Case officers kept their distance from the agents they deployed. They had to get to know them to predict how they would respond in moments of crisis but you never became comrades with a man you might be sending to his death.

'London staff officers aren't allowed to serve in enemy territory,' Annie heard herself say.

'Nonsense,' retorted Lusty. 'No one stops Yeo-Thomas popping off to France.'

'We'll find someone else,' she insisted.

'Not in time you won't.' Lusty gave her a piratical lopsided smile. 'Anyway, it'd be wrong for me to expect someone else to do a job I wouldn't do myself.'

A squall rattled the ill-fitting window panes. He glanced out through the glass at the wet roofs. There was a patch of blue away in the distance.

Cricklemarsh was at a loss. To give himself time to think, he asked: 'Remind us how you're part German.'

'My mother had a German mother and a Scottish father. When her father died in 1913, her mother returned to Germany. She was stranded there by the outbreak of war and remarried in 1918. My own mother died in the influenza epidemic the following year when I was three. My father was abroad a lot so I spent every summer and most holidays with my maternal grandmother in Germany. In a way, it became home to me.'

'You must have seen a lot of the Nazi Party.'

'I was an honorary member of the Hitler Youth.' He grinned at Cricklemarsh's surprise. 'I went back one summer to find all my friends had been forced to join up. The local Nazi Party *Kreisleiter* thought it a feather in his cap to have an English schoolboy in the *Hitler-Jugend*. I even met the HJ leader Shirach von Baldur.'

'Did you take the oath?'

'I had to – but I kept my fingers crossed. And I can shoot. It's perfect, you see. I know the operation, I know Christian Beck. I'm more or less the same height and build as him.' Lusty grinned. 'And I've always wanted to drive a tank.'

'You don't drive a tank in a recce battalion . . .' Cricklemarsh realized he had risen to the bait and tailed off. 'It won't be enough to play the part of Beck. You have to be him, a Panzer captain in a black uniform.'

'They don't wear Panzer black in Africa,' Lusty pointed out.

Cricklemarsh refused to be trumped. '*We* don't wear Panzer black in Africa.'

Annie swirled the teapot in both hands. 'Sugar, Christian?' she murmured.

The blue in the sky was growing. It was going to be a nice day after all. Lusty became aware that Cricklemarsh and Annie were staring at him.

'I'm talking to you, Christian,' said Annie severely.

He blushed. 'Yes, of course. I've a lot to learn.' Annie handed him his tea. 'May I have a piece of humble pie as well, please?'

'Would you eat it?'

A little while after Lusty had left, whistling 'Lili Marlene', Annie stood silently in front of Cricklemarsh's desk. It was a few seconds before he noticed she was there. He gave her a kindly questioning look over the top of his spectacles.

'Please don't let him do this.'

'Annie . . .' Cricklemarsh dropped his eyes.

'Please stop him.' Annie pulled an already damp handkerchief from her sleeve and twisted it between her fingers. 'What's prompted him to volunteer?'

'He thinks it's his duty to.'

Annie wasn't satisfied. 'There must be something deeper.'

'Why? You're wrong to delve too deeply for a motive. This is wartime. Men expect to fight. The civilized rules of rational logic do not apply.'

'But it's suicidal,' whispered Annie.

'No.' Cricklemarsh would not accept that. 'Dangerous, yes. Suicidal, no.'

'Do you honestly think he can get away once he's fired that shot? He'll be hunted down like a dog.'

On average, one in three SOE men and women did not come back, as Cricklemarsh knew. The odds against Lusty would be much higher. If Lusty returned, he would have to be very good – and very lucky.

'Annie, there's no one else. Lusty is right: it's him or no one. Purefoy won't give me any more time. He'll take the operation away unless I come up with an agent in the next day or two.'

'I'd rather that than lose him.'

'I'll bring him back,' said Cricklemarsh softly. 'I promise. Many years ago I went on a secret mission to an unfriendly land. I was betrayed by my own people for their own ends. I know what it's like to be on the run, hunted and friendless. I give you my word I'll get him back.'

'You got back?'

'Yes, I made it on my own.'

'What did your people say to you when you turned up?'

'I think they were rather embarrassed I'd returned.'

*

'Ding dong. Next stop Benghazi.' The bus lurched off past a South African sergeant being sick in a gutter outside Liverpool Street station.

'Oi, I want to go to Bethnal Green.'

'Get on with you, dearie.'

Lusty clung to the leather strap, listening to the banter in the packed bus.

'Wasn't it awful, that Jerry plane killing all those little kiddies in that school in Catford. I know what I'd like to do to that pilot. Call himself a man.'

'What do you expect? We bomb them. They bomb us. Tit for tat, ain't it?'

'I quite like the air raids,' said an old woman. 'While they're on, they make me forget about the war.'

Lusty was still grinning when he got off at Victoria Park. Bombs had left gaps in the rows of houses like missing teeth in a once smiling mouth. A blast had sheared off the entire front of one as if a giant hand had opened a doll's house. Yellow wallpaper with red flowers climbed the stairs to an intact paraffin heater on the landing where a mirror still hung, unscratched. A pink counterpane was draped over a single bed. Other houses were little more than piles of bricks and wooden beams with an armchair or splintered table sitting on top. Ragwort and rosebay willowherb grew everywhere. Lusty turned into an area of low terraced houses with a pub or a small shop on every corner. Children had turned the streets into playgrounds. Small boys were kicking a football between two crates while girls skipped with one end of the rope tied to a lamp-post.

'Got a fag, mister?' cried a lad in a cap three sizes too large.

'You're too young.'

'It ain't for me. It's for me big bruvver.' They always had an answer.

Ahead of Lusty a chubby urchin toddled across to plonk himself down next to two girls, aged six or seven, playing hopscotch in the middle of the road.

Bang. Bang. Two loud explosions made him jump.

'It's them new rocket guns in Victoria Park,' explained a woman as she anxiously searched the sky. 'They're always going off. Don't know why. There's no sign of Jerry.'

A horse-drawn milk cart trotted around the corner. A teenage girl jumped off, snatched up a crate of milk and carried it into the shop, ignoring the way the horse's ears were flattened against its head in alarm. Twenty yards away, the toddler was examining a partly sucked sweet. Lusty strolled on, hoping Doreen was in.

The rocket gun fired again. A short crack followed by a whoosh. The horse reared between the cart's shafts, sending bottles of milk crashing off the back of the cart. The girls froze in the middle of their hopscotch.

'Arthur!'

The girls grabbed at the boy to try to pull him to safety. Arthur did not understand. He wriggled free and sat down again in the middle of the road.

Lusty dashed to the horse just as it reared again. Its huge hooves flailed the air around his head as he clung on to the throat strap for all his life.

The milk girl flew out of the shop to grab the other side of the bridle. 'Shush. Easy, boy. Easy now, Sammy.' Slowly, the horse stopped rolling its eyes. The girl blew in his nostrils, then produced a mint. Lusty let go.

'That was brave of you,' grinned a short woman with curly hair.

Lusty thought he had seen her before but he couldn't place her. He smiled and began to walk away.

'I'm Polly.' She lengthened her stride to keep up with him. 'I live in the flat beneath Doreen.'

'Oh, yes, sorry.' Now he remembered her. Friendly and chatty but a little too short and plump for him. 'I'm on my way to see her now.'

'Is she expecting you?'

'No, I've been away so I just thought I'd pop in.'

'You shouldn't just pop in on a girl,' murmured Polly. 'Are you sweet on her?'

'Not really, but you can always have a laugh with Doreen.'

'Yes.' Polly gave a sideways glance at a US Army jeep parked outside their house. The upstairs curtains were drawn.

'She's not in. Told you.' She saw Lusty's hesitation. 'Would you like a cup of tea while you're here? I might even have a dash of rum to put in it, if you like.'

Lusty followed her into the downstairs flat, a replica of the one above: living room with kitchen alcove and bedroom with a shared bathroom on the landing.

Polly babbled on as she brewed the tea and added the dash of rum. Did he like *ITMA*? Did he know the king and queen listened to it? Wasn't it a scream? 'I love Mrs Mopp. When she says, "Can I do you now, sir?" I just crease up . . .' The noise from upstairs started softly – a creak, then the muted twang of a bedspring. Polly became even more voluble. 'How about the *Brains Trust*? I like Commander Campbell's stories but that Professor Joad is too clever for his own good.'

Boing. Twang. Thump. Polly could not help herself: her gaze travelled to the ceiling. In the room above, the headboard started bumping against the wall in a regular rhythm. Polly blushed crimson and gave a sick, wan smile.

She crossed the room to take his hand. 'They've got Camel cigarettes and nylons and more money than they know what to do with. Some girls . . .'

'Their heads are turned?'

'That's one way of putting it.'

He seemed so unsure, so vulnerable that Polly wanted to hug him but she didn't want him to think her cheap as well. Bloody Doreen – she had her pick of men. Little, dumpy things like Polly didn't get a look in.

God! They were going to come through the ceiling.

'Shall I bang on the ceiling? That'll shut them up.'

Lusty pulled her onto his lap. She went readily enough but then dropped her head in embarrassment. Lusty lifted her chin with his finger.

Polly did not want him to think her easy – but what the hell! There was a war on.

*

Purefoy stood nervously in front of Brigadier Gilbert's desk. 'I thought I should let you know that Cricklemarsh has finally found his gunman.'

Gilbert's head jerked up from the document he was pretending to read. 'Yes?'

'It's an unusual choice,' Purefoy began. Seeing the flash of exasperation cross Gilbert's sharp face, he hurried on. 'It's his deputy, sir. Lieutenant Lusty.'

'Lusty. Lusty. Do I know him?'

'Probably not, sir. Here's his file. All very straightforward: mentioned in dispatches at Dunkirk, fluent in German . . .'

'A little unorthodox, isn't it?' Gilbert scanned the two typed pages of Lusty's background and army career.

'Um, yes, sir, but Major Cricklemarsh's satisfied.' So was Purefoy. If Cricklemarsh had not found someone by the end of the week, he would have been forced to have called Nye in on the operation. That would have cost him a lot of pride but, worse, it would have given Nye the leverage to start prising away Purefoy's job.

'This isn't a false alarm like last time?' demanded Gilbert. 'Lusty's not going to suddenly shoot off to the Middle East like that Pole, is he?'

'No, sir. I can guarantee it.'

Gilbert put down the folder.

'If you're sure, then,' he said in a way that pinned Purefoy firmly against the wall. 'He must train alone. He mustn't be allowed to join any of the mainstream courses. We can't risk contaminating parallel operations. And he's not got long. Let's hope he's a quick learner.'

4

'Sit on the edge of the hole and give yourself a little push. Not too hard or you'll break your nose on the far side. Then spring to attention so the lines don't get entangled when the parachute opens.'

'Does that happen often?' demanded Lusty.

'Oh, yes.' The instructor enjoyed sharing bad news. 'We had an agent not long ago who ended up being towed behind the aircraft.'

'And?'

The instructor made a regretful sucking noise. 'Froze to death. Everyone tried to haul him back in but the slipstream was too powerful.'

Lusty made a mental note to snap to attention as he passed through the exit hole.

'One last thing, sir. It's worth making sure that the dispatcher has connected up your static line. They do forget sometimes.'

'You're joking.'

'Afraid not, sir.'

Lusty had spent hours learning the drill in the fuselage of a Halifax bomber at ST33 – the parachute training school at Altringham – until he could follow the procedure in his sleep. Sideways shuffle on hands and bottom, swivel, legs through the gap in the floor, wait until the red light turned green and the dispatcher brought down his arm and cried 'Go'. When it had come to the actual jump, he'd been surprised how much he'd enjoyed it. Now he had three parachute jumps into the grounds of Tatton Park under his belt.

Lusty also spent a morning in a London clinic under the knife of a Jewish surgeon who had fled from Heidelberg in 1938. The surgeon, a German army doctor in the Great War, apologized, explaining that his handiwork was normally much neater, but surgery near the battle front was necessarily crude and hurried. While his scar healed, Lusty studied the *Wehrmacht*, its customs, its methods and its equipment, with the help of a military intelligence officer. Once he had a sufficient grounding, he moved on to technical terms and military expressions, to Panzer Divisions and especially 21st Panzer. Cricklemarsh and colleagues from Oxford made sure he was well briefed about the Gestapo, the SD and the all-embracing role of the Nazi Party.

Cricklemarsh never allowed him to relax for a moment. Out of the blue he would demand in German, 'How did the Panzer Mark IIIs upgrade their gunnery last summer?'

'They—'

'What!'

'*We* mounted the short 75mm Kwk because high-explosive was more efficient than armour-piercing. Hollow-charge ammunition for the 75s improved its all-round usefulness.'

'When did you leave Naples?'

'31 January 1941. We were the 5th Light Division then.'

'Who commanded 21st Panzer last summer?'

'*Generalmajor* Georg von Bismarck. He was wounded in July, returned to us in August and was killed on the thirty-first, leading the division.'

Then Cricklemarsh would abruptly change subjects. 'Who wears black *Waffenfarbe*?' he demanded, referring to the background colour on *Wehrmacht* epaulettes.

'Engineers,' replied Lusty promptly.

'Grass green?'

'Armoured infantry.'

'What's the SS equivalent of Major?'

'*Sturmbannführer*.'

'Who comes directly under a *Kreisleiter* in the Party hierarchy?'

'*Ortsgruppenführer*.'

Cricklemarsh increased the pressure. After two weeks' cramming, Lusty knew the Afrika Korps's equipment – its trucks, half-tracks, machine guns and cannon – as well as if he fought with them.

And every day he lay under the sun lamp.

But Lusty's slowness in transmitting by wireless worried Cricklemarsh. Some took to it quickly – others, like Lusty, needed months to work up their speed. Lusty did not have that time. Cricklemarsh consoled himself that Lusty would not be sending long situation reports. He would be only passing on developments and seeking guidance. Still, he wished Lusty was faster.

'This is the latest transmitter. We call it the B2, although really it's the 3, mark II.' The technician in the brown overalls wore round glasses and the few strands of his hair were plastered flat across a domed skull. 'It has an output of thirty watts using two American valves called Loctal, transmitting between three and sixteen mc/s. It can also receive. As you can see, it's sturdy and compact and weighs just thirty-two pounds.'

Lusty regarded the attaché-case transmitter with interest.

'It has an ingenious built-in device. If mains power fails, all you have to do is throw this switch here and the set will immediately go over to its own six-volt battery.'

'Is that important?'

'Once the Gestapo narrow down the search for a set to one area of a town, they switch off the electrical current to different blocks while the transmitter's on air. When the transmitter goes dead, they know where the operator's hiding.'

'Oh.'

Lusty and Cricklemarsh settled on the standard German infantry rifle – the Kar 98k. The 'k' stood for *kurz*, meaning 'short', which was misleading as it was five inches longer than the original. Bolt action, five-round box magazine, barleycorn front sight and tangent-with-notch rear sight. Calibre 7.92mm. Weight 8.6 lbs. Muzzle velocity 2,476 feet per second.

'It needs to be German to make the Gestapo believe the killing's an own goal but we'll add a new barrel and prepare special rounds weighed to the exact grain for accuracy,' said Cricklemarsh. 'And we'll break the rifle up so you can transport it easier. The 23-inch barrel can go in your walking stick.'

*

Cricklemarsh thought long and hard about contacting Claude Ismay. On a personal level, he detested the beanpole's languid affectations; on a professional level he was loath to let SIS know what he was doing.

But . . . but Ismay had proved himself SIS's expert on getting people out of Germany for the past five years – an area where SOE itself had little expertise and where Cricklemarsh's own knowledge was out of date. Finally he forced himself to sublimate his dislike of the man for the good of the operation – and the chance of eventually getting Lusty out alive.

If he had known that Rupert Nye had been Ismay's fag at Harrow, he would have thought again.

Ismay suggested White's Club for the meeting. Cricklemarsh was not fooled. Just because it was not held in SIS's Broadway headquarters, it didn't mean their conversation wouldn't be reported back. It did mean that the notoriously stingy Ismay could drink at Cricklemarsh's expense.

Cricklemarsh bought him the obligatory large whisky and explained that he needed a safe route out of Germany, probably inside the next three weeks.

'Not thinking of having a chinwag with the forces of darkness, are we?' Ismay, an immaculately dressed six feet five with slicked back hair, assumed a supercilious hauteur that riled Cricklemarsh. 'All German contacts have to be channelled through us. That's spelled out in your charter.'

'We're not intending to make contact with anyone, officially or otherwise.'

'It's not that *we* mind. It's Joe Stalin and the Russkies. Paranoid about separate peace overtures and that sort of thing. Terrified we'll all gang up against them. Not a bad idea as it goes but keeping the Russians happy is what the Foreign Office wants. As you know, what the FO wants, the FO gets.'

'We're not talking to Germans,' repeated Cricklemarsh.

'Jolly good.'

'A safe crossing?' Cricklemarsh prompted.

'Ah, yes.' Ismay let his gaze crawl to the ceiling. 'Numbers?'

'One.'

'Hot or cold?'

'Probably hot.'

'Mmmm,' Ismay mewed in disapproval.

Cricklemarsh sat upright and arched his shoulders. It seemed to him that sometimes SOE and SIS spent more time fighting each other than they did the Germans.

'If it's too difficult then I must ask you to forget this conversation. I wouldn't wish to jeopardize or embarrass an asset.'

Ismay was curious. 'I understood this request had a, shall we say, high priority?'

'Not from me, you didn't.' Cricklemarsh looked around as if he wanted to end the conversation. The septuagenarian waiter took it as a signal to hobble over. Cricklemarsh shook his head.

Ismay pouted at the loss of another whisky. 'Where would you go?'

'We talk to the Americans a lot nowadays.'

'Ah yes, your acolytes. I didn't say it wasn't on. I just need to gauge the difficulty of the extraction. Are you expecting the crossing to take place at a time of heightened border security?'

'That's possible.'

Ismay took this to mean *definitely*.

'We have a chap in the *Abwehrpolizei* on the Swiss border. He's spineless, grubby and greedy. Any good?' Ismay turned and stared pointedly at the waiter.

'Happy with that, are you?'

Lusty laid down his rifle and rolled over on his shoulder to look up at a short, fierce sergeant with Royal Marine Commando flashes and a gruff Welsh accent.

'It's not bad.' To be honest, Lusty was secretly pleased with the five-shot group he had just drilled in the Figure 12 target at three hundred yards.

'I'm Taffy Jones, Sergeant Jones to officers.' Jones regarded Lusty as if he was a slug he'd found in a plate of salad. 'I'm told you want to be a sniper.'

'I need to *learn* to be a sniper, sergeant.'

'Quickly, too, I'm told.' Sergeant Jones made a tutting noise. 'Not easy.'

Lusty controlled his temper with difficulty. 'If you can't help, then we'll find someone who can.'

'If I can't teach you, no one can,' said Jones. He held up Lusty's target. 'You may as well have used a shotgun for that spread. Bloody awful.'

'Don't like officers very much, do you?'

'No. I don't . . . sir. But I do my job.'

'What did you do before the war?'

'I was a poacher, sir. Now I'm a gamekeeper teaching young gentry how to poach.'

'Humbug, sergeant. I bet you I can tickle a trout as well as you – or better. A fiver on it.'

'You could be right. I can't afford the fiver to gamble with – but I will bet you that you've never had to poach to survive.'

'You'd win your bet.'

'Ay, I knew I would.' Jones became businesslike. He picked up the German rifle and started stripping it while still staring at Lusty. 'The sniper's job is to kill with a single shot. Calmly and deliberately. Can you do that?'

'Oh, yes. I can do that,' replied Lusty, in little more than a whisper.

'You can kill? You have killed?'

'Yes.'

'I believe you.' Jones's lined, uncompromising face almost broke into a smile. 'You think you can shoot. But being a sniper means you must possess a natural—'

'Natural point of aim,' completed Lusty. 'Make the rifle an extension of the body so you point at the target without thinking, just as you'd point a finger.'

Lusty picked up another rifle, brought it to his shoulder, leaned forward and aimed. Then he turned his head towards Sergeant Jones.

'If the rifle is still on target after ten seconds then I have a natural point of aim.'

He continued to stare at Jones and then turned his head so his eye looked through the sight. The rifle pointed at the bull's eye. 'Wish to see?'

'Anything else you want to share?' asked Taffy, drily.

This was meat and drink to Lusty after all the hours and days he'd spent listening to the crack marksmen employed by his father's arms company to test their weapons and give impressive demonstrations.

'A steady shooting position needs support from the bones, not the muscle,' he began. 'When lying prone your left hand is forward, palm up. The wrist is straight and locked, the rifle lying across the relaxed palm of the hand; the left forearm and the elbow directly below the barrel . . . Breathe in, release part of it and then hold the rest while you fire. Never try to hold your breath for more than ten seconds or you'll get tense and invariably move slightly . . . Controlling the trigger is probably the single most important aspect of marksmanship. It's the key to firing without disturbing the way the weapon is lined up with the target . . . Instead of trying to hold the rifle perfectly still, work to perfect eye-hand coordination. Wind, light conditions, humidity and temperature affect the passage of the bullet. People shoot low on bright, clear days and high on overcast ones. Damp, humid air is thicker than dry air so the shot will strike low . . . Warm ammo works more efficiently than cold, making the round go high. If some ammunition is dry and some wet, you'll get different results. Better to have all of it wet.'

After a moment's silence, Taffy Jones said sourly, 'You've been well taught. Let's see how much of that you can put into practice.'

They spent the rest of day on the range dissecting Lusty's technique and stripping it back to the basic components to rebuild it to Taffy Jones's liking. By dusk, Jones had stopped niggling about his pupil's marksmanship so Lusty assumed he must be doing something right. But he still had to get close to his ultimate target. And that was a different matter altogether. *Wasn't it, sir?*

The following morning they drove to a clearing in the New Forest.

The grass was still wet and a thin wind made the tops of the trees moan softly. The rooks took exception to their presence, cawing shrilly as they climbed and wheeled away into the cheerless grey distance like angry black commas.

The two men brewed up in the lee of the Bedford lorry. When they were sitting on groundsheets, their mittened hands wrapped around tin mugs of scalding sweet tea, Taffy began his next lecture.

'I know you've done this in your basic training but forget it. *All of it.* That's usually easy for officers. You're going to start again – from scratch. You can't snipe if you can't stalk. So that's what we're going to practise today. The first thing is to make sure your equipment won't rattle or snag so check your clothing is soft, flexible and fits you well.'

Lusty ran his fingers over his battledress blouse.

'The material's all right but it's too loose on you,' said Jones. 'Baggy clothes can get caught on undergrowth. Secure the trousers with ties at the thigh and ankle to reduce any slack but don't use them anywhere else because they'll impair your circulation. Always wear a soft cap or balaclava to give you a blurred outline. Pare down your equipment to a minimum as weight reduces speed. Try to operate in conditions that'll obscure your presence such as darkness, fog, smoke or haze. You must always assume your area of operation is under enemy surveillance.'

'It will be.'

'Now you, if you don't mind me saying so, sir, do everything too quickly.' Taffy cocked an eye, inviting argument. 'You move quickly when you're stalking and you may as well announce your presence by megaphone. You must learn to take time; do everything slowly. You've just found a nice, safe position. What do you do? I'll tell you what you do. *Nothing.* Nothing for at least five minutes, understood?'

Lusty nodded.

'You just sit tight and breathe softly. Halt, listen and observe. Animals and birds are your friends, and also your enemies. They can alert you when the enemy is close but they can betray you similarly. OK, you've had your lay-up, and no one's detected you, so select your next move. Check for signs of enemy presence, work out and memorize your route to your next position. Avoid steep slopes and areas with loose stones, if you can.'

'I'm not sure if that's going to be possible.'

'Then we'll have to teach you how to move about without setting off a landslide, won't we?'

Taffy threw away the dregs of his tea and got up. Lusty followed him reluctantly. He spent the next hours crawling through the undergrowth until he was panting with exertion, his face scratched by brambles and his uniform soaking wet.

'You make any more noise and you'll have the camp guard phoning the circus to see if they've lost an elephant,' Taffy said derisively and with absolute contempt.

'Fuck off.'

'I'll tell you what, sir. You have a nice sit-down on that log over there and have a fag. Face towards the Bedford. I'm going to see if I can creep up on you from behind. I win a fag if I do. You get one if I don't.'

The ground behind Lusty was strewn with dead bracken and twigs. He cupped his hands around his lighter to shield the flame from the wind and lit a Players. Bloody smart-arsed sergeant! He crossed his legs in an appearance of nonchalance and strained his ears. He turned his head slightly to increase his hearing in the breeze and fought against the overwhelming temptation to turn around. As an afterthought, he pulled out his metal cigarette case. The wind murmured in the pines. He thought he heard a rustle but decided his imagination was playing tricks. He started wondering if this was a practical joke. Had Jones gone off and left him? Was he standing twenty yards away, grinning at the stupidity of the officer? Lusty took a final drag on the Players cigarette, dropped it to the ground and screwed the butt under his heel. Fuck him.

A hand fell on his shoulder. 'You're dead.'

Over a brew-up, Taffy chuckled about Lusty's attempted use of his cigarette case as a mirror. His willingness to cheat had broken the ice. 'Sneaky. I admire that. It needs to be more highly polished but nice try.'

Taffy dictated the golden rules for Lusty to write down and memorize.

'SSSSM. *Silhouette.* However good your camouflage, you'll be spotted if the light's behind you. See how the sun moves. What's good cover in the morning can be a dead give-away in the afternoon. *Shape.* The first thing guards look for is a familiar shape, like a man's body or a rifle. Blur your shape but don't turn into a walking tree. It makes too much noise. *Shine.* Dump watches and rings and dull the sheen of a gun barrel. *Shadow.* Check what sort of shadow you're casting. This applies at night and in moon shadow as well as in sunlight. *Movement.* Any movement can betray you, even working the action of your rifle. Got all that?'

'Yes, sergeant.'

'Call me Taffy.'

Heinz Voss did not look grubby, greedy or spineless, as Ismay had described him. He was precise and erect, with small glasses and straight, iron-grey hair. His colleagues, who thought him a dry old stick, would have been amazed to learn that under the correct and proper façade lurked a covetous, cowardly philanderer with unusual sexual tastes and a large collection of pornography and items of leather restraint.

And Claude Ismay, with his nose for detecting the rotten core inside the blooming skin, had sniffed him out back in January 1939. He had caught the faintest whiff as he sat in the bar watching the border guards drinking after they came off duty. It was easy to find out from their conversation that Voss's wife was ill. But it was only when he followed the German to an apartment rented in the name of the postman's widow and peeped through the window to see Voss wearing a horse's bridle and bit and tied to the four corners of the bed by reins that Ismay knew Voss was his.

Voss was in charge of the Gestapo-controlled frontier police at three crossings over the Rhine between Feldkirch and the Swiss town of Oberreit. He was the wrong side of fifty and saddled with the worry of his wife's debilitating illness. Worse were the growing demands from his mistress, fifteen years his junior. On quiet days on the frontier, peering down at the strong, confident waters of the Rhine flowing towards the Bodensee, Voss would often wonder how he had ever been sucked into a situation where he paid half the rent of Heidi's apartment. The cost of it was bleeding him dry.

But at other times, in her overheated pink bedroom, as she fulfilled his long-term fantasies and introduced him to new ones, the cost didn't matter at all.

So he had been happy to listen when a tall Englishman had started chatting to him in a bar on the Klobach road. After a few drinks the Englishman had made him a proposition: he'd pay Voss to look the other way while an old Jewish lady crossed out of Germany. The suggested sum would pay the rent of Heidi's apartment for two months and allow him to send his wife to visit her sister at Garmisch-Partenkirchen with plenty of spending money. The Englishman explained he was working for a Jewish charity so he needed a receipt for the money. You know what the Jews are like, he had said. Just sign any name you like.

With the help of his Swiss opposite number, Big Josef, Voss never looked back. By July the Englishman had been in touch twice more. Each time he had paid handsomely, once for a man to enter Germany to search for his sister, believed to be in a concentration camp, and the second time for a married couple to leave.

In August, the Englishman pointed out that it would be difficult for them to keep in touch if war broke out so why didn't he set up an account for Voss in a bank in St Gallen in Switzerland? He'd pay Voss a retainer every month and, of course, the usual fee when someone needed to pass in or out of Germany. Voss agreed readily. Messages were relayed through Big Josef and every six months an Englishman – he had not seen the original tall fellow since war broke out – treated him to a slap-up dinner among the spires of St Gallen. Voss was not stupid; he knew he was betraying his country – but not very often and not in any big way.

Four years later, this extra income was being taken for granted. But the fear that he would be caught was growing in Voss's mind like a malignant cancer. He had been physically sick when an English agent had arrived wearing a long leather coat and a felt hat – the unofficial uniform of the Gestapo. It had unnerved him so badly that he had had to be soothed with an extra-lavish meal. A bonus of a different sort appeared the following week in the shape of two escaped English prisoners of war. Voss had been quick to arrest them, receiving a commendation.

But the damage had been done. To make matters worse, his pliant sergeant was replaced by a former *Hitler-Jugend* leader, wounded on the Eastern Front. Berndt Schnitzler was a fanatic – and nosy. Voss began to believe he had been planted by the Gestapo to spy on him. The last time Voss had been called on to smuggle a man across the border, he'd thought Schnitzler had looked at him oddly when he'd been sent away on a spurious errand.

Voss's nerves were fraying fast. Soon they would snap.

One evening, bored with memorizing German uniforms, Lusty decided to search his bedroom, which overlooked an enclosed kitchen garden and what had once been the stables beyond. Within two minutes he discovered a microphone stuck underneath the bedside table. He dismantled it and went back to his reading – until it occurred to him that he had found the microphone remarkably easily. Perhaps he had been meant to. A thorough search, including taking apart light switches and electric plugs, failed to uncover a second one. Lusty concluded that the eavesdroppers were either woefully amateurish or else had been extremely cunning in concealing another microphone. He hoped it was the latter.

Two days later, on an evening out to the nearby market town, Lusty met a stunning blonde girl in the bar of the old county hotel. She worked in the administration section of the training house. They were both alone. They both belonged in the secret world so it seemed natural to have dinner together. The girl was bubbly, funny and naturally curious. Lusty did not know how he got so drunk but he was conscious, as the night wore on, of more and more watertight doors shutting in his mind. He vaguely remembered staggering up the broad stairs to a double room and tumbling into bed with the girl. He remembered she continued talking to him in the dark, stroking his hair and kissing his forehead. Then it was morning.

The girl reported that Lusty had held his drink even though she had laced one or two, that he was the soul of discretion and that he did not talk in his sleep. She did not report on his ability as a lover.

Lusty and Taffy continued stalking and sniping. By now Lusty could regularly get within a bowshot of the wary fallow deer that populated the forest. One morning he admitted he could not guarantee that his eventual target would be so obligingly stationary.

'Moving targets are the most difficult to hit.' Taffy scratched his nose. 'Impossible with any consistency over three hundred yards. I can tell you what the book says, but that's not the same as doing it.'

'What does the book say?'

'If the target's moving across your front from left to right aim at a point about four inches ahead at three hundred yards. If he's moving at forty-five degrees allow half that much lead, say two inches. If he's travelling from right to left, you must allow twice the lead since you'll be slower tracking a target against your firing shoulder. Remember to fire and follow through in case you need another shot.'

'I don't know if I'll get a chance for another shot,' admitted Lusty.

He practised firing at a dummy on a trolley that Taffy Jones towed back and forth across gaps in the butts.

Taffy decided that Lusty's side arm should be a Walther 9mm P38. He demonstrated the floating pin that protruded above the hammer when there was a round in the chamber. 'You can tell by a glance or a touch if it's loaded.'

Unarmed combat was taught by an evil dwarf called Marvin who delighted in showing how to kill a man with whatever was to hand, including a rolled-up newspaper and a teaspoon. Marvin's methods drew from the traditions of ju-jitsu and karate with rough-house brawling thrown in. He demonstrated how to snap a man's neck with a single blow and showed Lusty the body's nerve centres and how to paralyse them. The training gave Lusty the vital confidence that if he got into a fight – he would win.

'So what do you think of our Marvin, then?' enquired Taffy as they were having a smoke out on the range.

'Funny fucker.'

'You're right there but don't let him hear you say it. He's out on licence for murdering a couple of young girls.'

'Then he shouldn't be . . .' Lusty's amazement left him short of words.

'There's a war on,' said Taffy. 'And he's the best, believe me.'

Cricklemarsh called by regularly. 'How're you feeling?' he asked.

'Like a student cramming for exams.'

'You can still pull out, you know.'

They were walking under an avenue of beech trees. It was cold and damp and the ceaseless wind made the clinging brown leaves whisper and rustle in protest. There was a rawness in the air that caught Cricklemarsh's throat and he wrinkled his nose as they walked past the lingering, acrid smoke of a pile of smouldering leaves.

'I couldn't. Not now.'

'You are a volunteer, remember.'

Lusty had been thinking about this. 'Maybe this is what I was meant to do. Do you believe in fatalism?'

'Only so far,' replied Cricklemarsh gravely. 'I think I believe more in self-determination.'

'You mean how we influence our own destinies?' Lusty pushed his hands deeper in his pockets.

'If you like. There are certain times when the road branches. You opt to turn left or right.'

'Or maybe just stand at the crossroads.'

'That is seldom an option.'

'No.'

Their shoes crunched over the gravel surrounding the house. Behind them a door in the stable block banged in the gathering wind.

'There's going to be a storm,' observed Cricklemarsh.

'I couldn't quit now, anyway.' Lusty was speaking almost to

himself. 'I've thought about it. I've looked at myself in the mirror and asked myself: why, why, why are you doing this?'

'And what did the mirror reply?'

Lusty scuffed at a drift of rotting red and yellow leaves. 'It doesn't know. I'm not a mindless hero, I know that. Maybe it's patriotism. Love of one's country. It's just something you do – duty, if you like. I'm certainly not a fanatic. Isn't fanaticism what we're supposed to be fighting against?'

'You understand the risks.'

'Only too well. But if we never took risks, the world would be a dull and boring place.'

'You're in a sombre mood.'

'Just a passing flight of morbidity. I'll be a cheerful ray of sunshine in an hour.'

'Maybe we're working you too hard.'

'No, I'm enjoying it. I especially liked the lock-picking demonstrations. At least I'll have a trade to take up after the war – I'll become a burglar.'

'Your uniform is ready. The genuine article, as worn in North Africa by a captain in the DAK.'

'I hope it's been washed.'

They turned back towards the big house.

Cricklemarsh was like a fretful anxious parent. 'If we dropped you into France you'd be met by a reception committee. There'd be signal lights, bonfires, friendly hands waiting to greet you and escort you to a safe house. You'd be swimming with all the other fish in the sea. In Germany, you'll be jumping blind into a hostile world where every man's hand is turned against you. Remember, you're most vulnerable in the first hours after you land. You must walk that extra mile to avoid a village. Take to the woods and fields instead of the roads. Avoid children, they always talk. Pay for whatever you take from farmers. If it proves difficult to establish a base then accept discomfort. It's better to sleep safely in a ditch than be wakened in bed by the Gestapo. When you're in company, avoid politics and strong drink. Be a listener rather than a talker.'

'I'll be all right.'

'I'm still worried about your slowness in sending wireless messages. We lose too many RT operators in France because SOE underestimates the efficiency of the German tracking stations.' Cricklemarsh was prepared to repeat himself a dozen times to get this message home. 'The Germans keep a constant watch on every frequency. Any operator foolish enough to stay on air for more than ten minutes is going to find the Gestapo on his doorstep.'

'I know I'm not a natural. I'll try to make up in brevity what I lack in speed.'

'Don't worry if you are forced to miss a transmission, even two or three. You know the schedule. We'll still be here. If we have information for you, we'll keep transmitting until we know you've received it.'

'Thank you.'

Cricklemarsh blew into his pipe. 'You can't be too careful, you know.'

'I know. And I'm grateful. Honestly, I am.'

'Are you happy with things so far?'

'Yes. We've settled on an optimum range of four hundred yards.' They both realized it gave little leeway for escape after the shot. Neither man said anything.

'It looks as though Hitler'll move to the Berghof soon.'

'Has Purefoy been pressing you?'

'No. He understands you have to finish your training.'

This was not true. Purefoy was pushing every day but Cricklemarsh was absorbing the pressure. It was the last thing Lusty needed.

'Perhaps he trusts you after all.'

'I wouldn't think so.'

That night Lusty was woken roughly by a strong torch beam in his face and angry voices shouting at him in German. He was hauled up, hooded and made to stand for hours while he underwent a mock interrogation. He stuck firmly to the legend Cricklemarsh had created. By the time he was allowed to take off the hood, a steely dawn was breaking and his interrogators had disappeared. He was given a cup of tea and complimented on his resistance. Lusty considered the activities of the night an empty exercise. The Gestapo would use violence and torture as weapons of intimidation and interrogation. He was not sure how much he could stand.

Ismay not only worked in intelligence, he enjoyed purveying it; luxuriating in the sense of power in knowing something no one else did. Now he favoured Rupert Nye with that infuriating smirk that said he knew something Nye wanted to know.

Once Nye had ordered them whiskies, Ismay began to flirt, showing him a glimpse of the petticoat of his secret.

'Germany's your bailiwick, Rupert, isn't it? Solely yours?'

'You know it is,' Nye answered stiffly.

'I've been wondering why Cricklemarsh's been asking advice on how to cross the German-Swiss border.'

'Has he, then?' Nye was damned if he was going to show surprise or anger in front of Ismay.

'Well ... yes.' Ismay made the two words last for ever. 'He's apparently running an operation on your patch. Poaching, is he? Or did you already know of it? Thank you.' Ismay accepted his whisky gravely.

'I know there's something in the wind.' Nye dismissed the speculation irritably. 'Nothing's settled. Some preliminary explorations, feasibility studies, that sort of thing.'

Ismay enjoyed seeing his friends in distress more than his enemies. He timed his delivery perfectly. 'Cricklemarsh was asking about an egress in the next three weeks.'

'What!'

'Didn't they tell you?'

Nye's face had gone black with fury.

'Bit naughty, that?'

It was too late for Nye to attempt to disguise his anger. 'That operation should be mine.'

'Of course it should.' Ismay soothed him with the balm of vinegar.

Bastards! Encouraged by the odd hint from Purefoy, Nye had believed the operation had withered on the vine – like so many. Now it was going ahead, he was in a difficult position. He knew that he could only sustain his reputation as a thrusting section head for so long before he had to come up with the goods. At the same time, if this operation was successful, it would wreck his argument that it was impossible to achieve anything actually inside Germany.

He had to get control of the operation – or he had to kill it. If he himself couldn't profit from it, then no one else must be allowed to.

Lusty walked briskly along, attracting envious looks. It was illegal for shops to wrap goods so his box of chocolates stood out like the crown jewels. A couple of women called out to him that they hoped she was worth it. What would they have said if they'd known there was also a pair of nylon stockings carefully folded under the lid? Lusty was spending two days in London for up-to-date briefings on the Afrika Korps before going back to his solitary existence at the country house. Tonight, he was going to make the most of his freedom.

Doreen came bouncing out of the front door, her blonde hair swinging from side to side, when Lusty was only fifteen yards away. His heart lurched – then righted itself.

She saw Lusty and saw, too, the box of chocolates in his hand. Her face broke into an expectant smile. She put her hand near her throat in a gesture of surprise and pleasure.

'Are those for me? Goodness! I haven't seen chocs like that since before the war.'

'No, sorry, they're not.'

Doreen's smile faltered but held as he walked on past her.

'Where do you think you're going?'

Lusty rattled the door knocker.

'You can't be serious! You can't give those to little Polly. Really!' Doreen spun on her high heels and flounced away, her hips swaying in anger.

Polly stood in the doorway, smiling uncertainly. 'Go with her if you want. You don't have to . . . um.'

'Aren't you going to invite me in?'

'Yes, of course. It's nice to see you.'

'Here. These are for you.'

'Ooooh.' Her eyes opened wide. 'Where did you get them? They're not black market?'

'Just open them,' he said when they had stepped inside.

Polly squealed with excitement on discovering the nylon stockings. She held them up against her cheek, then threw her arms around him.

'Put on your glad rags and we'll make a night of it in the West End.'

'How much time do I have?'

'Exactly how long does it take you to put on your war paint?'

'No time at all . . .' Polly paused. 'Come and help me choose what to wear.'

It was as near an invitation to make love as she had ever dared make. What a little strumpet she was becoming.

Most of the cinemas had reopened and he let her choose. Polly contemplated *Dangerous Moonlight* because she said every time she heard the Warsaw Concerto it made her cry, but in the end she settled on the double bill of *Destry Rides Again* with James Stewart and Marlene Dietrich and *His Girl Friday* with Cary Grant.

They held hands as they watched and every so often Polly would offer him a chocolate or peck him on the cheek. Between the films the theatre organ, bathed in violet light, rose to play wartime hits, starting with 'The White Cliffs of Dover' and 'Shine on, Harvest Moon'. Polly sang along with gusto, setting their whole row swaying in rhythm. When they came out of the cinema, she did a little skip of joy and clung to his arms. Lusty derived greater pleasure from her show of uncomplicated enjoyment than from the films themselves.

A cab emptied its passengers in front of them and Lusty snaffled it. Polly protested when it pulled up outside the Grosvenor House Hotel.

'I can't go in there. It's too posh,' she whispered.

'I've booked us a table.'

The dining room seemed full of Americans and Free French accompanied by elegant young English women. Polly kept looking around to see if she recognized anyone famous.

When the waiter brought champagne, Polly squeaked excitedly. 'Wait until I tell the other girls at the bus depot about this.'

After the second glass, she embarked on a stream of personal anecdotes, most of which involved her putting her foot in it in some way or other. Lusty could not stop smiling with her as she succumbed to fit after fit of giggles.

A three-quarter moon shone overhead as they left, turning the streets of London silver and oddly romantic. The buses and Underground had long since stopped running so they sauntered arm in arm towards the City until they spotted a taxi with its light off heading east.

Polly put two fingers in her mouth and gave a piercing whistle.

'Bethnal Green?'

'Close enough, love. Hop in.'

But Polly's high spirits were spent. No sooner were they inside the warmth of the cab than she laid her head on Lusty's shoulder, snuggled up and fell asleep.

5

'Watch out, Annie. Christ!'

A police constable pedalled sedately out of the lane on their left. Annie hit the horn and the brake in that order. Lusty was thrown across the back seat against Cricklemarsh as she swung the wheel of the Armstrong Siddley. The policeman wobbled and toppled over, his black bicycle falling on top of him.

'I had right of way,' said Annie defiantly as she sped on.

'It doesn't matter if we're late, Annie,' said Lusty. 'He's not going anywhere.'

Drifts of thin snow lay under the hedges where the weak sun had failed to penetrate. A flock of fieldfares rose off the bare Hampshire fields and Cricklemarsh pointed out a redwing. Lusty, who was navigating, put his hand on Annie's shoulder. She resisted the impulse to press her face against his hand.

The prisoner-of-war camp with its two concentric rings of wire, guard towers, searchlights and machine guns was unlike the one with the few strands of barbed wire and relaxed guards Lusty had visited so often in North Africa.

'We can't take any chances. We have a core of dyed-in-the-wool Nazis here,' explained the commandant, Major Pewsey, as he escorted them to his office. 'Fanatical SS, real troublemakers – most of the prisoners are terrified of them. They impose their own discipline and hand out their own punishments.'

'I thought all the hard cases had been moved to Canada,' said Cricklemarsh.

'That's the theory. It never happens, of course. Everyone gets mixed up.'

'Tell us about Private Pabst.' Cricklemarsh felt uncomfortable in prisons of any sort.

'Never been in trouble – or at least never been caught. It was the chaplain who first mentioned it. Thought I'd better pass it on.'

'We're glad you did. May we see him?'

'Yes, of course. You can interview him in here.' Private Maximilian Pabst came to attention on the scrubbed floorboards across the desk from Cricklemarsh, his eyes squinting around the room, as if taking in every detail to store for future use.

'Sit down.' Cricklemarsh indicated the wooden chair. 'Cigarette?'

Pabst's small eyes lit up. Cricklemarsh left the silver cigarette case open on the desktop. Pabst sniffed and wiped his nose on the back of his hand while Lusty tried to analyse why he had instinctively taken a dislike to the man. Pabst had narrow features and shrewd eyes, now rheumy from a cold. To call him weasel-faced would be unfair to weasels. Ferret-faced, then? But what harm had ferrets ever done?

'You asked to see someone about information you possess,' began Cricklemarsh.

Pabst's eyes slid sideways to the window overlooking the parade ground. 'I only mentioned it to the chaplain. I didn't know it would come to this, did I?'

Yes, you did, thought Lusty. Cricklemarsh continued to gaze benignly at the prisoner.

'But then you saw the commandant?' he prompted.

'Yeh, well, he asked if I'd be willing to talk to someone else. He didn't say you'd be turning up so soon.' Pabst sniffed. 'I don't know I'm ready to speak to you yet.'

'And why's that?' continued Cricklemarsh in agreeable tones.

'Has to be worth my while, don't it? What I know must be valuable or you wouldn't be here, would you?'

Lusty had heard enough. He had placed Pabst now. A rat – a sewer rat. And an unpleasant one at that.

'You are addressing an officer,' he barked in best clipped Prussian military tones. 'You will say, "sir".'

'Yes, sir.' Pabst sniffed loudly to show his contempt.

It infuriated Lusty. 'If you have nothing to tell us, then you are wasting our time. Stand up. Stand up.'

Pabst scrambled to his feet.

'Attention! About turn. *Links rechts . . .*'

'Please, sir. I didn't say I wouldn't help you. It's all so sudden. I haven't collected my thoughts.' Pabst appealed to Cricklemarsh. 'But there has to be something in it for me, doesn't there, sir?'

'Of course,' agreed Cricklemarsh reasonably. 'You help us and we'll see you have a very easy ride. Another cigarette?'

As Pabst was reaching forward, Cricklemarsh produced a picture from his briefcase and placed it on the table.

'That's the Hotel zum Türken, sir,' said Pabst promptly. 'That's where Hitler's bodyguard are based. It's up the hill behind Hitler's house, the Berghof, sir.'

'This?' Cricklemarsh laid another photograph on the table. This time Pabst took his time.

'I think it's Göring's house but we never went there. He has his own guards.'

'Tell me about your time on Obersalzberg.'

'I worked in the kitchens of the Berghof, sir.'

'If you were down in the kitchens, how do you know Hitler's routine?' demanded Lusty.

Pabst curled his lip. 'The will of the Führer ruled. We had to anticipate his every need. We knew his movements better than the sentries did.'

Cricklemarsh was willing to accept that. 'Describe Hitler's normal day at the Berghof.'

'He never gets up before nine. He has a cup of tea – great one for tea is the Führer – then he sees his barber and goes for his morning stroll.'

'Where does he walk?'

'To the Mooslangerkopf tea house. I went there once to help get things ready.'

'He *always* takes a morning walk to the Mooslangerkopf?'

'Always. It's his favourite walk. It has a striking view towards

Salzburg.' Pabst was growing in confidence. 'But it's a headache for the guards because the Führer cannot stand being watched. If he catches sight of one of them, he shouts, "If you are so frightened of intruders, go and guard yourself." They have to stay five hundred metres away from him. They try to keep him in sight but it's impossible because of the winding path and the trees.'

The hairs on Lusty's neck had risen. Pabst's words were diamonds. Sheer brilliant diamonds.

'How long does it take him to walk to the tea house?'

'About thirty minutes. He takes tea and milk there, sometimes cakes. Then he carries on down the hill to where his armour-plated Mercedes-Benz is waiting. From there he's driven back up the mountain.'

'Does he go by himself?' Lusty tried to keep the eagerness out of his voice.

'No, there're always others with him but he's always in the lead, talking to someone or other.' Pabst made it plain that he did not want to speak to Lusty.

'How long does he spend there?'

'Forty minutes. Maybe less.'

'Show me this Mooslangerkopf on the map.' Cricklemarsh unfolded a detailed map of the Obersalzberg area.

A knock. The door swung open. A shaven-headed prisoner with a red armband stood at the door, holding a tray with three enamel mugs, a half-empty bottle of milk and a very small pile of sugar on a saucer. Major Pewsey swung into view at the far end of the short corridor.

'Thought you'd like some tea,' he shouted. 'Hope everything's going well.'

'Thank you,' replied Cricklemarsh. 'Most civil.'

But Lusty was studying Pabst. The colour had drained out of his face so that his skin resembled parchment. He was swallowing hard, transfixed by the trusty like a rabbit in front of a stoat. The trusty stared rigidly ahead, his gunmetal eyes cold and unblinking.

Lusty had to break the spell. He strode between Pabst and the trusty, smelling the sour sweat on the man's field-grey uniform. Wordlessly, he lifted the mugs off the tray and nodded to the trusty to leave.

Pabst was plainly terrified. He lit a cigarette, his hands shaking. 'You have to go.'

'Why?'

Pabst shook his head.

'Who was that man?'

'Please go. I have nothing else to say.'

'We'll transfer you out of this camp. Today, if you like. There's no need to worry about him.'

'You don't know,' spat Pabst. 'What do *you* know?'

The room fell silent. *What a bloody cock-up*, swore Lusty silently. Pabst might be a snivelling worm but he was a worm with something to sell. He had just been getting into his flow, too. Now he was scared for his life.

Pabst's eyes had wandered to the window. Across the parade square, a knot of German prisoners had gathered. They were looking hard in their direction.

Pabst shuddered.

Annie was handing Cricklemarsh his first cup of tea when Purefoy strode into their office.

'Hitler's preparing to leave the Eastern Front at last,' he announced. 'He's flying to Berlin to make a radio broadcast to the German people on Sunday and then he's going on to Berchtesgaden. Your man must be there before him. Is everything ready?'

'He's ready.' Cricklemarsh avoided Annie's eye.

'Excellent. I'll put 138 Special Ops squadron on standby. If the weather holds we'll get your man out tomorrow night.' Purefoy rubbed the back of one finger over his moustache in an exuberant gesture. 'I can't tell you how much is hanging on this. We're about to change the course of the war.' He bustled out of the room.

Annie stayed silent until Cricklemarsh was forced to meet her accusing stare.

'*Is* he ready?' she asked in a small voice.

'He's been training for over a month . . .'

'That's nothing and you know it.'

Yes. Most agents had a minimum of three months' preparation, longer usually. 'He's calm, level-headed, he thinks and speaks like a German.'

'But . . .?' Annie sensed that Cricklemarsh had reservations.

'Lusty's too decent. I'm worried he lacks that core of arrogance a real Panzer captain would both possess – and flaunt.'

'He's not a good liar, either,' said Annie, sadly. 'God, I hope he'll be all right.'

'What are you going to do for his last night?'

The question shocked Annie. 'Me?'

'I thought you were rather . . . sweet on him.'

'I told you I wasn't ever going to get involved in the office again.'

'Selfish?'

Annie's temper flared. 'It's up to me what I do in my personal life. Anyway, he's got a girl in the East End somewhere. No doubt he'll be seeing her tonight. Hell, I'm not like a cigarette you give to a condemned man.'

The silence hung like a mantle over the two men. Lusty rearranged pens and pencils in neat symmetrical rows while, as usual, Cricklemarsh took for ever to light his pipe.

Finally Lusty spoke. 'I'm glad the waiting's over.'

Cricklemarsh struck a match, its coarse phosphorus flaring and spluttering in an orange flame. 'I suppose you must be.'

Restlessly, Lusty crossed to the large-scale map of the Berchtesgaden region. On his way, he stopped briefly to pick up a new photograph on Cricklemarsh's desk. It showed Ken in a leather flying jacket standing proudly in front of his biplane, a torpedo slung under its belly.

For a moment, he envied the lad: a member of a squadron, sharing the comradeship, the laughter and the risks. Lusty had chosen a different, darker road. There'd be no one he could confide in, get drunk with. He was going to be alone, totally alone. And never once able to relax – because that was when they had you, said Cricklemarsh.

'You're happy with the plan?' insisted Cricklemarsh.

'It's the best we can do.' Lusty pointed at the map. 'Hitler will leave the inner prohibited zone around the Berghof to walk through the woods to the Mooslangerkopf tea house. His close-protection group, numbering around twenty, will be left behind at Hotel zum Türken. His bodyguard battalion, the *SS Leibstandarte*, is stationed further up the hill in these white barracks.'

'Guard dogs will be on leads because the Führer likes to walk his own dogs. By the time the guards react, you should have half a mile start getting away.' Cricklemarsh puffed heavily on his pipe.

'I wish we knew more about the outer fence.'

'It can't be very high, simply because it's so long. It's there to keep out the curious, not the determined assassin. Remember to make sure the getaway vehicle you steal matches the papers you're showing.' He held up his hand. 'I know this sounds obvious now, but you'd be surprised how easy it is to make the most basic error under pressure.'

The orders covering his getaway were sewn into the lining of his jackboots, and a false Gestapo identity disc and Gestapo papers, for emergencies, were hidden in the heel of the right boot. A silk map and one-time code pads were concealed in the left heel. To escape, Lusty would become a major in the 394th Mountain Regiment, which was known from signals intercepts to be currently training in the Alps. His new epaulettes and the colour tabs of the mountain regiment were concealed in the wireless set.

'Your documents and cover story will see you through police checkpoints but they won't stand detailed scrutiny from the Gestapo. All we're trying to do is buy time. If the Gestapo seriously begins checking into your background, get out fast – or you're dead. You have ten days within which to make the attempt.'

'Is that going to be long enough?'

'It'll have to be. The longer you're in Germany, the more danger there is of discovery. We can't keep the border crossing open indefinitely and, to be honest, if you haven't got Hitler in your sights within ten days, you never will have.'

'You're satisfied with the border crossing arrangements?'

'No,' said Cricklemarsh to Lusty's surprise. 'It's never good for an operation to rely on an outsider – but we can't help it. We're totally dependent on this Voss to see you into Switzerland, then give you a change of clothing and papers and tickets to St Gallen. He'll be on duty from four p.m. to midnight each day from 24 March to 30 March so you must reach there by the thirtieth. You can call him earlier if things go wrong but we're assuming you won't be in a position to make the attempt before the twenty-fourth.'

Once Lusty was close to the border, he would telephone Voss, saying, *'This is your cousin Georg. What time shall I come tomorrow?'* Voss would give a time. Lusty would deduct an hour and make for the crossing that same night.

'There's no way over without him?'

'You're going to need Voss's help not to get trapped inside Germany once the hue and cry goes up.' Cricklemarsh started playing with his pipe again. 'Even if you made it across the border by yourself, the Swiss police will pick you up. If the Germans work out who you are, they'll demand your return. The Swiss like an easy life, so I imagine they'd arrange a fatal accident to remove the embarrassment.'

Lusty swung round to face Cricklemarsh. 'Do you really think I'll even get as far as the border?'

'Yes. Yes, I do,' Cricklemarsh forced himself to meet Lusty's stare. 'I'll tell you why: because of the Nazis' craving for power. We don't know who else's going to be on Obersalzberg with Hitler, but one person is certain to be there – Martin Bormann. What do you know about him?'

'Bormann? He's a one of the Nazi bigwigs, but I don't know *exactly* what he does . . .'

The reply pleased Cricklemarsh, for he peered up through his spectacles like a benign old watchmaker. 'Quite. No one knows exactly what he does. Officially, Bormann is head of Hitler's secretariat. He was formerly Hess's deputy. When Hess flew to Scotland in 1941 Bormann was promoted to Minister in charge of Party headquarters. He's manoeuvred himself into a position where he's at Hitler's side day and night. He controls all access to the Führer. Bormann's made himself the second or third most powerful man in the Reich. Once Hitler's dead, he'll want to consolidate that power for himself.'

'You're saying that he won't announce that Hitler's dead?'

'It's interesting,' mused Cricklemarsh in the same tone in which he would conduct an analysis of evil in Goethe's *Faust*. 'The Nazis certainly won't announce Hitler's death to the German people straight away. Germany is run by the *Führerprinzip*. The will of the Führer governs. His and his alone. Take away Hitler and you'll have half a dozen Nazis fighting to be top of the heap. Bormann won't want to make it known, even inside Party circles, until he has secured the succession. Among other things, he'll be too frightened of an army coup.'

'Who else is in line for the job?'

'Hermann Göring is Hitler's appointed successor.'

'And you think Bormann will try to usurp him?'

'No doubt. And while those two are playing games, *you* should be making your escape to Switzerland.'

'In theory.'

'In theory,' agreed Cricklemarsh with a sigh.

Lusty inspected the index and middle fingers of his right hand – now scrubbed clean of nicotine stains. Cigarettes were in short supply in Germany, so this was a small detail that might help to keep him alive. Even though he was not allowed cigarettes, he now possessed a silver cigarette case with the initials 'CB' engraved by a German Jew working in Hatton Garden.

He had spent two hours in an amazing brownstone building in Brook Street. From the outside, it looked like any other Mayfair town house. Inside, it was an Aladdin's cave of all things German. Everything from belt buckles to fountain pens, from suits to toothbrushes, soap and suitcases. Lusty was kitted out with German army underwear and socks and the uniform of a Panzer captain in the *Deutsche Afrika Korps,* with Iron Cross first class, wound strip, and tank-destroyer badge. He was given a pen and a comb and German identity discs to wear. The picture of his dead girlfriend, letters, *Wehrmacht* papers and hospital discharge were in his wallet.

Lusty wiled away the afternoon in the flat Cricklemarsh had organized for him in Bryanston Square getting used to his German uniform. He practised buttoning up his greatcoat, sat down, stood up, walked around, working on his limp and becoming accustomed to his walking stick. Then he practised a fast draw in front of the mirror until he inspected his new German wristwatch and found it was time to meet Polly.

He heard a phone ring faintly behind him as he hurried down the stairs. He could not make out if it was coming from his flat or the one across the hall. If it was for him, it would only be the office. Bugger them. Whatever it was could wait until tomorrow. Nothing was going to spoil his last night.

Annie eventually put down the receiver, cursing herself for not having called earlier. At first she had found Cricklemarsh's accusation of selfishness insulting. When she stopped being angry, she began to reconsider. The more she thought it over, the more she agreed with him. She was being selfish and petty and cowardly. She was also being bloody-minded, obstinate, and was cutting off her nose to spite her face. And yes, Lusty did have a girl in the East End but only because he couldn't have Annie. Well, he could tonight.

A timid voice asked the old question: *What if he doesn't come back?*

Then at least they would have had one night together.

She called again – just in case she'd misdialled. Then she swore softly to herself in a most unladylike manner.

Polly was running late. At Old Ford the road had subsided into a wrecked gas main so she was behind schedule in getting back to the depot and even later getting home. She was relieved Doreen was not hogging the bathroom. Polly had a quick dip in tepid water and was dressing again when Doreen flounced in, cigarette in one hand, boredom written all over her face.

'Going out!' Doreen sounded surprised. She peered round for an ashtray, failed to find one and flicked her ash into a saucer. 'I'll come with you if you're off to the local palais.'

'I'm not.' Polly carefully opened out her new nylon stockings. 'Where's your Yank?'

'Americans only want one thing – and they can't even do that well.'

Polly translated that as meaning that once Doreen's GI had taken what he wanted, he'd moved on to pastures new.

'So where are you going, anyway?' Doreen enquired.

'Dinner dance at the Ritz.' Polly kept her head down so that Doreen could not see her smile.

'The Ritz!' Doreen picked a flake of tobacco off her lip. 'Who with?'

'It's Robin's last night of leave. He wants to push the boat out.'

'Oh, does he?' Doreen slowly and viciously ground out her Woodbine.

Polly opened her compact and dabbed powder on her shining forehead. She gave a hopeful little smile at herself in the foxed mirror. *I know I'm not beautiful. I know I'm too short and perhaps a little on the stocky side but I've an interesting face, an engaging face. And it's the only one I've got.*

Lusty slid along the wooden seat on the top deck of the bus. The moon was casting shadows down the canyons between Oxford Street's tall buildings. The same moon that would help him see his way tomorrow night was a guide for any German bombers tonight.

He felt he should be collecting these sights, recording his sensations and imprinting them on his mind. He knew the odds were against him ever seeing London again but, strangely, it did not trouble him. If he was killed, he would only have died in the line of duty – like so many other men before him. But not every soldier went to war with three special pills hidden in his uniform: blue benzedrine sulphate to keep him awake, white knock-out drops and his 'L' pill, cyanide coated in rubber so he had to bite into it to make it work. Then he'd be dead inside thirty seconds.

He made himself clear his mind of the mission ahead. Tonight was his, his and Polly's. They would make it a night to remember – for as long as he lived.

Doreen was a real cow, reflected Polly as she hurried along the white line painted on the kerb. An out and out cow. Doreen had done her very best to snag her new nylon stockings with that nail file. And her 'helpful' hints about make-up! *I don't want to end up looking like a painted doll. My hair's natural even if it is light brown – or mouse, as Doreen calls it. And now I'm late, oh so late. But if I hurry any more I'll start perspiring and then I'll be damp and that's not a very attractive way to meet him with my face all shining and my hair dank. Bloody Doreen. Just because she had nothing else to do. I don't foul up* her *nights out. Why does she have to try to foul up mine?*

Stuff her. I might be a mouse but I'm squeaking.

Lusty stood on the steps under where Eros hid in a mountain of sandbags. No chance of *him* burying his shaft down Shaftesbury Avenue until the war was over.

He had arrived early. Bad form if it had been an operation. Arrive early for a rendezvous and the Gestapo arrest you while you're waiting. Arrive late and they arrest your contact. Always arrive exactly on time, said the instructors.

Buses growled through the light-pooled blackness; dark figures drifted in and out of moon shadows. Was it like this in Germany, too? Was the whole continent of Europe in darkness?

Two policemen in capes and helmets loomed from around a corner. They represented all that was good and dependable but Lusty knew that if he saw policemen in Germany, he would feel threatened. He remembered Cricklemarsh's advice. If you feel you are under suspicion, go up and ask the policeman a question. Police are figures of authority; no genuine wrongdoer would ever approach one.

Say a policeman questioned me in Germany. Who am I? Christian Beck. Born 7 May 1916 in Cologne, son of Paul Beck and Renate Mann. Father born on 6 October 1884 in Cologne. Mother born on 20 February 1888 at Frankfurt a/Oder. We lived in Rheingasse 16. My father was a businessman and garage owner. I am single and Lutheran. From 1920 to 1925 I attended Volksschule in Ulmstraße. Then I went to the *Staatliches Friedrichsgymnasium und Realgymnasium* in Cologne. I graduated in 1934 and started working for my father . . .

'Get on with you, Dilys. The officer is waiting for someone.'

Lusty came out of his reverie to see the outline of a woman, with her hands on her hips, confronting the two policeman.

'I don't know what you're talking about.'

Polly was due soon, surely. An air-raid siren began its banshee moan to the east. Another joined in and then another. People stopped in their tracks, craned their necks towards the night sky and listened. Then they hurried on, leaving Lusty gazing up at the moon.

Polly was almost at the Underground station, clattering along the uneven pavements in her three-inch heels. The moon was so bright! She hummed to herself in her high spirits. She hoped she looked all right. She had done her best. She'd only worn this frock once before – to her sister's wedding. He'd like it, she knew he would.

A siren started to wail and Polly groaned. Bethnal Green Underground station was used as a deep air-raid shelter. It would soon be crowded and difficult to get through to the trains – if they were still running. Already people were streaming towards the station along Roman Road. Searchlights probed the sky. She strained to hear the deep *thrum* of the bombers' engines. Nothing. All was still

But most locals were not taking a chance. Now they had survived the Blitz, no one wanted to perish in a hit-and-run raid. Just last week, a single aircraft had dropped six bombs on Putney, hitting the Cinderella Dancing Club, a milk bar and a queue at a bus stop. Eighty-seven people had been killed and more than two hundred seriously injured.

The station entrance was thronged. Women in headscarves and

winter coats, carrying bedding and holding small children by the hand, jostled with boys in pullovers. Men with cigarettes hanging from their lips swapped banter with servicemen home on leave. It was a break in the monotony of the evening. They'd have a laugh and a sing-song in the shelter. Make their own entertainment, just as they had in the Blitz.

Polly fought to get to the booking office. Fought also to restrain her impatience. *He'll wait for me,* she told herself. *He'll know there's an air raid on. Oh, please, let him wait.* The press grew thicker. Polly had trouble keeping her balance. Those outside were pushing to get into the shelter. Halfway down the steep staircase, she was trapped, her hands pinned to her side, her face crushed against the shoulder of the man in front. Polly fought to breathe.

'Ease up, lads. Don't shove. Room for everyone,' called a man wearing a battered brown trilby.

There was an explosion as a salvo of rockets went up from Victoria Park. Polly jerked her head free and saw a woman poised at the top of the steps. She was carrying a child or maybe a bundle in her arms. As Polly watched, she slipped and fell forward onto those in front of her. There was a scream.

A surge of panic ran through the crowd, its ripple growing to a cresting wave.

A cry of anger. Another scream.

Men and women were toppling forward, tumbling like helpless tin soldiers down towards her.

'No,' cried Polly.

The all-clear had sounded ages ago but still Lusty waited. Everyone else had paired off, leaving him on his own and feeling miserable. He had no way of contacting Polly so he waited and waited, stamping his feet to keep warm and huddling deep inside his greatcoat. He kicked at the stone step in frustration. Why tonight of all nights? He realized how much he had been looking forward to the bright lights, to hearing Polly's infectious giggles and finally snuggling down with her in the narrow bed. *Hell and damnation.*

He thought about walking to Bethnal Green, but what would that achieve? Finally, with a heavy heart, he gave up. He decided to go home and feel sorry for himself.

On his way through the darkened city, he passed the end of the Mayfair street where Annie lived.

And where she lay in bed awake, staring sightlessly at the ceiling, her eyes leaking tears.

Lusty lumbered awkwardly out of the tender to stand in the shadow of the wing of the Halifax bomber, thinking it was a huge aircraft for just one man. It was lonely out here on the perimeter of the airfield, half a mile from the hangars and the administration blocks. Just one Halifax bomber and a subdued group of men, searching for the right words. A train bound for Scotland thundered past. The special-operations airfield in Tempsford, Bedfordshire was sandwiched directly between the main line to Edinburgh and the Great North Road. Amazingly, the Germans had never found it.

The straps of Lusty's parachute cut into the jumpsuit and he wriggled to re-distribute the weight, checking his pockets for his compass, flashlight, knife and short spade with retractable handle to bury everything. Cricklemarsh, muffled in a scarf and heavy topcoat, seemed more bowed than usual, as though the weight of the operation pressed on him. As the dispatcher made last-minute checks, an RAF car sped towards them. Annie leaped out and handed Cricklemarsh a piece of paper. He read its contents by the light of a hooded torch.

Polly's body had been formally identified. She had been one of one hundred and seventy-eight men, women and children suffocated or crushed to death as the entrance to Bethnal Green station was turned into a charnel house in less than fifteen seconds.

'Weather is good over the drop zone,' announced Cricklemarsh, folding the paper and putting it into his pocket.

Annie linked arms with Lusty. She had told herself that she was going to be brave. She was not going to cry. She was going to be jolly, even if it killed her.

'I phoned you yesterday evening.' She led him a few paces away from the others.

'I was out last night.'

'Come back safe.' Annie spoke so softly that Lusty could have imagined the words. 'Come back and I'll have that welcome-home present for you.'

'Promise?'

'Promise.'

There was a discreet cough from the other side of the shadowed aircraft, which told Lusty it was time to leave. For a moment at the foot of the ladder into the fuselage everyone stood around, unsure what to say.

'If you need to get out in a hurry, let us know.' Cricklemarsh's breath formed opaque clouds. 'We'll be listening.'

'Thanks.' Lusty nodded, wanting to climb into the belly of the aircraft and get going.

'Best of luck.'

They shook hands. Annie kissed him on the cheek, then Lusty clambered inside the cold, metal-ribbed fuselage, thinking again that this plane was too big for just one man.

As the Halifax lifted off, the lines from Lusty's poem echoed in Annie's mind.

'In balance with this life, this death.'

Lusty was 15,000 feet over the Eifel mountains on the German border with Belgium when the SS men came for Private Pabst. He was being held in protective confinement until he could be moved to another PoW camp. Neither he nor the camp authorities knew that the trusties had copied the internal keys. Pabst was no more safe than he would have been in Auschwitz.

He was woken by the scrape of the key in the lock. There was a rush of hard bodies. Before he could shout, a cloth was rammed in his mouth and the breath punched out of him. He was pulled out of bed. His knees crumpled but men either side of him held his thin arms in a vicelike grip. Pabst tried to speak but all that came out were muffled grunts. They punched him twice more in the stomach. Bile filled his mouth. Pabst retched and coughed until they removed the puke-saturated rag from his mouth.

'What were you telling those British officers?' demanded the shaven-headed trusty.

'Nothing. I made it all up,' croaked Pabst.

'You were looking at pictures of the Führer's Berghof, and there were maps.'

'I lied. I made it all up,' insisted Pabst

One of the men struck him across the face with a swinging backhand, splitting Pabst's lip so he tasted his own blood. 'Repeat your oath as a German soldier.'

'I swear before God to give my unconditional obedience to Adolf Hitler, Führer of the Reich and the German People, Supreme Commander of the *Wehrmacht* . . .' Pabst broke down, whimpering and sobbing. They tightened their grip. '. . . And I pledge my word as a brave soldier to observe this oath always . . . even at peril of my life.'

'You were betraying the Führer, weren't you? What did you tell the English about the Berghof?'

'Nothing. I know nothing.' The words tumbled out. 'I was a storeman on Party Chief Bormann's farm. I only ever saw the Führer twice.'

Huge shadows were cutting up the bed sheet, knotting one end to the high window grille.

Pabst was weeping helplessly. He wanted to wipe his nose but they still held his arms. Snot ran over his top lip.

'I made everything up. I swear on my mother's life.'

The shadows fashioned a noose.

'No. No.' Pabst pressed his chin against his chest. Someone jabbed two fingers into his eyes. He flung his head back.

The man who now thought of himself as Hauptmann Christian Beck was crossing the Rhine at the same time as they hanged Private Pabst.

PART TWO

6

Saturday, 20 March 1943

Beck snapped to attention. Throughout the flight he had concentrated his fears on not breaking his nose as he left the aircraft and making sure the dispatcher fastened the parachute's static line securely. Funny how the mind worried about such minor things when he could be dead in the next ten minutes. Then it all happened so quickly. The tap on the shoulder, the urgent shuffling to get into position, staring intently at the red light. Green for go. Beck plunged through the hole into black infinity. He was buffeted by a rush of icy air that snatched away his breath. Then the tumult ended and there was silence.

The countryside below lay in pale moonlight. He looked down on swatches of dark woodland, ghostly meadows and, here and there, patches of glistening snow. A small town stood on a hill in the distance. He made out a church with an onion-shaped dome and tall, sleeping houses huddling tightly together. Nearer was a large camp with a spur of a railway running towards it. Isolated farms and clusters of homes were scattered in the folds of the rich, rolling landscape.

Beck drifted down through the still night – with the growing and terrible realization that he had been dropped in the wrong place. He should have been landing on the outskirts of Munich. Instead, he was in the countryside.

Only two pairs of eyes saw the parachute descend. A dog fox sat square on its haunches and watched with an intelligent curiosity before stalking off in further quest for food. Under grubby rags, on straw that was his sleeping place in the barn, a Polish prisoner of war, put to work as a farm labourer, had been lying awake with toothache and the cold. Occasionally he would press his arms to his half-starved body and shake uncontrollably. Over in the warm farmhouse there were wood stoves and thick duvets. Here, in the barn, there were just hunger and that ever-present chill piercing his marrow. At last, the cold had driven the Pole to get up and walk around. At the doorway, he watched the parachute descend before shuffling on in his effort to keep warm. Looking out again a short time later he saw a figure striding down the lane towards the small town.

The fox was shot two days later by a vengeful farmer, leaving its pregnant vixen to fend for herself. The Polish farmworker kept secret his memory of that night – until the day they made him confess.

Cursing the RAF navigator who had dropped him miles off target, Beck hurriedly concealed his parachute and jumpsuit in the corner of a field and set off down dark lanes in the direction of the town, nervous enough to jump at his own shadow. Once he felt he was a safe distance from the drop zone, he made himself take the time to bury carefully his wireless transmitter and rucksack near three distinctive elm trees. He brushed the earth off his uniform, grasped his walking stick and case and slipped through the hedge back into the lane. Soon it joined a road heading towards the town. At a stream Beck paused on the bridge to stare down into the water. A water rat was paddling determinedly across, only its snout and whiskers visible. Reaching the near bank it looked up, spotted Beck and dived.

The day was breaking, grey and chill, when, after a mile and half, he reached a hamlet straddling a crossroads. A glimmer of light came from behind the curtains of an upstairs window of the first house. Smoke curled from the chimney of the next where a man could be heard noisily hawking up phlegm. Beck was twenty yards clear of the hamlet when he heard a door close behind him. Almost immediately, heavy footsteps crunched on the frosty ground. As Beck tensed, the footsteps stopped and then began to follow him in measured tread. He fought the temptation to turn around and look.

When a path appeared on his right. Beck turned along it, holding his breath. The heavy tread followed him. Beck swore and limped on, the confident steps behind him making no effort to close the distance.

He could feel eyes staring at his back. He had to turn round, glance over his shoulder. Hell's bells and damnation. A policeman! A thickset man in his late forties with a heavy, agricultural face. *Ordnungspolizei.* A bloody village bobby, but a policeman all the same, wearing a green greatcoat and a broad black belt.

Beck's senses tingled. Even a country copper must be wondering what a limping army officer was doing here – wherever 'here' was – at daybreak. Maybe the man was waiting until they got nearer the town, where there would be more people about and he could raise the alarm.

Beck remembered what Cricklemarsh had said: a policeman was a symbol of authority. Only wrongdoers ran away from them.

He forced himself to turn. '*Guten Morgen.*'

'Good morning, *Herr Hauptmann*.' The policeman saluted but his eyes were wary.

'Which way is the railway station?'

The policeman hesitated for a moment or, as Beck counted his own heartbeats, an eternity.

'Follow this lane until you come to the town, then take the first right and second left.'

'Thank you.' Beck fought down the impulse to explain his presence.

He limped on, the policeman following at a leisurely pace. Houses were becoming more frequent now, lights peeping from bedroom windows, the tantalizing smell of frying bacon. A cock crowed in the distance and a dog barked. Two women swaddled in shabby coats and headscarves emerged from the side of a house. They dropped their eyes when they saw the policeman. Beck slowed, the policeman did likewise. Another door banged and he heard a man shouting at a horse to stand still. Soon the road would be alive with people going to work. Beck made a decision. A sunken lane had appeared between a row of trees and a straggling hedge of holly and hornbeam. He quickly turned into it and stepped behind a tree, waiting.

At Dachau station Beck bought the Nazi *Völkischer Beobachter* newspaper and a ticket to Munich. Others on the platform were intent on keeping themselves to themselves. No one seemed willing to meet another's eye. Apart from a surly crowd of *Totenkopfverbände SS* with death's-head emblems on their caps, the early-morning passengers were mostly women and old men. The few men of military age wore the Nazi Party uniform. On the wall outside the waiting room an artist had painted a dramatic silhouette of a German soldier above an eagle grasping a wreathed swastika in its claws. Underneath was the legend, *Wo der deutsche Soldat steht, kommt kein anderer hin* – where the German soldier stands, no one else comes. No one seemed particularly impressed.

A long train of flatbed trucks carrying half-track troop carriers and 88mm guns was rumbling through the station. Beck guessed the arms were on their way to Italy and then to North Africa. Two minutes after it had finally disappeared, a steam engine pulled four cold carriages up to the platform. Civilians moved aside to allow Beck the window seat where he hid behind his newspaper. The inside back page was taken up with In Memoriam notices for those who had fallen on the Eastern Front. *Für Führer und das Vaterland*, read some. Others said simply *For The Fatherland*. Beck learned that enemy terrorist bombers had attacked a city in the Ruhr, but 'The city is remaining steadfast.' The *Wehrmacht* high command announced that German forces in the east were conducting an 'elastic' defence. Georg P, an antisocial from Frankfurt, had been beheaded for stealing pedals off a push-bike during an air raid.

Beck continued to keep his head buried in his newspaper, aware of being scrutinized by a man in steel-rimmed spectacles with a Party badge in the lapel of his top coat. He read on. In Africa, the DAK was holding a line against localized attacks . . .

A woman in a frayed black coat climbed hesitantly into the carriage. Unthinkingly, Beck rose to offer her his seat. As she turned, he saw on her right breast a violet 'P' inside a yellow diamond. He also saw the fear in her eyes and the astonishment on the faces of those around him. And he knew that he had just made a serious error.

There were three rings of security at Munich railway station. *Kriminalpolizei* hunting for runaway conscript labourers and escaped prisoners of war; military police, with shining metal gorgets on their chests, on the lookout for deserters; and the Gestapo, in long black leather coats, sweeping up the remains of the White Rose student protesters who had been bold and foolish enough to stage the only anti-Nazi demonstration of the war. Munich and its university were a hotbed of agitation. Ironically, the birthplace of National Socialism had turned against the Party.

The station, reeking of soot and steam, teemed with parties of schoolchildren evacuated from northern Germany and foreign workers with their cardboard suitcases on their way from the east to factories in the Ruhr. A leave train was arriving from the Eastern Front, releasing its load of gaunt-faced soldiers.

Beck fought down the urge to keep his eyes on the ground. He told himself not to hesitate or look furtively over his shoulder. *I am a German officer.* Other travellers were being made to produce travel orders and authority for their journey, but his limp, the walking stick and the Iron Cross did the trick. A Gestapo man leaned against the wall along from the booking office window as Beck, nerve endings twanging like taut guitar strings, asked in a level, commanding voice for a first-class ticket to Berchtesgaden.

He took his ticket and went to stand on the platform. As he waited, a pasty-faced teenager caught his attention. He could see the sweat on the youth's upper lip at fifteen yards, the way his eyes darted around ceaselessly. He was clearly scared stiff.

'You appear confused, captain.'

The Gestapo man had sidled up to him as he was staring at the youngster. Beck's heart took a salmon leap into his mouth.

'It's a little different here from the desert – or a hospital ward,' he replied evenly.

'Where have you come from?'

'Italy.'

The man began forming a word, his hand stretching out, when he caught sight of the teenager and forgot about Beck. A number of things happened at once. An engine let off steam with a tremendous hiss, there was a shout from somewhere and the teenager turned and darted towards the platforms. When two SS men emerged from behind a pillar, he ran back towards Beck, heading for the Bayerstraße exit. Beck was jostled from behind. As he stumbled and put out his walking stick to save himself, the teenager tripped over it and went flying. Before he could rise SS men were on him. The Gestapo man dragged him to his feet and punched him in the stomach until he was sick.

Beck sat alone in the first-class compartment, peering out at the choppy waters of the Chiemsee. It was beginning to snow. Just outside the window the first flakes were speeding past like white tracer bullets. Further away, as he allowed his eyes to focus on the lake, they seemed to be floating down so slowly and gently.

It was comfortingly familiar to be back in Germany – yet so strange. At heart she was a fat smiling land but her rulers had scarred her. And the people had changed: they looked inwards, frightened of the shadow that lay over them. Some exulted in their new-found power, a few strutted, but most shuffled along and averted their eyes.

Beck found his hands were still shaking. The two close shaves that morning had left him so jumpy that it would only take a mouse to squeak nearby and he'd be hanging from the luggage rack.

Relax. Float. Be a snowflake. But how could he relax? His face burned again as he recalled his mistake in offering his seat to the Polish woman. The scene replayed itself over and over in his mind's eye. The looks of astonishment from the other passengers, the amazement and fear that had come off the woman herself like the stench of vomit.

It had all happened in slow motion. Beck, glancing up from his newspaper, seeing the frail woman enter. Rising from his seat, polite smile on his lips. 'Please.' The woman half turning. The letter 'P' screaming at him, proclaiming her to be a Pole, one of the *Untermenschen,* the lesser humans.

The incomprehension, even anger, of those around him. The horrified look from the steel spectacles of the pen-pusher. The confusion as the woman turned her head away in shame as she muttered, 'No, no.'

Beck's face flaming in embarrassment, mumbling explanations before hiding behind his paper.

More mistakes like that and he'd be a dead man.

'I wonder what he's doing now?'

'You mustn't think about it.'

Annie gave a forced smile. Cricklemarsh wished he could reassure her but there was little he could say. His own stomach was quietly churning but he wouldn't let Annie – or anyone else – see it. They all knew Lusty's first hours on German soil were the most dangerous.

'It's in the lap of the gods, I suppose.'

'Yes, we've done all we can.'

'Have we?' asked Annie in a small voice. 'Have we done everything?'

'In the time allowed.' Cricklemarsh tried not to think of the hundreds of ways Lusty could slip up – and each one fatal.

Silence fell as each retreated into their thoughts. Around them, the Barley Mow was a hubbub of noise and laughter. Annie played with her drink. Operation Nightshade was out of their hands now but she couldn't help thinking of Lusty. She prayed with every fibre of her being that he would not suffer the same cruel fate that had befallen Paul.

'Here's Ken now.'

Annie smiled at Cricklemarsh's son. He had not changed in the two months: still the smooth-cheeked schoolboy in a Royal Navy sub lieutenant's uniform with pilot's wings. He blushed when he caught sight of Annie. Cricklemarsh did his usual magic with one eyebrow and a pint of beer appeared.

'On leave?' asked Annie, to put the boy at ease.

'Just passing through on the way to RNAS Hatson in the Orkneys.'

'What will you be doing up there?'

'Low-level torpedo practice and some anti-submarine bombing. I still haven't landed on a real carrier – just strips of grass pretending to be one. We'll be working up with one of the new carriers so I should get the chance soon.'

'One of the Woolworths escort carriers or a Fleet refit?'

Ken dropped his eyes. 'I can't say.'

'Oh, Ken,' exclaimed his father. 'Annie's English uncle's 2IC at Scapa.'

'Northern Approaches,' corrected Annie. 'No, Ken's absolutely right. Walls have ears.'

'How long's this course?' asked Cricklemarsh.

'At least two months.'

'So you're not heading off to war straight away, then?'

Annie saw the relief in Cricklemarsh's eyes. They both watched Ken at the bar as he queued for cigarettes.

'He's a fine boy,' she remarked.

'Yes, he is.' There was an infinite swell of pride in the words. 'He had twenty-four hours' leave recently, you know. The other pilots went out on the town but Ken chose to go to visit his mother.'

It was a rare reference to Cricklemarsh's wife.

'It'll have done her the world of good,' said Annie.

'Yes. We've not heard from Keith for months,' he continued sadly. 'We think he's in Burma, working on that bloody railway. Ken is all she's got until our other lad gets back.'

'Hello.'

Ilse Runge hurried through the *Stube*. An apologetic young officer hovered unsurely by the door. The first thing she noticed, she told herself later, was how pale he seemed around his eyes. No, that wasn't true. What struck her first was his slow, hesitant smile and the air of someone who wanted to please. The locals around the *Stammtisch* were watching curiously.

'I'm told you might have a room . . .'

'A room . . .' She knew she was appearing foolish.

'Yes, a room. You're my last chance. In fact, you're my only chance in the whole of Berchtesgaden.'

Ilse put a hand to her head, feeling how tightly she had drawn back her hair. 'Um . . .' Still she hesitated. He was tall and young. He took off his cap and brushed back a flap of hair, revealing a scar on his forehead. His eyes were soft and hazel. He leaned heavily on a walking stick with a curved handle. He had pulled off his gloves, revealing three fingers on his left hand. She saw all this but did not know what to say to him.

'I'm on convalescent leave. The doctors said I need mountain air for my chest.'

She hesitated. 'I'll see.'

Her husband, Gottlob Runge, was sitting at the kitchen table, dividing up the ration coupons he collected as a Party official. A fat *Leberwurst* lay on the oilcloth at his elbow.

'There's a man arrived,' Ilse stuttered. 'An officer who wants a room.'

Runge snorted, intolerant of being interrupted. 'Then *give* him a room.' He cut a thick slice of sausage with a jackknife.

'It's difficult with rationing and things.'

'Pah!' Runge picked up the sheaf of different-coloured coupons. 'What do you think these are?'

'But it's . . .'

He stabbed the sausage slice with the knife and transferred it to his mouth.

'It's money. If he's got money to spend, he might just as well spend it here as anywhere.'

'It'll mean more work.'

Runge rose to put away the coupons in the desk in the small adjoining office. Ilse followed him. A wraithlike girl scuttled through the kitchen as soon as Runge's back was turned. She paused in the doorway of the *Stube* to look at the officer. She thought he had a friendly face.

'You've got Vishnia,' said Runge. 'Make that lazy Ukrainian cow work harder.'

'She works very hard already,' protested Ilse. 'You know she does.'

'Tell the officer he can have a room. Go on, bloody well hurry up before he finds himself somewhere else.'

Ilse half ran back to the *Stube* where the officer was inspecting the signed portrait of the Führer. 'You are welcome to stay if you don't mind sharing what we have. It's not much. Everything is rationed, you see.'

'Thank you. I understand.'

Ilse heard Runge's heavy tread along the stone passage and her husband strutted into the bar.

'Captain Christian Beck.' The officer clicked his heels and gave a slight bow from the waist. Ilse was privately glad he had not saluted the Nazi Party uniform.

'My husband, *Herr* Runge,' she heard herself say. She knew what would be going through Beck's mind. *But he's old enough to be her father.*

'*Heil Hitler*,' barked Runge, throwing up an arm, his belly straining against his gaping shirt.

'*Heil Hitler*.'

'I will show you to your room,' said Ilse quietly. 'Have you travelled far?'

'From a hospital in northern Italy . . .'

He followed Ilse along the wide flagstone passage. 'You could get a coach and horses through here,' he exclaimed, peering up at the curved roof.

'That was the idea.'

'Oh, yes.' As they climbed the stairs he thanked her again for taking him in.

'That's all right. I'm sorry I didn't welcome you immediately. I didn't know what my husband would say.' She seemed to notice for the first time that Beck was limping. 'How thoughtless of me. Give me your arm.'

'It would be a delightful privilege but really it's not necessary.'

'I'm afraid there's a lot of stairs and passages,' apologized Ilse. 'They kept adding bits over the years.'

The room smelled of lavender and polish. A massive old painted wardrobe, decorated with edelweiss and enzian, filled one wall. A double bed, with a carved headboard, took up most of the rest of the room. Near the window, a blue-and-white ewer and basin sat on a varnished pine chest of drawers. The ceiling sloped down on one side so he assumed that he must be under the eaves. He instinctively went to look out of the window, Ilse following him.

'There's a lovely view from here on a fine day.' She peered up at the rain clouds, ragged and black. 'You can just make out the Jenner – that forested, cone-shaped mountain. And there's the Hohes Brett peeping out behind it. It's much higher – over 2,300 metres.'

She stopped, conscious of his closeness. He could have slipped his arm around her waist. She shivered slightly and moved lightly away. 'I'll show you them tomorrow when the weather's better. You can also see the Berghof from here. They say the Führer himself is expected any day.'

Beck made a politely interested noise.

Soon afterwards, the serving girl brought him a jug of warm water to wash with. She kept her eyes fixed on the ground and made a little curtsy.

'Thank you.' Beck took the jug from her.

Like a startled rabbit she looked up and blinked, as if suspicious of kindness from a man. She blushed crimson and ran from the room.

When Ilse brought him towels, he was stripped to the waist, the faint tan of his slim body stark against the ruddy bands of his collar and wrists. But most of all she noticed the jagged scar that ran across his chest like a flash of lightning.

Heinz Voss marched very correctly to the middle of the bridge over the Rhine and flung up his hand in a rigid Hitler salute. Big Josef replied with an affable wave.

'Is he still watching?' Voss spoke, scarcely moving his lips.

'Yes. He's in your office now.'

'Shit!'

Voss slowly turned around, looking at where the red-and-white Swiss flags fluttered, dwarfed by gigantic swastikas. Sergeant Schnitzler's blond hair jerked out of sight.

'I caught him looking through my desk yesterday. He follows me everywhere.'

'You're imagining things.' Josef shambled over to the parapet. Voss followed, placing Josef's bulk between himself and Schnitzler's gaze. For all he knew, the man could lip-read.

'I've had a message from our friends,' began Josef. 'They want you here on duty, four until midnight, from next Tuesday until the thirtieth. It's your cousin Georg.'

Voss took off his cap and ran his fingers through his grey hair. Twice he started to speak. Each time he gulped air instead. At last, he confessed, 'I don't think I can do it.'

'Oh, come on.'

'You don't know what it's like for me. That man's a Gestapo spy – I know he is.'

Wherever he went, the surly sergeant with the pale, staring eyes was never far away, moving softly, tweaking Voss's nerves until they twanged. He suspected Schnitzler had been through his papers during the first week. He regularly caught the man observing him, watching every movement. Schnitzler had taken to hanging around in the hall near the telephone extension. Voss was convinced he listened in on his superior's conversations.

'Why would they want to spy on you?' demanded Josef. 'You're letting little things play on your mind. Ignore Schnitzler, he's just a creep.'

That was easy for Josef to say, living safely in pleasant, comfortable Switzerland. He did not have to put up with a sergeant who was the sort of Nazi who would sell his own mother for the good of the *Reich* and the Führer.

'How am I going to explain the change of routine to him?'

His previous sergeant had been happy to accept Voss's explanation that his wife's illness demanded his presence at home on occasional mornings. The sergeant had been glad of the evenings-off in exchange and if he'd suspected anything at all, he'd have assumed that Voss was indulging in a little smuggling. And everyone did that.

'Why explain anything at all? You're the officer.'

'No, I'm sorry. Maybe another time. But I can't do it now.'

'Our friends won't be happy.'

Voss took off his glasses and began to rub his eyes. He suddenly stopped. Christ, he couldn't even do that without fear that Schnitzler was watching and would record him appearing upset over something.

'They're going to have to lump it.' Voss turned on his heel and marched very formally back to the Fatherland.

'He who wants to live must fight and he who does not want to fight in this world, when eternal struggle is the law of life, has no right to exist. Isn't that so, *Herr Hauptmann*?'

Beck thought the relatives of the three hundred thousand German corpses around Stalingrad might not see it that way.

'Indeed, Herr Runge. Didn't the Führer himself say that?'

'He wrote it in *Mein Kampf*. There's a copy in your room.'

The old men had left and their place at the *Stammtisch*, the locals' table, had been taken by Runge and his two cronies, Thurn, the postman and Leeb, the town hall caretaker, both in their Nazi Party uniforms. They had invited Beck to join them out of curiosity, he suspected.

On the left breast of his tunic, Beck wore the *Deutsche Afrika Korps* eagle, embroidered in light blue on a copper base. Around his left cuff, the word *Afrika* was flanked by palm trees in silver thread on dark green. His captain's stars sat on the salmon pink *Waffenfarbe* of the Panzers. But it was the Iron Cross and the badge on the right sleeve, an outline of a black tank against a silver background, that attracted attention. It told them that he had single-handedly destroyed an enemy tank. That he was a hero.

'More beer. Vishnia, you lazy slut. Four beers.' Runge stood beside the birdcage, occasionally cooing to the two linnets. 'They do not sing as they used to.'

Thurn put down his heavy china mug – known locally as a *Krug* – to enquire what Beck was doing here. He explained that he had been wounded at Buerat as they were withdrawing towards Tunisia.

'How's it going out there?' asked Leeb, a soft, plump man with ponderous jowls.

'So-so,' replied Beck carefully. 'We gave the Yanks a bloody nose at Kasserine. They have unlimited men and equipment, but we have Rommel.'

'War is for a man what childbirth is for a woman,' proclaimed Runge, again quoting Hitler. He gently poked a piece of bread through the bars of the cage. Beck found the bully's tenderness towards the linnets bizarre.

'Are you short of equipment out there?' asked the postman.

'After Alamein, we were down to thirty tanks and after the mauling in the Fuka, we were left with just four. The British could have walked over us then, but Montgomery's too cautious.'

'The Führer knows what he's doing. His genius will bring us ultimate victory.' Runge's pinhole black eyes glared at Beck, daring him to contradict. Runge had had run-ins with front-line troops before. They thought they knew better than the Führer just because they had seen a bit of fighting. How dare they come home on leave spreading gloom and despondency. The Party had laws to deal with such things.

'What's your unit?' asked Thurn.

'Third Motorized Reconnaissance Battalion, 21st Panzer.'

'Why aren't you in black, then?' demanded Runge.

'We don't wear black in Africa.'

'You're not in Africa now.'

'This is the uniform I was given in hospital. It's the only one I have.'

Runge half turned to glower towards the beer taps. 'For Christ's sake, Vishnia! What are you doing?'

'How did you win your Iron Cross?'

Beck shrugged modestly. 'A troop of Matildas cut us off in the Fuka. Their leader was standing up in the turret. In the dust storm, I was able to get close enough to shoot him and then drop a grenade into the hatch.'

Runge could not stand not being the centre of attention any longer. '*Ich bin ein Alter Kämpfer.* I am an Old Fighter. I, too, have a medal for bravery. Vishnia, bring me my medal.'

The girl, who had been putting the beers on a tray, produced a box from the till. She ran over to the table. Runge brought out a medal and held it up in front of Beck with smug superiority. It showed an eagle holding a wreath. Inside was the date: *9 Nov 1923–33*.

'*Der Blutorden*. The Blood Order medal.'

Beck inspected it. On the back was the number 730. Beck was at a loss. This was obviously something highly prized in Nazi circles – but what the hell was it?

He bowed his head respectfully. 'You do not see many of these.'

'You had to be there,' crowed Runge.

Suddenly the date rang a bell in Beck's memory. Hitler's attempted *putsch*. 'Of course.'

'I was in the *Bürgerbräukeller* the night the Führer wrested power,' boasted Runge. 'The next day I marched alongside him through the streets of Munich. We crossed the Isar together and together we told the police not to fire on their brothers.'

'But they did . . .' Beck cursed himself. Now he knew what Cricklemarsh had meant by the strain of keeping quiet. In his first few hours in Germany he had already let his distaste for this bloated Nazi overcome his training.

'But destiny was on the Führer's side. As we approached the *Odeonsplatz*, the police opened fire at point-blank range. I was just behind the Führer, alongside Göring when he was wounded. The Führer had linked arms with Scheubner-Richter. When *he* was shot, he dragged the Führer to the ground, so his shoulder was dislocated. His bodyguard Ulrich Graf was killed so I stepped in.' His piggy little eyes were gleaming. His cronies were making an effort to simulate interest. They had clearly heard the story many times before. 'I was the one who helped the Führer to his feet. Our doctor's little Fiat motor car pulled up but just as the Führer was about to get in, he noticed a wounded boy. He lifted the boy into the car and shielded the boy's body from the police with his own. Only when he was sure the boy was safe would the Führer allow me to help him escape the swine trying to murder him.'

This time Beck said nothing. He recognized Runge's account as a Nazi Party invention to hide the actual facts of Hitler's panic-stricken flight. The former army commander Ludendorff and his adjutant had calmly walked right on through the line of police bayonets as if out on a Sunday stroll. When the police opened fire, Hitler had thrown himself to the ground so quickly that he dislocated his shoulder. He had crawled along the pavement until he was clear, then he ran away as fast as his legs would carry him. When he arrived at a friend's house to hide, he was incoherent with panic.

'Well done, Gottlob,' chorused the others.

'Amazing story,' declared Beck.

Sturmbannführer Jäger saw the beating when he was still a hundred metres away. The local police recognized his car and redoubled their punishment.

'You're too late, Jäger. We've got the killer,' jeered Greim, his opposite number in the Dachauer *Kriminalpolizei*. 'We don't need hotshots from Munich to help us. We handle our own affairs.'

'Is this him?' Jäger nodded at the battered victim. Blood trickled from the man's pulped mouth. His eyes were mere slits in a face bruised yellow like a swollen, overripe melon.

'Yes. Belgian worker at the paper mill. These are his confederates.' A dozen workers, also bearing the marks of beatings, cowered together under guard. 'They walk past here on their way to work.'

'Has he confessed to killing Hamm?'

'He will do.'

Jäger ran a black, leather-gloved finger over his billhook of a nose. He could understand Greim's resentment that he had been called in, but a policeman had been killed. This local bunch of time-servers and Nazi Party thugs wouldn't have a clue. They'd find someone convenient and execute him and maybe two or three others, but they wouldn't necessarily be the right ones.

As if reading his mind, Greim said: 'We've got a witness, so it's cut and dried. We're convening a People's Special Court straight away.'

'No.'

Greim sneered. 'I don't need to remind you that since December, any anti-German behaviour is considered treason. We'll execute him this evening – and his accomplices.'

'Not until I've questioned him. And how do you know they're all guilty?'

'It's better to execute nine innocent men than to allow one guilty man to go free, says Judge Friesler.'

'Yes, it's not easy being innocent nowadays,' replied Jäger, dryly. 'Put him in the car, Wulzinger.'

The man struggled feebly as Jäger's shambling bear of a colleague pushed him onto the back seat. Jäger wished he was allowed to wear plain clothes instead of the brown shirt and black breeches and tunic of the SS. His black cap carried the silver death's head and on his left sleeve was a swastika armband. It was difficult getting a suspect's confidence when your uniform inspired fear. But since 1936, the detectives of the *Kriminalpolizei* had been placed under the control of the *Sicherheitspolizei*, the Security Police – which included the Gestapo. Then, three years later, as Himmler merged Party and state, the Security Police had been combined with the Nazi Party's own secret police, the SD, to make up the Reich Security Main Office – the *RHSA.*

'It was the Belgian.' A bloated old woman pushed forward to shake her fist at the figure huddled in the car. 'I saw him.'

'What did you see?' Jäger inclined his head steeply, glowering at the old woman through bushy eyebrows.

'I saw him running away while I was looking out of my window.' She pointed to the top floor of a house at the junction of an alley with the main road. Jäger guessed she spent a lot of time at her window. 'He kept looking over his shoulder. You should string him up.'

'Yeh, string him up.' The mob growled their agreement.

'What time was this?'

'About twelve o'clock. As he was going on shift. The others had already gone to work.'

'Do they normally work a full day on Saturday?'

'They work every day.'

'Did you see him actually attack the policeman?'

'He did it. I know he did.'

'Did you actually see him attack Hamm?' repeated Jäger, allowing irritation to creep into his voice.

'Didn't need to,' the old woman muttered sullenly.

'Let's see the body before it gets dark.'

Hamm's body lay under a stunted oak tree on the other side of the hedge. The temperature had not risen above zero all day and a sprinkling of snow covered his greatcoat as well as the shaded area alongside the hedge.

'Has the body been moved?'

'No, *Sturmbannführer*.'

Hamm had been a big man, more than a hundred kilos. Difficult to get the better of a man that size. There were no obvious marks on the body. Jäger examined the policeman's hands. No sign of wounds received while defending himself. It didn't appear as if he'd put up a fight. The body lay across a ditch, part of his weight supported by a fallen branch.

'What time was he last seen?' Jäger demanded.

'When he left home at six this morning to go on duty.'

'What time did it snow here today?'

'We had a little about mid-morning.'

With difficulty, Jäger and Wulzinger lifted the body. A hoar frost lay on the blackened leaf mulch underneath but there was no trace of snow.

'He was dead by then,' announced Jäger. 'When was he reported missing?'

There was no reply from the local policemen.

'Well, Greim?'

'Lunchtime.' Greim cleared his throat. 'His wife thought he was on duty but his colleagues assumed he was out following up a case.'

'Taking the morning off, you mean.'

'A Hitler Youth found the body. This lane isn't on Hamm's beat, nor on his usual way to the police station.'

'Talk to the youngster who found him, Wulzinger.' A wave of tiredness swept over him and he sighed deeply. 'I'll see what the Belgian has to say for himself.'

'He doesn't look very happy,' commented one of the local men as the detective climbed into the car.

'He doesn't like it when coppers get killed. Takes it very personally,' replied Wulzinger.

Jäger flopped on the back seat next to the handcuffed Belgian. God! The man's face was a mess. They would have beaten him to death in another ten minutes.

'Name?'

'Jean-Paul Lecotte,' the prisoner croaked with difficulty.

'Well, Monsieur Lecotte, I know you did not kill officer Hamm.'

The man moaned in relief. 'Thank you, sir.'

'So why were you running?'

'I was late . . . for work.' The words emerged as a distorted mumble.

Jäger lit a small black cigar. 'Don't lie to me.'

'Honestly.'

'Lie to me and I'll give you back to that lynch mob.'

The light of hope faded in the Belgian's eyes. Awkwardly, he raised his bound hands to his swollen lips. 'I was . . . checking snares . . . for rabbits . . . along the bank . . . on the way to work . . . saw the body . . . panicked . . .'

'Why didn't you report it?'

Lecotte's eyes strayed to the police outside the car.

'You thought you'd get a beating?'

The Belgian nodded, wincing with the pain.

Jäger drew deeply on the cheroot. 'Yeh, you're probably right.'

The Belgian relaxed perceptibly as Jäger opened the car door.

'Greim, take him away. Charge him with failing to report a murder and for hunting rabbits without a licence. See what the other Belgians know about poaching.'

'I thought you were my friend,' whispered the Belgian.

'You're in the Fatherland,' hissed Jäger, his face very close to the Belgian's. 'Not even your mother is your friend here.'

Wulzinger came to report that the doctor believed Hamm's neck had been broken.

Jäger pursed his lips. 'What do we know about this Hamm?'

Wulzinger consulted his notebook. 'Aged fifty. Badly gassed on the Somme. As a result, incapable of running more than twenty metres, say the local lads. Born and brought up here. Married the girl next door. Two sons: one missing in Russia, one serving in France. Basically, your average village bobby. So why would anyone kill him?'

'Because he saw something or stumbled across something,' replied Jäger. 'This place is off his normal route. Maybe something aroused his suspicions, he went to investigate and got himself killed. The main road is only eighty metres or so away. Pity the ground's too hard to tell if he was killed here or somewhere else.'

'He'd be a big man to carry.'

'There could be more than one killer involved. Find out what time that nosy old biddy took up station behind her curtains. She might have seen something else without knowing it. Hamm was certainly dead before it began snowing. See if there're escaped prisoners of war or concentration camp inmates on the loose round here. Personally, I'd put my money on black-market racketeers.'

'Black marketeers?'

'It makes sense. There're rumours of lorryloads of butter and eggs coming out of Austria and ending up in the Ruhr or Berlin. The gangs avoid Munich checkpoints by keeping to country roads. Dachau could be on a rat run.'

Beck paused in the corridor. From the *Gaststube*, the small room set aside for house guests, came a boy's soprano voice lifted in song.

> 'Die Fahne hoch! Die Reihen dicht geschlossen,
> S.A. marschiert mit mutig festern Schritt.
> Kam'raden, die Rotfront und Reaktion erschossen,
> Marschier'n im Geist in unsern Reihen mit.'

Runge's gruff baritone joined in on the last line.

Beck's blood froze. The Horst Wessel song. The Nazi Party anthem.

Through the doorway he saw a young boy in a black shirt with a leather cross strap and short blue trousers standing on a table, arm raised in the Hitler salute.

'Heil Hitler.' The boy stared coldly back at Beck.

'You know all the words,' smiled Beck, for want of something to say.

The boy's mouth curled in contempt. 'We sing it every morning at school.'

'This is my nephew Hänschen,' announced Runge as the boy climbed down. 'He's only eleven but already he's a standard-bearer in the *Pimpfs*.'

At the age of ten, every German boy joined the *Jungvolk*, known as the *Pimpfs*. At fourteen, they transferred to the Hitler Youth. Girls had their equivalent organizations.

'He's just come back from Party camp outside Munich.'

'Did you enjoy it?'

'I didn't go to camp to enjoy myself,' replied the boy scornfully. 'I went to study the thoughts of the Führer and help the Reich. I loaded trains going to the Eastern Front.'

'What did you learn, Hänschen?' asked Runge, keen to show off his nephew.

'That Jews are spongers, parasites, poisonous mushrooms, rats, leeches.'

What a little charmer! Beck kept his smile locked in place. 'So, little standard-bearer, tell me about the Jews.'

Hänschen glared for a moment, wary that he was being patronized.

'They encourage the spread of venereal disease to damage the Aryan race.' The boy struck a triumphant pose with his arms folded, one leg in front of the other, head high. 'We Aryans alone are the founders and the carriers of culture. We are the bearers of racial purity. The great civilizations of the past became decadent as a result of contamination of their races' blood. Just as the German tribes replaced the Roman Empire, so it's the destiny of the German people to replace the decadent civilizations of Europe.'

'Good boy.' Runge applauded. 'Isn't he a credit to the Party?'

'Um, yes,' said Beck.

God! It was chilling. The boy had been totally brainwashed. Hänschen had grown up indoctrinated with Nazi propaganda, one of a whole generation of German children who had been turned into mindless automatons to serve the Führer.

'Very good, Hänschen. But now it's time for bed. Would you like me to get you a mug of hot milk?'

'*She* can get it.' Vishnia had entered the room with a stack of plates. 'Put those things down and get me my milk.'

Vishnia appeared not to have heard Hänschen.

'Hey, I'm talking to you.' He picked up a wooden salt cellar and hurled it at the serving girl. It struck her on the elbow. 'Are you deaf as well as stupid? I said I wanted my milk.'

Beck waited for Runge to tell off the brat or, hopefully, clip him round the ears. Instead he too glowered at the girl.

'Do as you're told.'

'Why do we have to put up with *Untermenschen* in the *Reich*, uncle?'

'The German solider is needed at the front so we have Ukrainians like Vishnia to work in our homes and on the land.' Runge scratched his belly, sending the fat rippling across his sagging paunch. 'There are one and a half million foreign workers inside the Reich and seven hundred thousand prisoners of war on the land. We are the master race. They are our servants.'

Hänschen fixed Beck with an accusing eye. 'You should be away fighting.'

'I was wounded in North Africa.'

'Why are we retreating there? *I* wouldn't run away.'

'The enemy has more guns, tanks and men than we do there.'

Hänschen grasped his dagger in his fist. 'The source of a people's power does not lie in the possession of weapons but in its inner value, its *volkswert* – its race value.'

'It's not that simple on the battlefield,' said Beck mildly. Inside he was seething.

Vishnia returned with the milk in a white china mug. Hänschen snatched it from her. 'Where're my biscuits?'

Vishnia scurried out as Ilse entered wearing a long outdoor coat. She looked tired. 'Hänschen, are you still up! It's way past your bed-time.'

'I don't want to go to bed,' muttered the boy defiantly.

'For the Führer,' murmured Beck. He was rewarded by a fleeting grin from Ilse.

'Yes,' Runge agreed. 'You've had a long day. It's time you were asleep.'

Deserted by his expected ally, Hänschen surrendered. But first, he was determined to show off. 'Can I say my prayers down here? In front of his picture?'

Vishnia carried in a plate of biscuits. She gave the boy a wide berth.

'Certainly,' said Runge.

Hänschen turned to a picture of Hitler. There was one in every room. This one showed him smiling benevolently as he signed autographs for three flaxen-haired boys in Hitler Youth uniform.

'Stand still,' hissed Hänschen at Vishnia who had resumed putting the plates away. She winced as though she had been struck. He dropped onto his knees and put his hands together in prayer.

> 'Führer, mein Führer, by God given to me,
> Defend and protect me as long as may be,
> You rescued Germany in her deepest need,
> I give you thanks who dost daily me feed.
> Stay by me for ever and never take flight,
> Oh Führer, my Führer, my faith and my light.
> All hail to my Führer.'

Then he leaped to his feet, his right arm rigid in salute and began screaming, *'Sieg Heil, Sieg Heil.'*

He turned to shriek at Vishnia. 'You, give the Führer greeting.' She slowly raised her sticklike arm as if it weighed more than she could lift, a spasm of pain crossing her face. 'Say it, *Sieg Heil.* Go on, say, *Sieg Heil.*'

'Runge,' cried Ilse. 'Tell him to stop.'

'Sieg Heil. Sieg Heil. Sieg Heil. Go on, say it. *Sieg Heil. Sieg Heil.*'

Runge chuckled, deep in his throat.

'Hänschen, bed. NOWWW!' The force of the primeval scream wrenched from Ilse filled the room. Hänschen stopped dead, his mouth open.

Ilse stood white and shaking. Beck saw she held a six–inch hat pin in her trembling right hand. Runge put a protective arm around his nephew and led him awkwardly from the room. There was silence.

'Are you all right, Vishnia?' whispered Ilse at last.

Vishnia nodded, her eyes full of tears.

'I'm sorry,' Ilse apologized to Beck. 'Hänschen was being cruel, and I can't stand cruelty.'

'Where've you been?' Monika Jäger stood under the tasselled light shade in the hallway, her arms tightly folded. 'It's almost midnight.'

'Working.' Jäger brought out a thick piece of bacon from his pocket. 'Don't tell the neighbours about this.'

'Phew! I can smell the drink from here.' His wife pulled a face.

'You'll be able to smell more in a minute. I need to wash away the taste of society's dregs.'

He unbuttoned his jacket, wondering, as always, how, with the fuel restrictions, their over-furnished apartment always seemed so hot. He poured himself a beer, Monika watching him, arms still across her body. He wondered if she had stayed up this late just so they could exchange insults. Resentment was etched on her face and Jäger knew she was building herself up for another full-scale row. He knew what was coming. Shrill accusations of neglect and selfishness, of putting his job before his family.

'A copper's been murdered out near Dachau. I reckon it's down to black marketeers so I've been out rattling a few cages.' Such explanations were futile, of course, but at least he could tell himself that he had made the effort.

'The great detective! Always finding time for others.'

'Please, Monika, it's late. We're both tired.' But then he sensed she was holding something back. There was a specific reason why she had waited up. 'All right, what is it?'

She thrust a leaflet into his hand.

Jäger inspected it. A White Rose leaflet from the student resistance group, calling for Germans to break with National Socialism. So? They weren't that uncommon. Dangerous if the Gestapo found one in your possession but . . . Suddenly Jäger's blood ran cold.

'Where did you find this?'

'In Alix's bedside cupboard.'

'Where is she?'

'She's locked herself in her room. I told you it would come to this. You've let her run wild, get in with the wrong crowd . . .'

'I came back from France specially . . .'

But now was not the time to rework the old arguments. He scanned the leaflet, recognizing it as the sixth and final one. *'Students, men and women! The eyes of Germany are upon us! The nation looks to us to break the National Socialist terror . . . The dead of Stalingrad call to us!'*

The Gestapo estimated that three thousand of these leaflets had been run off. It would be inevitable there were still a few hidden away.

But this was not some mimeographed copy. This was typed – and corrected. Words had been inserted by hand. *'We will not be silent. We are your bad conscience.'*

God Almighty!

This was a draft.

An early draft of the one Hans Scholl and his sister Sophie had been throwing over the balcony in Munich University's entrance hall when they had been caught. The same university where Alix studied Medieval German History.

Jäger put a finger to his lips, carried the leaflet into the kitchen and set fire to it over the sink. He flushed away the ashes. Only then did he put his mouth close to Monika's ear.

'Has anyone unusual been in here during the past few weeks? Workmen, strangers? Have you ever left anyone alone in our apartment?'

Monika looked blank. 'The building superintendent brought a fire prevention officer around one morning.'

'Did you leave them alone?'

'I don't think so. Why?'

It didn't matter. The Gestapo could have got in while Monika was out queuing for the shops. He put his finger to his lips again, and began a detailed search of the whole apartment. Finally, he called to Alix through her bedroom door.

She did not answer.

'Alix, come out now or I swear I'll shoot the bloody lock off.'

She must have been standing right behind the door for the key turned instantly. She opened the door a few inches. He pushed past. Only when he was satisfied there was no microphone hidden in her bedroom did Jäger turn to look at his eighteen-year-old daughter.

She was paper-white, red-eyed but defiant.

'Ask her where she got it,' hissed Monika. 'She won't tell me. Go on, you're the great detective, ask her.'

It wasn't important. It wasn't the right question.

'Alix, do you have any more of these leaflets?'

'Of course she does,' cried Monika. 'The students took them home as souvenirs.'

Monika didn't understand. But Alix did.

'No, dad. It's the only one.'

Father and daughter regarded each other grimly. Alix blinked away tears. Jäger wished he could look at her in the same sardonic way that conned criminals into believing he knew what they were thinking – but Alix was his daughter, and he could only look at her as his daughter.

He did not know if she was telling the truth – and he could not take the risk.

He searched her room, briskly, expertly. Once he had finished, Alix went back inside and closed the door.

Monika meanwhile kept up her litany of accusation and resentment. 'Now you see what happens when you neglect your family. If you'd taken more interest, this would never have happened. I warned you she was mixing with bad company at that university. Why she wants to go there at all, I don't know. She should get herself married but she's got these fancy notions, and you encourage her . . .'

Jäger ignored her shrill complaints. He began to calculate. Hans and Sophie Scholl and their friend Christoph Probst had been arrested on 18 February. They were tried and guillotined four days later at Stadelheim prison. Another twelve members of the White Rose had been arrested and tortured. The ripple of ongoing arrests had spread wider and wider. So why hadn't Alix been picked up?

'Shut up,' he snarled at last.

Monika jerked as if she had been slapped in the face. 'Don't—'

'Just be quiet. In the morning, you will speak to your sister in Aachen and arrange for Alix to go to stay with her for the next few weeks, maybe months. I'll pay for her board and lodging. If she wants, she can attend university there – or she can become a land girl, for all I care.'

He noticed Alix standing in her bedroom doorway. A wave of weariness broke over him.

'Whatever happens, you will not go near the university here again, nor will you speak to any of your friends. In fact, you will not leave this house until I or your mother put you on the train to Aachen. Is that understood?'

The girl nodded silently.

'It's for your own good, you know that,' Jäger added in a softer tone.

'Ihr Geist lebt weiter,' Alix whispered so softly that Jäger strained to catch what she said. 'Their spirit lives on.'

7

Sunday, 21 March

When Beck opened his curtains next morning, he was in a different world. The sun was shining in a cloudless sky and, high above the valley, he could see sparkling, fresh snow on the mountain tops. The air, thin and pure, was intoxicating. There was a scratching at the door and Vishnia entered, bearing a jug of hot water.

'Thank you. Isn't it a beautiful morning?'

She looked down at her feet and stood rooted to the spot, her fingers intertwined behind her back. Her stance emphasized her bony shoulders and spare frame. Under her faded dress, her flanks were meagre and meatless. It occurred to Beck that she was nerving herself to submit to some act or other.

'Can I help you?' Vishnia shook her head. 'What's wrong? Cat got your tongue?'

Vishnia spun on her heel and ran out of the door.

Over breakfast of thin slices of sausage with rye bread and jam washed down by bitter ersatz coffee, Beck mentioned he had to go into Berchtesgaden to register with the civil and military authorities. Ilse had business in the town so she offered to show him the way.

'It's almost two kilometres. Is your leg strong enough to walk that far?'

'The exercise will be good for my leg – and my lungs.'

Ilse waited for him at the doorway of the inn. She wore cord breeches and boots, a thick hacking jacket and a Tyrolean hat with an enormous feather. The effect was stylish and incongruous at the same time. Beck was surprised. Here was someone who wanted to be noticed.

Ilse reached up and adjusted the Iron Cross at his neck. 'There, that's better. You're obviously one of those men who never uses a mirror, isn't that true?'

Yes, Beck admitted, it was true. Where was Herr Runge?

'He went off early to Salzburg on Party business. He won't be back until evening.'

As they left the inn, Ilse apologized for the scene the previous night. 'Hänschen is always worst when he comes back from a Party camp. Runge encourages him. *But I do not like cruelty.*'

'Is Hänschen staying here?'

'Yes, worse luck. His mother, Runge's sister, is married to the Party boss of Lübeck. It's dangerous there with all the bombing so Hänschen's come to stay with us.'

'I'm surprised you had any rooms available.'

'To be honest, Runge uses his influence so we don't have soldiers billeted on us. He says they're more trouble than they're worth and there's no money in it. We'll get busy when the Führer comes to stay.'

'Oh dear. You said last night that he was expected any day. Does that mean I'll have to move out?'

'No. The old Party members know he never sees anyone for the first fortnight or so while he recuperates but after that they'll pack the place while they try to get to see him. Poor Vishnia's rushed off her feet then.'

'She's very shy, isn't she? I can't get a word out of her.'

Ilse slapped her hand to her forehead. 'Oh! You don't know . . .' She grasped his arm, turning towards him. 'Vishnia never speaks. I don't know if she was born like that or whether something terrible's happened to her. Vishnia is dumb.'

'Oh, no! I asked her if the cat had got her tongue.'

'She won't mind. She likes you.'

'How do you know?'

'She took up your hot water before I had the chance to do so.'

'Oh!'

A convoy of *Wehrmacht* lorries rumbled by. A staff car with a motorcycle escort sped in the opposite direction. Soldiers were freshening up the white paint on the kerbstones and on the gratings.

'That shows the Führer is coming back soon,' observed Ilse. 'There are more soldiers than ever. You can't move for generals and field marshals when he's at the Berghof.'

Good.

'Tell me about yourself,' Ilse commanded.

'What do you want to know?'

'Where you're from. Do you have a family? A girlfriend?'

'I'm from Cologne. No, they were killed in the big air raid. So was she.' Beck went through the well-rehearsed story, punctuating it with hesitations and sadness when he came to describe the loss of all his loved ones.

'Oh, I'm sorry. I shouldn't have asked.'

'You keep saying sorry,' said Beck gently. In turn, he was curious to know how she came to be married to a fat, uncouth Nazi like Runge, who was a good twenty years older than her. But he couldn't think of a way of phrasing the question.

'Do I? Must be a guilty conscience.' Ilse perked up. 'I will name the mountains for you. That one straight ahead in the distance is the Watzmann, the second-highest peak in Germany. The one behind us is the Untersberg. There's a legend that Charlemagne and five thousand warriors sleep under the mountain ready to emerge when Germany is threatened.'

'Shouldn't he be stirring?'

Ilse glanced keenly at him. 'There is another legend that Charlemagne and his knights sleep at a great stone table in a hall within the mountain. When the emperor's beard curls seven times around the table they will wake.'

'That'll come as a shock to the Führer.'

'Oh no, he has already planned to make Charlemagne *Reichsminister* in charge of beards,' she laughed.

They set off alongside the river. Ilse chatted away, gay and brittle. The absence of Runge, the brilliance of the morning and the company of her own handsome, wounded officer had created in her a strange, febrile mood as fleeting and lambent as the tiny rainbows that hung in the spray over the Ache's spuming waters.

'You're not a member of the Party, are you?' she demanded.

'No.'

She was glad he said it firmly. She felt mischievous.

'There's a new game. You know the current fashion of abbreviating everything?' Beck didn't but he nodded anyway. Ilse hesitated for a moment and then blurted out, 'What's a *Gör*?'

'A *Gör*?'

'Yes, you know, short for Göring.'

'I don't know.'

'It's the maximum amount of tin a man can wear on his chest without falling flat on his face.' She clapped her hands like an excited schoolgirl. 'Didn't you know that, *Hauptmann* Beck?'

Beck chuckled at the reference to the number of medals Göring wore on his uniforms.

She went on. 'What's a *Goeb*, as in Goebbels, our beloved Minister of Propaganda?'

'Don't know.'

'The minimum amount of effort needed to switch off a million wireless sets at one time.'

'Is there a *Hit*?'

'Oh, yes. It's the most number of promises a man can make without keeping any of them.' She stopped dead. 'God! What am I saying! I don't know you. You don't know me.' She was gabbling. 'You're not an informer, are you? Most people can be, you know.'

'No, of course I'm not.'

'How do you know *I'm* not?'

Beck smiled down at her. 'You don't look like an agent provocateur. Are you?'

'No,' she replied in a small voice. 'I'm just me.'

She swung her gaze down to the foam-specked waters rushing beneath them. A bare branch was being carried down the edge of the current. She watched as it twirled round in an eddy and drifted into calm water. *What in God's name am I doing? What came over me? What happened to the wise daughter? Why am I babbling like a schoolgirl? What makes me want to shock and impress this man? And I laughed. Aloud. When did I last do that? I thought I'd forgotten how. And those things I said. I could end up in a concentration camp for just thinking half those jokes.*

Runge wouldn't help me. He'd be glad to disown me. But Captain Beck . . . Christian – she liked to think of him as Christian – *he is too trusting.* He was in danger from his own nature. Or perhaps he was a dissembler. Her thoughts tumbled like the waters of the Ache. The branch was moving now, turning slowly, carried away on the swirling torrent.

'Captain, you know that anything I say to you is not to be repeated.' It was unworthy but it had to be said.

'Do you think . . .?' He was frowning.

'Listen. This is a true story.' She put her hand on his arm. 'A mother lost her only son in the battle for Stalingrad. She was grieving as only a mother can grieve. Then a neighbour heard on Radio Moscow that he'd been taken prisoner. Out of the goodness of her heart, she told the mother. The mother reported her to the Gestapo for listening to the enemy wireless.'

'I didn't know things were as bad as that.'

'You've been fighting. Maybe there's still honour in real war. There's little here.' A sadness grew in her amber eyes. The moment had passed. The spell had been broken.

Ilse shook herself. 'No. It's too lovely a morning to be serious. Look, up there. That majestic slab of rock, the sun glinting off the crisp snow. That's the Hoher Göll. The border with Austria used to run along the top of the range. And there's the Berghof.'

Beck followed her pointing finger. Across the river, the mountain rose in gentle fields before steepening into a patchwork of dark forest and green meadows. Fifteen hundred feet above and just over a mile away, a white building stood on a shoulder of alpine pasture. He could make out other buildings further up the mountain.

'We're too low down here,' said Ilse. 'You'll see it better when we get to the town.'

'Perhaps we could go for a walk up there?'

Ilse laughed. It was a curiously bitter laugh. 'You need a special pass to go on Obersalzberg.'

'What! Even on the mountain?'

'The Nazi Party owns the mountain. It's theirs. They made everybody else move out.'

'Can't *you* go up there?'

'Not unless I'm invited. The guards in the *Führersperrgebiet*, immediately around the Berghof, have orders to shoot first and ask questions later. Not even a government minister can get in there without a special pass.'

'You *have* been up there?'

'Oh, yes. I was born near here. When I was a little girl we used to ride up on hay carts and have picnics in the meadows. I had many friends among the farmers' families before the Nazi Party decided they wanted the mountain for themselves.' She fell silent. 'Runge would be furious if he knew I'd even mentioned that.'

'I swear I will not say a word.'

Ilse lengthened her stride, forgetting for the moment Beck's limp. He struggled after her. Her mood swings unsettled him. She blew hot and then cold. One moment she was a correct *Hausfrau*, the next an indiscreet schoolgirl, delighting in salacious and forbidden gossip, and the next again a bitter, angry woman. Yet her face, in repose, betrayed little of the dark emotions that churned away inside her. With her corn-yellow hair and regular, almost severe, features, she was a picture of probity. She also had slightly protruding eyes, which in years to come would be medically recognized as an indication of an overactive thyroid gland – and full lips, kissable lips, trace-their-shape-with-your-finger lips.

Beck was not to know that in Ilse's dreams, in her fantasies, in the world she lived in most of the time because the real world was too awful to bear, she had already cast him as her paladin who would save her from her evil husband and his Nazi Party. Save her from her onsetting madness.

Beck hobbled to catch up till Ilse remembered his injury.

'I'm sorry, captain.'

'Please don't keep saying that. I have a favour to ask.'

'Yes?'

'Will you call me Christian?'

'When we are alone, I will call you Christian and you will call me Ilse,' she decided solemnly. 'But when we are in company it must be *Hauptmann* Beck and *Frau* Runge.'

'*Jawohl.*' Beck clicked his heels and bowed which made her smile. 'So, Ilse, tell me what happened on Obersalzberg. Remember whatever's said between us stays between us.'

'It was a lovely, friendly place. There was a children's sanatorium, a rest home for retired naval officers, Bechstein, the piano manufacturer, had a house up there and there were many old farms. There was only one steep, potholed road and in winter we used to sledge home to the smells of woodsmoke.' She leaned on the rails above the river and regarded the lost mountain. 'Then Hitler came. First he stayed with his friend Dietrich Eckard and then he rented a cottage to finish *Mein Kampf*. In 1928 he rented the *Haus Wachenfels*. Five years later, when he became Chancellor, he bought the house and started enlarging it. Party cronies moved in round him. Families who'd lived there for generations were threatened with being sent to a concentration camp if they did not sell up cheaply and get out quickly. The mountain belongs to Bormann now.'

'Bormann? The Führer's secretary?'

'He is more than that. He has wormed his way closest to the Führer's side.'

Beck was amazed at this insight into the Nazi Party. 'Is this true?'

'Oh, yes.' Ilse chose her words carefully. 'I have a friend who knows these things.'

'On the house, *Sturmbannführer*.' Hermann the barman placed two beers on the counter in front of Jäger and Wulzinger, and smiled nervously.

The small bar, hidden away in a narrow alley off Kaufingerstraße, was deserted apart from three men sitting at separate tables under photographs of Nazi parades and Hitler at Nuremburg.

'Has Squashy been in?' demanded Jäger.

'Not seen him all day,' said Hermann unnecessarily loudly. He scoured the inside of a glass with a cloth and let his eyes wander to the heavy green curtain partitioning off an alcove at the end of the room.

'You've heard about the copper killed near Dachau?'

'Yes. Shocking thing.'

Hermann made the mistake of moving within Jäger's reach. Jäger grabbed him by the throat.

'If there's something I hate more than low life, it's fucking hypocrites. You don't care if a copper croaks, you know you fucking don't.'

He flung the barman away.

'There was no call for that, *Sturmbannführer*,' gasped Hermann. 'You know I've always cooperated with the *Kripo*.'

Even Wulzinger was looking strangely at Jäger. *Bollocks.* He couldn't apologize now. But he had to get out of this thieves' kitchen and pick up Alix. She was booked on the 14.30 train to Aachen and he was going to make sure she got on it.

Wulzinger ripped the green curtain aside. A short, muscular man with cropped hair sat by himself at a table. He wore a Party badge in the lapel of his expensive suit. He lifted his glass in a gesture which was at the same time unperturbed and patronizing.

'Squashy, how nice to see you. Fetch our beers, Wulzinger. We're going to have a little chat with our black marketeer friend here.'

'That copper's murder is nothing to do with me,' said Squashy.

'Not been running any trucks out Dachau way?'

'Dachau?'

'Or know anyone who might have been?'

'Nah.' He gave a small shake of his head.

'Thanks.' Jäger took a long pull of the beer. It tasted good. He could do with a few beers, might make him less tense. Maybe, after he'd put Alix on the train.

'Where were you yesterday morning early?'

'Yesterday . . .' Squashy gave an elaborate shrug. 'How the hell do I know? That was a long, long time ago.'

'Tsk.' Jäger made a regretful sound with his tongue.

Crunch. Wulzinger grabbed Squashy by the hair and slammed his face into the table. The man's nose broke with a grinding of splintered cartilage. He gave a muffled scream as blood spurted everywhere.

'Look at that. All over your posh suit,' observed Jäger.

'God. You bastards.' Squashy was trying to hold his nose and pull out a handkerchief at the same time. 'Why the fuck . . .'

Large drops of blood dripped into his beer, heavy red swirls in the pale golden liquid.

'Again,' said Jäger.

'Wait, wait.' Squashy's eyes welled with tears of pain. 'I was inside. Gospel. I got into in a fight in a bar in Pullach. I spent the night in the cells there. They didn't let me out until ten yesterday morning.'

'You should have told us that sooner.'

'You've broken my nose.'

'We'll start on your fingers next. Who's running trucks through Dachau?'

'There's a mob in Stuttgart . . .'

'How convenient,' interrupted Jäger. 'No one from Munich.'

'. . . No, listen. They're ruthless bastards – deserters, some of them. They wouldn't think twice about killing a copper who got in their way.'

Jäger knew there was more. 'Yeh, go on.'

Squashy regarded Jäger with pure hate. 'Word is, they're moving a load of eggs. You remember those railway wagons that got unhitched last week outside Innsbruck? Yeh, those. Apparently, they're taking the eggs up to the Ruhr in dribs and drabs rather than risk a whole convoy being nicked.'

'When's the next run?'

'I don't know. Honest.'

'Find out. And put the word out. Pond life in Munich is going to have a hard time until I find whoever killed Hamm. And don't drip into your beer.'

As he passed the bar, Hermann nodded towards the counter. Jäger swept up the packet of cheroots without a word.

Beck was relieved to find that many wounded officers came to the area to convalesce. There was safety in numbers but Beck's case was different. Others had their billets arranged for them. Beck had arrived under his own steam. Yet, because he was one among many, his papers were stamped without hesitation and he hoped he was now part of the larger system.

As he came out into the cobbled square, he was accosted by Party members collecting for Winter Relief. Beck knew most of the money found its way into Nazi funds but not to give would draw attention to himself. A gang of Hitler Youth clustered around the water fountain under huge swastikas hanging from the ancient palace walls. Almost everyone was in uniform: even young women were clad in the blue skirts and white blouses of the *Bund Deutscher Mädel* – the League of German Maidens. Only the older inhabitants, making their way to church, were in traditional Bavarian costume.

Under an arcade, carved on stone tablets set in the wall, Beck found the town's memorial for those who had died in the First World War.

'A *Pfennig* for your thoughts.' Ilse stood beside him.

'I was just thinking how we do not learn.'

Ilse pointed to the names Andreas and Rupert Hölzl. 'The only Hölzl brother who survived the last war has already lost three sons in this one. Hans was killed in Poland in the first month and Andreas and Johann both fell in Russia. I grew up with them. They were lovely boys. Now there's only Michael left. I say prayers for his safe return.'*

Beck came to attention and saluted. An army salute.

Ilse had never seen anyone do that before. It was a wonderful, chivalrous gesture. Her paladin grew in stature. 'Thank you,' she whispered.

She led him up a flight of steps from where they could see over the roofs to the Obersalzberg mountain. There were more buildings up there than he'd first thought.

'Bormann razed the old ones to start again,' explained Ilse. 'So they're almost all new except for the Hotel zum Türken. It used to be owned by Karl Schuster and his family. Ten years ago Hitler wanted to create a new drive up to the Berghof. When Herr Schuster protested, he was put into a concentration camp and the Nazi Party confiscated the hotel. The family were made to leave in the clothes they wore. They were banned from living near Berchtesgaden and forced to promise never to reveal the story.'

'Then how do you know?'

* Michael, too, was to die on the Eastern Front.

'Therese Schuster was my best friend. I cried buckets when she left. Her father died of a heart attack a year after they were forced out. I still write to Therese. She and her mother swear they'll return one day.'

'What's happened to their hotel?' Beck already knew from briefings in London but he had to show natural curiosity.

'The Security Services took it over. The house up to the left is Bormann's and Göring's is above that. The big building is the SS barracks.'

'What's that shining?'

'The greenhouses reflecting the sun. Bormann uses them to grow flowers for the Berghof while people go hungry for food. The white building on the right is the Platterhof Hotel for Party VIPs.'

'What are the huts?'

'That's where the building workers live. There's even a bordello near Unterau, although nice girls aren't supposed to know about that.' Ilse giggled. 'I still have a couple of things to do so why don't you wait for me in the Hotel Post?'

They were about to part when a small woman with a huge smile approached in her Sunday best. She was bursting with news.

'*Frau* Runge, *Frau* Runge. My boy Artur is safe.'

'That's good news, *Frau* Reintaler.' Ilse clasped the woman's hand. 'I'm so pleased.'

'Yes. He's coming home on leave from Russia and then he's going to be posted to France. He's safe.'

'Thank God.'

'I'm on my way to church to say a thank-you for Artur's life and a prayer for Wolf, lying somewhere in Greece.' *Frau* Reintaler crossed herself.

Heinz Voss wrapped the beige civilian raincoat tightly around himself, braced his shoulders and entered the inn as if it was the condemned cell. Back in the car, Big Josef looked up and down the quiet country road near Kohelwald, satisfied himself they had not been followed and opened a newspaper.

A man attempting to conceal a military bearing was sitting at a far table.

'My name is Peter. I'm your contact for this operation,' said the Englishman in faintly accented German.

'I'm not involved in any operation.' Voss had rehearsed how he would play the scene. Straight talking right from the start. Show who was boss.

The serving girl hurried out of the kitchen, and Voss ordered a beer. When she had left, the Englishman with the long face smiled pleasantly. 'We need your help.'

'My wife's not well. I have to be home in the evenings to look after her.'

Peter nodded sympathetically. 'Surely you can afford a nurse.'

'That's my decision.' Voss steeled himself. 'It's better if we end this association.'

When the beer arrived, Voss held the glass in both hands, unwilling to met Peter's eye.

'Is there anything worrying you? Anything we can do to help?'

'Nothing. Just leave me alone. I don't want you to contact me again.'

'You don't *want*. Oh, dear.'

Peter's mockery annoyed him. 'Enough is enough.' Voss spoke in the clipped tones of someone who had made up his mind. 'I don't need your money.'

'I'm sure Heidi does,' said Peter.

Voss shuddered at the mention of his mistress. The fact that this Englishman knew about her unsettled him.

Peter reached slowly into his pocket. For a moment, Voss thought he was going to pull a gun, but instead he brought out two pieces of paper, which he inspected with slow deliberation before placing them on the table. Voss recognized one as the receipt for the first payment he had received four years ago. The other was a statement from the St Gallen bank recording all the monthly deposits.

'Neither of them is in my name,' muttered Voss.

Peter regarded him with sympathetic eyes, as though he hated doing this. 'The handwriting on the receipt is yours. The name on the receipt matches the holder of the Swiss account.'

The Englishman did not need to spell it out. It was illegal for a German national to hold a foreign bank account. One word to the Gestapo and the contents of the whole can of worms would crawl out – all over Voss and Heidi.

'This is the *last* time,' he whispered.

'Of course.' Peter became businesslike. 'Our man will be wearing the uniform of an officer in a mountaineering regiment. Josef will give you a change of clothing for him, together with travel documents and railway tickets to St Gallen and then on to Zurich. Make sure he's in time for the last train from Oberreit to Altstitten.'

'All right.'

Peter's next words sent a dagger into Voss's heart. 'There may be a national emergency on at the time so the border will be closed. It's up to you to get our man across.' Peter placed a thick brown envelope on the table before him. 'Now I have a present for you – and one for Heidi.' Gently, he laid a ladies' gold Swiss watch on top.

The stick and the carrot. Perfect to get a donkey to do as you want.

Beck sat in the old inn and sipped a glass of weak beer, feeling a thrill of anticipation. It had been one thing to see aerial photographs and study maps of Obersalzberg back in a London office. Now he had seen the real thing. The Nazi domain was protected on the west by the river Ache and on the east by a range rising over two thousand, five hundred metres – almost 8,000 feet of snow, ice and vertical rock face. He hadn't yet spotted the Mooslanger tea house. He must also find out more about the three security zones. He'd slip in questions to Ilse sometime.

She was an enigma: what went on in her head? She looked so proper but . . . still waters ran deep but did they run straight? There was a seam of bitterness imbedded in her like a fault line. Did that make her a potential ally – or just unpredictably dangerous?

Beck was dragged from his thoughts by raised voices. Two old men, faces like sandpaper, were shouting at each other in a thick local dialect, rich with rolled Rs, as though they were struggling to make themselves heard over the roar of a mountain torrent.

'What are they saying?' he asked an elderly waitress.

'Ach. Those two! Albrecht is attacking the Kaiser and his family. He is demanding to know which other family in Germany had six sons left alive in 1918.'

'Are they always like this?'

'Always. They are true Bavarians. A Bavarian will quarrel with his best friend over drink, kill him with his beer mug and then repent. The police always find him in church praying for forgiveness. I'd better stop them before they go too far and say something that will land them in trouble.' The waitress went across and began scolding them like naughty children.

'I'll come and see you tomorrow, father. We get deliveries in the morning and Runge's away again so it'll be easier.'

'Don't take any risks, Ilse.' Dr Meissner put his arms on his daughter's shoulders. 'Promise me.'

'Of course.'

'Runge's away a lot at the moment.'

'He comes home every night,' she said bitterly.

'I'm sorry.' He dropped his arms.

'I didn't mean it like that. Father, believe me.' Ilse was instantly desperate to be believed. She grabbed his arms and made him look in her face. 'You know I wouldn't . . .'

'Nothing lasts for ever, Ilse. Not even the war. Remember what Goethe said, "Better an end with suffering than suffering without end".'

People were looking at them. They stood out. The doctor, distinguished and grey-haired, and his daughter, as erect as a man, with her strong features and corn hair. Both were well known.

'I haven't told you, we've a wounded officer staying at the Red Ox.'

'Is he agreeable? Someone you can talk to?'

'Yes, I think so. There he is now.' Beck was standing in the doorway of the inn. 'Come. I'll introduce you. I think you two'll get on.'

Beck limped out into the square to meet them.

'My father, Dr Meissner. Captain Christian Beck.'

'Grüß Gott,' said Dr Meissner, using the Bavarian greeting. 'May God greet you.'

'Grüß Gott,' replied Beck.

'My daughter tells me you are recuperating in the mountains.' Dr Meissner was taller than Beck, with a tired, lined face and a smile at the same time quizzical and rueful. 'The air here is the best in Germany. Even the Führer thinks so.'

'It is also very beautiful,' said Beck politely.

'Yes, nothing can change the scenery.'

The two old men came out of the inn arm in arm. They waved to Ilse and her father who waved back.

'They've just been having a terrible row,' exclaimed Beck. 'Now look at them.'

'If Albrecht and Ludwig didn't have each other to argue with, they'd die of boredom.'

'The waitress was worried they'd go too far.'

'Last week Albrecht was heard to declare that the Russians were getting the better of us. Fortunately, it was in dialect so few understood,' said Dr Meissner.

'But surely it's true. Especially after the defeat at Stalingrad.'

'My naïve young friend, what has truth to do with it?'

'Is it defeatist to say we lost a battle?'

'It is when the Führer proclaims that total victory is inevitable.'

Beck bit his lip. He must learn to curb his tongue. Cricklemarsh had been right about the strain of keeping silent. Being a listener, not a talker. He was in a police state where everyone was a potential informer.

Dr Meissner smiled understandingly. 'My friend, it's easier to believe in false victory than to walk around Berchtesgaden without your head. Maybe you can speak freely at the front. In the Fatherland, we have the German look . . .' Dr Meissner demonstrated by glancing quickly over his shoulder as if to make sure no one was listening '... and the *Flüsterwitze*: the whispered jokes.'

'Father!'

'Did you know there are now forty crimes punishable by death, including a new one of undermining the fighting ability of the people?'

'That sounds very vague.'

'It's not intended to secure justice, of course, only to destroy the enemies of National Socialism. Ouch!'

Ilse kicked her father on the ankle.

'Yes, all right, my dear. Captain, we now have a mutual hold over one another. You inform on me and I'll inform on you.'

'But that's terrible.'

'That's the way things work in Germany.'

'No chance it was suicide?' Cricklemarsh looked out of the commandant's office window at the ranks of German prisoners of war standing to attention.

'None at all. There were bruises on his arms and a considerable amount of ... um ...' Major Pewsey glanced uncomfortably towards Annie '... excrement, consistent with the hanging having been murder.'

'I thought he was supposed to be kept in a secure unit, away from the SS thugs.'

'So did I.' Major Pewsey reached into his desk drawer. 'We turned the place upside down after the death and found these keys. We've stripped the trusties of their privileges but I'm afraid it's a case of locking the stable door after the horse has bolted.'

'Or in this case been murdered.'

'Er ... quite. The ringleader's that chap who brought you a cup of tea when you interviewed Pabst. Fellow called Werner Mayr.'

'He did put the fear of God into Pabst. Let's see him, then.'

Werner Mayr stood rigidly to attention, his unblinking gunmetal eyes fixed on a point on the wall above Cricklemarsh's head. There were scratches down one side of his skull-like face.

'Where did you get those marks?' demanded Cricklemarsh in German.

'Was?'

'The scratches on your cheek.'

'What scratches on my cheek?'

'Don't try to be funny,' barked Major Pewsey, losing his temper. 'This is a murder inquiry. I'll see you dangling on the end of a rope, if you carry on.'

'About turn. Three paces. Halt.' Cricklemarsh manoeuvred the German so he was out of line with the window. 'The scratches?'

'I tripped and fell against the wire around the cookhouse.' Mayr could not resist letting his eyes slide towards Annie.

Cricklemarsh nodded as if it was the obvious answer. Why hadn't they thought of it sooner? 'Why did you kill Pabst?' he enquired in a mild tone.

'Sir?'

'Why did you and your comrades kill Private Pabst?'

'How do you know we did?'

'I wouldn't have thought he'd put up much of a fight, a weasel like him,' said Cricklemarsh, almost to himself. 'Still, he struggled enough to scratch you, Mayr. Careless of you, wasn't it – or couldn't you handle him?'

'I've nothing to say.'

A silence fell over the room. Cricklemarsh had expected this. A hardened SS veteran like Mayr was not going to crack under the sort of pressure Cricklemarsh was able to apply in such a short time.

'At ease,' said Cricklemarsh. 'We're not going to get anywhere like this. Cigarette?'

Mayr took one from Cricklemarsh's case, lit it and inhaled deeply. He blew a cloud of smoke to one side of his benefactor's face. Just close enough to show contempt but not close enough to incur punishment.

'Do you know any of your fellow prisoners who might have been involved?' enquired Cricklemarsh in an offhand way. 'Come over and look. Well?'

Mayr stood in the window and smirked. 'No. Absolutely no one.'

'Do you like American cigarettes?' Cricklemarsh pointed generally at the ranks of prisoners. 'Or do you prefer English?'

'American.'

Cricklemarsh placed a friendly hand on the prisoner's shoulder, threw back his head and laughed. Annie caught his quick glance towards the German and then at the window. She understood.

'Major Pewsey, a word outside, if I may,' said Cricklemarsh. 'You'll be all right with Mayr, won't you, Annie?'

Once they were alone, Annie sidled up to the German. 'It's a shame we didn't meet in different circumstances.'

The German sniggered. She was eating him with her eyes. He could not help but respond. Annie gave him a tantalizing come-to-bed half-smile and let her gaze drop to his groin. Mayr groaned. He was reaching out towards her when the door opened and Cricklemarsh and the commandant returned.

'Thank you for cooperating, Mayr . . .'

'I didn't.'

'. . . You may leave. Take this packet of Players with you.'

'Over here.' Annie grasped the lapel of Mayr's tunic and pulled him gently away from the window.

Mayr was suspicious. 'Why? Why give me these?'

'As I said, for cooperating.'

'But I've told you nothing.'

'Really! Your comrades have just seen you smoking, laughing, talking – even flirting with a beautiful woman – while they've been standing to attention outside in the cold.'

'What!' Mayr threw the cigarettes onto the desk as if they were on fire.

'They'll wonder what you were doing to earn such friendliness. They will come to the conclusion that you cooperated.'

'I'll make sure the story's all over the camp in half an hour,' added Major Pewsey.

'They won't believe you,' said Mayr in a tone at once both defiant and doubting.

Major Pewsey flung open the door. 'Sergeant, escort the prisoner back to the cells. He's been very helpful. Put him in solitary for his own protection. Give him a special guard.'

'Wait. Wait,' pleaded Mayr. 'You're compromising me.'

'Yes,' agreed Cricklemarsh. 'Yes, I suppose we are.'

'Thanks for twigging so smartly,' said Cricklemarsh as he and Annie drove away. 'You're a born actress.'

'Who said I was acting?' asked Annie, keeping her eyes on the road.

They had been back in their Baker Street garret less than five minutes before Colonel Purefoy strode in to demand a report on the murder. Cricklemarsh was sitting alone.

'The SS prisoners killed Pabst because they thought he'd tell us more about Hitler's routine at the Berghof,' explained Cricklemarsh. 'At least we managed to find out about the regular morning walk.'

'He should have been moved to proper safety. Have we heard from Lusty?'

'Not yet.'

The colonel tutted in disapproval. 'The Gestapo could have him by now. For all we know he was picked up as soon as he landed. All agents are instructed to announce that they've arrived safely. He should have done so.'

'We always recognized that recovering the set was going to present a problem,' argued Cricklemarsh. 'We agreed it was too dangerous for him to carry it through Germany until he knew the lie of the land.'

'We can't have Lusty operating without control,' carped Purefoy. 'He's not a fully trained agent. You knew I had reservations about his selection . . .'

No. Cricklemarsh hadn't known Purefoy had had reservations. The man had never mentioned them before.

'. . . I hope we're not going to get egg on our faces. It'll hand the Nazis the propaganda coup of the war if Lusty talks.'

There was a tap on the door and Annie entered, clutching a piece of paper. 'Michaelhouse have just received this, sir.'

Cricklemarsh took the signal and read aloud. 'Hitler's arrived in Berlin. He's travelling on to Obersalzberg tomorrow.'

Purefoy stroked his moustache with the back of his finger. 'This will give Lusty the chance to show what he's worth – if he's still alive.'

'He's alive,' said Cricklemarsh, firmly.

An uncomfortable silence fell over the *Stammtisch* as the Führer finished his broadcast. Not only had he failed to mention the disaster at Stalingrad but the whole speech lacked Hitler's normal fervour. Instead, he had spoken rapidly in a low, leaden monotone. Even to an outsider like Beck, it was an embarrassment.

'Our beloved Führer is exhausted,' decided Runge finally, switching off the wireless set. 'He needs a rest. He cannot carry the nation single-handedly.'

'But if he doesn't protect Germany, who will? Not the generals, that's for sure,' exclaimed Leeb.

There was no one in the bar apart from Runge, his cronies, Beck and the boy.

'Do you know what I think?' Thurn the postman lowered his voice. 'I don't believe that was our Führer. It didn't sound like him.'

The door opened. Beck was surprised to see Dr Meissner enter.

'Grüß Gott.'

'Grüß Gott,' replied Leeb and Thurn.

'*Heil Hitler.*' Runge snapped up his arm.

'You must have missed the Führer's speech, Dr Meissner,' said Thurn. 'But I was just saying, I don't believe it was him.'

'So who was it?' enquired Dr Meissner, unbuttoning his coat.

'Who do *you* think it was?' growled Runge.

'How do I know?' replied Dr Meissner mildly. 'I was on my way here.'

'Maybe the Jews have poisoned him.' Thurn wiped off the froth that hung on his wispy moustache. 'The Party's keeping it secret until he's recovered and then he'll rip out the Jewish, Communist conspirators, root and branch.'

'What do you think, *Herr Hauptmann*?' asked Leeb, stifling a belch.

That you are all barking mad, flashed through Beck's mind. 'I wouldn't dare offer an opinion about the Führer.'

'It didn't have his usual . . . fire.' Thurn was not going to let the subject go.

'Not like Goebbels's speech last month,' agreed Runge. He made no effort to offer Dr Meissner a drink. 'Now, that *was* a speech. Did you hear it, captain?'

'No. I was in hospital then.'

'Don't they have wireless in hospital?'

'I might have been unconscious.' *Don't be too clever*, Beck heard a little voice inside him warn.

'Well, I was one of the honoured few to hear Dr Goebbels speak in person. He told us straight that if we don't purify ourselves, thousands of Mongol tanks will destroy Western civilization. The German working classes will be reduced to Bolshevik-Jewish slavery to provide worker battalions for the Russian tundra. The only way to stand against them is Total War. Were we prepared to make sacrifices? Did we want Total War, he demanded. Yes, we cried. Total War. We cheered him to the echo.'

He locked his hands together and cracked his finger joints slowly, one by one.

'It's a shame the Party doesn't follow its own acclamations,' murmured Dr Meissner.

'What's that supposed to mean?'

'Simply that there're too many Party officials filling their bellies while our soldiers in Russia go hungry and cold.'

A hush fell over the table. Runge's face mottled with fury.

'How dare you attack the Führer and the Party!' His eyes bulged over his huge, sinister underlids.

'I didn't mention the Führer. You just did.'

Veins in Runge's thick neck pulsed purple. 'Scum!'

'All I said was, too many Party officials slide out of making the same sacrifices they demand of the German people,' repeated Dr Meissner in a reasonable voice. 'I've followed Party guidelines and only had a one-course meal today. What did you eat?'

'What the fuck's it got to do with you?' Runge swayed to his feet.

'Father?' Ilse came running out of the kitchen. 'What's going on?'

'Tell this man to shut his fucking gob or I'll shut it for him. He'd find himself before a people's court for half the filthy, treacherous things he's just come out with.'

Ilse put her arm around her father's shoulder and led him into the kitchen.

'Get him out of my sight,' screamed Runge. 'I'll have the bastard put away. Put away for ever.'

Later, as Beck was going to bed, he met Ilse on the stairs. The electricity had failed and they were using some of their precious oil supply in small lamps. Ilse wished him good night, then hesitated as if she had something else to say.

'I'm sorry about the row earlier.' Vishnia slipped past like a ghost on her way to her room diagonally across the top-floor corridor from Beck's. Ilse waited until Vishnia turned the corner. 'My father ought to have know better.'

'It's only what soldiers at the front are saying. The Party is corrupt.'

'Yes,' she whispered. 'It's full of selfish hypocrites who call for sacrifices while stuffing their faces. But my father was asking for trouble, saying anything like that in front of Runge.'

'Runge was very quick to defend the Party.'

'He knew my father was right.' A draught blew down the corridor, making the lamps' flames gutter and flicker so that they cast huge distorted shadows over the walls.

'I hope your husband's threats were ... empty ones. I wouldn't like your father to get into trouble.'

A deep, calm intensity infused Ilse's face. 'He wouldn't dare hurt my father. He knows the day he does will be his last.'

Her icy resolution unnerved Beck. She mistook his uncertain smile for one of doubt.

'Christian, my father is all I have in the world. All I care for. If anything happens to him, then I will not care what happens to me.'

Beck could not get Ilse out of his mind. He lay awake under his thick goose-down cover and wondered again at the conflicting emotions and competing tides that carried this ice queen, so serene to look at, so desperate underneath. *A swan,* he decided. She was a swan. On the surface she glided through the waters of life, elegant and untroubled, regal in pale beauty. Underneath, ungainly webbed limbs were furiously thrashing away just to keep her in the same place.

He climbed out of the snug bed to stand by the window, his feet cold on the thin linoleum. The waning moon was golden in the indigo sky. In the distance loomed the jagged, treeless peak of the Hoher Göll, an immense mass of rock rising above a sheer face. Beneath it were black forests of pine and there, in its large clearing, was the Berghof. It looked so peaceful, its white walls reflected in the moonlight. The roads were ghostly ribbons. From the trees a guard's torch blinked once.

He gazed at the silent mountain peaks and felt forlorn and vulnerable. He was alone, far from home. It didn't do to dwell on the dangers and difficulties ahead so he thought of Annie and her promise. He smiled. That was something to look forward to.

Why had Polly stood him up? It wasn't like her. He wondered if something had happened to her. He should have been worrying about her rather than feeling hurt and indignant. But his last day in London had been so busy.

Beck heard heavy footsteps coming along the corridor. A door opened and closed. Then the scrape of a bed on floorboards. A muffled cry. A little later Runge belched as he padded back downstairs. Vishnia sobbed for a long time before she got up to shut her bedroom door.

8

Monday, 22 March

'Please, captain, please.'

'You don't know what time the Führer's arriving.'

'Yes, I do. Midday. Uncle Gottlob phoned the stationmaster.' Hänschen, remembering he was asking a favour, managed to stop himself gloating.

The boy had pounced on Beck's announcement that he was going for a walk to ask to be taken to watch Hitler arrive. Beck had planned to reconnoitre along the river in the hope of finding a footbridge linking the small farming communities on the far side with the main road so his first reaction was to resent spending time with Hänschen when he should be getting on with the operation. Then again, what better cover than to be accompanied by a young Nazi? And watching Hitler arrive would allow him to assess local security.

'It'll be a treat for the boy,' said Ilse, who did not want Hänschen hanging around under her feet, either stealing food or bullying Vishnia, who was even more tearful than usual this morning.

So Beck limped off with Hänschen in his best *Pimpf* uniform. Soon the boy was telling stories about his time at the Nazi camp, consisting largely of how he'd got the better of other *Pimpfs*. One boy had accused him of taking his candle.

'I put glue in his scabbard so when he went to present his dagger for inspection, he couldn't get it out.' Hänschen chortled gleefully.

'And did you take his candle?' Beck's eyes were scanning the far bank of the river.

'What if I did? No one steals *my* things. Do you know the best bit?

We watched the Gestapo raid a house and take away a Jewish family. I threw a stone that hit the ugly old woman on the head.'

They were alongside a wide, shallow stretch of river. Beck studied a broken ribbon of rocks running from bank to bank, before ruling them out. A crossing there would be too visible by day and suicide by night.

'Why do you hate the Jews so much?'

Hänschen stared at him as if he had two heads. What was this man on about? He had been taught since his first kindergarten that Jews were the incarnation of all that was evil.

'Everyone hates the Jews,' replied Hänschen firmly.

'But why?'

'What do you mean, "why"?'

'Why do you hate them yourself?'

Hänschen frowned. When you'd been told for so long that Jews were a bad thing, it became difficult to recall exactly why.

'Because they have no homeland of their own, they've become parasites,' he said finally. 'They can't build their own state so they batten onto the creative activities of others. Jews led the Communist Revolution. It's Jewish capitalists who plunge nations into war. The Jew is the eternal enemy of the Aryan.'

Beck interrupted the boy's flow. 'When did you last talk to one?'

'What! A Jew? Never.'

'You've never met one?'

'Yeuk.' The boy screwed up his face and pretended to be sick.

'Then how do you know they're so evil?'

'The Führer says so. Why do you keep looking across the river?'

'Looking for otters,' replied Beck glibly. It was a timely reminder that never but never, must he let down his guard near Hänschen.

'I've never seen one.'

'Sometimes deer come down to drink. How do we get to the other side?' Maybe the boy knew a way. But he mustn't push his questioning. Suspicion and denouncement had been inculcated into Hänschen from infancy.

'You can't.' The boy grinned smugly. 'It belongs to the Party.'

'But *you* belong to the Party. Aren't you allowed in?'

'There's an old footbridge near Unterau but Ilse says it's dangerous because it's likely to fall down. Sometimes, if the guards see you near it, they'll shout at you.' He caught sight of the clock on a church tower. 'Hurry up. We're going to be late.'

The square outside the white-stuccoed railway station was bedecked with long red and black banners hanging from tall flagpoles. More swastikas hung from the station façade itself. An SS guard of honour, with white gloves and polished coal-scuttle helmets, was drawn up to attention in two ranks, their bayonets glinting in the sun. Dignitaries in brown Nazi Party uniform fussed over last-minute preparations. Six Mercedes-Benz cars waited outside the triple arches of the Führer's personal exit.

Hänschen was beside himself with anxiety. He complained that he could not see properly and tried to push his way through the outer cordon.

A man in a long coat materialized alongside them. 'You're forbidden to go any closer.'

Recognizing the voice of authority, the boy for once did not argue.

There were similarly dressed men deployed at regular intervals in the sparse crowd, noted Beck, but there were no guards on the station roof. No men with binoculars scanning the surrounding countryside. He could have a decent shot at the station from either of the two hotels across the road bridge that led to Königssee. Less than three hundred yards, a downward shot, over the heads of the guards. And a fair chance of escape. Definitely an option to remember.

The *Führerzug* pulled in. The band struck up the Horst Wessel Song; a hoarse command and the honour guard goose-stepped towards the triple arches. Beck inspected the hotels again. There was no one watching from their windows; no one leaning out, waving and cheering. By this stage of the war, glum acceptance had replaced enthusiasm.

Hänschen was climbing onto a brick pillar set among the railings above the foaming river, fifty feet below.

'Get down from there.'

'I want to see better.'

At that moment Hitler emerged, followed by party officials and high-ranking army officers.

'Sieg Heil,' screamed Hänschen, throwing out his right arm.

Hitler was smaller than Beck had expected. He recognized the squat figure of Martin Bormann talking earnestly at Hitler's side and, just behind, the severe features of the army chief of staff, Field Marshal Keitel. Hitler, he noticed, was shuffling like a tired old man.

'Heil Hitler. Heil Hitler.' Hänschen's shrill chant rent the air as he tried to catch the Führer's attention. Hitler was reaching the end of the first rank. It was the closest he would come to them. Hänschen was jumping up and down with excitement. Then he missed his footing, his arms flailing like windmills as he desperately sought to regain his balance.

'Nooo!' With a high-pitched scream of sheer terror, he toppled backwards into the abyss. Beck dived at the railings and caught Hänschen's ankle with his left hand. His arms slammed against the railings, almost forcing him to release the boy. Men were shouting. Hänschen, upside down over the foaming waters, screamed for his mother in distant Lübeck. Beck feared his forearm would snap; his biceps were on fire. He couldn't hold on much longer. Then other arms were thrust over the side. The weight was taken from him. Hänschen was hauled back over the railings. Beck slowly stood up as the first car in the motorcade passed alongside. Hitler sat in the front passenger seat. As Beck rubbed his tortured arm, Hitler turned his head towards the commotion and Beck felt the man's pale, incurious eyes upon him.

Beck was lost. He was in an old, run-down quarter of the town and he was alone. Hänschen had been taken away by a nursing sister from the National Socialist Women's League. Beck had slipped away as soon as he decently could, but by then the damage had been done. A Party official had taken his name and the commander of the SS guard had congratulated him on saving the boy's life. Beck smiled ruefully. If his mental reactions had been faster, he might have conquered the impulse that had sent him diving to grab Hänschen. But he couldn't have left the boy to die. They weren't waging war on children, even though those children would grow up to be fanatical Nazis.

Beck found himself in a cobbled lane flanked by workshops and small factories mixed with tall old apartment houses. He could not tell how long he had been walking. Ahead, the figure of a woman looked familiar and he realized with a start that it was Ilse. How she had got there or where she had come from, he did not know. She seemed anonymous today in a drab, brown coat, headscarf and flat heels. She carried a wicker basket with a cloth over the top, which she transferred from hand to hand as if it was heavy. Beck was about to call out to her when she turned into a narrow alleyway. A masonry bridge linking the two buildings on either side of it bore a sign: *Runge & Meissner. Printers.* From the workshop on the right Beck caught the thud and clang of a printing press. Suddenly he became aware of Dr Meissner approaching

'Grüß Gott. What brings you to this part of town?'

'I was just strolling when I thought I saw your daughter here. But she seems to have disappeared.'

'No. She's inside. Come in and have a coffee and schnapps with us.'

Beck followed Dr Meissner along a gloomy passageway, up a flight of narrow, wooden stairs and into a compact office, dominated by a roll-top desk and sheaves of long galley proofs hanging from nails around the room. A silver-framed studio photograph of a pretty woman with a reflective smile and a young schoolgirl held pride of place on the desk.

'Ilse and her mother,' announced Dr Meissner, pouring two glasses of local enzian schnapps. 'That was taken in Augsburg when we were on holiday there in 1928. Ilse always liked Augsburg. She attended university there for two years until the few places left for women were taken exclusively by Party members.'

'I didn't know you and Ilse's husband were in business together.'

'There was a time a few years ago when it was mutually beneficial for us to become . . . partners.'

The only other picture in the room was familiar and notorious.

Taken in May 1933, it showed Nazi students hurling books onto a blazing bonfire.

'You may ask why a printing company should keep such a stark reminder of the destruction of learning.' Dr Meissner chuckled. 'Runge does not understand the significance. He sees it only for what it is but whenever I look at it I remember Heine's words, *"When one burns books, one ends up burning people."* Ah, Ilse, I was explaining to our guest how that photograph serves as a reminder of ignorance and brutality.'

Ilse smiled indulgently at her father. 'Sometimes he is a little free with his explanations. But what are you doing here, *Hauptmann* Beck? I thought you'd taken Hänschen to see the Führer.'

Beck could not face recounting what had happened. 'I did but I seem to have wandered here afterwards and then I caught sight of you.'

'I saw him standing outside and invited him in.'

'And now I will show you the way home.' Ilse swung the basket on her finger. 'Is your leg all right today? It's not hurting too much?'

'No, it's fine. Really.'

'Good. Come on, then.'

Outside, the gloom was gathering. Already the cobbles were covered with silver patches of frost. It was going to be a cold night. For a while, Beck's stick tapping along the stones was the only sound.

'It's hard to imagine Runge and your father as business partners,' he said at last.

'Or me and Runge as married partners.' She stilled his incipient protests with a sharp movement of her hand. 'I know what you must be thinking. What did my father say?'

'That a few years ago there was a time when it was mutually beneficial for them both to become partners,' he quoted.

'Huh!' Ilse gave a humourless laugh. 'For once, daddy was being discreet.'

'I'm sorry, I don't mean to pry.'

'No, it's well known. There are few secrets in this town.' Ilse ran her tongue over the corner of her mouth. 'My father was a teacher who lost his job. As you know, anyone who doesn't hang out a swastika flag on special occasions is noted down by the local Block wardens. Daddy was too proud, too independent to let the Party do his thinking for him. He was therefore marked down as politically unreliable. Fortunately, he had the old family printing business. It was *Meissner & Sohn* in those days. Daddy's father had been the *Sohn*. Then daddy . . .'

'It's all right. You don't have to tell me.'

'Why shouldn't I? I'm proud of it.' The words rushed out in a torrent. 'Daddy forged an exit visa for one of his workers who was Jewish. The papers gave the man time to sell up and get his family out of Germany to start a new life in Hungary. Runge was the Party official in charge of tracking down local Jews. Unknown to daddy, the worker was already on his list. When Runge found out what daddy had done, he turned up in the office. If the offence came to light, daddy would be sent to a concentration camp. He could even have been executed and the business confiscated by the Party. Runge offered a deal. He demanded two things. In return for his silence, he wanted a half-share in the printing firm – to be an equal partner. It was a good deal. Half a business is better than none. And daddy still had his life. My mother was very ill at the time. We thought any additional strain would kill her. As it happened, she died three months later anyway.'

There was a silence broken only by the tap-tap of Beck's stick on the cobblestones. He had to ask her even though he knew the answer. 'You said Runge wanted *two* things.'

'I was the other thing. He wanted me for his wife. By the way, you remember *Frau* Reintaler, the woman we met yesterday who was going to church to say thank-you for the life of her son?'

'Yes. She said he was coming home from Russia on leave.'

'He never made it. His leave train was bombed by the English at Anhalt station in Berlin. Eighty died, including Artur. She's lost both sons now. Prayers don't seem to work, do they?'

Allen Welsh Dulles lived at Herrengasse 23 in the oldest part of the medieval Swiss city of Berne. The war had not robbed Berne of its air of bourgeois contentment. Its burghers still continued their favourite pastime of slowly devouring heavy meals while its arcaded streets suggested a mercantile cloister. The city was self-satisfied and uncomplicated and it suited Dulles down to the ground. Dulles was the European head of the American Office for Strategic Studies – wartime predecessor of the CIA.

In March 1943 Switzerland was a neutral island in the middle of Nazi-occupied Europe. Its frontier posts were closely guarded and the only airline flight was run weekly by Lufthansa from and to Berlin. Dulles and just two assistants had found themselves marooned in Switzerland since the Germans had occupied southern France. The shortage of staff was slowly being rectified by the increasing number of US aircrew who managed to nurse their damaged bombers over the Swiss border.

The OSS went under the cover of the US Office of War Information, housed in two adjoining houses across the river Aare from Dulles's home. Dulles himself was the 'Special Legal Counsel' to the American Minister, Leland Harrison. His real role was common knowledge, especially to the Swiss *Fremdenpolizei* who kept an eye on embassies and all foreigners, looking out for violations of Swiss neutrality. Swiss counter-intelligence was good, very good. Just as well they were neutral, joked both the Germans and the Allies.

Allen Dulles was forty-nine years old, grey-haired and bespectacled, resembling, said those who met him, a Nonconformist minister. The Americans had come late to the war and to the intelligence game. They were considered naïve at best and dangerously gullible at worst. Britain's SIS, especially, accused them of throwing money at problems, of believing that the more they paid for information, the more it had to be worth.

But Dulles had a special reason for his willingness to listen to anyone touting a tale. In 1917, in Switzerland during the previous war, he had turned down the opportunity to meet a Russian revolutionary calling himself Lenin. Dulles had been compensating for his error of judgement ever since.

His visitor this night was a short, balding senior clerk from the

Foreign Ministry in Berlin. Waldheim Krenzler made irregular visits to the German embassy in Switzerland as a courier. He used these trips to carry copies of a wide range of documents that he claimed he and a small circle of spies had abstracted from various government departments. Krenzler was paid $20,000 for each delivery and had already been promised American citizenship when the war ended.

This time, Krenzler's prize offering was the complete order of battle of von Manstein's Army Group Don that, against odds of seven to one, had just recaptured Kharkov on the Eastern Front. As Dulles received Krenzler's trophy in his book-lined study, he was aware not only of the magnitude but also the ephemeral nature of the information it contained. Today, it was pure gold. In a week, it would be out of date. It had to be sent to London immediately.

Leaving an aide to pour Krenzler another brandy, Dulles went up to a permanently locked room on the fourth floor. He bolted himself in and began encrypting the message in the latest code, which had come into use only during the last month. It was midnight before he had finished. Then, rousing the wireless operator, he set out for the OSS office with an armed guard. There he stood at the shoulder of the operator as the long signal was transmitted to London.

That evening Beck slipped out of the Red Ox. The pitch-black night crackled with frost. A path led down from the road to the old river footbridge that Hänschen had mentioned. Beck had tried to explore earlier but the lie of the land meant he was unable to get near the bridge without being spotted and challenged by the guards. The last thing he wanted was to draw attention to himself again.

Reaching the path, he crouched and ran lightly to the bridge. He halted, listening to the stillness before slowly making his way onto the planks. The bridge, supported by thick cables, swayed under his weight. The ice-crusted handrope stuck to the skin of his palm. The cold was intense, piercing his clothing and scratching at his face with its bitter nails. Any sentry on duty was going to be muffled to the eyeballs. As Beck inched forward again, his foot landed on thin air.

His heart bulged into his throat. He dropped to his hands and knees, feeling ahead in the blackness. A plank was missing. He stepped over the gap, then halted to let the jackhammer of his heart slow down.

The smell of tobacco smoke drifted over him. Since the air was very still, the smoker had to be near. An owl hooted and hooted again. Beck gratefully expelled the breath he had been holding. He could almost feel the other's presence. *Where the hell are you?* His eyes quartered the trees on the bank. It was so dark! The blackness had an intensity, a solid quality that held and suffocated. He could not see his hand in front of his face.

The bridge creaked. If anyone happened to shine a torch on him now he would have a lot of explaining to do.

He glimpsed the glow of the cigarette. There was a crunching noise to his right.

'How's it going?' A torch beam momentarily caught the hunched figure of a guard in a greatcoat, rifle slung over his shoulder.

'Fucking freezing.'

'Yeh, it's bloody cold up there, too. You want to watch that fag, I could see it from my post.'

'No one in their right mind's going be out on a night like this.'

'Don't you believe it. The *Feldwebel*'s always turning up when you don't expect him.'

A dog barked in the distance.

'Hell! That could be him now. I'd better be getting back.'

Beck began inching back across the bridge. There was clearly no way through that way. There were two roads up to Obersalzberg: the old one from Berchtesgaden and a new one from Unterau built by Bormann. Both were closely guarded. Getting up to the tea house would prove harder than he had expected. And he still needed to return to Dachau to unearth his rifle and radio.

The anonymous stone building behind the high walls could have passed for a school if it were not for the huge array of wireless aerials on the roof. Few in the Austrian town of Bregenz near the Swiss border realized that the building housed the wireless-monitoring post run by the *Abwehr*, the intelligence service of the German High Command, to intercept Allied radio traffic coming out of Switzerland. Those who did know kept it to themselves.

A reinforced team of listeners had been on duty for four hours, sitting with headphones in front of their sets. The room, smelling of warm dust, was silent apart from a muted electrical hum. Sitting at his raised desk behind the rows of monitors, Major Neurath could not keep a look of triumph off his face as two operators rapidly jotted down the meaningless sequences of letters coming out of Berne.

Major Neurath picked up the direct line to *Abwehr* headquarters in Tirpitz Ufer in Berlin. They would be delighted. Soon he would send the jumble of letters to the cryptologists to work on. It would be a relatively easy task to break the code by comparing the message with the original text – the one giving the order of battle of von Manstein's Army Group Don.

The intelligence had a long way to go. In London, it would be processed, considered, chewed over and then sent to the Americans' liaison office in Moscow, which would pass it on to the *Stavka*, the Supreme Command of the Soviet Armed Forces. Naturally, they would distrust any American intelligence, as they always did. By the time it filtered down to the Russian army commanders opposing von Manstein it would be history.

But meanwhile the *Abwehr* would have cracked the new American code.

Yes, the old tricks were the best tricks.

9

Tuesday, 23 March

'Why didn't you let that little sod drown?'

'I couldn't. I was supposed to be looking after him.'

'Do you have to take your responsibility so seriously?'

Beck examined Ilse's expression for traces of irony or humour, but failed to find any. He was still waiting for Hänschen to say a word of thanks for saving his life. He had the idea he'd wait a long time.

'Christian, you're driving on the wrong side of the road!'

'Sorry.' Beck cursed himself for making such a silly mistake. 'There aren't many roads in North Africa. We tend to make it up as we go.'

'Make it up here and we'll never get to Munich.'

'We're all right. There's no traffic about.'

'That's because there's no petrol.'

'Then how do you manage?'

'We're engaged in Party business,' giggled Ilse. 'There's always petrol for Party business.'

It was another beautiful day. To the south, a flock of fluffy, flat-bottomed clouds grazed over the twin snow-covered peaks of the Karkopf and the Keikopf. Elsewhere the sky was a deep, deep blue.

Over breakfast Ilse had announced that she had to deliver newly printed posters to the Brown House, the Nazi Party headquarters in Munich. Beck had volunteered to accompany her, wondering whether he could use the opportunity to collect his buried equipment. Ilse had hesitated. She had some private business to conduct, she said. But if he did not mind amusing himself for an hour or so, he could keep the car to drive around. Beck could not believe his luck, especially as the red 'V' on its number plate was guaranteed to let the car pass unhindered through police checks and roadblocks.

'Good for the Party!'

'Runge blew up at my father yesterday because he knew he was telling the truth. How do you think we've got soap at the inn?'

'Soap?'

'Most people can't get soap for love or money. You're supposed to be able to exchange five kilos of bones for a soap coupon – except there's no soap available.' She stared straight ahead. 'Typical man, don't have a clue about rationing, do you?'

No, if he was honest Beck would have to admit he didn't. 'Um . . . Is it that bad?'

'Party officials and their families get a special food supplement. We get added vitamin C; the C stands for connections, but most people find it hard to make ends meet, especially now we've got Prussian evacuees staying here. Those women don't work, so they can afford to queue all day long. Fighting the British in North Africa is nothing compared with battling with a Berlin housewife in the shops.'

'Did you know there's a Gestapo man hidden in the back listening to every word you say?' Beck asked.

'Don't joke.' Ilse punched him on the arm.

She was instantly contrite. 'Oh, sorry. That was harder than I intended. Is this better?' She stroked his biceps with the palm of her right hand. Beck felt an electric charge pass between them. Ilse must have experienced it, too, for she withdrew her hand quickly. She was looking at him in surprise, her lips slightly apart in a strange half-smile. For some reason, his thoughts turned to her husband.

'Where's Runge today?'

'Organizing Winter Relief collections. The Party keeps us very busy. You know the story? The girl says, "My father's in the SA, my elder brother's in the SS, my younger brother's in the Hitler Youth and my mother's in the National Socialist Woman's League. I'm in the League of German Maidens. We only meet once a year – at the Nuremburg Rally".'

Beck's chuckle encouraged her. She tucked her legs under her and twisted sideways to study him as he drove.

'Shall I tell you the story of Little Red Riding Hood – *Rotkäppchen* – in Nazi-organized Germany?' she asked in a mischievous tone.

'Yes, please.'

'A long time ago, just before the war, there was a forest in Germany that had not been tidied up by the Nazi Labour Service. In it there lived a wolf. One day a little girl in a red hat walked through the forest to pay a visit to her Aryan grandmother who lived in a Nazi Party old people's home. All of a sudden, the wolf appeared. He wore a brown coat so that no one would guess his un-German intentions. *Rotkäppchen* was not suspicious: she knew all the enemies of Germany were locked away in concentration camps. "*Heil, Rotkäppchen!*" said the wolf, raising a right paw. "Where are you going?" "To visit my granny." "Why don't you pick these nice flowers that the Department for Forest Beautification has planted?" said the wolf. As Little Red Riding Hood began picking flowers for a posy, the wolf ran to the old people's home, gobbled up the grandmother and dressed himself in her clothes. He put on her Nazi Party Women's League badge and got into bed. Very soon, *Rotkäppchen* arrived. "*Heil Hitler, Oma!* How are you?" "I am well, my dear." "Why is your voice so strange today?" asked Little Red Riding Hood. "Because the Party speaking course was very strenuous." "Why do you have such big ears?" "All the better to hear the whiners with, my dear." "And why do you have such big eyes?" "All the better to detect the fifth columnists with, my dear." "But why do you have such a big mouth?" "Because I'm a member of the Nazi Party cultural debating society" – and with that the wolf gobbled her up, fell asleep and snored loudly. Just then the District Master of the Hunt passed by and thought to himself, "Can an Aryan grandmother really snore in such a non-Aryan manner?" So he went in, saw the wolf and shot it – on his own responsibility – even though he didn't possess the special wolf-hunting licence. When he cut open the wolf's belly, he found both the grandmother and *Rotkäppchen* alive and well. There was great rejoicing in the Nazi Party home. The wolf's carcass was handed to the *Reich* Food Estate where it was potted as venison. The Huntsman was allowed to wear a gold-embroidered wolf badge on his uniform. *Rotkäppchen* was promoted to corporal in the League of German Maidens and her grandmother was invited to a Strength-through-Joy trip on one of their new ships. Now isn't that a nice story?'

'Very nice.' Beck grinned broadly. 'That's the first fairy story I've heard in a long time.'

'Well, you can't have been listening to Radio Berlin much. I'll tell you my favourite joke, shall I?'

There was no stopping Ilse. She glowed happily.

'Go on, then.'

'There's a Jew who wants to change his name, so he goes to the Party official at the town hall. "What's your name?" asks the official. "Adolf Stinkfoot." The Party official considers. "Okay, I understand," he says. "What do you want to change it to?" "Maurice Stinkfoot," says the Jew.'

Ilse put back her head and laughed. It was a merry, infectious laugh and Beck could not help joining in. They were still laughing when they came to the police roadblock.

Jäger watched the Volkswagen pull away and wondered idly what an Afrika Korps captain was doing driving a Party car. Probably having it off with the pretty young wife of the Party official. It was no concern of his – as long as they were both Aryan. He looked at his watch. The black-market lorry was due soon, according to Squashy's tip-off.

The Munich underworld had become an even more unpleasant place since the murder of *Unterführer* Hamm. Jäger was rattling the cage. Black marketeers had been arrested, warehouses raided, homes searched. Informants were dragged in and illegal shipments intercepted, but Jäger knew he had to get a result quickly. Too many Party members regarded the black market as a profitable sideline for him to sustain the pressure on it for much longer.

At least Alix was safely away in Aachen. That wouldn't save her if she was named in the ongoing investigation but it stopped her falling into any Gestapo trap in Munich. Jäger was puzzled, though. If Alix had been at the heart of the conspiracy, and her possession of the draft leaflet suggested that she had been, why hadn't the Gestapo interrogations thrown up her name? He didn't understand.

Wulzinger's shout brought him back to the present. A convoy of *Luftwaffe* lorries was rolling past. Tacked on the end, just as Squashy had said, was an unmarked truck with a tightly closed canvas back. Wulzinger lumbered into the nearside lane, waving his arms. For a moment it looked as if the lorry was going to continue on. Jäger was fumbling to undo his holster when it reluctantly pulled over. The driver, in SA uniform, leaped down, surly and belligerent. He strode towards Jäger. Another Brownshirt remained in the cab.

'I am on Party business. You've no right—'

'What do you have in the back?' Jäger cut him short.

'This is Party business,' the man repeated. 'Don't poke your nose in where it doesn't belong.'

'My nose, your business,' drawled Jäger.

Wulzinger opened the passenger door.

'What the fuck!' He let out a roar – and the passenger was sent hurtling out of the cab onto the road. Wulzinger kicked him once in the head. The man lay still. 'The fucking toe-rag pointed a Schmeisser at me.' He held up the sub-machine gun, which looked like a toy in his hands.

'Your mate should never point a gun at a policeman,' said Jäger. 'Let's see your *Kennkarte*. Where are you heading?'

'Essen.' The man's eyes flicked nervously to the policemen undoing the straps holding down the canvas covering.

'And coming from?' Jäger sensed the man was getting ready to run. Wulzinger moved behind him.

'Salzburg area.'

'*Sturmbannführer*. Look!'

Wulzinger gripped the driver's shoulders to stop him escaping.

Jäger already knew what his men had found. Eggs. Thousands of eggs. If motorists driving past knew what was in the lorry, he'd have a riot on his hands. His own men would help themselves to a dozen each, and he'd do the same. He could exchange them for cheroots.

Squashy's tip-off had been right. But did it make the driver Hamm's killer? Or was it just a convenient way for the Munich underworld to get rid of a competitor – and take the pressure off themselves?

'This load's for *Gauleiter* Amann. You'll have him to answer to,' blustered the driver.

'Yeh, yeh.' Wulzinger eased on metal knuckledusters. The driver was led to the nearside of the lorry.

'When did you last make this run?'

'I don't know what you're talking about.'

Wulzinger hit him in the kidneys. The man howled with pain.

'Let's try again.' Jäger lit a cheroot. 'Where were you three mornings ago? Say, between six and eleven.'

'Three mornings ago? I can't—' He screamed as Wulzinger hit him again.

'Try and remember. We don't like cop-killers.'

'Cop-killer! No. Not me. Three mornings ago, I'm thinking.' The driver was panicking. 'Yes. Oh, yes. I'm the neighbourhood *Blockwart* . . .'

Jäger inhaled on his cheroot and did not hide a sneer. After the Gestapo, *Blockwarts* – the Nazi Party's eyes and ears on the streets – were the most hated breed in Germany.

'. . . This family lost their boy in the U-boats. They were going to hold a memorial service. The next thing, they're celebrating. The word was how they'd heard on the BBC that their boy was a prisoner. I knew they hadn't tampered with their wireless, so they had to have one hidden. The Gestapo raided their flat at dawn three mornings ago and I went with them. We found the set behind the false wall of a cupboard. If you don't believe me, check with the Gestapo.'

'I will do,' said Jäger. 'Now tell me about other members of your little black-market gang.'

The *Autobahn* ended at Munich's suburbs. At one side of the road the *Kohlenklau* – the coal thief, with his walrus face, cloth cap and a sack over his shoulder – scowled down from a large poster. Beck couldn't understand why such a grotesque image had been chosen to represent the war against waste.

'You obviously know your way,' he remarked to Ilse as they drove under a banner strung across the road. *Juden sind hier unerwünscht.* Jews not welcome here.

'I come this route about once a week. Runge's Party connections are good for business.'

They turned into a street of bomb-damaged apartment houses, craters and rubble everywhere.

'A stick of bombs fell along here just a month ago. Luckily, most people were safely in the shelters. When you see this destruction and hear of all the dead on the Eastern Front, you wonder if it's worth it, don't you?'

'Do *you* think it is?' Beck was surprised how Ilse could switch from skittish humour to morbid compassion within seconds.

'Sometimes I'm so weary of this war, I don't care who wins. All right, not the Russians but life under the British or Americans couldn't be any worse than things are now. There's no fun in living any more, only hardships.' Ilse sighed. 'I want some fun. Dancing's been banned since we went to war with Russia. What harm does dancing do? Some nights, when we know it's safe, Vishnia and I listen to Swiss radio and dance together in the kitchen.'

Beck decided to test the water. 'A British prisoner of war once told me that Germany started the war . . .'

'No.' Ilse was indignant. 'No. The Versailles Treaty was totally unjust. The Führer was only getting back what rightfully belonged to Germany.'

'But we invaded Poland . . .?'

'It was the French and English who declared war, not us. It wasn't Hitler's fault. Left here. Mind that tram.'

An old-fashioned Number 6 tram to Sendling clattered past, ringing its bell. Ahead two SS sentries stood guard in front of the plaque adorning a huge colonnaded stone edifice.

'That's the memorial to those who died in the Nazi *Putsch*. Everyone who passes must give the Hitler salute.' Ilse chuckled. 'So many people use the parallel Viscardi-Gasse that it's known as Drückeberger-Gasse – Shirkers' Alley.'

Now they were near the end of their journey, Beck asked again if she wanted the car. He fervently hoped she didn't.

'You hang on to it. Use it to explore Munich.'

'What are *you* going to do?'

Ilse placed a slim forefinger alongside her nose. 'I have some private business to attend to.'

The penny dropped. For the first time, Beck noticed she had make-up around her eyes and was wearing lipstick. She wore a fashionable green skirt with a matching jacket that made her look smart and attractive, if a little severe. Maybe that was the way her lover liked to see her.

'Sorry, I shouldn't have pried.'

'That's all right. Here . . . no, not here.' Too late – he had turned off into Türkenstraße. 'This is the Gestapo headquarters. Go left and left again. The Brown House is on the next block. I'll see you back here in, say, an hour and a half.'

Ilse swung a large black leather bag onto her shoulder as Hitler Youths started carrying the boxes of leaflets into the three-storey building.

'The Englischer Garten is a lovely place and there's always good sausage and beer in the *Löwenbräukeller* in the Stilmaierplatz because the Party uses it for meetings.'

She was like an anxious mother fussing over her child. Perversely, a mental image of Ilse, naked, sweating at the moment of climax, sped through Beck's mind. Maybe she sensed the thought because she drew back from the car window.

'An hour and a half, remember.'

She wasn't giving herself much time for her assignation, Beck thought sourly.

'Your table will be ready in five minutes, brigadier. Would you and Mrs Gilbert like a drink while you're looking at the menu?'

Marjorie Gilbert gave an exasperated sigh. 'Oh, very well. Gin.'

They pushed their way through to a small table in the crowded bar. 'It's so difficult to get into restaurants nowadays with all these blasted Americans,' complained Gilbert.

'I'm surprised they allow other ranks in here. Look at the American sergeant with that huge cigar. It's obscene.' Marjorie leaned forward. 'Any more news overnight?'

Gilbert chortled. 'Not a word. Purefoy's having kittens. He's already starting to shift the blame onto Cricklemarsh for sending out a half-trained agent.'

'And how's this Cricklemarsh coping with it?'

'I haven't asked. I can't be seen to have anything to do with the day-to-day running. Delegation, as I've told Purefoy, is everything.'

A waiter placed two drinks in front of them.

'But shouldn't you have heard by now?' asked Marjorie, once the waiter had moved away.

'In the normal run of things – but this isn't a normal operation.'

'Do you think the Gestapo have picked him up?'

'It's highly likely. German agents parachuted into this country are normally arrested within four hours of landing. Forty-eight hours was the longest anyone remained on the loose last year. I wouldn't have thought it'd be much different in Germany.'

'How will you *know* if he's been arrested?'

'We'll look closely at his first message to see if the security checks are in place.' Gilbert picked up the menu. 'They've got cod tonight.'

'It'll be left over from the weekend. You'd be better off with the roast beef.'

'It was tough last time.' He gave a bark of a laugh. 'You really should see Purefoy and Nye. Purefoy's guarding the operation like a dog with a bone while Nye keeps circling, looking for the chance to nip in and grab it.'

'So, all in all, Operation Nightshade's going as you planned.'

The head waiter stood over them. 'Your table's ready now, brigadier. I'm sorry for the delay.'

Gilbert followed his wife in single file. 'Oh, yes,' he said. 'You could say that Nightshade is going splendidly.'

They did not see Annie as they walked past, sitting with her oldest English friend Penelope Hardinge at the table immediately behind a black lacquer screen near the dining-room entrance.

Annie frowned, her fork halfway to her mouth. It *wasn't* going splendidly. She and Cricklemarsh were becoming more worried by the hour. What was that man Gilbert on about? And what the hell was he doing talking to his battleaxe of a wife about a top secret operation in the middle of a restaurant?

'Are you all right, Annie?'

Annie became conscious that she was still staring after the couple as they made their way to their table.

'Sorry.' She dropped her voice to a whisper. 'Pen, you know Operation Nightshade . . .'

Penelope, the senior secretary to the director-general of SOE, shook her head. 'No.'

'You must do.'

'I promise you I've never heard of it.'

Beck found his way back to the hidden equipment ridiculously easily. He knew he had to head north-west. As he drove along Brienner Straße he came, as Ilse had predicted, to Stilmaierplatz. The first of three roads branching off it bore the sign 'Dachauer Straße'. It led directly to the town of Dachau itself. His luck was clearly in. From the railway line, he tracked his way back until he came to the hamlet where the policeman had lived. What was the legend about a murderer always returning to the scene of his crime? He drove on slowly, constantly checking in his rear-view mirror. The road looked very different in the sunshine. Just as he was beginning to think he'd gone wrong, he recognized the three elm trees in the corner of a field. He pulled into the adjoining lane. People seeing a Party car in the countryside would associate it with the black market and look the other way. If he was challenged, he'd say he was answering a call of nature. He did not spot the farmworker resting his horses in the shadow of a copse under the brow of the hill.

Beck loosened the rear seat to make a hiding place. It would serve as long as the car was not searched thoroughly. In that case, it'd be as much good as a wet paper bag.

The short-handled spade was still concealed under leaf mould in a thicket of blackthorn and bramble. Beck measured four paces from the elm standing furthest from the lane and began digging in the soft soil. Within minutes there was a satisfying clunk as the spade hit something solid. Beck quickly hauled out the rucksack and the transmitter wrapped in waterproof oilskins. It had all been so easy.

The farmworker put his hand to his aching face and watched with interest as the car sped away. Anything to take his mind off his pain. One side of the Pole's face was swollen like a pumpkin but the farmer would not pay for him to see a dentist. He reckoned he was going to have to remove the bad tooth with pliers as soon as he got back to the barn.

He began to wonder if the mysterious package the man had unearthed was connected with the parachutist he had spotted landing a few days ago. That policeman had been killed the same day. He'd been questioned during the murder investigation but he'd had a cast-iron alibi. The cows were milked at 6.30 a.m. regular as clockwork and he'd been working around the farm all the rest of the morning.

He slipped their nosebags over the horses' heads and set off towards the three elms. The man had hidden his short-handled shovel there. That would come in useful, that would.

Beck was experiencing mixed emotions. On one hand, he was elated that the pick-up had gone so easily. The rifle and transmitter were now concealed under a box of Nazi posters Ilse had collected earlier to take back to Berchtesgaden. On the other hand, he realized he was jealous. It was absurd. How could he be jealous of Ilse's lover? He had only known her three days. What right had he?

On the way home Ilse was calmer than she had been on the journey into Munich. She was still in high spirits but whatever she had been up to had brought her peace and contentment.

Bitch!

'I was thinking,' she said, swinging round to face Beck and locking her fingers together on the back of the seat. 'You know an awful lot about me but I know very little about you.'

'What do you want to know?'

'Were you and Ingrid very much in love?'

Beck didn't have the answer to that one. 'We were engaged to be married.'

'But you've no one now? No one at all?'

'No. We weren't a large family.'

She put a sympathetic hand over his, squeezed it gently and released it. 'What do you think you'll do when the war's over?'

'I don't know yet. Let's get there first. How about you?'

'I'll have fun,' she cried, throwing her hands in the air. 'Lots of fun.'

Ilse had talked about having fun on their outward journey. But she didn't appear to be a dizzy flapper, out for a good time and to hell with the consequences. On the contrary, she was sensible, staid and, at times, determinedly demure. Yet he had already witnessed how Ilse's moods could swing from somersaulting, high-flying gaiety to melancholy – all within a space of five minutes.

'You're not really the type.'

'That shows how little you know me,' Ilse replied pertly.

'Will you have fun whoever wins the war?'

Ilse saw the trap and pursed her lips. She would never have fun as long as she was married to Runge. 'I don't think Germany will win the war.'

'No.'

'I'll have fun,' she repeated determinedly.

Beck thought of the missing hour and a half in Munich.

'I'm sure you will.'

'Your voice was hard as you said that. You despise me . . .'

'No. Where will you go for your fun?'

'I don't care, as long as there's happiness and laughter. You know, because I have no love of Hitler or the Party, I worry that I have nothing to protect. Nothing to defend. I feel like a mother denied children.'

Dusk fell quickly. As the car climbed to Berchtesgaden, Ilse became visibly nervous, twisting her gloves in her lap and turning her head to stare into the blackness, so the trickle of conversation dried up completely. Beck was surprised to see about a dozen cars parked outside the Red Ox. Ilse ran indoors without a word. Beck picked up the box of posters and followed slowly.

Even before he pushed through the blackout curtain, he could hear Runge's raised voice.

'How can it have taken you this fucking long to get to Munich and back?'

'The posters weren't ready. I had to wait for them.' Ilse sounded calm and collected – lying though her teeth. 'You know how inefficient the Brown House is. Remember that time you went along and they didn't have the order number so you came back empty-handed.'

Beck limped in with the box. Runge glowered at him with reddened eyes.

'I hope these are worth it,' said Beck. 'We had to wait for ages.'

A babble of voices came from the large beer hall. Leeb and Thurn swaggered past them in their Nazi uniforms, their thumbs hooked in their belts. Beer fumes and smoke billowed out as they pushed through the door.

'You knew very well I had this important meeting tonight . . .' Runge had clearly been drinking. He was trying to pick a quarrel.

'There was nothing I could do about it.'

Beck headed on upstairs. He had already prepared a hiding place in a junk room in a dead-end corridor where he had made space between some dusty tapestries, a listing linen chest and a parrot's heavy cage on a stand.

He stayed on the landing and listened until the shouts faded before making his way back to the ground floor. Inside the beer hall, a man was making a patriotic speech in a harsh, guttural voice. The rest of the inn seemed deserted. Beck slipped out into the night and closed the door behind him. Then he stopped dead. The car was gone.

'This beer is piss,' complained Jäger, wrinkling his nose. Wulzinger shrugged. The beer wasn't any thinner than usual but receiving the news that the lorry driver's alibi had stood up had soured Jäger. The alibis of other members of the Stuttgart black-market gang were being closely examined but it didn't look hopeful. Back to square one, then – if they had ever left it.

They faced each other across their desks in their gloomy, cluttered office in police headquarters, drinking beer and eating sausage and sauerkraut sent in by the local bar. The rest of the *Kripo* floor was almost empty at this time of night but Jäger regularly worked long hours, and Wulzinger was there because Jäger was still there.

'Maybe we're asking the wrong questions.' Jäger balanced a forkful of sauerkraut in one hand while turning the pages of a report with the other.

'What other questions can there be?' asked Wulzinger, chewing steadily.

'That old biddy was ensconced in her window by nine o'clock, and says she saw nothing else unusual. Hamm left his home at six . . .'

'. . . And was killed before eleven.'

'His body was where we found it by eleven,' corrected Jäger. 'That's not the same thing. But if the old biddy is telling the truth, and there's no reason to disbelieve her, then he was killed before nine. It has to be earlier rather than later because no one else saw him. No one saw him because he was already dead. And since we haven't come up with a single sighting of him, it's likely he was killed within minutes of leaving home.'

'Makes sense.'

'Who's up and around at that time in the morning?'

'Farmworkers, men on early shift, night watchmen heading home, office cleaners, people catching the first train into Munich.'

'Let's roust those lazy bastards in Dachau and get them out on the road at six tomorrow morning. Talk to everyone who's about at that hour.'

'You'll be popular.'

'Fuck them.'

'What about the plane? There were reports of a low-flying aircraft that night.'

If Jäger had still been in France he would have expected a British team to have been parachuted in, but no foreign agent had ever dropped into the Fatherland. 'You're right. Check with the *Luftwaffe* to see if there was a night fighter or a training mission up. It could even have been an enemy bomber in difficulties. There's been nothing more on that report of a covered lorry passing through at first light?'

'Afraid not, boss.'

Jäger scratched the tip of his nose with his thumb. In his heart, he still believed the murder was down to the black-market thugs. 'We're going to have to move quickly. We won't be given the manpower much longer. Esser's more concerned about shagging Poles than investigating a murdered cop.'

Wulzinger made a warning signal with his hand. They glanced through the glass partition to the corridor outside to make sure no one was listening. *The German look* – not even policemen were exempt from it.

They both knew what Jäger meant. *Standartenführer* Esser was obsessed with racial purity. He was waging a personal crusade against foreign workers who had sex with German women. Jäger preferred to catch murderers. Like most Bavarians, he had nothing against Poles or French workers. They were fellow Catholics. The decree forbidding Poles to attend church or visit inns was largely ignored around Munich. Jäger certainly had no intention of enforcing it.

'Yesterday, Esser arrested a pregnant Polish woman who'd had a one-night stand with a *Wehrmacht* squaddie on leave,' whispered Wulzinger.

'Poor cow.' The woman would at least be allowed to give birth before the child was taken from her and she was sent to a concentration camp. A child for the Führer.

Jäger turned another page. There was so little to go on.

'There's been no report of any burglaries or thefts. We'd be hearing of food being stolen if there was a vagabond still in the area.' The tramp who had been seen hanging around the previous day had vanished, probably a foreign worker on the run. Anyway, he could easily have escaped the old policeman, and he could not have killed him with a single blow.

'Just one blow, wasn't it?' mused Jäger. 'One blow to the neck.'

'It'd take one hell of a blow to break Hamm's neck.'

'So who could do that? And why? We're back on *why* again. I'm sure he must have seen something.' Jäger stretched his spare frame and reached for his coat.

'Going home?'

Jäger shook his head. 'There're some cages out there yet to be rattled. I still reckon the black market provides the motive and the opportunity. We know they wouldn't hesitate to kill a cop. And if it wasn't black-market racketeers, who the hell was it?'

Beck sat alone in the small *Stube*, waiting for the car to return. The linnets began chirping with pleasure as Vishnia poked a crust of bread through the bars of their cage. The only time he heard them sing, he realized, was when Vishnia was near them. Once she'd fed the birds, she brought him a beer and stood fingering a heart-shaped locket on a chain around her neck while Beck scanned the short menu. He chose *Linseneintopf*, a dish of lentils and sausage. Vishnia shook her head and pointed to the large hall where the Nazis were gathered.

'Goulash?'

The waif nodded brightly, glad she was able to please.

'That's a nice locket.' Beck had not noticed it before. 'What is it?'

Vishnia's hand closed around it as if he was about to snatch it off her.

'Sorry.' Beck held up his hand, palm forward, to show he meant no harm.

Vishnia held out the locket warily. It was the closest she had ever come to him. Beck caught her scent, a combination of steam, soups, garlic and, somewhere, the hint of flowers.

The locket was made of base metal and dented. To Vishnia, it was beyond price.

'Is there a photo inside?' Vishnia stroked the locket with her forefinger and shook her head. 'Something precious. A keepsake? A memento?'

Her pinched features lit up and for the first time he noticed that she had cornflower-blue eyes. Trembling, she pressed a catch. The locket opened to reveal a tightly curled strand of rich chestnut hair.

Her lover's? No. No, of course not. 'Your mother?'

Yes, her mother. Vishnia put the locket to her lips in an act of love and reverence and kissed it gently. Beck felt sad and humbled.

Vishnia heard the car before he did. She looked nervously away and dropped the locket back inside her blouse, rearranging her hair around her neck to hide the chain. She fled back to the kitchen. Beck watched from behind the curtain as Runge and three other SA men climbed out of the VW. From the boot, they produced two cases of enzian, four crates of beer from the town brewery and a huge smoked ham. Runge bawled for Vishnia to come and help them as he struggled with two of the crates. He clipped her around the ear for being slow as she staggered away under the weight of the ham.

They all disappeared into the kitchen.

When Vishnia finally brought his thin soup, Beck saw she had been crying. He reached out and squeezed her hand.

The arrival of the extra drinks brought renewed cheering and shouts. Beck waited until the hubbub had died down before he headed for the car. The weight of the Nazis had pressed the rear seat back into position so he needed the wheel brace to prise it up. He was halfway back up the first flight of stairs with his prize when a surge of noise warned him someone was coming out of the meeting. Beck was down the narrow corridor and into his room before he dared draw breath. He locked the door, shut the curtains and turned on the light.

A gingerbread man lay on his pillow.

Everyone who knew Magda Hocherlin said she was vain. Boys who tried to know her better groaned that she was a cockteaser. Men who succeeded in getting to know her complained that she set her own price and that frequently it was too high. As the seventeen-year-old daughter of the local Nazi Party *Ortsleiter*, she could more or less do what she wanted – and she did.

But there were some gifts she would accept gratefully, and honour. The panel of silk, for example, that she was now holding against her cheek. Magda stroked its exquisite softness. It was beautiful – so beautiful that she hardly noticed Erich's hands pawing at her breasts. She would get the maid to start fashioning a blouse out of it first thing next morning.

Wincing, she knocked away Erich's hand as he pinched her nipple. Then she grasped his hair and began to kiss him, forcing her tongue deep into his mouth. She hated sex in the back of cars at this cold time of year but she had to be nice to Erich in case he came up with more silk.

She knew better than to ask how he had acquired it. She loosened his belt and undid the top fly buttons. Two of a kind, they were: the devil's children. Except she was more the devil and he the child.

'Beer, skittles, racket, wolf.' Cricklemarsh smiled up at Annie, his face haloed in the light of the desk. 'Or, to be exact, befr, skittles, sacket, wolf. That means the Gestapo doesn't have him.'

It was the first time Annie had seen Cricklemarsh relax for days. Apart from going to investigate the murder of Private Pabst, he had not left the Baker Street attic since Beck's departure – even sleeping on the camp bed.

'Thank God he's safe and well,' she smiled back.

'Safe is a relative description,' cautioned Cricklemarsh, packing a celebratory pipe.

Signals were usually received at SOE's home station at Poundon on the Oxfordshire-Buckinghamshire border and relayed by teleprinter to the signal and cypher department at nearby Michaelhouse. But Cricklemarsh had successfully argued for their own wireless transmitter and an operator based in Annie's office.

The message just in contained security checks confirming that Beck was not yet in the hands of the Gestapo. There were two types of checks hidden in agents' signals from occupied territory: random and routine. SOE favoured routine. In Beck's case, this meant a deliberate error involving one letter in transmission on both the third and thirteenth letters of the message. The Gestapo had soon learned of this device so agents now used two security checks – one to give up under torture and the real one.

'Befr, beer – I have not been detected,' recited Cricklemarsh, through clouds of smoke. 'Skittles, I have found somewhere to stay. Racket, I am fully equipped. Wolf – this was a mistake. Hitler's well known to have used this alias – it means the Führer has arrived at the Berghof. All in all, cause for a drink, wouldn't you say?'

The Barley Mow was more crowded than usual. Too late, Annie remembered the send-off party being given for two officers going out to Cairo. She would have preferred somewhere quieter, and so, she sensed, would Cricklemarsh. Purefoy, standing with a handful of senior officers by the fire, ignored them totally. Cricklemarsh bought Annie a gin and it, and a whisky for himself. Several officers were casting hopeful looks in her direction but getting a glacial shoulder in return.

'One odd thing,' remembered Annie. 'I overheard Brigadier Gilbert telling his wife over lunch that the operation was going splendidly. He couldn't have known that before us, could he?'

'No,' said Cricklemarsh. 'Perhaps he has more faith in us than Purefoy has.'

'Aren't you going to at least tell him the good news? It might stop him going on at you.'

Cricklemarsh squeezed his way over to Purefoy, his stooped shoulders and bald head looking out of place among all the young officers. He spoke quietly into the colonel's ear.

'Your man's turned up at last.' Nye, head of the German Section, materialized at Annie's shoulder.

'Sorry?' Most other men would have died a little on the spot, then crawled away. At her abrupt haughtiest, Annie could choke off a water main.

'Your man's surfaced.'

'Has he?'

'That should be my operation by rights.'

'Gee, really!' Annie turned her back on him to continue watching Cricklemarsh.

Nye changed tack. 'Perhaps you and I could have a drink or dinner together. Bury the hatchet.'

'I'm not carrying a hatchet.'

'You might find you'll want to come and work in X Section.'

'Why should I do that?' *I'd blow my brains out first.*

'You won't have a job anywhere else.'

The Gestapo liked to boast that they could identify the building from which a wireless operator was sending anywhere in Western Europe within thirty minutes. Beck's two-minute transmission was picked up at Gestapo HQ in the Avenue Foch in Paris where relays of thirty clerks kept up a continuous watch on every available frequency. Once a new transmitter opened up, it showed itself on a cathode ray tube. The frequency was read off and the direction-finding stations at Brest, Augsburg, Berlin and Nuremburg were alerted to take a cross-bearing. First, unmarked detector vans closed in on a fifteen-kilometre triangle. Then, if the operator was foolish enough to still be sending, the Gestapo would narrow the search area to within two kilometres. Finally, portly men in raincoats, hiding small detection sets strapped to their waists, would move in. Soon, too soon for many, they would be knocking down the door.

Beck was off the air before the Germans could manage anything more precise than a general direction. The first indication that the new signal came from the Salzburg area was greeted with scepticism. Although the location was outside the triangle of normal cross-bearings, the DF stations insisted they were correct. Two detector vans set off from Munich to Salzburg, ready for the next time.

In the meantime, Gestapo cypher experts got to work to crack the code. Something that, Cricklemarsh knew, was impossible.

10

Wednesday, 24 March

The fog wrapped Beck in a silent and unreal world, at once both bright and gloomy. He could see no further than the blurred trunks of trees less than fifty yards away. The fog was a blessing and a curse. It covered his ascent up the Mooslangerkopf but it made navigation difficult. Better map-readers than Beck had got lost in pea-soupers like this.

Ilse had been surprised when he had asked her earlier for local hiking maps.

'Surely you're not going out in this weather.'

'The doctors said a little damp's good for my chest. Will this cloud extend right up to the peaks?'

'Sometimes yes, sometimes no.' She was being formal this morning. The previous intimacy of their shared journey together was over. She had still not thanked him for backing up her lie to her husband.

He found the bridge over the Ache at Kilianmühle unguarded. The lane from the bridge petered out at a farmhouse and became merely a hill track. Beck climbed a stile and pressed on up through the meadow, his greatcoat already damp with the mist that wreathed and swirled, pressing in and confusing him. He reached the road leading to the hamlet of Stanger where he used compass and map to take a bearing on the tea house. Further to the left, towards Stanger and its fellow hamlet of Spornhof, patches of alpine meadow appeared in the middle of the forest like bald patches in a thick head of hair. He must be sure not to drift too far in that direction.

As Cricklemarsh had predicted, the outer fence was not a serious obstacle; ten feet high, topped by three strands of barbed wire –

intended to keep out the curious and the sightseers, rather than the professional assassin. Beck listened intently. Somewhere out beyond his foggy little world were SS guards and dogs.

He was over the fence in seconds and into longer grass. Beck paused and was rewarded by spotting the hidden tripwire, ready to set alarm bells ringing at the nearest guard post. He stepped over the wire and entered a ghostly forest where tree trunks loomed up from nowhere and the mist hung in tatters off the ends of sodden branches. The pine needles were soft and yielding underfoot; the damp air heavy with the scent of resin. Beck came to a track that climbed diagonally across his path. He heard muffled voices but didn't have a clue which direction they came from. He moved on over the track and into another strip of forest where a brown rill rushed past, forcing him to keep to the right. He clambered over a bank – onto a paved path.

That shouldn't be there.

Beck halted, confused and disorientated. *Read from the ground to the map,* he reminded himself. *Do not impose the map onto the terrain.* He worked out that he was crossing the woodland walk that followed the 700-metre contour from Mausbichl towards Spornhof. He had drifted too far to the right. To compensate, he tracked two hundred paces back before continuing to climb. Soon the slope grew so steep that Beck was hauling himself up by clutching at branches and saplings.

Stunted conifers grew on the edge of a rocky outcrop to his left. He crabbed towards it, only to find that the lie of the land deceived the eye. The outcrop was close now but the trees were fifty yards further away. He climbed over the rocks into a perfect miniature glade. A stream tumbled over mirror-smooth black rocks into a pool surrounded by ferns set in a dew-drenched meadow that was hemmed in by the surrounding forest.

This hidden basin made such little topographical sense that he climbed up to one side to try to get an overview. It proved impossible. The trees were too dense for him to be able to see into the dell from above, and as soon as he moved only a yard into the forest, the glade had disappeared. Magical! Beck consulted the map again to find that the glade had never been charted.

Beams of sunlight were forcing their way through the thinning clouds. Suddenly the fog streamed away in pale wisps and, for a second, he was standing under a brilliant clear sky, looking towards the peaks of the Brandlberg and the Kneifelspitze rising out of the cotton wool filling the valley. He turned his head. Not four hundred yards above him, through a gap in the trees, he spotted the red-brick tea house set into the steep hillside. In front of it extended a grass viewing promontory protected by wooden rails. Steps led down towards the clouds below.

As Beck stood spellbound, bank after bank of fog rolled back in. He pressed on upwards through the murk until he thought he must be level with the track leading to the tea house. He shrank behind a tree as two SS guards emerged. They marched silently past him, rifles over their shoulders, and receded into the fog. Beck did not know if Hitler was solely a fair-weather walker, so he waited. Shame he had not brought his rifle.

'So what did you talk about?' demanded Runge as Ilse reached up to unpin one end of the long banner.

'Nothing much.'

Vishnia loosened the other end of the banner and the women walked towards each other, folding and refolding.

'You must have spoken about something. You were together long enough. Did you stop anywhere for a drink?'

'Of course not. If you'll empty the ashtrays, please, Vishnia, I'll take down the rest of the flags.' Cigarette rationing was severe – three cigarettes a day or twelve cheap cigars every ten days – but Runge and his cronies never went short. 'And watch your feet on the broken glass.'

'What does the gallant captain reckon about the war?' Runge stood with his hands on his hips, making no effort to help them tidy up after his SA meeting.

'He thinks it may be a long, hard slog,' replied Ilse carefully.

'Did he have anything to say about the Party?' he continued suspiciously. Too many soldiers came back to the Fatherland thinking they owned it just because they had fought at the front. They had no respect for what National Socialism had achieved. He ignored Vishnia's efforts to reach past him for an ashtray, making her go all the way around the table instead. 'Did he ask you anything about me?'

'No.' Ilse glanced at him. 'Why should he?'

'How I came to own this place, for example?'

'No. What are you thinking?' Ilse knew how Runge had forced its previous owners to sell him the Red Ox at a fraction of its true value by claiming they were *Mischlinge* – half-Jews.

'Don't you think it's strange that this captain turns up here out of the blue?'

'You were the one who agreed to take him in.'

Ilse wondered exactly what Runge was thinking. You could never tell with him. He was barely literate but he possessed an animal cunning that had seen him prosper with the Nazis till he was now a man of considerable property and status in Berchtesgaden. He had been a humble brewery labourer when he had first joined Hitler in the early 1920s. The Nazis had needed thugs like him, while Runge needed the Nazis to legitimize his violence and his thieving. But even they had recognized his limitations. Unlike many of the other old fighters, he had not been appointed *Ortsleiter* – town leader. Instead he was allowed to continue as a fixer, a go-between, taking a percentage here, confiscating a property there.

'He comes from Cologne, doesn't he?' insisted Runge.

'His family owned a chain of garages there but they lost everything in the air raids. Take this as well, please, Vishnia,' said Ilse, draping a towel over the girl's arm. Vishnia carried the stack of ashtrays towards the kitchen.

'The *Mischlinge* I got this place from had relations with garages in Cologne . . .' His speculations were interrupted by a tremendous crash. Vishnia staggered back into the room and collapsed. A metal pail rolled on the floor, slopping water. Hänschen emerged through the door, holding his sides in mirth.

'I put the bucket on top of the door . . .' Tears of laughter ran down his cheeks.

Ilse's patience snapped. Grabbing the boy, she rammed his head into the bucket, then began beating him on the backside with the broom handle that she snatched up. When Hänschen finally wriggled free, his face was red with fury.

'My uniform. Look what you've done to my uniform,' he screamed. 'You've insulted the Führer. I'll tell them. I'll inform on you.' He aimed a kick at Vishnia, still on her hands and knees on the floor, then fled the room, hurling insults over his shoulder. 'I'll get even with you, you bloody cow. I'll put you in a concentration camp.'

'You'll have to do something, Runge.' Ilse helped Vishnia to her feet. A lump was already rising on the girl's forehead.

'He's only a boy,' shrugged Runge.

'He's a spoilt brat who needs a man's hand. He doesn't listen to me. You control him or he's going. I'm not having him here.' She found herself screaming, then dropped to a gentler tone. 'I'm sorry, Vishnia. Let me look at your head. It was a wicked thing to do.'

Vishnia was lying on her thin mattress, pressing a damp cloth to her head, when she heard Runge's heavy tread on the stairs. She began to tremble but the footsteps halted outside Captain Beck's room instead. Alert and wary, she sat up as she heard the jangle of keys. Runge was trying to get into Beck's bedroom. Finally, he found the key that fitted. Vishnia stood up, wincing with pain.

She feared what would happen to her once Runge had finished in Beck's room. She would be safer in the kitchen. Grimacing, her head still on fire, she tiptoed down the corridor, pausing to listen for a moment to the sound of Runge opening and closing drawers.

'You're not going back there now, are you?' Penelope Hardinge raised a well-plucked eyebrow more in despair than surprise. 'They'll start charging you rent if you keep on like this.'

'Cricklemarsh is sleeping in the office these days,' replied Annie evenly. 'The least I can do is be on hand for the scheduled transmissions.'

Penelope gave an evil grin. 'There's a squadron passing through London tonight from Yorkshire. I know a couple of the flight commanders and it promises to be quite a party.'

'Thanks, Pen, but I'm not in the mood.' Annie felt she was being disloyal just popping out to the local Lyons Corner House.

'You're not taking things too personally again, are you?'

Penelope thought Annie should have learned after the business with Paul. She knew Annie as well as anyone. They had become schoolfriends, aged ten, when Annie's father had been posted to the American Embassy in London. The girls had stayed in touch, visiting each other when Annie had moved to Dublin. Even when Annie had gone back to America and had been at school at Vassar, her mother had contrived to bring her back for most of the season in England, so the two girls had seen a lot of each other. Finally, they had successfully plotted to spend a year together in a Swiss finishing school. In fact, Penelope probably knew Annie *better* than anyone.

And Penny remembered how Annie had wept for weeks after Paul had been taken by the Gestapo. She had sworn blind then that she'd never do it again, never fall for a man in uniform.

'I've told you, no,' retorted Annie with enough asperity to make a sailor and his girlfriend glance up from the next table.

'Fine, then.' Penelope looked away from her and out of the window. 'That's a funny colour for a bus.'

Annie followed her gaze. 'West Mon,' she said automatically. They no longer played Spot the Bus from the garret office any more – so this reminded her all the more of Lusty. It was not right to be out enjoying herself while his life hung in the balance.

A Nippy put down a teapot, a metal water jug, a small milk jug, a smear of sugar and a plate of scones. Penelope pulled two sachets of sugar out of her handbag. 'Those two Canadians are giving us the eye.'

Annie didn't even look round.

The scones, made with powered eggs, were dry and crumbled in their hands. The gooseberry jam was thin and tasteless.

Annie eventually gave up and lit a Camel cigarette. 'Do you

remember yesterday when Brigadier Gilbert and his awful wife walked past our table? I overheard him say something about the operation going splendidly.'

'So?'

'But we only learned later that Lusty was safe. There's no way Gilbert could have known.'

'Maybe he picked up on a radio intercept.'

'No.' Annie delicately plucked a piece of tobacco from her lips. 'No, Lusty sends directly to Cricklemarsh.'

'Maybe he was talking about some other operation.' Penelope determinedly squeezed together the last dry fragments of her scone.

'He mentioned Nightshade by name.' Annie reflected. 'And I didn't like the way he laughed. It sounded malicious. Listen, do me a favour, see what paperwork they've got on your floor on Nightshade. Who originated it, who's sponsoring it, that sort of thing.'

Penelope looked doubtful. 'You said Purefoy was pulling the strings?'

'I've got a feeling someone else's pulling Purefoy's strings and that that someone may be Gilbert.'

'While I remember,' said Penny. 'I finally got that roll of film from the Christmas bash developed.' She delved in her handbag. 'Here's a good one of you with Cricklemarsh and Lusty.'

Annie inspected the photograph of herself flanked by her two male colleagues. God, Lusty looked boyish with his open face and honest grin.

'May I keep it to show Cricklemarsh?'

'Of course. It's yours.'

Beck shivered. The cold had risen up through the soles of his boots till now he could not feel his feet. He had waited all through the morning and much of the afternoon in the hope of seeing Hitler. Now, the sun was dipping towards the Gernhorn on the far side of the Königssee, a red ball through a latticework of spruce branches. Clearly, the Führer would not be going out for a walk today. Still, Beck was satisfied with the day's work. He had penetrated the outer zone and found the route leading to the tea house. He also knew that pairs of sentries patrolled every thirty minutes. They were young, smart and even marched in step but they looked relaxed because they didn't seriously believe anyone would try to kill the Führer.

Beck turned and plunged back into the mist, intending to descend past the same small clearing. But although he carefully followed a stream, it turned out to be a different one and he missed the glade. Confused, he pushed on through the fog, which now cast his own dim twilight shadow back at him.

The sentry wore a steel helmet and a long white coat with a fur collar. His rifle was slung over his shoulder and he was urinating. The man half turned at Beck's approach. Guilt infused his face at the thought he was about to be caught out by an officer. His look changed to incomprehension as he made out Beck's *Wehrmacht* greatcoat – and then to panic. He went to unsling his rifle but first had to stop pissing and do up his fly. Nothing in his SS training had prepared him to challenge an intruder with his cock hanging out.

'Achtung!'

The sentry instinctively straightened at the stranger's command.

Beck jabbed swiftly at his throat. As the sentry staggered back, choking for air, Beck seized him by his head and hooked his legs away. It was one of Marvin's favourite nasty little tricks at training school. 'Breaking a man's neck is easy,' he would say. 'Simply make use of their own weight while you twist a little. You break the neck at the atlas: the first cervical vertebra that supports the skull. It's like taking the top off an Ovaltine jar.'

The sentry's neck gave a muffled *snick* and the man went limp. Beck lowered him to the earth. He was a big, handsome boy, a good two inches taller than Beck. Only the tallest and the best were good enough for the Führer's SS bodyguard. *Sad bastard,* thought Beck, *he should have been doing something useful like fighting on the Russian Front.* Now he was dead and Beck had to find a way of camouflaging his death.

The sentry lay on his back, his head twisted at an obscene angle. He had urinated over his overcoat and trousers during the brief struggle. His open fly gave Beck an idea. He pulled the dead man's belt from his trousers and flung it over a seven-foot-high conifer branch. Taking the sling off the rifle, he fashioned a primitive noose and placed it around the German's neck. Now came the difficult part. Beck hauled the sentry into a sitting position. Then, kneeling in front of him, he tucked his shoulder into the dead man's midriff and straightened.

Time was not on Beck's side. The sentry would have a comrade not far away. Beck fastened the sling through the belt buckle and slowly let the branch take the weight so that the sentry's toes just scuffed the pine needles.

Beck lowered the man's trousers and underpants. It wasn't very pretty but it would take a pathologist to discover the sentry had not hanged himself in a frenzy of masturbation. Beck's betting was that this was one death the garrison commander would want to cover up. Knowing soldiers, he was pretty sure that it would merely give the rest of the bodyguard a good laugh.

Beck had already crossed the path when he felt the breeze getting up. Soon, too soon, he could make out the planet Venus, golden and twinkling, in a magenta sky over the Untersberg. Reaching the edge of the trees, he cleaned his coat with the clothes brush he had brought. He could do nothing much about his sodden boots.

It was going to be a dry, clear night. He made out the shape of the farmhouse and, across the river, the glimmer of headlamps from a convoy moving along the road towards Austria. The chain link fence was more exposed than he had thought previously. He would be visible for more than one hundred metres in either direction. A dog barked. Beck fancied the sound came from the woods behind him. He gathered himself and ran. The ground was heavy and slippery. He leaped at the fence, one foot brushing the tripwire. Beck was up the barrier faster than he'd ever managed in training. Too fast, maybe. At the top, the barbed wire snatched spitefully at the knee of his breeches. He stopped and inched backward to prise free the barb.

The dog barked again. This time it was answered by another off to the right. Beck jumped down the other side and ran hell for leather down through the meadow until he came to the track leading to the bridge. Panting in the shadow of a farm outhouse, he saw torches approaching the stretch of fence where he had crossed. A scout car drove up and halted. The guards had reacted alarmingly quickly. They were now casting around on the ground with their torches. Beck hoped they would assume a fox had brushed against the wire. But in the morning light, they might find a patch of his trousers on the barbs, if they came back to inspect.

He retrieved his stick from its hiding place and emerged onto the road, mentally preparing himself in case he bumped into a patrol. *Where have you been? What have you been doing? Where are you going?*

I've been up to the Ochshütte. It took longer than I expected because of my leg. I fell and ripped my breeches. I am returning to the Red Ox inn.

The phone rang at one minute past four. Voss's heart stopped. It couldn't be the English agent! Not already! Not yet!

He steeled himself, as through his open office door, he saw Schnitzler stride along the corridor towards the extension phone. *That bloody man.* How Voss hated him!

Voss snatched up the receiver. 'Yes?'

'Schaanwald crossing, major . . .'

Voss deflated in relief. He hardly listened as the corporal told how one of his men had just had his foot crushed under a lorry. He eventually came off the phone to find Schnitzler regarding him from the doorway with knowing, mocking eyes. Schnitzler had that knack of forcing eye contact, his gaze boring into his own until Voss had to look guiltily away.

'Yes? What do you want?'

Schnitzler came smartly to attention. 'There's a Swiss banker from St Gallen who claims he's travelling to Frankfurt on business.'

'So? Are his papers in order?'

'Yes, but it's an odd route to get there. It would be much more direct to go north.'

'What's his explanation?'

'He says he's visiting friends en route.'

'That'll be Bruno Waldheim. He makes the crossing regularly. He has a school friend in Ulm.'

Schnitzler was eyeing him as though Voss and Waldheim were in some sort of conspiracy. Why hadn't the man gone off duty? He had been here since six this morning.

'You were due off at four,' Voss reminded him, making an effort to sound pleasant. 'I'll be taking evening duties for a while.'

'Of course. Though I don't know why you'd want to.' There was just that hint of insolence that infuriated Voss while at the same time undermining his confidence.

'It's good for morale for the men to see their senior officer prepared to share unsociable hours. It also lets me check that standards are not being dropped in the evenings after I've gone.'

'I can assure you . . .'

The phone rang again and Voss jumped.

Schnitzler was again staring at him strangely. 'Shall I get it, sir?'

'No. No one answers this phone but me.' Voss found he was shouting. 'Understand?'

This was only the first day. There were another five to come. He didn't think he would be able to get through them.

Beck was fifty metres away from the Red Ox when he heard cars coming up behind. They slowed, then a large black Mercedes-Benz overtook him to halt right outside the inn. Beck limped briskly through the door. Out of the corner of his eye, he saw the following car was full of SS men.

Ilse stood just inside, dusting a portrait of the Führer. 'You've been out a long time.'

'I stopped to rest for a while.'

I won't be taken alive. I'll fight. I'd rather die on my feet than be tortured to death. And I'll take a few of them with me.

He loosened the flap of his holster and moved away. There was the clatter of jackboots. The floating pin on the Walther automatic told him there was a round in the chamber. The blackout curtain was ripped aside and Beck felt his insides coil like a tightly wound spring.

A blonde woman in a tweed jacket, roll neck sweater and trousers entered. As she saw Ilse, she broke into a broad smile.

'Ilse.'

'Evi.'

The women embraced. A pair of Highland Terriers dashed in and ran around their legs, barking in excitement. Ilse remembered that Beck was still there.

'Christian, let me introduce you. *Hauptmann* Beck of the *Deutsche Afrika Korps. Fräulein* Braun.'

Beck clicked his heels and bowed. '*Fräulein* Braun.'

'Come into the small *Stube.* It's cosier there. How are you?' Ilse fussed around her visitor. 'You come too, Captain Beck. You don't mind, Evi? Captain Beck's a friend.'

Beck limped in after them, hoping that this woman with the round face would not notice how his hands were shaking. He surreptitiously refastened his holster as she flopped heavily on a chair next to the stove and pulled off her woollen bobble hat. She ran her hands through her wavy shoulder-length hair.

'I've been skiing all day.' The white dog tried to jump up on her lap. 'No. Down, Stasi, down. Those two think they can do what they like. Negus is the black one and this white tearaway's Stasi. You're a monster, aren't you?'

'What would you like to drink?' enquired Ilse.

'Cider, if you have it. What are you doing all the way out here, Captain Beck?'

'I was wounded in the desert. Doctors say I need plenty of pure air. *Frau* Runge is kindly putting me up for a short time.'

'Why do you need pure air for a bad leg?' the woman asked, smiling. Beck had the impression she smiled easily.

'I was careless . . . I was hit in the chest as well.'

She gave a rippling peel of laughter. 'I'm sorry. I'm always putting my foot in it.'

'Captain Beck was so far ahead of our troops that he was shelled by our own guns,' proclaimed Ilse.

'That's very brave.'

'Foolish,' he corrected modestly.

'And how are things with you, Evi?' asked Ilse. She pressed the service bell for Vishnia but nothing happened.

'Bit better now he's here. He's totally worn out. He needs a long rest – not that they'll let him enjoy one, of course.'

Ilse scowled. 'I don't know what's happened to Vishnia. I'll fetch your cider. Captain Beck, what'll you have?'

'A beer, please.'

Ilse appeared to notice Beck for the first time. 'What have you been doing? Your boots are soaking.'

As Beck looked down at his boots, his greatcoat opened.

'And you've ripped your breeches,' giggled the blonde woman.

Beck coloured. 'I caught them on a thorn bush. I walked too far and my leg gave way. I fell down into a ditch. I'd better go and change.'

'You poor thing. You *will* come back and talk to us?' Her voice carried the tone of one who expected to be obeyed.

'If you wish.'

'Yes, do.' She bent to tickle Negus behind his ears. 'It's nice to meet real people.'

Ilse followed Beck out. 'You've made a hit there. Evi's normally more reserved with strangers. People assume she's stuck-up but in fact she's shy – and in such a difficult position.'

'Is she? In what way?'

Ilse tilted her head on the side. She opened her mouth to speak but paused. 'You realize who she is, don't you?'

'No.'

Ilse suppressed a grin. She dropped her voice. 'That's Eva Braun. Hitler's special friend.'

Beck returned to find Ilse and Eva Braun chattering merrily about clothes and fashion. Eva indicated a chair at her side. Now he knew her identity, he could not keep his eyes off her. He guessed she was thirty or thereabouts – slightly older than Ilse. Fresh-faced and pleasant rather than beautiful; quite short, with a firm, athletic body. She possessed an appealing gaiety and a willingness to laugh but Beck sensed that, under the surface, there was a core of determination and an awkward pride in her unique position in the Reich.

She made no attempt to explain to Beck exactly who she was. She was just herself and got on with it. Beck liked her for that.

Finally, Vishnia brought in a plateful of cakes. The dogs sat expectantly but Eva pulled a regretful face.

'I shouldn't really but I do love your cakes.'

'You're always on a diet and you don't need to be.'

'That's what the chief says. He doesn't approve of me losing weight. Oh, I didn't tell you . . .' Eva tapped Ilse on the knee. 'That vulgar Valkyrie Emmy Göring has really overreached herself. Last week she invited everyone on the mountain for tea at her house. *Everyone,* even little Milli Schellmoser, the hairdresser. She sent out her invitations in alphabetical order so she put me under "B", as Braun, Eva. She knows she should have put me first. The chief was furious when I told him. He's banned her from the Berghof.'

'Good.'

'Oh, dear.' Eva Braun stopped herself. 'Captain Beck . . . I'm sorry, I was being indiscreet.'

Beck hastened to reassure her. 'I've a terrible memory. I forget everything. *What* were you talking about?'

'You're very kind.' She smiled warmly. 'I can talk so easily to Ilse. We've known each other since I started coming here.'

'We were only girls then,' said Ilse.

'Life was easier too,' agreed Eva, crumbling a cake into pieces for her dogs. 'We could come and go without having to fight our way through building sites and barbed wire. What Bormann's done to the mountain makes me weep.'

'Is he still . . .?' It was Ilse's turn to be indiscreet.

'If it wears a skirt, he'll chase it. He makes me sick. How his wife puts up with his philandering, God only knows. I suppose she must be used to it.'

'Maybe with ten children to look after she doesn't have time to notice.'

Eva laughed. 'It is so nice to see you. My sister Gretl's staying for a fortnight but she's only got eyes for Fegelein so she's no company any more.'

Beck had a dozen questions he would have loved to ask but he didn't want to appear over-familiar. But, at the same time, he couldn't sit just there like a stuffed puppet.

'You're going to be very busy . . . now?' he ventured.

'There are no official visits for the next fortnight but most of the General Staff have accompanied him. The *Gauleiters* and Party bosses will turn up in droves once they get the word that he's willing to see them. I'm keeping them at arm's length as long as possible. But, of course, Bormann's around *all the time*.' Eva remembered the time. 'I must be going. He'll worry if I'm late.'

As if understanding, the dogs ran to the door and started scratching to be let out.

Eva extended a hand to Beck. 'It's been a pleasure to meet you, captain. I hope you'll be able to get those breeches sewn up.'

'I'll see if I can mend them,' said Ilse.

In the corridor, Eva halted to say goodbye.

'At least you have the Führer here now,' said Ilse.

'He's so tired. The war's exhausting him. The treachery on the Eastern Front . . .' Eva brightened as a thought hit her and she turned to Beck. 'Perhaps it would do him good to speak to an officer from the *Afrika Korps*. They've been so courageous.' She did not seem to know the DAK was in full retreat. 'He likes to meet front-line soldiers. He says he finds them more honest than any of the *Junkers* on the General Staff. But, either way, you *must* come and see me at the Grand Hotel.'

'Sorry?' Beck did not understand.

'How can anything be called a *Berghof*, a mountain farm, when it's got thirty rooms? I'll send passes for you both to visit as the Führer's guests.'

'Do we really need a pass?' asked Beck innocently.

'My dear captain, Bormann has decreed that not even a government minister in uniform is allowed inside the inner zone without a pass. Even I have to carry a pass.'

There seemed to be a void once Eva Braun had left. Beck returned to the warmth of the stove to digest the latest development. Ilse came in with a mischievous glint in her eye.

'Now you've met one of the *Reich*'s secrets.'

'I'd no idea.'

'Few do. But in spite of all her privileges, I wouldn't swap my life for hers. Evi doesn't have a happy time. Her only friends on that mountain are *Reichsminister* Speer and his wife. The wives of other Party high-ups gang up on her. She has to stay in her bedroom when dignitaries visit. She's only allowed to be seen with the Führer when they are among old and close friends. She's very lonely.'

'She seems very chatty.'

'She's desperate to talk.'

Claude Ismay liked OSS parties. He did not particularly like Americans but he enjoyed their endless hospitality. The sumptuous living room of the flat in St James's was full of elegant women and men in well-tailored uniforms speaking in loud, confident voices. He positioned himself near the makeshift bar where the servants began their circuits with trays of canapés and waited for his host to return.

OSS officers were so gung-ho. You'd have thought these Ivy League scions of old families would show more decorum – but give them a war and they mounted their chargers, drew their sabres and galloped straight towards the guns. Of course, they'd never fought a real war. Ismay conveniently forgot about the bloodletting of the Civil War and held out his glass in exchange for another cocktail. He wondered if he could ever persuade the committee of White's to serve Manhattans. He thought not. The Americans did attract some fine specimens of female, though, not that Ismay bothered with them. He was content to stand there on his own, eating and drinking – and thinking. No, the Americans had never fought a real foreign war. They'd bashed a few tribes of Indians and taken their land, squabbled with Spain over Cuba, and entered the first war only in 1917 when the other nations were on their knees with exhaustion. They hadn't had suffered the previous three years of carnage. Ismay used his beanpole height to deftly collect a clutch of cocktail sausages on sticks from a waiter's tray.

There was still no sign of J. Edward Jollison, acting head of OSS Europe. Jollison, Ismay had decided, was a snob with a chip on his shoulder the size of Alaska. Like most Americans, he was in awe of SIS, hoping that by frequent association some of its mystique would rub off onto his callow organization. He had sought out Ismay in one of his early forays on the cocktail circuit and carefully cultivated him. Ismay was flattered – but watchful.

When Jollison emerged, looking flushed and excited, he took Ismay's arm and steered him towards the red velvet curtains at the windows and away from the food.

'The darnedest thing. We've just had a signal from Berne . . .' He checked himself. 'I'd like to bounce it off you, totally off the record, you understand?'

'Of course.' *Silly boy.*

'Does the name Antonescu mean anything to you?'

'Romanian Army leader, threw in his lot with King Michael after Carol abdicated.'

'Er, no. Not that one.'

'I'm afraid he's the only one I know.' Ismay watched a tray of meatballs passing just out of reach, the waiter determinedly avoiding his eye.

'This other Antonescu represents the Romanian state oil company, claims to be in big with Nazi industrialists. He approached our Berne people a while ago.' Jollison moved even closer. 'He's come up with a scheme to assassinate Hitler.'

Ismay jumped as though someone had stuck a pin through the seat of his pinstriped trousers. 'And . . . um . . . how far has Mr Antonescu progressed with this scheme? Just between us, you understand.'

Jollison smiled, showing perfect white teeth. 'He claims he can gain proximity to Hitler through his connections. Our boys in Berne think he might have a chance.'

Ismay swore to himself. This meant he had a decision to make. He did not for one minute believe that this Romanian was anything but, at worst, a Nazi plant or, at best, a self-serving scoundrel after American dollars. But, but . . . he couldn't afford to take the chance.

'Look, old boy. This is very much *entre nous*.' It was Ismay's turn to go through the motions of sharing a confidence. He chose his words carefully. 'We already have an operation under way to the very same end. I'm informed that our chap's virtually *in situ*.'

Jollison gave a low whistle. 'You don't say. You Brits! You let everyone think you're sitting around on your butts and all the time . . . Wow!'

Ismay recoiled at the puerility of such hero-worship. 'You'll appreciate it's important not to rock the boat.'

'Gee, yeh. Think of the consequences if this Romanian guy goes off half-cock. You'd never get another crack . . . Softly-softly, catchee monkey, yeh?'

'If you put it that way. We'd be grateful if you'd hold off – just for a while. Of course, we don't know whether our chap will be successful or not. If he fails then we'll be delighted to do everything we can to weigh in and help you.'

No, they wouldn't. SIS would hinder and obstruct the Americans under the pretence of offering advice and caution – but first Ismay had to scupper the OSS operation. It was not often that SIS went out of its way to help Baker Street but his friend Nye had his eye on this operation. He expected Nye to pull it into his own orbit once it looked like succeeding.

You scratch my back and I'll scratch yours. Yes, thought Ismay, *it would be nice to share a bath with Nye again.*

11

Thursday, 25 March

'I'm a busy man. I haven't got time to waste hanging around for some detective or other.' *Ortsleiter* Hocherlin flexed the bullwhip he carried.

Wulzinger refused to be intimidated. '*Sturmbannführer* Jäger is in conference regarding the murder of a police officer.'

'Huh!'

Hocherlin and his daughter Magda followed Wulzinger up the stairs of the Munich police headquarters to the *Kripo* floor. Even in her BDM uniform, Magda managed to turn heads. Her skirt was two inches too short and her blouse tight across her full breasts. Wulzinger, a stern father of three, thought she was a little trollop.

He was angry that Jäger had been assigned to investigate Hocherlin's complaints – as if they didn't have enough on their plates. He showed Hocherlin and his daughter into the cramped office and produced two hard chairs. Jäger bustled in, a sheaf of papers in one hand and a black cheroot in his mouth.

'*Heil Hitler*,' barked Hocherlin.

Jäger nodded.

'I'm not used to being kept waiting.' Hocherlin slapped the whip against his jackboot.

The slight policeman with the axe nose ignored him. Squinting through the smoke curling around his eyes, he placed the papers in a buff folder on his desk. He then searched through the middle tier of the three wooden in-trays until he found the report he wanted and added it to the folder. Finally he took the cheroot out of his mouth.

'How may I help you?'

Hocherlin bristled. 'I'm the Party leader of Karlsfeld.'

'Yes?' Karlsfeld was the town between Munich and Dachau.

'Last night we went to the shelters when the air-raid sirens sounded. It was a false alarm but when we returned two pairs of Magda's shoes had been stolen.'

'They were fine leather shoes,' added Magda.

Jäger leaned back and pressed his knuckles into his eyes. He was trying not to yawn. When he reopened his eyes, he found himself staring at Magda's breasts. Accustomed to the attention of men, Magda crossed her legs and favoured him with her most alluring smile. But this policeman was different. He didn't return her smile, nor did he blush. He furrowed his brow as if in pain and kept staring at her breasts.

'The Dutch gardener from the house next door took them.'

When it became obvious Jäger was not going to speak, Wulzinger asked, 'Where were the shoes at the time?'

'In the scullery. The maid hadn't got round to cleaning them. The gardener was watching me when I put them out for her. He took them, I know he did.' Magda sat back, spiteful and vindictive.

'You heard my daughter. What are you going to do?'

Jäger continued to frown at Magda's bosom as if mesmerized. She folded her arms defensively across her chest .

'You're fortunate to own three pairs of shoes,' observed Wulzinger.

'Oh, I've plenty of shoes,' Magda replied airily, her pride running ahead of her wits. Shoes in Germany were so scarce, you had to swear that you possessed only two pairs and that one was beyond repair to get a permit to buy another pair, and then their soles would be made of wood.

'That's not the point.' Hocherlin bent the whip almost in two. 'My daughter's shoes have been stolen. I want the thief punished, executed . . .'

'Of course.' Jäger came out of his dream.

'These foreign scum must be taught a lesson, once and for all.'

'Yes, yes, of course. That's an interesting blouse, *Fräulein*.'

'Thank you,' simpered Magda before she registered the tone of his voice.

'Is it new?'

'What's it got to do with my shoes?'

'Where did you get it?'

'What's this got to do with my daughter's shoes?' echoed Hocherlin.

'Well, *Fräulein*?' Jäger ignored the Nazi.

'Our maid made it for me.' Magda was alert now, mouth quivering.

'Where did she find the material?'

'I don't know,' the girl replied, as if that were none of her concern.

'You don't even know where your maid got such fine material. Silk, isn't it?'

'Yes, of course it's silk.'

'I've had enough of your impertinence.' Hocherlin leapt to his feet, slamming his whip down across the desk. 'I'm going to see your superiors right now. This'll be the last time you treat a senior Nazi Party official in this way . . .'

Jäger had not taken his eyes off Magda's face. 'It's actually rather special silk,' he said softly. 'It comes from a parachute. In fact, it comes from a British parachute.'

Magda swallowed nervously.

'You're crazy,' bellowed her father. 'Come, Magda, we're leaving. God, you'll pay for this.'

He grabbed Magda's arm and backed towards the door. He came up against Wulzinger's bulk and stopped.

'What will your maid say when we question her?' demanded Jäger.

'She'll lie. They all do,' shouted Hocherlin.

'I gave her the silk,' confessed Magda, sullen in defeat. 'I didn't know it came from a parachute.'

'How do *you* know it does?' her father asked Jäger.

'I spent six months in France hunting English spies.' Jäger answered him for the first time. 'Where did you get it, *Fräulein*?'

'That's my business,' she spat.

'My colleagues in the Gestapo may think differently.' Jäger reached for the phone. 'I don't believe Party connections will be any help to you from here on.'

Crack. The whip fell across Magda's shoulders. She cried out in pain.

'Tell him, you brazen little cow of hell. Tell him before you drag our whole family into the shit.'

'Papa,' Magda's eyes filled with tears. 'Please!' She fell back cowering in the corner.

'Don't try that with me, you bloody slut. If you involve me and your mother with the Gestapo I'll . . .'

'It was Erich. His father is a commandant at the *KZ* in Dachau.'

'When did he give it you?'

'Just two days ago. I didn't know it came from a parachute. Honestly, I didn't.'

'Maybe I believe you,' said Jäger, reaching for the phone anyway.

'Do you really think we'll be invited to visit Obersalzberg?' enquired Beck, giving voice to his thoughts.

Ilse turned in the passenger seat. 'Why are you so keen to go there?'

'It'd be fascinating to see how the other half lives.'

'In India one man starves for the millions, in Germany millions starve for one man.'

'Ilse. Hush!' He pulled out to overtake a convoy of empty *Wehrmacht* lorries. Soon they would be reaching the outskirts of Munich. The printers had worked through the night to get new ration notices ready by three o'clock. Beck had expressed surprise that Runge had the contract for the city of Munich until Ilse explained this was the Party's way of looking after its own.

'It's only you, and I know I can trust you.' She squeezed his arm. 'Eva will keep her word, if she can.'

The prospect of an invitation to the Berghof had really cheered Beck up. He had still been hugging himself in glee when Ilse had announced that she needed to drive to Munich. Beck offered to accompany her. Spending an afternoon with Ilse was an appealing prospect, especially as she had said nothing about going off by herself this time. He assumed she hadn't had sufficient time to organize a rendezvous with her lover.

He'd thought of telling London about Eva Braun but had decided not to risk it. The desire to share the ups and downs of any operation was inevitable, Cricklemarsh had warned him. *Wait until you have decided on a date for the attempted hit or need guidance. Don't 'send' just to have a chat, never mind how lonely you feel.*

With Ilse around, Beck didn't feel lonely at all.

He recognized the Coal Thief poster and turned towards the city centre along a straight, cobbled street lined with tall apartment houses.

'How long have your friend Eva and the Führer been . . . um . . . together?'

'About ten, eleven years, I suppose. Certainly before the *Autobahn* was built. The Berghof was much smaller then – only a couple of bedrooms – so Eva had to be smuggled in. For appearances' sake, she used to turn up with the secretaries a couple of hours after Hitler.'

'How did they meet?'

'You know what curiosity did to the cat.'

'It's natural.'

'And they say it's women who are nosy.' Ilse pretended to tut in disapproval. 'Evi was working in Hitler's official photographer's shop. The very first time they met, she was up a ladder. She'd just shortened her skirt and was worried if her hem was even. She claims she didn't know who he was.'

'Is she telling the truth, do you think?'

'Well, twenty-year-old girls have other things to think about than politics but the Führer was well known then. There's no doubt she set her cap at him.'

'What sort of woman becomes the mistress of a dictator?' Beck was waved through a police checkpoint.

'A clever one,' replied Ilse tartly, then softened. 'No, that's not true. There's no art or cunning in Evi. Maybe she did fall in love with him, I don't know. I do know that she was so unhappy about him ignoring her in those early years that she twice tried to commit suicide.'

'Were there other women?'

'I don't think so. Does the Führer having a mistress shock you?'

'No, it makes him seem human.'

'Do you *want* our Führer to be human?'

'Yes, if he's to lead other men.'

The engine spluttered, coughed and died before restarting with a bang that had pedestrians diving for cover.

Ilse groaned. 'Not now. We've just got to get back home in daylight. Those mountain roads are a death trap without headlights.'

'Is Eva the love of his life?' The car coughed again.

'My dear Captain Beck, how can you say that? You know that the Führer has but one love and that is for the German people.'

Beck gave her an old-fashioned look. He did not know what to make of her when she spoke like this.

Ilse had assumed her innocent little girl's face. 'I'll tell you another fairy story. Are you ready?'

'Yes.' Beck was already smiling.

'Once upon a time, before Hitler was Chancellor, there was a very beautiful girl called Geli Raubal. Turn left here. She was gay, elegant and only wanted fun.' Ilse sighed. 'She was the daughter of Hitler's half-sister and Hitler fell in love with her. He wanted to control her. She was given a room in his luxurious new apartment and stories emerged about what he did to her. Stories that a young girl like myself could not even begin to understand. It's said that he used the excuse that he was an artist to sketch parts of her anatomy in intricate detail. Hitler was very possessive of her so he was furious when he discovered her either kissing or making love to his chauffeur. I prefer the second version. He wanted her as a caged bird and she needed her freedom. Turn right here, by the *Bierkeller*. It was one September afternoon in 1931 and the *Föhn* wind was blowing, which always frays people's tempers. Hitler was leaving to make a speech in Hamburg and he and Geli had a terrific row. Geli was pleading to him from the balcony to be allowed to study in Vienna. Neighbours later spoke of the despair in her voice but Hitler shouted back up from the street below, "For the last time, no!" Once he had gone, Geli shut herself away in her bedroom. She wrote letters and in the evening she phoned a girlfriend to chat about nothing. Next morning, when she couldn't be roused, the servants broke into her room. They found her in a blue nightdress, lying at the foot of a sofa. Take the second left. She had been shot through the heart. The revolver was on the sofa. Evi told me Geli had wrapped a damp facecloth around the gun to muffle the sound. She was just twenty-three years old and she died . . . right there.'

Ilse pointed to an elegant five-storey apartment block with SS guards outside.

'This is Prinzregentenplatz. Hitler still keeps the apartment on the second floor. There's the balcony Geli pleaded from.'

'What happened?'

'It was hushed up. The . . . death was investigated by a Munich detective called Müller. He's head of the Gestapo now. Müller declared it was suicide. The Bavarian Minister of Justice quickly agreed. Some said Geli's body was badly bruised and that the bridge of her nose was broken. But I don't believe it. I believe the fairy story. I believe poor Geli committed suicide.' Ilse fell quiet, her lips compressed.

Beck wondered whether Ilse was mentally comparing Geli's position with her own. Both of them trapped in unnatural relationships. One thing was certain: Ilse was full of surprises – and not all of them pleasant ones.

They pulled up at a warehouse in Schellingstraße, behind the offices of the Nazi Party newspaper, *Völkischer Beobachter*, to unload the notices. The car refused to start. Warehouse men had to push them until the engine exploded into life with a bang and a cloud of black smoke. It was already getting late and Ilse was growing increasingly worried that the car would break down on the way home, leaving them stranded. She knew of a Party garage nearby in Schwabing.

The mechanics shrugged when Beck explained the problem. Sounded like dirt in the petrol or a blocked fuel line, said one. They wouldn't be able to look at the car that afternoon. Perhaps in the morning, depending how much official Party work they had to do first. Ilse produced two packets of cigarettes from the glove compartment. Very quickly, the VW's rear bonnet was up and a mechanic was dismantling the fuel pump. They should have it fixed in an hour, they estimated. Another packet when the car was going, promised Ilse.

She suggested they fill the time by having coffee in the Englischer Garten. Beck found they were in one of the poorer areas of the city. The narrow cobbled streets were flanked by meagre shops with empty windows, and shabby apartment buildings in need of a coat of paint.

'What really happened to Geli Raubal?' Beck was still fascinated by the story.

'Who knows? There were stories there were pictures of her of a rather delicate nature that went missing. They were brought back by a Nazi priest who was later found in a wood with three bullets in him. It's all a mystery and anyone who was involved ended up dead.'

'So you don't think Hitler killed her?'

'No. She was probably the only woman Hitler really loved. He wept openly at her funeral. He still preserves her room in the Berghof just as it was before her death. But other Nazis could have killed her to head off a scandal.'

'But . . .'

They turned the corner off Adalbertstraße to find SS troops with fixed bayonets blocking their path. A crowd of working-class women had clustered around the soldiers, muttering angrily among themselves. Two covered lorries bearing SS runes stood at the kerbside with their tailgates lowered.

Suddenly, there were shouts and screams and a party of Jews began spilling out of the open door of a crumbling apartment house. An old man with a Homburg hat came first, holding hands with an elderly woman with pure white hair, parted in the middle and pulled back to emphasize her high cheekbones. A couple in their late thirties followed, the woman weeping with a handkerchief pressed to her eyes. Her bespectacled husband, carrying a cardboard suitcase, was trying to reassure her, putting himself between her and the bayonets. Next came a pathetic, shambling, broken old man with a shawl over his shoulders, peering around in utter incomprehension. Then came a pretty, curly-haired girl, balancing a toddler on her hip. She murmured softly to quieten the frightened child, holding it in place with one arm while in her other hand she grasped a torn rush basket from which a teddy bear's smiling face peeped out.

Ilse put her hand to her throat and she turned as pale as porcelain.

Beck thought she was about to faint. The last Jew to emerge from the entrance was a teenage boy with wide-open eyes and slender hands. Only some of them wore the Star of David so Beck guessed that a Jewish family had been discovered sheltering other Jews.

'Into the truck, you scum.' The SS men herded them with their rifle butts towards the first lorry.

'Shame. Shame on you. Leave them alone.' The women shook their fists at the soldiers. 'Leave them alone, you bullies.'

The *Feldwebel* in charge spun around to confront them. 'Shut your mouths, you stinking old harpies. Shut it or you know where you'll end up.'

His threats only goaded the women into greater fury.

'Why aren't you lot at the front? Go and pick on the Russians.'

The *Feldwebel* took a couple of steps towards the women, raising his rifle like a club. But instead of backing off, the women advanced. One spat at him.

'Try it, you fucking little coward, and we'll rip your balls off – if you've got any.'

The *Feldwebel*, realizing he could not intimidate the women, took out his spite on the Jewish girl. He gave her a vicious shove to send her sprawling, the child spilling from her hold onto the cobbles.

'Let them go!' Ilse burst forward. 'Let them go!'

Everyone turned to stare at her. The nearest SS man raised his rifle. Ilse knocked it aside and dashed through the cordon to the child who lay weeping on the cold stones. Beck forgot his limp and sprinted after her. He wrapped his arms around her and lifted her bodily off the ground.

'Let me go. It's wrong. Let me go.'

Beck carried her, kicking and struggling, back to outside the cordon.

The old man slipped as he was forced onto the back of the lorry. He fell, smashing his nose so that blood spurted over his white shirt. The teenager clambered up and offered his hand to help. The mother and her child were last. She passed up her baby and hauled herself up after him. For a moment she stood looking back at freedom. She smiled once towards where Ilse was still fighting to break free from Beck's hold. It was a sad smile, maybe her last smile ever, and it pierced Ilse's heart. She sent up a demoniacal scream and went limp.

The SS men slammed shut the tailgate.

'We'll see what you all have to say when the Gestapo get here,' shouted the *Feldwebel*, climbing into the cab.

'Cowards. Bastards. Bullies. Why aren't you at the front?' The lorries set off at high speed, the jeers and taunts of the women ringing in the ears of the SS men.

Ilse, her hands shaking with impotent fury, recovered enough to push herself away from Beck. Tears streaked her face. They walked in silence.

'What'll happen to them?' he asked.

For a while he thought she was not going to speak. At last, she replied. 'They are taken to be resettled in the east. At least, that's what they tell us. But there are rumours. No one ever comes back. Those left behind never hear from those who have gone. They . . . they disappear. Why did you stop me?'

'You couldn't have done anything.'

'You're as bad as they are.'

'That's unfair.'

It was true that Ilse could not have helped the Jews but Beck had a selfish motive. He could not afford to become involved in anything that might bring him to the attention of the Gestapo. Only he could not tell Ilse that.

'I was expecting more of you,' she murmured sadly.

'What could I have done?'

She stopped and, for the first time since the incident, looked up into his face. 'Do you know that someone once said that all it needed for evil to flourish was for one good man to do nothing? That's all. One man to do nothing. *You* did nothing.'

Jäger frowned up at the message in wrought iron spanning the concentration camp gate. *Arbeit Macht Frei.* Work Makes Free. That was not true. In this hell-hole, only death made free.

'Ever been in here before?' muttered Wulzinger as the guards checked their papers.

'Only once. I couldn't wait to get out.'

'Me, too. The place stinks.'

Long low huts stretched as far as they could see. The stench was unbearable. From a white-painted block on their left came a piercing scream followed by a shot. Human scarecrows in rags watched Jäger and Wulzinger with dead eyes as they were escorted to the commandant's offices.

By 1943 Dachau concentration camp held 30,000 inmates. It had been built ten years earlier to house 5,000 anti-Nazis, communists, gypsies, homosexuals and common criminals. Now unfortunates from all over occupied Europe were huddled together in those endless huts behind the moat and the barbed wire, guarded by *Totenkopfverbände SS*. Dachau, the model for the later extermination camps of Treblinka, Auschwitz and Majdanek, served as a holding camp from where thousands were sent to their deaths elsewhere; the sick and the handicapped to gas chambers near Linz, the Jews to extermination camps further east. In time, almost 32,000 would be officially calculated to have perished in Dachau during the war, including four women members of the British SOE, who were tortured and murdered there. The true number of dead would never be known.

'You want to see my son?' *Unterkommandant* Frick did not invite them to be seated. He was a big man, as tall as Wulzinger, but he had gone to seed. Jäger strolled to the window, looking over a huge yard thronged with gaunt, pinch-faced men. The smoke he'd seen earlier was coming from a crematorium chimney to his left.

'Where is he?' Jäger swung around, unable to look out any more.

'Why do you want to see him?'

'That's between me and the boy.' The lad had no criminal record but, given his father's influence, that did not mean a great deal. Paragraph 42 of the *Reich* Criminal Code said that habitual criminals and offenders against morality could be arrested on suspicion that they *might* go on to commit an offence. Criminality, Nazis believed, was in the blood. A petty thief could be executed for repeated crimes because he *'displayed an inclination towards criminality so deep-rooted that it precluded him ever becoming a useful member of the community.'* Conversely, Nazis themselves could, and did, get away with murder.

'Then I cannot help you.'

Time to deflate this overblown warder. 'I believe he has knowledge of an enemy agent.'

'My son's been brought up a good National Socialist. He would never harbour an enemy of the state.'

'You aren't listening,' said Jäger coldly. 'I didn't say an enemy of the state, I said an enemy agent, probably English.'

'Who is telling these lies? I'll have them horsewhipped.'

'The daughter of the Nazi Party leader at Karlsfeld.'

A couple of minutes later the boy oozed into the room, wearing the uniform of a cadet in the Death's Head SS. Jäger disliked him on sight. He knew his type – the sort who would load the gun and then give it to someone else to pull the trigger.

'Come to see the *KZ, Sturmbannführer*?' enquired the eighteen-year-old.

'I've come to see *you*, Erich. Where did you find the parachute?'

'Parachute? I don't know anything about a parachute.' The boy was a natural liar. He did not colour or hesitate – and he had the effrontery to look Jäger straight in the eye.

Jäger played along. 'You gave Magda Hocherlin a panel of silk two nights ago.'

'She's crazy.' The indignation sounded convincing. 'We fell out and she's just saying that to drop me in it.'

'She's succeeded,' said Jäger, sweetly. 'When did you last see Magda?'

Erich pretended to try to remember. 'Dunno,' he said at last.

'You went for a drive together . . .'

'Did we?'

Wulzinger slammed the boy up against the wall, gripping him by his throat, his feet off the floor. 'You're so sharp, lad, you're going to cut yourself,' he hissed.

'Stop it!' Frick hurried around his desk but Jäger stood in his way, his hand on his holster.

'Violence upsets you, does it? Or is it only seeing your own whelp squirm?'

Wulzinger released the boy who slithered, choking, to the floor.

'You found a parachute somewhere and you thought of all that lovely silk you could barter,' shouted Jäger, contempt rasping in his voice. 'You didn't stop to think that the person who used the parachute might be an enemy agent. You put your own greed before the good of the Fatherland. That's treason, you sack of pus. You have committed treason.'

'I didn't know it was a parachute.' Erich's cockiness had deserted him.

'What did you think it was, then?' shot back Jäger before the boy could catch up with his own admission.

'I don't know. It was partly buried. I thought it was left there by black marketeers.' The excuse appealed to Erich and he rallied, his confidence returning. 'Yeh, black marketeers, that was it.'

'Did you see them bury it?'

'No, but . . .'

'Where's it now?'

'Under my bed. I'll fetch it . . .'

As Erich reached for the door handle there was a *snick*. He looked at his handcuffed wrist in amazement. 'What are you doing? Dad, stop them. They can't come in here and do this. Not in this camp.' He started sniffling.

'This doesn't have to get out, does it?' whispered Frick. 'I'm sure we could do a deal. The SS are not ungrateful to those who do them favours.'

'I know,' replied Jäger. 'I'm wearing the SS uniform, if you hadn't noticed.'

'But you're a copper . . .'

'Exactly. I'm a copper.'

It was a short drive to the field where Erich Frick pointed out where he had dug up the parachute. He had been shooting pigeons when he had come across the disturbed earth where a fox, scrabbling in the loose soil, hunting worms, had exposed a few inches of the parachute.

'Did you find anything else?' demanded Jäger.

'No.' The boy continued to lie.

'The agent's jumpsuit?'

The boy indicated a pile of leaves. He hadn't been able to think of an immediate use for the garment so he had covered it up again. He said he had been meaning to tell the authorities, honestly.

Jäger didn't believe him but it didn't matter now.

The parachute had not been buried long. And anyone setting out for Dachau station from here would pass close to the spot where Hamm had been murdered. He had been right to suspect the policeman had seen something suspicious but wrong to assume that that 'something' concerned black-market gangsters. The single blow that had killed the policeman was part of the training given to agents. It all fell into place.

Air-raid sirens started wailing across the fields around Dachau but Jäger barely heard them. He was lost in thought. If there was a British agent on the loose in southern Germany, what was his mission?

On a hillock a quarter of a mile away, a farmworker walked steadily behind two horses as they turned furrows for potatoes.

The boy, Erich Frick? The Gestapo could have him. He was as good as dead.

Claude Ismay enjoyed being the guest of other services' messes. It meant that no one expected him to put his hand in his pocket. Broadway had its own mess, of course, and Ismay made a point of inviting his guests there once – but only once, just to impress: a technique, it pleased him to think, like casting his bread on the waters and watching a bakery arrive on the incoming tide.

Ismay was especially enjoying his evening at Baker Street because he was savouring the delightful sense of power that came from knowing something Nye would gag for. All evening he had looked forward to the final *coup de théâtre* when he would disclose his secret, a revelation that would be followed by Nye's astonishment and his gratitude – to be redeemed at some point in the future. And, all the time, someone else was paying. Wonderful.

Ismay folded his long body in the armchair and surveyed the surrounding company through the bottom of his third whisky and soda.

'Well?' Nye had grown increasingly impatient at Ismay's hints as the drinks bill mounted.

'Don't be in such a hurry, you silly boy. Good things are worth waiting for.'

'You're not getting another drink.'

'All right, then.' Ismay realized he could not spin out the performance any longer. 'You know Cricklemarsh's man, Lusty?'

'Of course,' snorted Nye, impatiently.

'Did you know he was never vetted for covert overseas service?'

'You're joking! How do you know?' demanded Nye.

'It . . . emerged, shall we say?'

'But we don't just send our agents off without positively vetting them. It takes weeks. Lusty could be a German for all we know.'

'A quarter German,' corrected Ismay, enjoying the shock etched on Nye's face.

'*Quarter* German!' Nye's startled yelp stilled the bar.

'On his mother's side. I'm told he was even a member of the Hitler Youth.'

'But . . . but you can't send someone like that to Germany. You can't be sure where his loyalties lie.'

'Quite.' Ismay almost hugged himself. Nye's reaction was everything he had hoped for.

'How did he slip through the net?'

Ismay took another delicate sip. 'He was only perfunctorily vetted when he joined SOE because he was a serving army officer at the time, although, and this is the killing bit, he was taken on in mistake for someone else.'

'What!'

'Isn't it too delicious?' chortled Ismay. 'They thought they were getting Ronnie Lusty of the Grenadiers, only some twerp of a clerk got it wrong.'

'So?' The implications were sinking in.

Ismay spelled it out. 'So Lusty was given the standard cursory security check when he joined the British army. Since then he's penetrated SOE and now returned to the Third Reich where, for all we know, he's supping at the right hand of Heinrich Himmler.'

It was dark when Beck and Ilse arrived back at the repair garage. The car was still not ready. The rear engine cover was up and the petrol pump lay in pieces on the floor. The mechanics were working instead on a black Mercedes-Benz that hadn't been there an hour ago. Clearly someone had offered a fatter bribe or made greater threats. Ilse had begun remonstrating with the mechanics when the men froze, heads cocked to one side. From far away came the tremulous wail of an air-raid siren. It was joined by one nearer.

'Meier's hunting horns,' exclaimed the foreman.

'Oh, come on. You don't know the bombers are heading this way,' argued Ilse.

'Sorry, lady. I'm not taking the chance – and if I was you I'd get myself into a shelter quick.'

The garage men threw on coats over their overalls and hurried out through the Judas door, not even bothering to lock up. Ilse and Beck were left alone as more sirens started up their morbid wailing.

'What did he mean, "Meier's hunting horns"?' asked Beck.

'Göring once said that if any enemy aircraft ever bombed Germany, we could call him Meier. So air-raid sirens are known as Meier's hunting horns. I'm surprised you didn't know that.' She eyed him curiously.

Shit! Beck turned away to hide his embarrassment. It was always going to be some little thing – something that genuine Germans took for granted, but which was alien to him, that would catch him out. He scrutinized the petrol pump to give himself time to think of a reply.

'I've obviously been away a long time,' he said, with what he hoped was a grin. 'What shall we do now?'

'I couldn't go into a public shelter. The RAF scored a direct hit on one a month ago. More than two hundred people were trapped and suffocated.' Ilse put a hand on his sleeve. The harsh neon lighting made her face appear drawn and hollow. 'I couldn't stand that. I'd go mad.'

'We'll do whatever you want.'

The first searchlights had begun piercing the sky, their beams criss-crossing the night. A single AA gun fired well away to the west.

'I know somewhere. Let's hurry.'

She took his hand and led him through the rapidly emptying streets. Under the rising and falling wail of the sirens, drivers abandoned trams in their tracks, leaving their passengers to fend for themselves. A young boy in a dog-tooth check coat, many times too large for him, jogtrotted past, holding a quivering ginger cat in his arms. A horse-drawn dray careered around the corner, the carrier standing up in the box to whip the matching greys into a gallop over the uneven cobbles.

They hurried on, past entire families clutching suitcases and bundles and peering up fearfully into the clear sky. Beck, managing a compromise between limping and covering the ground, was totally lost. They came to a wide avenue full of monstrous white buildings like temples before they plunged back into deep urban canyons punctuated by roundabouts where abandoned trams huddled.

A heavily pregnant woman waddled down the middle of the tramlines towards them.

'Can we help you?' asked Ilse, as the drone of aeroplane engines floated on the breeze.

'The hospital. I must get to the hospital. It's my time.'

Ilse took her arm. 'Come with us. We'll look after you.'

Very faintly came a sound like someone beating a giant carpet.

The woman shook herself free. 'I must get to hospital for my baby.'

She stumbled away, a crazed look on her face. Ilse took a few steps after her, then stopped as the ground beneath them heaved under the shock of high explosives.

'I'm sorry,' she whispered after the woman. 'I'm sorry.'

She grabbed Beck's hand and led him across a park – where Beck caught sight of the moon's reflection in a small lake – and then along an alley at the side of an old apartment building where she pushed open a brown door. At the rear of a dim foyer another door opened onto a flight of steep stairs. Beck descended into a whitewashed cellar lit by one weak bulb hanging on a cord. Haunted faces regarded them with fixed, incurious eyes.

They found a space in a corner and slumped against the wall.

'Why here?'

Ilse was reluctant to reply. 'I used to live in this block. I feel safe here,' she said at last.

Ilse did not tell him of her father's apartment up on the third floor – or of its present occupant who could not hide in the cellar with the others.

The men and women around them remained silent, listening intently for the whine of each falling bomb, flinching at each thud. Everyone wore their best clothes for fear of losing them in the bombing. Suitcases were piled up against one wall. The explosions were coming ever nearer.

'Now you know what we civilians have to go through.'

Beck had never been comfortable in enclosed spaces either. Maybe Ilse sensed his fear, for she squeezed his hand. He concentrated his attention on a printed notice on the wall and fought down the panic rising inside him.

In the event of being buried, knock on walls with a hard object or scratch with fingernails. Do not shout: you will use up oxygen. Make sure you have a chisel in the cellar, as well as rags and water to make a moist mask to filter out dirt and dust.

A stick of bombs fell in the adjoining street, making the walls leap and ripple. As the dust trickled from the ceiling someone began sobbing. The anti-aircraft guns kept firing unceasingly. The light bulb swung madly, sending distorted images of hell looming around the cellar.

Ilse was finding it increasingly hard to breathe. The pressure from a nearby explosion pressed on her eardrums. Then the air was sucked out of her mouth. *Pressure. Suction. Pressure. Suction.* She heard a soft rustle like a flock of doves which, she knew, was a bundle of stick bombs falling apart. Every bomb they dropped had its own signature and Ilse recognized them all. A short sharp explosion meant a twelve-kilogramme incendiary bomb, capable of spreading fire eighty metres in all directions. A noise like a bucket of water splashing was a fourteen-kilogramme firebomb that dispersed liquid rubber and benzine around for fifty metres. Fire canisters sounded like wet sacks landing. A definitive crack chilled the heart. It meant a 112-kilogramme firebomb that could cover walls of buildings with thousands of flaming cow-pats of benzol and rubber. And then there were the explosive bombs and the mines that tore out doors and windows to provide additional oxygen inside buildings to feed the flames.

Oh, yes, Ilse knew all the sounds of the RAF bombs.

Beck put his arm around her and Ilse rested her head on his shoulder. After a minute she slid her hand across his chest and nuzzled into his neck. He kissed the top of her head and she mewed with pleasure. Intimacy in the face of death.

Time lost its meaning. The cellar became hotter and hotter. Someone should have gone to check if a firebomb had fallen on their building – but everyone was too scared to move. When the light went out, Ilse's hand became a claw grasping at Beck's flesh.

'Shhussh. Gently.' He stroked her hair.

It seemed the most normal thing in the world for Ilse to turn her head, her nose brushing his cheek. From there it was natural for her lips to find the corner of Beck's mouth and then his own lips. In the blackness, she held his face in her two trembling hands as if it was a chalice and drank from his lips with a desperate thirst that unnerved him.

She drew back and began weeping, her body juddering in spasms. Beck gathered her closer to him. She crept inside the folds of his greatcoat and made small, frightened sounds like some young animal whimpering for its mother.

'Are we going to die?' she whispered.

'Of course not,' Beck whispered back.

She gave a defiant little sniff. 'There's so much to live for. So much I want to do.'

They clung together in the blackness that grew denser and hotter until she felt she could knead it into the shapes of demons.

The light came back on. They gasped with relief when there came a clatter and an almighty rumble. The air rang. The floor heaved beneath them, walls buckling. Dust swirled thickly around the cellar as if the house was about to collapse on top of them. Ilse was panting in furious, shallow bursts.

Beck bitterly remembered those newspaper articles he'd read back in London about the bravery of the RAF bomber crews. They alone were taking the war to the Germans. He had never expected to be on the receiving end of it.

The odour of faeces filled the cellar. Through the tumult, they heard someone frantically tapping from the basement next door. Beck grabbed a metal bar and tapped back.

'Somebody must be trapped there,' exclaimed Ilse.

Beck began to attack the soft mortar, scraping and hacking away. After a moment, others joined in. Overhead the bombs continued falling but now the inhabitants of the cellar had something to do. They were passive sufferers no longer. At first one brick came loose, then another. A bleeding hand appeared from the other side and pulled the next one free. Soon the hole was big enough for a man, in his sixties, to climb through. He was wearing a dinner suit, his white hair standing up as if he had received an electric shock. He pulled an enormous leather suitcase after him. He faced the people in the cellar and bowed formally. The suitcase fell open to reveal a straw hat and a jar of marmalade. The man slowly and deliberately picked them up, fastened the case, bowed again and slid down against a wall.

The sense of unreality increased when the light went out again. Ilse didn't know if she had dreamed the elderly man or if she was going mad. She closed her eyes and rested her head once more on Beck's shoulder. Again time lost its meaning, the seconds being measured by the pressure and suction of the falling bombs against the endless barrage of anti-aircraft guns.

Ilse supposed she must have dozed off because she gradually realized that the din had eased. The bombs had ceased falling and the guns seemed to be much further away.

'Come.' She was desperate to get out of that suffocating tomb. Outside there was a sky, freedom. Whatever was out there could not be worse than it was in here.

Ilse was wrong.

With the dawn came the firestorm. Apart from the building next door, their street had escaped serious damage, but all around raged a fire mountain like Vesuvius. Every window, every door, every tree, everything that could burn was blazing. The flames were incredible in their ferocity and the variety of their hues – blood red, orange, crimson, blue, even white. Helpless firemen, with dry hoses, slumped exhausted beside water dribbling from the cracked mains. Dazed survivors staggered through the sulphur-yellow smoke. An ambulance clattered past, its bell ringing, swerving around the piles of rubble and debris. There was the stench of burned flesh, heavy acrid smoke, hot steam. A man dashed out of a burning shop, his clothes and hair on fire. As Beck and Ilse watched, he plunged into the lake in the park in a cloud of steam. As he climbed out, the phosphorus coating his back ignited again. With a scream from hell, he blundered blindly back into the burning building.

Ilse and Beck looked down on the bodies of foreign workers, trapped under massive slabs of concrete in a marshalling yard. The dead had black faces from the concussion. One screaming man had been almost cut in two by a sheet of metal. A *Wehrmacht* officer was approaching him from behind, a drawn pistol in his hand. Beck hurried Ilse away but worse was to come. At the corner, not one hundred metres from where they had last seen her, was the charred corpse of the hysterical mother. Alongside, on the pavement, still joined to her, lay the blackened remains of her tiny newborn baby.

Ilse sank to her knees and wept as she had not believed she could ever weep. She wept for the baby and its mother. She wept for the dead, the burned, the mutilated. She wept for Germany and its people

– and she wept for herself. When she had wept until she had no more tears to shed, Beck helped her up but her legs gave way and she flopped like a rag doll. Beck half carried, half supported her back to the murk of the cellar where she fell asleep instantly.

12

Friday, 26 March

Ilse slept for almost three hours, a sleep of nervous exhaustion and relief. She woke to find her head on Beck's lap. She opened one eye and watched his chest slowly rising and falling. He had covered her with his greatcoat to keep her warm, its collar reaching over her head. Half asleep, she went to nuzzle back down before realizing she was burrowing into his groin. She'd thought about Christian's member before – and now she was touching it through his clothing. She wondered what it was like. What was he like as a lover?

She moved her hand slightly so that it rested on the inside of his left thigh. Snores and grunts filled the cellar. No one could see what she was doing under his greatcoat.

There were those who said the proximity of death created a yearning for sex, a subconscious imperative to spawn before extinction. Others said that if you were going to die tomorrow, you should make bloody well sure you had fun today. Ilse didn't analyse her current actions. She just felt mischievous and sexy. Under the greatcoat, she began to brush Beck's trousers with the fingertips of her left hand. She found a softness. She wasn't sure. She slid her forefinger down and something gave, something soft and round. She stroked it once, twice and started slowly on her return journey upwards. There it was, curling over to the right. She traced the outline of the slumbering cock until it became lost in the trouser folds. She repeated the motion and it stirred under her touch. Ilse extended the lengths of her finger strokes and it grew with her. Daringly, she lifted a fold of constricting material to allow it to spring out to its full length. Her fingertips whispered up its length, seeing how long she could make the journey last. Finally she reached the tip. Snug in her own hidden world, Ilse stroked Beck's long, hard member. Now she wanted to feel the texture of its skin, to enjoy its heat. Cradle it in her hand and rub it against her cheek.

She was toying with the first fly button when she looked up to find Beck's eyes had opened. For a second Ilse froze. Then she resumed her ministrations.

'I was just saying "Good morning",' she whispered.

Alongside them, someone coughed loudly, clearing the dust of the night from their throat. Soon others were struggling to their feet. The moment was lost.

Outside, the firestorm had at last subsided. A pall of grey and black smoke lay over the western part of Munich where whole rows of houses had been turned into smouldering skeletons. A tram lay obscenely on its side next to a bomb crater. On a charred doorpost, a woman was writing a message in chalk. *'We're alive.'*

To be alive was everything. *Überleben* – survival was all.

Ilse and Beck walked close together, their sleeves brushing, but they did not hold hands. Out in the daylight, Ilse felt embarrassed and ashamed of her behaviour. At the same time, the unwanted interruption had left her irritable – as though she had unfinished business.

Beck said nothing.

The car was still not ready. There was no sign of the foreman so Ilse bullied the mechanics to abandon the Mercedes-Benz and begin work on their car instead. As the older man suspected, there was dirt in the carburettor. He'd said that at the start; he'd known it wasn't the fuel pump. In an hour he had stripped and rebuilt the carburettor and the fuel pump, had made sure that the fuel line was clean and, for good measure, had checked the points and plugs. Ilse paid him in cigarettes and by ten o'clock they set off, glad to be leaving the city's smouldering ruins. They stopped at the rest area at Chiemsee, conscious that they had not eaten or drunk since the previous evening. Ilse had a shock when she inspected herself in her compact mirror. Her eyes were bloodshot from smoke and lack of sleep. There was a large black mark under her left eye and a greasy smudge on her forehead.

'Why didn't you tell me I looked such a mess?'

'I hadn't noticed,' Beck replied truthfully.

'And look at you.' Ilse tutted. 'Stand still a moment.'

She produced a plain white handkerchief, dampened it with her tongue and dabbed at a mark on his cheek. She added more spittle and rubbed harder. He yelped.

Ilse giggled. 'Oh, I'm sorry. It's a bruise. Just stand still and don't be a baby. There's something on your forehead, too. There, that's better.'

Ilse stood in front of him and brushed his shoulders. She would have readily given herself to him there and then, finished what she had begun in the cellar. If only he'd touched her, kissed her, just made the first move, she'd travel the rest of the distance. But he merely smiled pleasantly, avoiding her eye. Just as they were about to enter the rest house itself, Ilse threw her arms around him and pressed her face to his chest.

'Thanks for looking after me last night.'

'I thought *you* looked after *me*.' He slipped his arm through hers before she knew it, and guided her up the steps.

Alone in the lavatory, reapplying her make-up, Ilse told herself that he was being honourable. Other men would have taken advantage of her overwrought state. They would have taken her, as she had wanted – and later she would have felt used and guilty.

How decent he was being. *Damn him!*

She did not know that Beck too was suffering a conflict of emotions. He had known exactly what Ilse was offering, but he knew he had to decline. It did not matter so much that Ilse was married – a brute like Runge deserved to be cuckolded. Countless men and women in wartime enjoyed the amorality of opportunity. But ultimately he had a job to do. Killing Hitler had to come first, last and always. But – Christ, it had been so tempting with their sexual chemistry charging the very air around them.

Back at the Red Ox they found an letter from Eva Braun.

'I told you she'd be as good as her word,' said Ilse. 'She's invited us both to tea.'

'When?'

'Today.' The implications sank in. 'This afternoon! We can't possibly go today. Look at the state of us. I need a bath and I must wash my hair. You need to get your uniform cleaned. Your boots are filthy. Vishnia! Vishnia, where are you?'

One step nearer Hitler, thought Beck as a storm of domestic activity broke around him.

Major Charles L. Donovan broke the first rule governing a rendezvous with another agent by turning up early. He broke the second rule by failing to make absolutely sure that he was not being followed by the Swiss *Fremdenpolizei*, and he made his third mistake by taking a table right in the middle of the old brown café, where his view of the door was also obscured.

Chuck Donovan was too open and too good-natured to be an intelligence officer. Until four months ago he had been a lead navigator in the 41st Combat Wing, flying B17 Fortresses out of Molesworth, Cambridgeshire. Then a Focke-Wulf Fw190 had taken off the elevator and most of the tail of his plane *Good Girl Ginnie* over the chemical plant at Schwenningen. The pilot had held her together until they'd crossed the Bodensee into Switzerland and then the crew had jumped. Donovan had been interned for three months before the OSS in Berne had succeeded in press-ganging him on the strength of his degree in physics and a rudimentary knowledge of German.

Anton Antonescu was much more careful. He had changed trams twice on the way to the *Treff*, spent ten minutes window-shopping along a largely deserted street and then doubled back to hail a taxi to take him to the Berne café. He knew for sure he had not been followed. Having been thorough and correct in his approach, he swore softly when he saw Donovan occupying such a prominent position. It crossed his mind to blank him and demand to fix another meeting but time was not on his side. He needed to know how the OSS was going to react to his offer to assassinate Hitler.

Antonescu went through the motions of being surprised to encounter the American. Donovan rose to shake his hand. He liked Antonescu: the man looked you in the eye. He had perfectly manicured nails. *A fastidious man*, thought Donovan. Antonescu lowered himself in the wicker-back chair and hoisted his trousers a good foot, to reveal black silk socks. They exchanged pleasantries in English about the unseasonably mild weather until Antonescu's coffee and cake arrived. Then the Romanian bent forward.

'I have to return to Bucharest tonight. Have your people given any further thought to my proposal?'

'Absolutely.' Donovan gave an upbeat smile as he remembered his briefing. *Keep the guy sweet but keep him at arm's length.* 'This went all the way back to London. We ran it up the flag pole and, boy, oh boy, did people salute.'

Antonescu leaned forward, turning a mother-of-pearl cuff link. 'Yes?'

'We like the idea – like it very much. But, for the moment, we're putting it on the back burner.' Donovan never found it easy to say no.

Antonescu frowned. 'I'm sorry. I don't understand this "back burner".'

'They like the idea, sure, but they want to hold off for a while.'

'I see.' The Romanian's mobile face collapsed into a lugubrious mask of disappointment. 'So my efforts have been for nothing. All my planning . . . You can't "put it on the back burner", as you say. Hitler is not someone you can get near every day. There is a trade and oil mission visiting Germany within the next fortnight. That would have been—'

'We understand all that and we're very grateful that you contacted us.'

'But you do not want to help me. Maybe I'll go to the British instead.' He nodded to himself, as if he'd just thought of that. Antonescu lifted his cup, little finger crooked at a right angle. 'Yes, I'll try the British.'

'Gee, no.'

Antonescu continued to appear hurt. 'Maybe I'll go ahead and do it myself. You'll be grateful when Hitler is dead, back burner or not.'

Donovan sucked his teeth. 'Look, buddy, please don't take this badly. We love the idea and we're pleased you came to us but . . . but the time just isn't right.'

'What do you mean, the time isn't right?'

'Just between you and me, okay? This must go no further. There's no point in going to the Limeys. They already have an operation under way.'

'You don't say!' Antonescu's eyes opened wide in astonishment.

Gratified by the response, Donovan hurried on. 'That's why we're asking you to wait for a while. Just so we can see if the Brits pull it off.'

'Do the British really think they can get closer to Hitler than I can?' Antonescu's tone implied disbelief.

'They have a man there already.' Donovan feared he might have said too much. 'For Pete's sake, this is between us, all right? Not a word, okay?'

The Romanian whistled soundlessly. 'Now I understand. I am glad you told me. I can see that you are right.'

'Good,' said Donovan, relieved that the meeting had gone smoothly. 'We'd like you to keep in touch. I've got five hundred dollars for you – a retainer, if you like.'

'That is kind of you,' said Antonescu, gravely. 'Of course, I will keep in touch.'

Back in his OSS office, Donovan reported that Antonescu had agreed to put his assassination attempt on hold. Donovan's information was encoded and sent to London within the hour. He thought it better not to mention that he had been forced to reveal the British operation.

Runge was beside himself with jealousy.

'How come Beck receives an invitation and I don't?'

'You weren't here when she called,' replied Ilse simply, sitting in front of the dressing-table mirror in her petticoat. She hated him to see her in any state of undress but Runge insisted on talking and she did not have time for a scene.

'I'm an Old Fighter. I deserve to see the Führer more than that man does.'

'We're not going to visit the Führer. We're just having tea with Eva. If you'd been here at the time, no doubt you'd have been invited too.' Actually, she doubted that very much. Eva knew what Ilse thought of her husband.

But Runge was spoiling for a fight. 'It's not enough that my wife spends the night in Munich with Captain Beck, now she goes off to tea parties with him.'

'Don't be ridiculous.' Ilse hurried to finish powdering her face so she could pull on a dress. 'Do you think we'd *choose* to stay in Munich during an air raid? We were almost killed. God, you're pathetic.'

As Runge raised his fist, Ilse turned to face him.

'Go on. Hit me,' she taunted. 'Go on. Let Hitler know that his Old Fighters are really cowards who pick on women.'

Runge turned and stormed out, slamming the door behind him. In the mirror Ilse watched him go, a look of pure hatred contorting her features.

'Oh, Annie.' Penelope halted in the corridor, her arms full of buff folders. 'I was hoping I'd catch you.'

'Late night, then?' Even under the weak bulb, Penelope's face looked drawn under her make-up. Annie wondered if she herself had ever looked this terrible.

'It was worth it.' Penelope gave a small smile. 'I met this New Zealander. We're going out tonight. He's got a stack of pals and they're all very presentable.'

'I'm sure they are.'

The women moved to one side to let a documents trolley pass.

'I can't tempt you, then? All right. It's up to you. Now, what was I going to tell you? Oh, yes. You asked what paperwork we had on your op.' Penelope took a breath. 'Well, we don't.'

'What!'

'We don't have any. There isn't any.'

'But there must be. God! Even a request for paper clips has to be done in triplicate.' It crossed Annie's mind, uncharitably, that Penny hadn't really bothered to look.

'Annie, I would know. Believe me.'

'Yes, of course, I'm sorry. But you must admit, it's very odd.'

Penny's headache didn't allow her to admit anything that needed further thought.

'Well, Hans?' Admiral Wilhelm Franz Canaris, the head of the *Abwehr*, German Military Intelligence, looked up from behind his large old-fashioned desk.

His friend and chief assistant Hans Oster closed the door behind him and looked meaningfully around the dark-panelled room on the fifth floor of the Tirpitz Ufer.

'I checked for listening devices this morning,' said Canaris grimly. 'I don't trust Himmler any more than you do.'

Oster still spoke in little more than a whisper. 'We have another intercept from OSS Berne – on agent Vernon.'

'Our would-be assassin?' Alarm crossed Canaris's face. 'I trust you—'

'Of course. All copies to me, marked "Eyes Only". No one else has seen it except the cypher clerk. He can be trusted.'

'Good. So what are our American friends telling us today?'

'They want Vernon to hold fire.' Oster held out the decoded signal. *As ordered, Vernon instructed not to proceed until further notice. He is willing to await events.*

Canaris read the message through again. 'Stranger and stranger.' He frowned.

'I wish we could read London's side of this radio traffic.'

'I don't think we need to, do we? Berne is telling us all we need to know.' Canaris steepled his fingers under his chin. 'Sit down, Hans and we'll run through it together.'

'Okay. Two days ago, OSS Berne signalled London with a proposal to assassinate the Führer. An agent, code name Vernon, claimed that he'd be able to get close to Hitler as one of a party of visiting Romanian industrialists.' Oster counted off the points. 'We know such a meeting is scheduled to take place at the Berghof in around ten days. We've identified Vernon as Anton Antonescu, a Romanian adventurer who does indeed have links with the Ploesti oilfields. What we don't know is whether the offer's genuine or a piece of coat-trailing either by the Swiss or our friends in the SD.'

'But that doesn't matter now, does it?' argued Canaris. 'What's important is that London has instructed Vernon to wait. That can mean only one thing – that they are mounting another attempt. And it must be due very soon. London doesn't want this Romanian amateur doing anything that might jeopardize their own operation.'

'They must be feeling pretty certain they'll succeed,' murmured Oster.

'The Führer's certainly more accessible now he's at the Berghof. The last thing the British would want is for something to happen that would make it more difficult to get near him.'

The two men looked at each other in silence.

'That is the only copy of the signal,' said Oster. 'I've checked the signal log and the cypher clerk's schedules.'

'Good.' Canaris walked stiffly to the small stove burning in a corner. The paper flamed blue briefly. Then he poked at the ashes until there was nothing left.

Beck settled into the rear seat of the Mercedes-Benz, inhaling the rich smells of luxury. He ran his hand along the smooth worked leather and eyed the shining walnut veneer, the deep carpets, the curtains clipped back at the windows.

Ilse picked a thread of cotton off his shoulder and thought how handsome he was. Since last night, she was conscious that she had begun to regard him differently. She was appraising him now as a potential lover, rather than just as a wounded visitor. With a fingertip, she gently touched the crescent-shaped scar high on his forehead.

'Does that hurt?'

'Sometimes, when I'm very tired.'

'How did it happen?'

The SS driver was partitioned off in the front but Beck would bet a *Pfennig* to ten *Reichsmark* that he was listening to their conversation.

'A war wound.'

Ilse touched it again. His eyes had more flecks of green in the hazel than she'd previously noticed. She was glad he wasn't blond and cold, like so many Germans. She could not have stood him looking like a Nazi propaganda poster. He was kind, gentle, considerate, honourable. An honest man. Everything her swine of a husband was not.

The *SS Leibstandarte Adolf Hitler* guards on the bridge demanded to see their passes, identity papers and residence permits. They were taking no chances, noted Beck who was also made to hand over his pistol. Immediately beyond, the road began to climb between trees. Beck, committing every detail to memory, was surprised at the steepness of the hill. Soon they came to another sentry box and a side road leading up to a dark wooden house.

'That's *Reichsminister* Speer's,' announced Ilse.

A few hundred yards further on, the ground fell away to the left and Beck glimpsed a long, low tiled building.

'The model farm where Minister Bormann rears prize *Haflinger* mountain horses,' said Ilse, who from her formal tone obviously also suspected they could be overheard. 'The Berghof is straight up this road ahead.'

But to Ilse's surprise, they swung off on the right-hand fork before the reached a roadblock marking the perimeter of the inner security zone.

Ilse slid open the glass panel to speak to the driver. 'This isn't the way.'

'No. *Fräulein* Braun is expecting you at the Kehlsteinhaus,' he replied, coldly.

'What's that?' enquired Beck.

'It was built just before the war. I've never been up there.'

They were skirting the inner zone. Sentries, in long coats with fur collars, patrolled alongside a high, chain link fence topped by barbed wire. They drove past the Platterhof hotel and then the three-storey SS barracks topped with swastika flags.

'*Fräulein* Braun requests that you close the curtains for the remainder of the journey,' instructed the driver. 'She wants the view to be a surprise for you.'

Beck drew the dove-grey curtains. He sensed they were climbing a winding road but only once did they turn a hairpin bend, tipping Ilse against him. After ten minutes, it grew very dark. Beck expected them to re-emerge into daylight but instead the car slowed and halted. The door was flung open and they stepped out to find themselves at the far end of a long, wide tunnel bored into the heart of the mountain. Recovering their surprise, Beck and Ilse entered an ornate lift of polished brass and bronze with Venetian mirrors and plush green leather seats. It began to rise.

Eva Braun was waiting at the top, smiling in welcome.

'Forgive the melodrama but the weather's so perfect I wanted you to appreciate the view from here at its best.' She hooked her arm in Ilse's and led them out onto a snow-covered terrace.

The panorama took Beck's breath away.

They were perched on a rocky shoulder 1,800 metres high. Around lay the splendours of Berchtesgadener Land with its scoured mountains and lush alpine pasture. In the distance, the cold, blue waters of the Königssee reflected the stark, snowed-capped peaks of the Watzmann and the Hochkalter. Directly behind them soared the Hoher Brett and the Höhe Goll. Across the broad valley stood the bleak mass of the Untersberg. Looking down, they could make out small, rounded hills, each with its own scattering of farms and settlements. The countless meadows were separated by darker swathes of pine. To the right, in the distance, lay the archbishop's castle of Salzburg, a white jewel amid the blue hills of Austria.

As the sunset light cast its long shadows, Beck had the impression he was floating in space above a wild and eerie fairy story.

Eva was pleased by their exclamations of delight. Stasi and Negus picked up on her pleasure and began barking in unison.

'The German people built this place for the chief's fiftieth birthday. I love it here. It's my favourite place in the whole world.'

'It's really magnificent.' Ilse's breath formed a cloud in the cold air.

'A French diplomat who came here called it the Eagle's Nest.'

'A perfect description,' agreed Beck.

'They keep the access road open all year so I can come up here. Sadly, Bormann also likes it so we have to sort of take it in turns.'

'Does the Führer himself ever come here?' enquired Beck.

'Oh, yes. He likes the peace and quiet. Sometimes it's just the two of us, other times he comes up here with Schaub or one of his adjutants. They sit around and talk about old times.'

An SS guard took their coats in the stone hallway. Two more guards sprang to attention from a cupboard-like duty room as they descended into a large room lined with Scots pine and elm. The afternoon sun streamed in through five windows set in the thick walls. Armchairs had been placed around a massive oval table and a log fire roared in the red-marble fireplace.

'The road up to here was carved out of solid rock and the house itself finished in just thirteen months. The tunnel under the mountain is 124 metres long – exactly the same length as the lift shaft – and the road is 4.2 kilometres.' Eva threw out the figures without any comprehension of the magnitude of the builders' achievement. 'Electricity comes up from Berchtesgaden but in case of a power failure, we've a U-boat engine to provide our own. The carpet is a present from the Japanese emperor Hirohito. It weighs five hundred kilogrammes. Ah, now here is my little tea room.'

They followed Eva into a smaller room with views towards the Königssee. Another fire in the hearth reflected off the wood-clad walls and ceiling. Outside, the mountain dropped vertically away to where, far below, Beck made out a meadow where smoke was curling from the chimney of a low farm building.

'That's the Scharitzalm,' said Eva, following his gaze. 'We often used to walk down there from the Berghof before the war.'

'Do you still do much walking?'

He noticed two guards from an alpine regiment were making their way up a steep path alongside the fence that stretched across an almost sheer rock face.

'We used to. The chief loves walking. Sometimes we'd walk as far as Königssee but then it got difficult because people used to want to welcome him, or even touch him. In the end they used to almost mob him. Now, would you like chocolate, coffee or tea?'

'Chocolate, please,' Ilse decided for them.

Beck's missing fingers had started throbbing as they had done on the flight out. He had removed his gloves and was rubbing his knuckles before he noticed that Eva Braun was staring at him.

'Forgive me. My fingers hurt even though—'

'But your glove . . .?'

'Two of its fingers are stuffed.'

They sat in easy chairs while their hostess perched on a brick ledge next to the fireplace and played with the dogs. It was all very informal until an SS guard in black trousers and white shirt arrived with the chocolate and an array of cakes.

Eva motioned towards the cake stand. 'Please help yourselves. I'm sorry they're not as nice as the ones you make, Ilse. One day, you must bake your special *Linzertorte* for us – it's the chief's favourite. He says it's better than any he's had in Linz. Now tuck in, but excuse me for not joining you.'

'I know, you're on another diet,' laughed Ilse.

The two women began chatting about fashions and the closure of the fashion magazine *die neue linie.* Eva admitted she had protested about it to Hitler but she couldn't complain too much, considering the paper shortage. She had made the Führer stop stupid Party officials banning Munich people from going skiing.

'How is the Führer?' Beck took the opportunity to ask.

'Very tired now. He needs a long rest away from those stupid generals. He must look after himself.'

'He is the father of our country,' said Beck reverentially.

'If he's the father of Germany then I must be the mother.' Eva clapped her hands delightedly at the notion.

'*Mutti* Evi,' laughed Ilse.

'A fortune-teller once told me that one day the world would talk about me and my great love.' Eva sighed. 'But what's the point if it has to be kept secret . . .'

She noticed Beck squinting up at a photograph on the wall. It showed the British Prime Minister Chamberlain sitting on a long leather sofa with Daladier of France and Mussolini of Italy.

'That was taken in the living room of the chief's Munich apartment. It's just as well that sofa can't talk.' Eva giggled.

Beck found himself increasingly drawn to the woman's spontaneous gaiety but at the same time marvelling that someone as ordinary as Eva Braun could become mistress of the Führer. He had the impression that she didn't understand or even worry too much about the war. She appeared vacuous, yet driven, and clearly believed implicitly in the genius of Hitler.

'It's important the Führer builds up his strength,' said Beck. 'I heard he likes a morning walk.'

Eva looked surprised. 'No, the Führer's not a morning person at all. He works till late at night and rests through the morning. We can't even take a bath in the Berghof before eleven o'clock in case the sound of running water disturbs him.'

'I'm sure I read somewhere how the Führer regularly walked to the Mooslangerkopf tea house,' he persisted. 'I must have got it wrong.'

Ilse was regarding him curiously.

'That used to be the chief's favourite walk,' conceded Eva slowly. 'Every afternoon about three or four o'clock we'd troop down there for tea and cakes but never in the morning, and we haven't gone there once since the war began.'

'You're looking very thoughtful.' Marjorie Gilbert cocked an eyebrow at her husband.

'I've just had an extraordinary conversation with Rupert Nye. He came to me with the amazing story that Lusty is actually one-quarter German. Apparently he bypassed Five's security checks because he was already in SOE. Nye was trying to suggest that Lusty was really a double agent using Operation Nightshade as a way of returning to the Fatherland where he's now personally debriefing Himmler.'

'Surely not!'

They were walking briskly around the outer path in Regent's Park where secretaries, wrapped up against the cold, were feeding ducks with their sandwiches.

'It's true Five didn't vet him for overseas service but I can't believe he's a double agent. Still, it shows the depth of Nye's ambition if he's prepared to stab Purefoy in the back like that.'

'Does that change things?'

'I don't know. I chewed out Purefoy – just to keep him even more on edge.' He chuckled.

'Why haven't the Gestapo picked up Lusty by now?'

Gilbert pursed his lips. 'It appears that Cricklemarsh put together a better operation than we gave him credit for.'

'When did you last hear from this Lusty?'

'Three days ago. Just a straightforward message to say he had arrived safely. Nothing since.'

Marjorie grasped his arm. 'This operation must fail. Whatever happens it must fail.'

Gilbert was taken aback by his wife's fervour. 'Yes, of course, dear.'

'There's no "of course" about it. It's your plan, your idea. You must have the courage to see it through, whatever it takes. You've let them walk over you before.' Gilbert winced under the familiar whiplash of her contempt. 'This is your moment. Nothing must stop you. Nothing.'

'You're right, Marjorie,' he said stoutly.

Of course, she was right. She knew she was. She also knew that, ultimately, he was a mouse. Which was why she had taken to meeting him during his working day to keep abreast of the operation and to strengthen his resolve. There was no going back now.

'Can't you warn the Gestapo?'

'What!'

'Tell the Germans about Lusty. I'm sure there are ways.'

There were but he hadn't considered it because he hadn't thought it would ever be necessary. He'd expected Lusty to be caught quickly. Irrationally, part of him rebelled at the idea of betraying a British agent to the Germans. His wife was right: he lacked the killer instinct. He'd been perfectly willing to let Lusty be captured, tortured, executed. But the idea of actually handing him over to the Nazis – he found that distasteful.

'There're ways all right, through Lisbon or Stockholm, but there's not enough time now and it's too risky,' he said.

Marjorie glowered at him, uncertain if he was telling the truth or just being weak.

'How's it risky?'

'I'd have to use a go-between. If it ever got back . . .' His blood ran cold. 'And there really is no time. This sort of thing takes ages to set up.'

'We'll see,' said Majorie firmly.

Marjorie saw things differently. Her husband had sabotaged this operation. So what! It served those people in Baker Street right. It was nothing to how he had been betrayed and belittled by them. Marjorie was playing for altogether different stakes. Her over-vaulting ambition made her willing to ignore the risks and dangers. Her husband did not know just how much she wanted him to get the D-G's job – and the knighthood that accompanied it. *Lady Gilbert.* She liked the sound of the title; relished it in her head, where she could hear head waiters and hotel managers use it in obsequious deference.

She knew her husband was weak. He would try to back out – not that she would let him. She thought of him as a horse without stamina or determination, always ready to shy at the big jump. She was his rider. She would push him on over that one last fence – then he would be in the home straight.

Standartenführer Esser fidgeted nervously, adjusting his tie in the ante-room's gilt mirror while Jäger stood by the adjutant's desk, smoking another cheroot and wondering morosely why he was here in Berlin when he should have been out and about on the Munich streets.

'This is a great honour for us, for you,' fluted Esser.

'Indeed.' Whatever Jäger's private misgivings about wasting an entire day to hand over the parachute and the jumpsuit in person, he was not about to articulate them in Gestapo headquarters in Prinz-Albrecht-Straße. Up on this floor, the rooms were elegantly decorated and exquisitely furnished; but in the basement were the interrogation cells and torture chambers. Jäger knew when to button his lip.

'The *Reichsminister* will see you now.'

Esser pumped himself up and virtually trotted through the double doors. Jäger stubbed out his cheroot and followed in his wake. He caught the eye of the adjutant, as cold as that of a dead fish.

'Heil Hitler.'

'Heil Hitler.'

A giant of a man stood next to the parachute, which was laid out on a side table.

'So we have you to thank for this breakthrough. Let me congratulate you on good work, *Standartenführer.*'

'Thank you,' beamed Esser.

Prick, Jäger muttered silently behind him as he took in *SS Obergruppenführer* Ernst Kaltenbrunner. God, he was big! Six feet seven, if he was an inch, with a duelling scar down one cheek and a coarse Austrian accent.

And, after Himmler, the man in charge of the whole of *Reich* security, including the Gestapo, SD and police.

'How did you discover it?'

'Um . . . My subordinate noticed that a local girl was wearing a blouse made out of parachute silk . . .'

He ran out of words. Kaltenbrunner snorted. He held a panel of silk up to the window before turning to confront Jäger with a half smile. 'There's a former colleague of yours here who speaks very highly of you, *Sturmbannführer*. Remember Müller?'

'Of course,' said Jäger, starting slightly.

Kaltenbrunner sat down at his desk, his eyes still fixed on Jäger. 'You are convinced this English spy killed the copper.'

'It is too much of a coincidence . . .'

Kaltenbrunner nodded slowly in agreement. 'He was killed last Saturday, six days ago. The spy could be anywhere by now. Do we know if he was alone? Was he met?'

'At the moment there's nothing to suggest there's more than one man, *Obergruppenführer*. And I don't think he was met. It looks as if he was making his way to the railway station in Dachau. We have to assume there was something about him that aroused Hamm's suspicion.'

'You've questioned every possible witness?'

'I requested an early-morning trawl of the station regulars from Dachau yesterday morning, before we'd even found the parachute. It didn't throw up any new sightings . . .' Which was not surprising since Jäger knew Greim had detailed just two reluctant men for the early-morning duty.

'Why has it taken you so long to realize the killer was a spy?'

Jäger did not think it had taken particularly long but he did not have a chance to answer.

'*Sturmbannführer* Jäger believed the murder was the work of black marketeers,' replied Esser, quickly.

Jäger could not resist shooting him a sardonic glance. 'No enemy agent has ever successfully dropped into the Reich before,' he pointed out.

'Why would the spy have been dropped near Munich, do you think?' There was a silence. '*Standartenführer* Esser?'

'Oh . . . um . . . Jäger has a theory,' Esser blurted out.

Bastard! 'The agent's arrival might be connected with the White Rose protest group in Munich.'

'To help rally them? Yes, I thought of that. But then another idea crossed my mind . . .'

'If you would, *Obergruppenführer*,' said Esser eagerly.

'The Führer travelled to the Berghof at the beginning of the week. On Tuesday, there was a coded radio transmission from somewhere south of Munich. Assuming it's the same man, he'll transmit again. We sent two detection vans to the area. We'll dispatch two more, immediately.' Kaltenbrunner picked up a pencil, which looked tiny in his hands. 'The other organs of state security will obviously also be hunting for this spy but I've been persuaded to leave the investigation of the copper's murder to you. You have my authority to use whatever resources you need. *Reichsführer* Himmler agrees.'

Jäger felt physically sick. It was bad enough to have the head of the RHSA on the case but to have Himmler looking over your shoulder . . .

'Thank you, sir.' Esser clearly imagined Kaltenbrunner was talking to him.

'Anyway, well done. There's a reception this evening at the Opera House. You will both attend as my personal guests.'

Esser preened. 'Thank you, *Obergruppenführer*.'

Jäger cleared his throat. 'It's kind of you, sir, but *I* should be getting back to Munich.'

'Really?'

'Tomorrow it will be exactly a week since Hamm was killed. With your authority, I'd like to conduct a dawn dragnet in and around Dachau station. There might be some once-a-week travellers who saw something suspicious.'

'Your diligence does you credit, Jäger. Any problems with man-power, refer them to my office. All right, I won't detain you.'

Out in the ante-room, Esser could not contain his anger. '*You* want to get back,' he mocked. 'I'll make you sorry for showing me up in front of the *Obergruppenführer*.'

'You stay,' replied Jäger mildly. 'I can cope.'

A man in a civilian suit was bending over the reception desk by the door, his back towards them.

'I won't forget this in a hurry.' Esser brushed impatiently past the man.

The man turned around. 'I bet Kaltenbrunner fifty *Reichsmark* you wouldn't stay for the reception,' he said to Jäger.

'Müller!' gasped Jäger.

If Kaltenbrunner was striking in his appearance, Heinrich Müller was nearly invisible. Average height, average build, nondescript features. He looked insignificant – which was his genius.

Esser halted to scowl at the interloper.

'Introduce us, Jäger,' ordered the man, eyeing Esser, now bristling with anger.

'*Standartenführer* Esser. *SS Gruppenführer* Müller.'

Esser went grey. He put out a hand as if to steady himself. This was 'Gestapo' Müller – the operational chief of the secret police.

'You can go.' Müller dismissed the little man who was now swaying to and fro in fear. 'Still smoking those disgusting cheroots, Jäger? Good. I'll have one. How is Munich?'

'Full of pond life.'

'Yeh. Some things don't change.'

Jäger had once shared a desk with Müller when he'd been a young copper, without knowing Müller was a closet Nazi. Once the Party gained power, Müller had been transferred to Berlin, some said as a reward for declaring Geli Raubal's death to be suicide. Now he was head of the SS RHSA Amt IV and one of the most feared men in the *Reich*.

Müller coughed as he lit the cheroot. 'I was thinking about the old times only a few weeks ago. Remember when that pimp went for me with a knife at the top of those stairs? I reckon he'd have had me if it weren't for you. I owe you for that, but there's no room for sentimentality in the *Reich*. We're fighting a war – a war on many different fronts.'

Jäger was wondering what was coming next when Müller changed tack.

'Do you really think the English spy came to link up with those White Rose traitors?'

'I don't know. Are there any of them left to link up with?'

'Oh, yeh. They're still out there. Not just in Munich, either. There's a branch in Freiburg, about fifty or so in Hamburg calling themselves the North Branch of the White Rose. Even a very small cell in Aachen, which has just grown by one new member.'

Jäger didn't blink. 'And you're expunging them root and branch?'

'The main centres of infestation, certainly. The smaller ones may eventually just wither on the vine.' Müller drew on the cheroot, becoming accustomed to its strength. 'I think of these traitors like TB bacilli inside a healthy body. A single bacillus may stay inert, it may evolve and become healthy by itself. That's fine. But if it continues and works to infect the body then I must act to stop it. I must cut it out. *Heil Hitler*.'

*

Beck slid home the bolt on his bedroom door and wedged a chair under the handle. Downstairs Runge was getting morosely drunk, still angry at being excluded from the visit to the Eagle's Nest. To avoid trouble, Ilse had gone to see her father. Beck had to transmit his news to London. The assassination plan had been based on Hitler walking along a given path at a given time and out of sight of his guards.

Now Beck knew that was a fairy story.

But, on the plus side, he had been up on the forbidden mountain. He might even get the chance to meet Hitler himself. He couldn't give up. Something must come out of his new friendship with Eva Braun.

Beck pulled off a jackboot and twisted the heel to reveal a thin pad of one-time cyphers. He began drafting the message. In the first part of it, he passed on the bad news that Pabst's information had been false. In the second part, he explained why he thought it was worth continuing. He encoded the signal, inserting the safety checks. When he was ready to transmit, he tiptoed to the door, slid back the bolt as quietly as he could and stuck his head out into the dark corridor. From downstairs came the sound of breaking glass and shouting.

Beck plugged the wireless transmitter into the wall socket and watched it glow into life. He began tapping out his message. He was slow. The period of training had not been long enough to overcome his heavy-handedness on the Morse key. He recalled Cricklemarsh's warnings on the efficiency of the Gestapo radio-detector vans and made himself concentrate.

In the Avenue Foch, Gestapo clerks 'sweeping' the cathode ray tubes picked up the signal immediately. The radio-direction stations were alerted before Beck had finished the third group of five. Beck's time was running out.

The RD vans that had been dispatched to Salzburg after his last broadcast immediately began reducing the arc of uncertainty. Fortunately, Beck had the mountains on his side, especially the Untersberg and the Watzmann that distorted his signal. But the operators could tell that the transmitter was operating somewhere between Salzburg and Bad Reichenhall. And, from the strength of the signal, somewhere closer rather than further. In four minutes a van was out on the road with an SS motorcycle escort.

Beck sat under the single tassled light shade, tapping away, and hoped to God his message was getting through without being corrupted. He transmitted the news of Pabst's treachery and paused to wipe away the sweat on his brow.

Now for the good news.

There was a scratching at the door. Beck's heart somersaulted into his mouth. The scratching was repeated. Once, twice, growing in urgency.

'Who's there?'

Beck hesitated. The scratching became frantic. Terrified animal noises filtered through the door. Beck had no choice. He switched off the set. In his hurry to unplug it, he tugged the cord too hard, so the transmitter fell onto the floor with a thud. Beck swore and slid it under the bed. He rumpled the duvet, stepped swiftly to the door and removed the chair.

'I'm coming.'

Vishnia rushed past him into the middle of the room, wide-eyed and trembling like a hunted animal. A door below slammed and Beck heard Runge swear as he stumbled up the stairs. Vishnia pleaded with her eyes for sanctuary.

'Don't be frightened.' Beck closed the door.

She looked about to scramble under the bed.

'The wardrobe. Get in the wardrobe. He won't hurt you, I promise. You're safe here.' Beck led her by her matchstick arm.

'Where are you, you Ukrainian slut? It's no use hiding from me.'

Beck unnecessarily put his finger to Vishnia's lips for silence and softly closed the wardrobe door. *Crash.* He heard the door to her room fly open, banging against the wall. From the noise, Runge was blundering into all the empty rooms along the corridor towards them. He would get here in a minute. Beck pulled on his boots, adrenalin pumping. If Runge wanted a fight, he was ready for him. He'd enjoy giving the Nazi bully a beating he'd never forget.

But no. Whatever happened he must not get into a scrap. He must stay cool, give Runge no reason call the police. Beck was still struggling to control his emotions when the door flew open and Runge staggered in. His eyes were blood-red, his face purple beneath sweat-stained hair.

'Where is she?'

'Who?' Beck moved towards Runge, blocking off his access to the rest of the room.

'You know who. That bitch Vishnia,' slurred Runge. 'Where are you hiding her?' The idea took hold in his mind. 'You're hiding her, aren't you?'

Beck gestured around the empty room. 'Do you see her?'

Runge lost his balance and staggered towards the bed. As Beck put out a hand to steady him, Runge knocked it aside.

'Don't you push me, you bastard. I know she's in here.'

Beck stared at Runge. 'If you're calling me a liar . . .' he said in a voice as cold as Toledo steel.

There was something chilling about the menace in those few words. His eyes had turned empty; the eyes of a killer. Runge flinched and his stomach heaved. Retching, he slapped a hand over his mouth, then stumbled from the room, leaving a thin trail of vomit.

'So Pabst lied.' Cricklemarsh folded one hand over the other and rested his chin on them.

'Bloody man, I could kill him,' agreed Annie, staring at the newly arrived signal.

'Others have beaten you to it,' replied Cricklemarsh drily. 'It's ironic, isn't it? Pabst was murdered for lying to us.'

'Where does that leave Lusty?' She glanced at the photograph of the three of them, now propped up on the mantelpiece.

Cricklemarsh sighed. 'With a near-impossible task. He's got to discover where else Hitler's going to be at any given time. We know how unpredictable and paranoid the man is about his security.'

'If the story about Hitler insisting on being left alone occasionally is make-believe, then . . .'

'. . . Then it's going to be very difficult to make the hit and escape safely. Given luck and determination, an assassin will always get through – getting away again is not so easy.'

'Are you suggesting that Lusty won't get away?' Annie's dark eyes clouded with concern.

Cricklemarsh busied himself with his pipe. 'It's unlikely.'

Annie read through the signal again. 'It's odd that he says nothing about his plans.'

'Perhaps he was disturbed. You know he's slow at transmitting. Maybe he'll send more later.'

Annie slumped on the camp bed. It was all getting too difficult. She was still perplexed as to why there was no paper foundation to the operation on the Sixth Floor, as there should be. Cricklemarsh did not seemed as concerned by that as she was, suggesting that Gilbert might be the title holder with all the paperwork residing with him. But Annie had an orderly mind, and she knew organizations like SOE were run by paperwork, never mind how inspirational some individuals liked to think themselves. This wasn't right, somehow. *It wasn't as it should be* – but for the moment there were larger, more immediate worries.

'Today's Friday. The border will close midnight Tuesday,' Annie reinded Cricklemarsh.

Cricklemarsh watched the pipe smoke curl towards the brown ceiling. 'How does he *know* for sure that Hitler does not go for a daily walk?'

'Sorry?'

'He must be sure of his information or he wouldn't have risked transmitting. He doesn't say he's pulling out.'

'True.'

'Maybe he has another plan . . .'

His words died as he sank into thought. Annie's heart went out to the older man. He'd put so much into this operation. Too much emotionally, she feared. This wasn't merely about a case officer running an operation; this was personal. Cricklemarsh slept on that camp bed every night, waiting all the time for news. He had been elated when Lusty had reported his safe arrival in Germany, and had lived in hope ever since. Now his hopes were dashed. The window of escape on the Swiss frontier would remain open only until Tuesday – then it would be up to Lusty to make his own way out.

Annie, too, found reasons to stay late. She had not had a night out since Lusty had left. Somehow, she didn't fancy it any more.

By ten o'clock the streets of Berne were empty. The good burghers were keeping warm and cosy in their homes, and out of the frosty night. The trams were deserted, which made it easy for Antonescu to check that he was not being followed. He was the only passenger to climb down onto the traffic island in the middle of the long, gloomy street. He turned up his overcoat collar against the piercing wind and watched the occasional snowflake swirl past the amber street lamps, suggesting a blizzard was on its way. The streets would be white by morning. His tram rattled away around the bend and he was alone.

A minute later, an old Renault car pulled up and the passenger door was pushed open. Antonescu slid onto the seat, grateful for the warmth.

'Sonya sends her love.'

'I trust she is better today.'

'Who thinks up these stupid recognition codes?' snarled the driver, pulling away from the kerb.

'I once had to ask someone if the peacock had drowned. If I'd picked the wrong man, he'd have thought I was barking mad.' The driver, wrapped up in a coat and wearing glasses and a beret, was not the man he had been expecting. 'Where's Gunter? I normally deal with Gunter.'

'Tonight you report to me. You can call me Willy. Well, what have you got?'

The car reeked of stale smoke. It was like sitting in an ashtray. Antonescu coughed and tried unsuccessfully to wind down the window. 'It seems they don't want my services.'

Willy shrugged. 'I never thought they would.'

His supercilious tone infuriated Antonescu. This Willy was too sure of himself, not like the quietly spoken Gunter who treated him respectfully. He coughed again, delicately, into the back of his hand.

'Don't you even want to know why not?'

'Yeh, all right. Tell me.'

'The British already have an assassin in place.'

'What!'

'Interesting, isn't it?' Antonescu savoured his moment.

'Who told you this?'

'An American called Donovan.'

'He's not a regular?'

'No, I believe he was previously an airman.' Antonescu recounted their conversation. Before he had finished the driver was shaking his head in disbelief.

'He really said that? He really said that the Brits have a man in place? Where?'

'He didn't elaborate,' replied Antonescu, primly.

'I bet he didn't.' It was obvious Willy did not believe him.

'All he said was, the Limeys have a man there already but the Americans want me to stay in touch in case the British attempt fails.' Antonescu did not recognize the street they were in.

'You're not just coming out with this shit to put your price up, are you? Not stringing us along?' growled the driver.

'Certainly not. Where are we, anyway?' It cost Antonescu a lot to remain sounding composed.

'Don't worry. Nothing's going to happen to you. Maybe the American just made up this story to let you down gently.'

'No. He was telling me something he shouldn't have. He made me swear not to tell another living soul. I can tell when men like Donovan are lying. Americans are so transparent.'

'Compared with Eastern Europeans, you mean?' They turned a corner and the railway station lay ahead of them.

'What shall I do now?'

'Everything the Americans expect you to. You said you were going back to Romania. So go there. We'll find you if we need you.'

Antonescu knew he was being dismissed. 'I am telling the truth,' he insisted.

'Yeh, yeh. And pigs fly.'

Smarting at the injustice, Antonescu walked briskly away without a backward glance.

Willy Pickel, too, was angry that his time had been wasted when he could have been sitting in a bar. Bloody Gunter. It should have been his job to service this little fantasy merchant. Now he was going to have to write up the report of the meeting, which meant he wasn't going to get a drink tonight. Not even a parachute would open in Berne after eleven o'clock. He pulled the old Renault into an underground garage and two minutes later left in a Mercedes-Benz bearing German diplomatic number plates. Willy drove straight to the German legation and used his keys to enter a locked suite of rooms on the first floor.

For Willy Pickel was a member of the SD or *Sicherheitsdienst*, the original Nazi intelligence organization that competed with the *Abwehr*. He did not believe Antonescu, and said so in the report he sent directly off to Berlin.

'What's wrong with you?' Blonde Heidi, with the areolae like pink saucers, could not decide whether to be concerned or annoyed. This wasn't like Voss. He might appear prim and proper but in bed he was an inventive tiger.

'I'm just tired.'

'We're *all* tired. I'm tired of queuing, tired of not ever being able to buy new shoes, tired of nettle soup and tired of the war. We're all tired!'

'I'm sorry.'

Heidi snorted in exasperation and rolled onto her back. Out of the corner of his eye, Voss could see her staring at the ceiling, her lips pursed. It was rumoured locally that she had killed her postman husband through her excessive sexual demands, and Voss could believe it. Normally his own appetite matched hers, but at the moment it wasn't surprising that he couldn't get an erection.

The strain of the last two days was just too much. Every time the phone rang, his stomach plummeted to his boots. He'd caught his sergeant eyeing him curiously more than once. Those endless hours under the French bombardment outside Verdun in 1916 had never been as bad as this – and they had been known to drive men mad. The last time he had answered the phone, he had had to wipe the receiver because it was so clammy from his sweating palms. He had barely eaten, he could not sleep, he could not concentrate. What chance did he have for enjoying sex?

'Wake up!' bawled Heidi. She sat up abruptly sending the rolls of fat rippling around her hips, then slapped his cock with the back of her hand. 'Come on.'

Voss bit his lip to stop himself crying out.

Just when he thought his cock couldn't stand any more abuse, Heidi plumped herself down so that it disappeared into her crimson-painted mouth.

But even that didn't work. Rejected and furious, Heidi gave up.

'It's me, isn't it? You don't find me attractive any more.'

At that moment, he did not find her at all attractive. All he could see was the smeared lipstick, a belly filled with lard and gravel and a spare tyre that would have fitted a small tractor. On a good day, she seemed comely and arousingly voracious. On a bad day, like today, she was just a fat, sex-crazed slut.

'I do. Of course I do,' he lied.

He could not tell her why he could not perform. Having no one to confide in was a large part of the problem. But dread of being denounced lay in every German's mind. How would Heidi react if she learned that the English were paying her rent? Probably go straight to the Gestapo, if only to try to prove she was ignorant of its provenance.

'I don't know what's wrong with you today but I'm fed up with it.' She grasped his cock in her hand and peeled the foreskin right back in one savage jerk.

He yelped in pain.

'No, please. Please, pull it back up,' Voss pleaded through gritted teeth.

'Do it yourself.' Heidi heaved herself off the bed – leaving Voss tied to the brass bedhead, squirming in discomfort.

13

Saturday, 27 March

Jäger liked the hour before dawn. The hour when the frail, the sick and the old surrendered up the ghost and slipped quietly to another world. The hour of the day that concentrated the mind. He lay partially dressed beneath the thick duvet in a freezing cold room of the Dachau inn, listening to Wulzinger snoring in a rasping bass, and cursing the loss of the past twenty-four hours in Berlin. There were still a dozen men to be eliminated from their inquiries. The vagabond had never been identified, although Jäger doubted whether the British agent would have been disguised as a drifter who would naturally attract any policeman's attention. Yet again, no one had accounted for the Nazi Party car spotted parked in a nearby lane four days after the murder.

And then there was the Polish farmworker. The more Jäger thought about the transcript of the local police interview, the more it worried him. Seemingly, it had been difficult to get any sense out of the Pole because he had been in such agony. He had taken out a bad tooth with a pair of pliers. The Pole's gums had turned septic but no one would waste valuable medicine on a prisoner of war. He was going to have to put up with it.

Yet the very nature of his work would keep the Pole out in all weathers and at all odd hours of the day. It was exactly someone like him who would be at hand to notice something unusual. Jäger made a mental note to interrogate the Pole and other local farmworkers again.

At least Jäger now had the manpower he needed to seal off Dachau railway station, board every train, question every passenger and, at last, do things properly. Appeals for information were about to fill the local newspapers and huge posters were being plastered up over the region. No mention was made of the parachute. As far as the public were concerned, this was a hunt for a cop-killer.

But Jäger had other worries. Thanks to Müller, he knew the Gestapo were watching his daughter Alix. He had been flown back to Munich last night and had driven directly to Dachau. When he finally got home, he'd have to talk to his wife about how they could make Alix give up these stupid protests before she found herself in a concentration camp.

He looked at his watch in the growing light. Time to get up. He hurled a boot at Wulzinger to stop him snoring.

Willy Pickel stood on the concourse under the vaulted glass roof of Berne station, scanning the faces of passengers boarding the morning's first train out of Switzerland heading east. He was trying to relax so that he would not stare too hard at the flow of passengers until they became just one blur of movement. But every time he remembered that phone call he turned cold.

The ringing had slowly penetrated his deep sleep. Grumpily, he had reached out to locate the telephone on the bedside table. He had fumbled, dropping the receiver on the floor before finally putting it to his ear.

Two seconds later, Willy Pickel was standing to attention, rigid with fear. He had knocked over the table lamp and a glass of water in his haste to rise, so he was standing in the darkness in a pool of water and listening to a deep Austrian voice demanding to know every detail of his interview with Antonescu.

'I want to talk to him personally. Accompany him on the first available train into the *Reich*. I'll have a plane waiting near the border.' Maybe it was Pickel's silence that aroused Kaltenbrunner's suspicions. 'Where is he now?'

'At his hotel.'

'I hope he is – for your sake.'

But he wasn't.

When Willy Pickel put on the light, he found it was 3.30 a.m. He dressed and went straight to Antonescu's hotel, roused the night porter and learned that the Romanian had checked out the previous evening – before their meeting – without leaving a forwarding address. Pickel had pressed the panic button, turning out the whole of the SD section, its agents and their stringers. Within an hour men were watching the American legation and OSS offices and staking out the railway station, the major hotels and all Antonescu's known haunts. Pickel knew that such activity would attract the attention of the Swiss *Fremdenpolizei* but he had no option.

But Antonescu seemed to have vanished into thin air the moment he had stomped away from the old Renault car the previous night. Pickel's heart sank when Antonescu did not turn up at his favourite café on the Bolligenstraße where he inevitably took breakfast. His only hope was that no train had left to the east, towards Romania, since ten o'clock last night. The first one, to Vienna, was due to leave at eight o'clock. With only five minutes to spare before the train departed, he saw one of his men at the side entrance raise his arm. Willy let out a sigh of relief. There was Antonescu, fastidious in his Homburg, dark topcoat and spats, following a porter pushing a trolley with two large leather suitcases edged with brass.

'Herr Antonescu.'

'Ah. Willy, isn't it?' The Romanian eyed him coldly. 'Yes?'

'I've been looking everywhere for you.' Pickel gave what he hoped was an ingratiating smile. 'I'd like you to come to Berlin with me.'

'Why?' Antonescu did not stop walking alongside the train.

'There's been a change of plan.'

'Really! You just told me to go back to Romania, and that's where I am going.' He scanned the coaches, looking for the right one.

'You must come with me now.'

'Must! You forget we are in Switzerland.' Large men were gathering ahead and behind him. 'You would not dare try anything on a Swiss railway station.'

Pickel tried a softer tack. '*Obergruppenführer* Kaltenbrunner himself wants to interview you. He believes you may have something to offer us.'

'Ah, I see.' Antonescu stopped. 'He at least believes that I am telling the truth.'

'I don't always get to see the whole picture,' mumbled Pickel.

'No.' The Romanian was enjoying his moment of victory, but he continued walking. The porter stood at the steps of a first class carriage.

'We'll fly you to Berlin and back to Bucharest. You'll be there at the same time as you would if you took this train.'

Antonescu motioned for the porter to wait. 'You want me to go voluntarily to Gestapo headquarters in Berlin. You think that I am mad?'

'It's not like that.' Pickel was becoming desperate. Swiss *Fremden-polizei* were drifting onto the station. 'You are our friend. We are grateful for your help. We will pay you five hundred dollars for your inconvenience.'

'And I'm to believe that you will then let me go?'

'The Americans say they will contact you in Bucharest, so you must be there for them. You're of no use to us in Albrechtstraße.' Pickel held his breath. The Romanian could not win. He would be picked up as soon as he crossed the border into Austria, but Pickel would be held to account for letting him go. He must accompany Antonescu, personally.

'All right,' said Antonescu, who had made the same calculations. 'One thousand dollars.'

Esser was in a foul temper. He was cold, short of sleep and unused to being out at six-thirty on a raw morning. It was all right for Jäger maybe; Esser was a Nazi Party official first and a policeman second. But after the way Jäger had spoken so intimately with Gestapo Müller, Esser dared not let him out of his sight. If there was another break-through, he had to be on hand to take the credit.

He stamped his foot to break a shallow pool of ice just as a grizzled *Wehrmacht* sergeant with a Winter War medal turned away to avoid saluting Esser's SS uniform. That was the final straw! He had been out in the cold long enough. Esser bullied the stationmaster to use up his entire day's supply of coal, then hogged the fire until Jäger and Wulzinger came in to report on their dragnet. They had already eliminated six men from their inquiries.

'There're another four to go, plus two women – although I can't really see a woman being capable of killing Hamm with a single blow,' said Jäger.

'We had a bit of luck,' added Wulzinger. 'We interviewed one man who'd been travelling with a soldier going back off leave. So that we eliminated two birds with one stone, so to speak.'

'Don't talk to me about soldiers,' snapped Esser. 'They're forgetting their place. I even read a report about some officer who tried to give up his seat on a train to a Polish woman.' Esser spat in the fire in contempt, sending a globule of phlegm hissing onto the hot coals. 'Somewhere near here, it was.'

'One of the men we're failing to eliminate is an army officer,' remarked Wulzinger, inspecting his list.

'Probably returning to the front,' declared Esser dismissively. 'You'll never find him.'

'Wait a minute.' Bells had begun jangling in Jäger's head. 'Say that again.'

'What? About the soldier on leave?'

'No. About him standing up for a Polish woman.'

'A Party member complained that an officer had risen to offer his seat to a Polish woman. She, of course, refused.'

'Where did this happen? When?'

'I don't know. There's a report in the office. I'll look for it when I get back.'

'I need it *immediately*.'

Esser made a fuss of calling Munich Police Headquarters. He finally put down the phone. 'Party member Walter Bunting complained to his section leader at the Munich City planning department that some officer had tried to offer his railway seat to a Polish woman. The train was the 6.43 from Petershausen and the incident took place around Obermenzing at approximately 7.25 a.m. The train was running late because—'

'The Petershausen train comes through Dachau,' exclaimed Jäger. 'When did this happen?'

Esser inspected his notes. 'On the twentieth. A week ago today.'

'And we still have this army officer left to find.' Jäger felt a tremor of excitement.

'You're clutching at straws, aren't you?'

'Maybe, but straws make bricks and bricks make walls and walls make houses. Listen. Imagine you've just landed by parachute. Your nerves are jangling. You're not thinking clearly. You see a woman standing, you're playing the part of an officer and a gentleman so you offer her your seat. Then you see others staring at you and you sit down again. Let's talk to Bunting.'

Ilse was avoiding Christian Beck like the plague – and he didn't know why. He had tried to strike up a conversation earlier but she'd answered monosyllabically before hurrying out of the back door with her basket covered in a red cloth. It seemed a shame. Runge had left early on Party business and it was a perfect morning. Beck would have liked to have spent some time with Ilse.

He was puzzling over her mood swing when Vishnia sidled up to the table and produced a boiled egg. She put a finger to her lips in mimicry of his gesture the previous night. It was a disarming display of gratitude for his protection. He had tried to call London after Vishnia had left, but the transmitter was dead. He had replaced the two valves but it still refused to work. Runge was still rampaging drunkenly around the inn so, to be safe, Beck had hidden the apparatus away. First thing this morning, he had retrieved it to find that a wire had come loose from the plug when he had tugged it out of the wall socket in his hurry. He repaired it in seconds. According to the schedule, if London had anything for him, they would transmit at six o'clock this evening. Half an hour later he could send the rest of his original message. Meanwhile, at a loose end, he decided he'd take a stroll and visit Dr Meissner.

The clang and thump of the printing presses echoed around the cobbled lane as he approached. Beck paused in the hope of catching sight of Ilse before pushing open the outer door. No one answered his calls as he climbed the steep flight of wooden stairs, feeling the vibrations from the machinery under his feet. The only light in the first-floor corridor came from Dr Meissner's office. Beck went to knock and stopped in amazement.

The wall, which had been festooned with galley proofs, had a gaping black hole in the middle. In the room itself, a small man was bending over the roll-top desk. He sensed Beck's presence for his birdlike movements slowed down until he became absolutely still. Then he turned round, his eyes widening at the sight of Beck's uniform, and toppled back against the desk as if pushed by an invisible hand.

Beck found himself staring at a gnomelike man with white hair, very red cheeks and bright blue eyes, which twinkled with mischief even in his fear. He wore a black waistcoat and a collarless shirt, buttoned at the cuffs. His creased black trousers, seemingly part of a funeral suit, were held up by red braces. On his feet were felt slippers.

'Now you know our secret.'

Beck spun around. Ilse was standing behind him, Dr Meissner at her shoulder.

Beck felt guilty he had intruded. 'I'm sorry. I was passing by so I thought I'd drop in to say good morning. I did call out, honestly.'

A smile played on Ilse's lips in acknowledgement of the irony that Beck was the one who was doing the apologizing. 'Let me introduce you. Hugo Guttmann, this is *Hauptmann* Beck.'

Beck bowed formally.

'I've heard a lot about you, captain. I'm pleased to meet you, although I think I'd experience greater pleasure in a different time and place.'

'What were you thinking of, Hugo?' remonstrated Dr Meissner.

'I wanted to find a book. I should have checked that the downstairs door . . . I'm sorry.'

Ilse slid past Beck to place her basket on the desk. She turned to face him, a challenge in her eye.

'Well, *Hauptmann* Beck. What will you do now?' She could tell he did not have a clue what to do. He was still trying to work out what he had stumbled upon.

'I'm going to have a schnapps,' announced Guttmann. 'I find it helps in times like these. Captain?'

'We'll all have one,' said Dr Meissner.

'If you want to see?' Ilse waved a hand towards the hole. Beck peered into a room not ten feet by ten, with one tiny, high window. The space was crowded with a double bed, two chairs and a desk. When he stepped back, Ilse pushed the secret door closed. The room vanished without a trace, leaving the wall once more covered by schedules and sheaves of proofs.

Dr Meissner sighed. 'I do not know if there's any way we can influence you, Captain Beck, but at least we can tell you the facts, if you care to hear them.'

Beck accepted a glass of Enzian from a grave-faced Ilse who stood watching him as if it was she who was sitting in judgement.

'Hugo is Ilse's godfather. Germany is not a safe place for any Jew at the moment, especially one who's had the temerity to criticize the Nazi Party. They've been hunting for him for more than two years.'

'My friends here have risked their own lives by sheltering me and my wife.'

'Hugo's wife is in Munich,' explained Dr Meissner. 'We smuggled her there just after Christmas when her mother was dying. Now it's too dangerous to bring her back.'

'And you've been hiding here for two years?'

'Yes. The interior of these buildings is a rabbit warren so it wasn't difficult to lose a few square metres.'

'Didn't the workers suspect?'

'We've been very careful up until now,' said Hugo Guttmann. He perched on the edge of the desk, his feet barely touching the ground. 'I am a mouse who creeps about quietly. I only usually come out on Sundays or at night when no one is here.'

'Don't you ever go outside?'

'I went out last Christmas Eve because Ilse told me the stars were so beautiful they made the risk worthwhile. That's been the only time.' Guttmann threw back his head to swallow the schnapps in one gulp.

Dr Meissner was studying Beck's face, mistaking the man's shock for disbelief. 'You don't appear convinced. What if I told you that ten years ago there were almost eleven thousand Jews in Munich? Now there are fewer than five hundred, most of them in hiding. Last week three hundred and sixty Jews were deported from Augsburg alone. Others committed suicide to avoid being taken.'

'Where do they take them?' Beck had already asked Ilse the same question but he wanted to hear what her father had to say.

'In theory, to camps in the east where they are put to work. But no one ever comes back and rumours are growing of extermination camps.'

'Don't the ordinary people protest?'

Guttmann give an eloquent shrug, his whole body contorted like a marionette's. 'There are one or two brave enough to stand up to the SS but the majority of Germans don't care.'

'We cannot hope to convince you,' murmured Ilse, resignedly.

'I do not fear death any more,' said Guttmann. 'Death would be like waking from a nightmare. But I implore you not to involve these brave people. I will come with you to the Gestapo right now if you'll say you discovered me elsewhere in Berchtesgaden.'

Beck's involuntary shaking of his head allowed Ilse a spark of hope.

'We are in your hands,' she said.

'The hands of a German officer,' added her father.

The room held its breath. Beck stepped forward and offered his hand to the strange little man. Slowly, almost in disbelief, Guttmann extended his own.

'I give you my hand and my word as an officer.' Beck subtly corrected Dr Meissner. 'I will never betray you.'

Everyone expelled a sigh of relief together. Dr Meissner grabbed Beck's hand and shook it. Only Ilse held back, watching him, partly in fear, partly in pride.

Meissner removed the cloth from the basket to reveal a piece of smoked ham, blood sausages, brown rolls, cheese, a tub of sauerkraut and two eggs. 'Courtesy of the Party,' he announced.

Guttman saw the surprise on Beck's face. 'According to the Nazis I am racially a Jew but it doesn't mean that I practise that religion. I think of myself as a German first and an atheist second. I eat pork; in fact, nowadays I eat anything I can.'

'Where is your wife?' Beck asked Guttmann.

'Hiding in Dr Meissner's apartment in Munich. Ilse goes there to make sure she's all right when she gets the chance,' replied Guttmann.

'Remember a few days ago when we took those leaflets to the Brown House?' smiled Ilse.

'I thought . . .'

'What?'

'Nothing.' He started, suddenly divining why Ilse had chosen to shelter in that one cellar during the bombing raid.

As if reading his thoughts, Ilse said, '*Frau* Guttmann couldn't hide with us but I wanted to be near her. I checked she was all right while you were asleep in the morning.'

Beck turned to Guttmann. 'I don't know how you cope.'

'I feel like a tapeworm, moving among brown masses and expecting all the time to be purged.'

'Most of the Jews left in Germany have gone into hiding,' said Dr Meissner. 'Those who decided not to are now in an impossible position. They aren't allowed decent jobs. Their ration cards do not entitle them to meat, bread, milk or eggs. Every parcel addressed to a Jew is opened. If it contains tea, coffee or one of a hundred other banned goods, then it's confiscated. If they're delivered, the contents are deducted from the ration allowance – even if things are damaged.'

'And they always make sure they are damaged,' added Guttmann. 'They are very hard with us. You know, an SS officer arrests a Jew and he says to the Jew, "I have a glass eye. If you can guess which one it is, I'll let you go." The Jew guesses correctly. "That's amazing," says the SS officer. "How did you do that?" "Easy," says the Jew. "I chose the compassionate one." '

Guttmann tapped the end of his crooked nose with a fingertip and beamed.

'It's hard to remember that when the Nazi Party first came to power, they were welcomed. It was a change from a republic with a hole in its heart,' said Dr Meissner. 'But it soon changed as power corrupted them. The Nazis put themselves above and beyond the law . . .'

'Father!' warned Ilse.

'Ilse, Captain Beck already holds our lives in his hands. Do you think a few truths said here will make a difference? The so-called "People's Courts" make no attempt to administer justice, only to guillotine those who dare to stand up against the Nazis.'

Hugo Guttmann obviously found the atmosphere becoming too serious, for he jumped up from the edge of the desk. 'An orthodox Jew is denounced for killing a Nazi at ten o'clock one evening, then eating his brains. But the Jew has a cast-iron defence. The Nazis have no brains, orthodox Jews will eat nothing that comes from a pig, and at ten o'clock everyone is listening to the BBC.'

'Now you know why he gets himself into trouble,' laughed Ilse.

'I make up jokes to cheer myself up. Sometimes I tell my wife jokes, even though she is not here to hear them.' The merriment leached out of Guttmann's eyes. 'I try to follow the advice of the poet Rilke. The best way is not to attempt to work things out or add things up but just to go on growing like a tree, which can stand up to spring storms because it knows that summer must follow, and so it will, but only for those with patience who go on living as though all eternity lies before them, quiet, carefree and vast.'

Beck offered the little refugee his hand again.

Ilse felt a warmth swell inside her. Unknowingly she moved closer to Beck, proud of him, grateful to him, growing more in love with him.

Walter Bunting was a good Nazi and a diligent civil servant. He had joined the Party in 1932 – just ahead of the ultimate victory when he could see which way the wind was blowing. He had stayed as true as a weathercock to the fortunes of the Party ever since. When he was picked up his first thought was that he was going to be late for work.

Then he panicked. He had recently entertained defeatist thoughts. He was sure they were only thoughts, he had never articulated them – but what if he spoke in his sleep and his wife had informed on him! Such things did happen!

Jäger put the man's mind at rest. He knew instinctively that this pompous, bespectacled clerk was desperate to do the right thing and within a minute he had made Bunting feel he was the only one who could help them in their hunt for Hamm's killer. Bunting did his best. Yes, he remembered that wintry morning. The train had been held up to allow flatbed trucks to pass through. Quite right: arms came first. He had been sitting diagonally opposite a soldier who had worn a greatcoat, an officer's cap and who carried a walking stick. No, he couldn't remember the colour of the epaulettes or recognize the man's rank. He was sorry but he was only a civil servant and didn't know much about *Wehrmacht* insignia. The walking stick? Just a normal walking stick. Description? Not very tall, nor very short. When he'd stood up? Er, yes. Say around five feet ten but you understand . . . Yes, Jäger understood. So, average build. Clean-shaven. Fair hair. Shape of face? Bunting hesitated over that.

'Long and thin, full, oval?'

'Um . . . sort of average. Firm chin. Yes, a firm chin.'

'Were there distinguishing marks of any sort?' So far, Bunting was reinforcing the bromide description they had already built up from interviewing other passengers, but Jäger did not want to pressure the man into inventing a description just to oblige them.

'No.' Bunting shook his head and clutched his old leather briefcase more tightly to his body.

'Describe how this officer tried to give up his seat.' No other passenger had bothered to report the incident. Consequently, no one else was now willing to admit witnessing it.

'I was astonished. I mean. To one of those *Untermenschen* . . .' He caught the impatience in Jäger's stare and hurried on. 'I was studying an office report when I noticed a Polish woman get on at Allach. The officer was reading his newspaper. He looked up and saw her. He began to rise from his seat. The woman turned away. The officer realized his mistake and sat down again quickly.'

'Why do you think he stood up at all?'

Bunting screwed up his face. 'I don't know. It was as if he was so lost in his paper, he just instinctively responded. I mean, a German officer would certainly give up his seat to an Aryan woman – but this one was so obviously a Pole.'

'Do you think he didn't notice her badge with the "P" in it?'

'Possibly not, but it was so obvious from her clothes, her looks, her bearing that she wasn't a German woman.'

'And then what?' demanded Jäger.

'He looked flustered and hid behind his paper. I remember he was blushing. He lifted up his cap to brush the sweat away from his forehead.' Bunting paused. 'There was something, you know. Something different.'

'A mark? A distinguishing feature?'

Bunting took off his glasses and polished them on a pressed handkerchief. Eventually he shook his head in despair. 'I don't know.'

'It'll come to you – and when it does, call me.'

Bunting nodded dutifully.

Jäger's confidence about making a breakthrough suffered a setback at Munich railway station when one of the Gestapo men who'd been on duty a week ago came forward to recount how an officer with a limp had helped them apprehend a dissident student.

'The boy tried to do a runner but the officer tripped him up with his stick.'

'That's not in your report,' complained Jäger, knowing the Gestapo man had deliberately omitted the officer's intervention so as to enhance his own part in the arrest.

'Not every detail gets into our reports.'

'Do you have this officer's name?'

'I was too busy at the time.'

'His rank?'

The man shook his head.

'What branch of the army? Infantry, engineers, artillery?'

'I didn't notice.'

'You must have seen the epaulettes. What was the *Waffenfarbe*?'

'I told you I was very busy.'

This was unforgivable. Jäger seethed. He could understand Bunting's failure but the Gestapo was trained to observe such details.

'Did he leave the station or was he waiting for a train?'

'I had the impression he was waiting. He was standing near a pile of luggage, so one of the bags may have been his. He was near the platform for Berlin.'

'Did you actually see him board a train?'

'No. I had to attend to my prisoner.' The Gestapo man's impatient manner implied he was more accustomed to asking questions than answering them.

Bloody useless. Jäger gave up.

There were also reports of a nervous man, probably a foreign worker, seen lurking near the Regensburg platform but disappearing whenever a policeman or Gestapo man approached. Jäger set Wulzinger on his trail.

But Jäger had a good gut feeling about the limping officer. The timing, just after eight in the morning, certainly fitted, but otherwise the trail had gone cold.

For the moment, anyway.

'Where are we going now?'

'I want to show you something secret.'

'You're full of secrets.'

'Wheee!' Ilse caught Beck's hand in hers and swung it upwards in a gesture of high spirits.

They walked over the Kilianmühle bridge and passed a farm. Beck recognized it as the same way he had come the other day when he'd climbed the mountain in the fog. The day he had killed the sentry. But instead of heading on up the mountain, Ilse turned towards Stanger and led the way along a cart track between pine trees. The track petered out as the ground rose ahead of them. Ilse was like a playful child, laughing and chattering, and every so often allowing her body to touch his. They wended their way through a thickening forest, heavy with the scent of resin.

'So what did *you* think I was doing in Munich?' she demanded.

'I don't know,' Beck stuttered, embarrassed.

She put her head on one side. 'You thought I'd gone to see my secret lover, didn't you? Confess.'

'Yes.'

'And were you jealous?'

'Yes.' Christ, why had he admitted that?

'Good.' Ilse swung his hand up again.

They came soon to a broad swathe of open ground where the trees had been cut down, leaving only the trunks. Across the clearing, a fence topped with barbed wire marked the perimeter of the outer forbidden zone. The ground, covered in brown pine needles, was criss-crossed by miniature ditches scoured out by the waters that tumbled down the hillside. Ilse pointed to one section of fence where a stream had washed away the soft topsoil to leave a gap of at least two feet beneath the barrier.

'How did you find this?' asked Beck.

'It was my mountain long before it was theirs.'

'What about the guards?'

'They've never caught me yet.'

The trees grew right up to the fence on the other side and a conifer had fallen across the dip, hiding the gap from view. They ducked under it.

'It gets a bit steep here. Do you think you can manage, with your leg?'

'I'll try,' replied Beck. The hardest part was remembering to feign his limp as he climbed up behind Ilse who moved with the speed and sureness of a mountain goat.

'I'll be worthwhile. I promise.'

They pressed on for another fifteen minutes under a canopy of trees that grew taller and closer together. Suddenly, he found himself in a small glade where a cascade of water tumbled over smooth rocks into a pool.

It was the lost glade. Ilse had come to it from another direction.

'Welcome to my secret.' Ilse took his hand again. 'You're the first person in the whole world I've ever brought here.'

'It's incredible.' Beck wondered again at the miniature alpine meadow with its soft, springy turf surrounded on three sides by a dense wall of trees and on the other by the vertical escarpment. He knew the Mooslangerkopf tea house lay just above them – but he couldn't see it.

'No one can ever find us here,' declared Ilse. 'Even I can't locate it from above because it's hidden by the cliff – and I know where to look. I think it deliberately hides itself away because it doesn't want anyone to come here apart from me – and now you.'

A miniature rainbow shimmered elusively in the spray above the pool.

'I come here sometimes to be alone – to think.' Ilse ran her fingers over the damp fronds that grew at the water's edge. 'Sometimes I just lie in the sun. Sometimes I bathe in the pool. The waters have magical properties.'

'Do they really?'

'Oh, yes. They can cure all ailments and they help you forget your troubles. Forget the world outside. Now, if you will be a gentleman and turn round, I intend to bathe.'

'How can I carry on talking to you with my back turned?' asked Beck, turning nonetheless towards the trees.

'I don't mind you seeing me naked. I only object to performing a striptease for someone I hardly know. You can occupy yourself by undressing, too. You'll find the waters good for your wounds.'

When Beck turned round eventually, Ilse was standing up to her thighs in the pool, splashing water over her body so that her pale skin glistened and her nipples stood hard and proud. She was slimmer than he had thought with a narrow waist and swelling breasts. As if conscious of his examination, her eyes, in turn, dropped to his groin.

'Won't be like that for long,' she smiled.

The coldness of the water took his breath away. He waded out until he was up to his navel and facing her. The world fell silent. She traced the lightning scar on his chest with her forefinger, watching the trail of tiny beads of moisture that she left behind. Then they were kissing. She pressed against him, shuddering and hungry. Her finger followed the scar to its end, then slid under the water. She squeezed him as hard as she dared before flinging her left hand around his neck and pulling his head down so his mouth was pressed on hers. She felt as if she was tumbling towards the edge of her being, her passions wildly out of control.

Voices. Men's voices. Above them. On the path to the Mooslangerkopf?

Beck drew back, anxiety clouding his eyes, but Ilse reassured him. 'You'll see.'

Hand in hand, they stepped out of the pool. Ilse led him over to a narrow ledge of soft grass under a rocky overhang at the side of the waterfall. They lay down side by side, invisible to the outside world, listening to the voices retreat. As they did so they rediscovered their nakedness. They kissed, touched each other, and, slowly and silently, began to make love.

Nothing but steel-grey water. For as far as the eye could see, there was a forlorn emptiness. Beneath them, the freshening wind formed whitecaps on the deep, uneasy swell. Above them, the clouds loomed dark. Ken Cricklemarsh had never felt so alone.

Where the hell was their aircraft carrier? It should be in sight if his calculations were correct.

'Someone's moved our home,' shouted John Ellis, his observer gunner, down the voice pipe.

'Can't be far away. They're just hiding,' replied Ken, leaning out of the open cockpit of the Swordfish. The lightness in his tone concealed his growing fear that something had gone wrong, seriously wrong.

Five hundred miles off the Western Isles of Scotland in the North Atlantic: as desolate and lonely a place as you could wish for. The escort aircraft carrier *Blaster* must be somewhere near – but where?

They had left the carrier almost two hours ago on an exercise to locate and then simulate a torpedo attack on a cooperative merchantman posing as an enemy vessel. That had been fun, especially as they had first attacked another ship by mistake. Ken and Ellis had still been laughing about it, blaming each other light-heartedly, when they'd spotted another freighter.

'Is that the right one?' demanded Ken.

'Hang on.' Ellis fought to steady the powerful binoculars in the rush of wind that buffeted him as soon as he peered over the cockpit rim. He shivered: it was bloody cold, despite the layers, including flannel pyjamas, they wore under their flying suits. He raised his goggles over his leather flying helmet so he could press the binoculars to his eyes.

'Yeh, that's her. SS *Patna*.'

The old freighter was already turning away to port to present her stern to the attack. Ken turned on the cameras to record his attack, banked the biplane to port and began a sweep to come out low on the *Patna*'s beam. He heard the bracing wires sing as he picked up speed in the dive and felt the throb of the big Bristol Pegasus radial engine.

Ken was trying to lay off the Stringbag by means of the pre-set torpedo aimer, a row of small bulbs across his line of vision on top of the instrument panel. At just fifty feet above the sea and doing the Stringbag's maximum 120 knots, he levelled out. The waves raced past, the distance narrowed. Finally he pressed the tit to release the imaginary torpedo.

He pulled back on the joystick and the Stringbag lumbered through a climbing turn over the ship. They waved to the crew. Ken thought how different it would be to attack a German pocket battleship, flying into a wall of lead. He had no illusions about surviving *that*.

Just as well this was an exercise. Time to report the completion of their mock attack and go home.

Shit! The radio was dead. Stone dead.

'The radio's U/S,' he reported to Ellis

'I thought they were supposed to have fixed it after the last time it conked out.'

'It was all right earlier.' Ken felt around the set in case it was something as simple as a loose wire. 'It's totally dead. Oh, well, we'll just have to find our way home without it.'

The carrier was somewhere off to the north-east. Ken set to working out their course. The reciprocal of their outward course of 210 was 030. Allow for a fifteen-knot wind coming from the west and build in for the carrier to continue on its west-north-west course. Say for twenty-five miles.

Ken looked up from the circular slide rule. The bad weather was closing in. The good visibility was breaking up, with ominous black tails hanging from the heavy cloud base. He set course for 025. Even if he was off by ten miles or so they would still be able to pick up one of the flotilla spread over the ocean. After that it would be simple to find the carrier itself.

After thirty minutes, they encountered unexpected squalls. These were localized and easy to fly around, but the effort drained fuel and put them off track. All the time the ever-lowering cloud base forced them to descend, until they were down to 2,000 feet. Ken had calculated forty minutes to the carrier. After fifty minutes he was getting worried.

'Shit! Where the hell have they gone?' Ellis echoed his fears, his voice taut with anxiety.

Ken forced himself to stay calm, trying to think rationally. Now that the carrier was not where he had placed it, it could be anywhere. Had his calculations been faulty? Had the carrier group changed course? The low cloud stopped them climbing higher to see. In this sort of weather, you needed to navigate spot on – and he obviously hadn't.

'I'll do a figure-of-eight search. Keep your eyes peeled.' Ken turned ninety degrees to port and pressed the stopwatch. After five minutes he altered course again. They had completed five legs when he was forced to switch to the emergency fuel tank.

Ken tried to recheck his calculations but his mind was getting scrambled. Panic rose inside him until it was almost impossible to think straight. In such a situation, it was all too easy for mistake to pile on mistake until you were totally confused – and totally lost. He tried the radio again. If he could only get through, they could give him a fix.

'What the fuck's happening?' demanded Ellis.

'I don't know,' Ken was forced to admit. Then there was a shaft of sunlight. The clouds were breaking up. 'Hallelujah.'

He turned towards the cloud break. A hint of blue sky. Get high enough now and they could see for ever. He pulled back the stick to climb. The engine coughed, spluttered and restarted. Ken turned on the petrol pump. He willed the old Stringbag to carry on for just a few more minutes. Its ceiling was barely 11,000 feet but from there they'd be able to see for almost fifty miles.

The engine stopped.

For a second, the silence was ghostly. Then Ken heard the wind whistling and twanging the wires. He put down the nose.

'Break out the life raft. It seems we're going for a sail.'

All was not lost. The Stringbag should stay afloat long enough for them to scramble into the raft, which contained food, water, a compass and flares. There were legendary stories of Stringbag crews who had survived for days until they were picked up. One crew had even paddled to mainland Scotland from out in the Western Atlantic.

The glide down seemed interminable. Ken sent out a Mayday just in case someone could hear them. As they got lower, he saw that the sea was restless and unhappy, and the swell was greater than he'd thought.

He held up the Stringbag's heavy nose for as long as he could, pulling the stick into his stomach. The tail wheel skimmed the surface. Too late, he saw the swell had backed so that he was landing across it.

There was an explosion of spray and a wall of green water exploded over him. He was flung against his harness and jolted sideways. Then he toppled forward until he was hanging face down. Slowly the Stringbag turned over onto its back.

Ilse was finding it difficult to keep her hands off Beck. She wanted to touch, hold, caress him, to run her fingers through his hair. Vishnia was peeling potatoes by herself in the kitchen of the Red Ox when the couple returned. She sensed immediately that something had happened between them. They shared the intimacy of lovers, standing that inch closer, their hands regularly brushing. As Beck took off his greatcoat, Ilse picked a long, blonde hair off his shoulder.

It was as plain to Vishnia as those massive Winter Relief posters that Ilse had fallen head over heels in love. Vishnia was pleased for *Frau* Runge. She wasn't sure if Beck felt the same but it was harder to tell what a man was thinking or feeling. *Frau* Runge's new-found happiness made Vishnia think of her own miserable state. She pulled out her locket and stroked it as she always did when she felt especially homesick and alone.

Meanwhile Ilse bustled around the kitchen, preparing coffee and finding any reason she could to be near Beck. After a while, she caught Vishnia eyeing her in a knowing way. She flushed and wrinkled her nose in a gesture that was part admission and part embarrassment. She was so happy that she didn't care who knew.

To her surprise, Vishnia reached out and grabbed Ilse's and Beck's hands together. She squeezed them as if to say, *I know your secret and I'm happy for you.* Then, before she could help it, a tear escaped.

'Oh, Vishnia,' cried Ilse, pulling the girl to her breast. 'Poor child.'

Right then, she had joy to spare and she wanted Vishnia to be as happy as she was. It dawned on her that she knew so little about the mute serving girl. No, untrue – she knew absolutely nothing about her.

'Are you very homesick?' she ventured.

Vishnia nodded.

'Show Ilse your locket,' Beck urged.

Shyly, Vishnia opened her palm.

'That's Vishnia's most precious possession,' explained Beck. 'It holds a lock of her mother's hair.'

Ilse wondered how Beck knew this when he had been here only a week, while Vishnia had been working at the inn since Runge had acquired her last summer, just one of the million Ukrainian women transported to the *Reich* to work in its factories, its fields and the homes of important Nazi Party members.

'Does your name – Vishnia – mean anything?'

The girl nodded. Smiling, she mimed picking some kind of fruit and putting it in her mouth.

'Apple? No, smaller. Plum? Cherry?'

Vishnia clapped her hands.

'Cherry?'

She nodded vigorously, her face glowing with delight.

'Are you from Kiev?' asked Beck.

Vishnia pulled a face.

'Krivoy Rog, then?' The two towns were the limit of Beck's Ukrainian geography.

Vishnia held her nose. She spread her hands, wiggling her fingers. Seeing their incomprehension, she made shovelling motions, then crouched down and imitated milking a cow.

'You lived on a farm?' Ilse hazarded.

Vishnia's eyes burned bright with a strange intensity. She started to dance, fluttering around the kitchen, holding the hem of her skirt between her thumb and little finger while her feet performed impossible steps and her head rolled back and forth like that of an excited puppet. But her miming turned darker, the dance slowed and stopped. She tolled a great imaginary bell and cupped a hand to her ear while peering fearfully upwards.

She held back her thin arms as wings before scything the air with a flattened hand. *Dive bombers*, thought Becks. She threw her hands up, cheeks bulging, to indicate the explosions as the bombs burst, engulfing the farm. At last, eyes glassy from the pain of remembrance, she stared dully at the floor.

Ilse wanted to ask why the girl couldn't – or wouldn't – speak but she was afraid of the answer.

'Your father?'asked Beck softly.

A shrug.

'Your mother?'

Vishnia put both hands together as if in prayer and inclined her head on them.

'Brothers?'

She shrugged.

'Sisters?'

Such a painful look scoured Vishnia's face that Ilse wanted to weep for her.

'How did you come here?' asked Beck.

She was giving something, taking something, exchanging with her right hand. With her left, she seemed to be holding onto someone smaller. Smiling down at them. Then fear careered across her face, her eyes darting this way and that, like a desperate, trapped animal. Violently she shook her head, hands raised in entreaty. Now the face was ugly and hateful. Jabbing and prodding with a rifle. She reached out her arms as far as they would go, fingers extended, mouth wide open, pleading. She staggered as though she had been struck. Now she was begging on her knees. She was shoved violently again. Grief disfigured her until finally Vishnia slowly dissolved into a sad, dreamy smile.

A chill settled over Beck's heart. Ilse spoke in a flat, empty voice.

'You were rounded up when you were with your little sister and loaded onto a truck. You don't know what happened to her. You were brought here. Oh, God, oh God.' Her voice rose to a wail. 'I'm sorry. I'm so sorry.'

She broke down, weeping her heart out while Vishnia clutched at the locket of her mother's hair and silently comforted her.

She was still consoling Ilse when the Gestapo arrived to check Beck's papers.

Purefoy waited nervously outside Gilbert's office and braced himself. Operation Nightshade was now seven days old – and he was beginning to wish he had never heard the name. Gilbert had turned against the mission for some reason while Nye, with the skill of a consummate office politician, was spreading rumours about the unsuitability of the agent, Purefoy's inept handling, Cricklemarsh's advanced years and God knew what else.

The green light came on and Purefoy entered. By the way Gilbert deliberately did not look up from the papers on his desk, Purefoy knew he was in for an unpleasant time. He stood to attention and waited.

'Well, how is Operation Nightshade going?' Still Gilbert did not look up.

'Bad news, I'm afraid. A message came in from Lusty last night.' Purefoy steeled himself. 'The premise on which the operation's based has turned out to be false.'

'What are you on about?' Gilbert glared at him like an angry bird of prey.

'It seems Hitler does *not* go for an unguarded morning walk. Our informant lied to us.'

Gilbert gave an exasperated sigh. 'So what's your man doing about it?'

'I don't know, sir, but Major Cricklemarsh reckons Lusty must have made some progress – if only to know that Hitler doesn't take the walk.'

'I'm told Major Nye has been making rather disquieting remarks about your choice of agent.'

'I don't know what Major Nye has to do with this.'

Brigadier Gilbert's eyes gleamed like coal. 'Ignoring Major Nye's comments, would it interest you to know that Albrechtstraße are pulling out all the stops to catch an English agent who's reported to have parachuted into Germany?'

'How could the Gestapo know that?' gasped Purefoy.

'They've found the parachute,' snapped Gilbert. 'Your man didn't bother to bury it properly. According to an in-house study, it demonstrates a desire to show off, a subconscious desire to be caught.'

'Surely not?'

'It gets worse. German intelligence in Berne has picked up the notion that we're about to assassinate the Führer. Not surprisingly, the Gestapo has linked such an attempt to the parachute drop. Security on this operation seems rather a joke, wouldn't you say?'

'I . . . I can't think how it might have happened.'

'No.' Gilbert's eyes bored into him. 'Nothing on paper, is there?'

'I don't think so, sir.'

'I hope not, colonel. I do hope not. Time to distance ourselves now. The whole thing's deniable, of course. Just another of Clubfoot's fairy tales.' He gave an oleaginous smile. Purefoy would see that smile in his mind for a long time: a sickly, death-laden grimace. 'Time to pull your man out, I think – or cut him adrift. He must not be allowed to contaminate any other operation. Just make sure there's nothing to link him to SOE. How's he getting out, anyway?'

'An SIS frontier guard will see him over.'

'Stand him down. Stand him down *immediately*. If the Gestapo run your man on a long lead and they happen to uncover one of Six's prime assets, they'll be furious.'

'Yes, sir.' Purefoy picked up that Lusty was now 'your man'. Yesterday he had been 'our man'.

'Maybe Major Nye should be the one to untangle this mess as it's his patch. Should be done as soon as possible, I feel, but I'll leave that up to you.'

Once Purefoy had gone, Marjorie Gilbert came out of the small cloakroom in the corner. 'Masterly, my dear. I didn't know you had it in you.'

'It seemed the obvious thing to do,' replied Gilbert modestly. He had secretly been pleased to read in that morning's radio intercepts from Bletchley that Albrechtstraße were on Lusty's trail. It stopped Marjorie from carping at him to tip them off. All he had to do now was to help the Gestapo along without appearing to do so.

'Now the pack have his scent, we have to stop up the escape holes. We don't want the fox running to earth,' agreed Marjorie.

14

'*Hauptmann* Beck? I am *Hauptsturmführer* Diels, *Geheime Staatspolizei*. I wish to ask you some questions.'

Beck fought to calm the panic that threatened to engulf him like a tidal wave. Gestapo men could smell fear. He made himself nod in a polite but curious manner. Ilse offered Diels beer and sausage.

'I am on duty, *Frau* Runge.'

'As you wish. Go into the *Gaststub*e. It'll be warmer in there.'

Beck limped into the small room, thinking quickly. As a *Wehrmacht* officer, he did not have to submit to a Gestapo interrogation. The army had their own bogeymen – but to refuse to be questioned might start a whole chain of events over which he'd have no control. It was better to speak to this man now.

Beck tried to appear unconcerned as Diels scrutinized his papers. This was the first real test of his documentation. If London had made a mistake, he was a dead man. He watched Diels for the smallest indication that he had spotted something suspicious but Diels's dead eyes gave nothing away. He made a few notes, then handed back Beck's papers. The linnets sat silently in their gilded cage.

'You belong to the 21st Panzer Division. Where and when were you injured?'

'On the Mersa-Brega line at the beginning of December.'

'What happened?' Diels made notes in pencil in a small black leather-bound book.

'I'm in the reconnaissance battalion. I stayed behind to observe the advance of the British and got hit by our own artillery. Fortunately my driver, Schwegg, managed to get me into the Siegfried and high-tailed it to our own lines.'

'Wounds?'

'To the chest, leg and hand.'

'How did you come to leave Africa?'

Beck cleared his throat in a semblance of embarrassment. 'The adjutant of the hospital in Tripoli was a old comrade from the 5th Light Division. He arranged for me to be shipped to Italy due to the severity of my wounds.'

'Where in Italy?'

This was starting to get potentially risky. 'A military hospital. Santa Christina outside Naples, as you can see in my discharge papers.'

The hospital was genuine. They'd chosen it because the Americans had bombed it by accident last month. They hoped the records had been destroyed. If not ... How long would it take the Gestapo to discover that the hospital had never heard of *Hauptmann* Beck?

'What was the name of the hospital ship?'

That question threw Beck. One fact they had not thought of. 'Oh, really! I was on a stretcher when I embarked and in a coma, as a result of a secondary infection, when I disembarked. I wasn't very well, to put it mildly.'

Never know everything. You can seem too *word-perfect.*

'Who was your CO?'

'At the time of my injuries, it was General-Major von Randow. He assumed command after General-Major von Bismarck was killed leading the Division into battle. He was a brave man. We would have followed him anywhere.'

Diels gave a bleak smile. 'You are not afraid of me.'

'During the shelling at El Alamein, the men on either side of me were blown to bits. Fear is relative.'

'How long do you intend staying in Berchtesgaden?'

'I've reported my address and medical condition to Southern Army Command. I expect a medical board sometime in the next fortnight.'

'Yes?' For the first time Diels fixed his gaze on Beck's face.

'I hope to be passed fit for light duties.' Beck found it unnerving answering questions from someone like Diels who was totally unresponsive. He could not tell what the Gestapo man was thinking, what impression he was making.

'Thank you. That will do – for now, anyway.' Diels started to put away his pencil and notebook. 'One more thing. Why did you choose to come here?'

'I met a major in Santa Christina who spoke warmly of *Berchtesgadener Land*. He recommended the air for my lungs and the hill walks to build up my leg. Why are you asking me all these questions?'

Diels reopened his notebook and scribbled briefly. 'We're questioning every soldier in the area who's not on active duty here. When did your parents marry?'

'Um . . .' Beck's mind went momentarily blank. A complete blank. *Start at the beginning! Father Paul, mother Renate.* 'Nineteen-thirteen, October.'

'Thank you. Oh, and what colour are the trams in Cologne?'

'Blue, but why do you ask?'

Back in his room, Beck found he was trembling. It was obvious the interrogation had not been just a routine security check – but what did it mean? As a parting shot, Diels had asked about his journey up from Naples. Beck had not only been able to tell him the exact train times but also about the connecting tunnel between platforms at Bolzano where he had needed to change.

But the Gestapo would check his story. His time was running out.

Thanks to Ilse, Beck now knew a secret way onto the forbidden mountain. But he had lost his target. If Hitler did not walk to the Mooslangerkopf tea house, Beck would have to penetrate the inner security ring around the Berghof itself. It was Saturday today. His border crossing with Switzerland would close at midnight on Tuesday. Would he have that long?

Freed from nervous tension, waves of tiredness washed over him. Beck heard Runge's car drive up and Hänschen calling for Vishnia – then he fell asleep.

Purefoy was a coward, and the other side of a coward was a bully, thought Annie when she heard his voice raised as he berated Cricklemarsh. Her boss was attempting to reason quietly, but was being drowned out by the tirade of invective. Annie suspected Purefoy was being needlessly unpleasant because he had received a roasting in turn. She would set her spies to work to find out more.

In a very unladylike gesture, Annie spat in the cup of tea that she was making for Purefoy.

'But the operation's only got three days left to run. Why not let it go its natural course?' argued Cricklemarsh. 'If Lusty doesn't manage to get a shot at Hitler, we'll use what he's learned as a basis for our next operation. Hitler will be staying at Obersalzberg for several months. We'll have time to go back – and this time we'll know our way around.'

'Lusty won't have even three days, the way this operation is leaking out,' snapped Purefoy

Annie entered, carrying two cups of tea. She was careful about which one she handed to Purefoy. She busied herself tidying the files piled up on Lusty's desk. Purefoy was too busy scoring points to object to her presence.

'The discovery of the parachute *may* be down to Lusty,' conceded Cricklemarsh. 'But the leak from Berne can't have anything to do with him. That's something we should be concerned about . . .'

But Purefoy was already setting up his next target to shoot down. 'He didn't bother to bury his parachute properly because he was inadequately trained. How you could send a half-trained agent into the field is beyond me.'

'He was not half-trained . . .'

'Of course he's half-trained. And he wasn't properly vetted, either. I didn't know he was part German.'

'The King's got more German blood in him than Lusty has,' exclaimed Annie. Purefoy turned to scowl at her but Annie's imperious stare was more than a match for him.

Outside, in the dark London afternoon, a storm was gathering.

'The operation has been a farce from the beginning,' continued Purefoy, moving to stand with his back to the map of Obersalzberg, as if fearing someone would creep up behind him. 'You've got just twenty-four hours to pull Lusty out. The border crossing will be closed at midnight tomorrow. We can't risk compromising Six's tame border guard.'

'I don't know we can get through to Lusty in that time.'

'That's entirely his lookout,' retorted Purefoy, brushing his moustache with brisk aggressive movements of his index finger. 'The odds are the Gestapo will pick him up within the next twelve hours, anyway.'

Annie sank down into Lusty's chair and, unseen by the others, ran a hand over his desk. It made him seem closer, more tangible.

Pleased with the impact he'd made, Purefoy ploughed on. 'And if you yourself are not prepared to wrap up the operation, I'm sure Major Nye would be delighted to do so.'

With a curt nod, he strode out of the door, leaving it wide open. Annie and Cricklemarsh sat in motionless silence, listening to the sonorous tick of the old wall clock. Annie felt sick with fear for Lusty and furious at Purefoy's bullying. Cricklemarsh began twiddling with his pipe as though he'd reached the end of a college seminar.

'The bastard,' she swore viciously at last.

'When we planned this operation, we rather skipped over the matter of communications.' Cricklemarsh shook his head sadly. 'I didn't think they'd be important because it's not a fact-gathering mission. I was wrong. I didn't appreciate the amount of interplay there'd be between London and the field. I should have drawn up a tighter transmission schedule.'

With a heavy heart, he prepared a coded one-word message. *Poison.* The signal to pull out instantly. At five o'clock – six o'clock in Germany – he and Annie stood anxiously at the shoulder of the wireless operator as he began tapping out Lusty's call sign: dot-dash-dot, dot-dash-dot-dot.

Conditions were not good, said the operator. They were sending and receiving at the limit of the set's range. The mountains around Berchtesgaden would obscure the signal and you really needed perfect atmospheric conditions to communicate with reasonable clarity. The weather wasn't helping, either. The signal was stronger at night but there were storms over much of Europe and the area of low pressure was expected to deepen as the evening wore on. Not a night for trying to make contact.

'Beggars and choosers,' muttered Cricklemarsh.

He's not there, sensed Annie. *He's not there.* She had an image of the wireless transmitter sitting at the bottom of some wardrobe. 'He's not there,' she said dully.

'There's no reason why he should be.'

'But if we can't make contact with him tonight he'll be abandoned.'

'It hasn't come to that yet,' said Cricklemarsh, biting at the stem of his pipe.

Beck woke with a raging thirst, worrying that he had missed his six o'clock slot. If he had, there was still a call scheduled at nine o'clock and a final one at midnight but he found he had ten minutes before he needed to switch on the set. The memories of the recent Gestapo interview and the magical morning with Ilse vied for his attention like two powerful currents. Beck chose to think of Ilse. She was infatuated with him. He hadn't meant it to happen. He wasn't to know that she, like Vishnia in her way, was crying out for affection, for a kind word.

Ilse had made love with a jagged-edged intensity that frightened him. Even when guards had been in earshot, she had been desperate and unbridled in her passion. He'd needed to slap a hand over her mouth to stop her crying out. But instead of sharing his fear she'd stared back at him with mad, daring eyes and thrust harder against him, taking herself to higher ecstasies.

He remembered the semi-hysterical way she had acted that first time they had walked together. He'd suspected then that she was a little unbalanced. Now, maybe, he understood why. Not only had she been blackmailed into a loveless marriage to Runge, but she was forced to endure the daily stress of hiding Hugo Guttmann and his wife, knowing that at any time they might be discovered and herself denounced. It was enough to drive anyone to the brink of sanity. Then a handsome, wounded officer had come along. All too easy for her to fall in love as an escape from the tensions of the real and terrible world.

But he could not afford to love her. If he was successful in his mission, he would be her death warrant. The Gestapo would torture and murder everyone he had been close to.

Beck felt guilty about using Ilse – loving, mentally frail Ilse. But he knew that he must never allow himself to feel *so* guilty that he would stop using her. *Use her, yes – but do not fall in love with her.*

He limped into the *Stube* just as Hänschen was ripping the locket from around Vishnia's neck.

Vishnia clutched at her throat, her eyes as wide as saucers. She held out her hand imploringly but Hänschen danced away from her, smirking in triumph.

'I've got that stupid girl's pendant, Uncle Gottlob,' he gloated. 'I'm going to throw it in the stove.'

Runge glanced up from the *Stammtisch* where he sat flicking through a tattered pile of *Nordic Physical Training* and *Heath and Beauty* magazines, and merely grunted.

Vishnia banged the flat of her hand on the table in frustration as she again failed to grab Hänschen.

'Quiet, you Ukrainian cow,' growled Runge.

The boy leaped on a bench, still holding the pendant out of her reach. Vishnia made a whimpering noise at the back of her throat.

'Give it back to her,' commanded Beck.

'Shan't, and you won't make me.' Hänschen drew his *Pimpf* dagger and began to prise open the locket. 'I want to see what's inside.'

Runge rumbled with laughter. Encouraged, Hänschen pressed harder to break open the locket. As Vishnia flung herself at the boy, her flailing arm sent a set of antlers crashing to the floor.

'You clumsy bitch,' yelled Runge. 'You'll wreck the place.'

Hänschen cawed in triumph.

Something snapped inside Beck. Moving amazingly quickly, he grasped Hänschen by the scruff of the neck, threw the boy over his knee and brought his walking stick down as hard as he could.

'This – will – teach – you – to – respect – others,' rasped Beck, punctuating his words by blows. The boy squealed but Beck held him in an iron grip. 'You – are – a – spoilt – brat – who – deserves – to – be – taught – a – lesson. Do – not – bully – others, understand.'

He tore the locket out of Hänschen's hand, then hurled the boy away.

Tears ran down Hänschen's face. 'I hate you. I hate you. You're a traitor. I'll denounce you.'

Beck examined the locket. Apart from one dent there was no harm done. He handed it back to Vishnia. Out of the corner of his eye, he saw Runge watching with a contemptuous leer on his unshaven face.

Suddenly, Vishnia snatched at his arm and jerked him forwards. Caught off balance, Beck stumbled and fell to his knees. He looked up to see Vishnia standing over him, wielding a chair to fend off Hänschen. The boy held the dagger in his hand. He would have stabbed Beck while Runge watched and said nothing.

'Another stab in the back,' sneered Beck. He brought his stick down on Hänschen's arm with almost enough force to break it. The boy dropped the dagger and fled screaming from the room.

Beck's fury was out of control. He snatched up the dagger and raised it above his head. Runge's eyes bulged over their huge underlids. He shrank back, and a stench of shit rose off him. The dagger flashed as Beck stabbed it into the *Stammtisch* with all his might, impaling the pile of soft-porn magazines.

It was only when Beck returned to his room that he found he had missed the six o'clock transmission.

Annie waited with a dry mouth and an increasing sense of gloom and foreboding. After the allotted ten minutes, the operator had given up.

'Come on,' said Cricklemarsh to Annie. 'I'll take you for a drink. We've not been out of this place all day.'

'You've not been out for three days.'

'Is it that long? Good gracious! Some fresh air will do me good.'

The sky was slate grey with torn, black clouds, like smoke from exploding shells, scudding over the rooftops. Strong gusts of wind sent ripples across the puddles on the pavements. Annie turned up her collar and linked her arm through Cricklemarsh's just as the full force of the wind caught them at the corner.

'Gee. This is fearsome,' she shouted.

'Exhilarating.'

They fell through the door of the Barley Mow as heavy rain began to drum down and were lucky to find a table in one corner. Cricklemarsh fumbled for his pipe and started the lengthy ritual of scraping and reaming it.

'There's a saying in the intelligence world that shit rolls down the mountain.'

'And we're at the bottom of the mountain?'

'No. Sadly, Lusty is.' He sucked through the stem.

'Do you really think we're wise to call it off?'

'No, not yet. So the Germans found an abandoned parachute! It doesn't tell them who was wearing it. Lusty's miles away by now. But Purefoy claims the Gestapo already know there's a British plot to assassinate Hitler . . .'

'How do we know they know?' Annie interrupted.

Cricklemarsh had friends and colleagues at Station X at Bletchley regularly cracking the German codes. He had used their product in Oxford but the existence of Station X was one of the most closely guarded secrets of the war. Immense care was taken to disguise the provenance of intelligence gathered by the code-breakers.

Cricklemarsh dropped his voice. 'I can only assume we've been reading their signal traffic.'

'But how do the Gestapo know our plans?'

'The Gestapo work on the assumption that there're plots to assassinate the Führer all the time,' replied Cricklemarsh, relieved that Annie had not pursued the subject of the code-breakers. 'The only difference this time is that they seem to know that there's an attempt being made *right now*.'

'But they can't know what Lusty looks like or anything about his cover.'

'Exactly. I wish I knew what was behind our masters' loss of confidence. How did they learn Lusty wasn't properly vetted or find out about his German connections?'

'I bet that creep Nye had something to do with it. Speak of the devil,' exclaimed Annie as Nye entered the bar. 'He's doubtless been getting at people. You know what he's like. Hell! He's coming over this way.'

Nye was unable to keep a smug look off his face.

'I gather your little expedition is coming to a premature close.'

'Yeh! Go to hell,' said Annie with American bluntness.

'I'm not surprised.' He ignored her. 'Half-baked scheme with half-trained personnel. It never stood a chance.'

'What do you know about it, anyway?' Annie's eyes flashed but Nye ignored the danger signs.

'I've friends.'

'Then I suggest you tell your friends to keep their noses out of our affairs,' hissed Annie.

'There'll be the post-mortem,' taunted Nye. 'Lots of questions to be answered.'

'Let's get our man home first,' said Cricklemarsh, speaking for the first time. 'Compared with that, whatever else may happen in the future isn't important.'

'You don't really have much of a future, do you?'

Annie leaped up and landed him a stinging blow with the flat of her hand.

The bar fell silent. The larger of two Australians drinking nearby said, 'If he's bothering you, miss, we'll sort him out.'

'Thank you, but I can deal with his kind.' White patches of fury sat high on her cheeks.

'You'll regret that, you Yankee bitch. I promise you, you'll regret that.' Nye marched out, the jeers of the Aussies ringing in his ears.

'Oh, Annie,' sighed Cricklemarsh. 'Why did you have to do that?'

Because I was standing up for you, because I was standing up for Lusty, because I was standing up for friendship and decency.

'He annoyed me,' she said simply. 'I'm sorry.'

'Don't be. I'm proud of you.'

'But now he'll go and start putting in the poison good and proper. Don't you have any friends in high places to turn to?'

'You're the well-connected one.'

'If we were in America, I could maybe call some of daddy's friends in Washington,' she mused. 'But mummy's side are all navy. If you want a battle cruiser for the weekend, I could probably organize it.'

'I'll remember that,' smiled Cricklemarsh.

'We need someone fighting our corner,' insisted Annie. 'It's not enough in Baker Street to get on with your job, you have to be a politician as well.'

'Come on, let's get back. We must try to contact Lusty again.'

But once they were back in their garret, Cricklemarsh left Annie alone to resume her vigil alongside the wireless operator while he went to make some phone calls.

'*Grüß Gott*,' Ilse greeted Thurn and Leeb as they hurried into the bar room out of the rain. 'What can I get you to drink?'

'Beer and schnapps, please, *Frau* Runge.'

'Move nearer the stove and dry out while I tell *Herr* Runge you're here.' She hurried out, humming to herself.

The two men adjusted the swastika armbands on their brown shirts and exchanged glances. '*Frau* Runge seems in a very good mood,' whispered Thurn.

'Yes, normally she won't pass the time of day with us,' agreed Leeb.

Ilse was trying hard not to show her feelings but she was just too happy. She couldn't stop smiling, her eyes younger and brighter than they'd been for years.

'Well, you know what makes a woman happy, don't you?' winked Leeb, wiping froth off his wispy moustache.

Runge strutted into the bar. 'Ready, men?'

'Hang on,' protested Thurn. 'We're only halfway though our drinks.'

'If you want a lift you can come now, otherwise you can sodding well walk.' Runge strode away, leaving the two men trying to gulp down the contents of their glasses.

They drove away at a snail's pace, the windscreen wipers barely coping with the downpour.

'I don't expect there'll be much of a turnout tonight,' forecast Leeb.

'Don't talk shit. An opportunity to hear Julius Streicher speak! They'll all be there. Streicher's newspaper is the only one the Führer reads from cover to cover,' declared Runge.

A small imp made Leeb say, '*Frau* Runge's looking good. She's positively blooming.'

'You obviously know how to keep a woman happy,' sniped Thurn, still angry at being forced to hurry his drink.

'The secret's to give them a good seeing-to every night.' Runge had the uncomfortable feeling that Thurn and Leeb were laughing at him.

'It's a remarkable change, anyway,' said Leeb. 'Only two days ago she bit my head off for spilling beer on the table.'

'I've told you, it's because us Old Fighters know how to satisfy a woman.' Runge was growing angry at the way the two men kept harping on about his wife's new-found happiness. He hadn't noticed it. In fact, she'd threatened him with a carving knife that very morning.

They pulled up outside the four-storey *Berchtesgadener Hof* on the edge of the town. The swastika flag over the doorway hung soaking and limp. Inside, glass chandeliers glittered at the top of the broad, red-carpeted staircase where an imposing bronze bust of Hitler glared down over the vestibule crowded with brown and black uniforms. A figure in a leather coat materialized at Runge's side.

'A word, if you please.' Diels steered Runge into a corner. 'What exactly do you know about the army officer staying at your inn?'

'Very little. He just arrived out of the blue, asking for somewhere to stay,' replied Runge defensively. He knew Diels to be one of the late influx who had joined the Party overnight when Hitler's success was guaranteed. They were mockingly referred to as *Pfepferlinge*, or mushrooms, by the older fighters who had been pushed into the background by the younger, brighter wave. Runge had no time for Diels' kind but no one sneered at the Gestapo. Not openly. 'Is anything wrong?'

'How do you find Captain Beck?'

'He's got airs and graces like many army officers. He belted my own nephew when the boy was wearing his *Pimpf* uniform and he stood up for some Ukrainian girl who works for me. I put him in his place, I can tell you.'

'Of course.' Diels continued to regard him with his unblinking eyes. 'How does he spend his time?'

'Walks, stays in his room . . . I don't know. I'm too busy with Party business to be watching the man twenty-four hours a day.'

'Does he spend any time with *Frau* Runge?'

Again those insinuations. 'They got caught in the RAF raid on Munich so they had to spend a night together in an air-raid shelter.'

'Have you searched his room?'

'Yes, but there was nothing. What is this about?'

Diels produced two cigarettes from an inside pocket and offered one to Runge, as if signifying the interview had reached an informal stage.

'Most soldiers who come to Berchtesgaden to convalesce have their billets arranged by their own units. Your Captain Beck made his own way here.'

'You think he's an impostor?'

'There's no doubt Captain Beck exists. He was awarded the Iron Cross in North Africa, and his family was definitely killed in Cologne. We're trying to check further but the air raids are making communications difficult.'

'So?'

'Search his room again sometime. Keep an eye on him and get your nephew to do the same.'

'You have a hunch?'

Diels was scornful. 'Gestapo officers do not need to rely on hunches. We have powers.'

Runge took his seat in the front row, gleefully excited by their talk. It could be a chance to get rid of Beck and kill two birds with one stone. He'd seen Leeb and Thurn sniggering with friends, throwing sideways glances in his direction. He'd teach them to laugh at him, suggesting there was something going on between his wife and Beck. The very idea! Staid, conservative Ilse who would not undress with the light on. He didn't believe his wife had the imagination to be unfaithful, but it was bad enough that others thought it. If Beck was having a fling with his wife, it'd be the last fling he'd ever have.

Runge listened with only half an ear as Julius Streicher, arch anti-Semite of the Third Reich, trademark bullwhip in his right hand, wound himself up into a fury against the Jews. *'There is a documented case of a racially pure Aryan girl who was preyed on by the bestial lusts of a Jew. Fortunately she managed to escape the clutches of this lecher and later she married an Aryan. Yet she and her husband produced Jewish-looking off-spring, meaning her hereditary properties had been permanently corrupted by her encounter with the Jew.'*

Runge cheered with the others, but his mind was elsewhere, planning and willing the downfall of the man he was coming to hate.

Beck hunched over the transmitter, listening to the hum of the valves and smelling the warm dust. There was something wrong. He'd sent out his call sign half a dozen times but all he was getting back was static. Once he thought he had discerned the answer-back – but it could have been wishful thinking. The storm could be interfering with reception or maybe he had damaged the set. He began sending blind.

Operation going well. Have found entrance to maze. Have struck up relationship with close friend of Wolf . . .

He paused. Every time a floorboard creaked or a gust rattled the window, his heart stopped. Once he stopped to tiptoe to the door when he thought he'd heard a sound in the corridor.

Invitation to maze possible.

A lorry ground its way up the road past the inn. He froze, staring at the blackout curtain until the noise of the lorry had faded into the night, heading towards Austria.

Can you extend border opening if needed?

Beck was taking longer than the safe four minutes set down by Cricklemarsh but still all he was getting back from London was an earful of static. By the time he'd finished sending, Beck felt mentally and physically drained. He turned out the light and drew back the curtain. He lay on the bed, letting the tension trickle out of him as he watched the faint headlights of a car create shadowy ripples on the white ceiling.

It was strange to think that a little over a mile away Hitler himself was doing whatever he did in the evenings. Was he poring over military maps of the Eastern Front flanked by generals from the High Command? Earnestly debating the conduct of the war with his advisers? Or was he reading a book, sitting in an armchair across the fireside from Eva Braun, the pair of them a picture of domestic tranquillity? Beck found it hard to imagine Hitler doing any of these things.

'Christian.'

He sat bolt upright, eyes wide open, wondering if he had imagined the voice.

Someone was turning the door handle.

'Christian.' Ilse was calling softly to him. *Hell!* He was cursed by interruptions each time he established contact with London. He unplugged the set, pushed it under the bed, removed the chair from under the handle and unlocked the door in one rapid movement.

Ilse slid into the room.

'Hello,' he whispered.

Ilse did not reply. Instead she wrapped her arms around his neck and pulled his mouth down onto hers. Beck gasped at the electricity pulsing from her body. She pressed harder against him, chewing at his lower lip. Like a serpent's, her body was writhing, coiling around his own. As she felt him grow hard, she mewed deeply at the back of her throat. Naked animal lust consumed her. Breathing heavily, she pushed him back towards the bed, fighting desperately with his fly buttons, uncaring if she ripped the material.

When Beck entered her, Ilse's mouth set in a manic rictus before widening in a silent scream. She thrashed wildly with arms, legs, pulling, biting, scratching in a maelstrom of emotions, her back arched and taut as a bowstring.

Her climax was as piercingly shrill as the wind on a mountain ledge, as the keening of an eagle soaring and circling on ever-rising thermals.

When she regained consciousness, she found she was still lying on her back, her frock pulled up around her naked belly, her legs wide open as if giving birth. Beck lay panting next to her, his trousers around his knees. There was no beauty and little dignity in their post-coital state. Only a sense of the ridiculous and of shame.

Ilse rolled on her side to face Beck, making no effort to pull down her dress. Instead she reached out to hold his balls and kissed him gently on the moon scar marking his forehead.

'Sorry,' she whispered. 'I'm not usually so . . . I needed that. I hope I didn't scare you.'

Beck shook his head, unwilling to admit to her that it was the closest he had ever come to being raped. It was an unsettling experience.

'Only after this morning . . . you must think me sex mad. I promise you I'm not.' The words were tainted with bitterness. 'Runge takes Vishnia like that. He makes her have sex with him. Suddenly, forcibly so she can't object. I feel sorry for her but I don't say anything because when he's doing it to her, he's not doing it to me. Isn't that terrible! It's for my sanity, you see,' she ended simply.

Beck wrapped his arms around her.

'It's not Vishnia's fault,' Ilse continued, talking to herself as much as to Beck. 'She fears Runge'll send her to a *KZ* if she objects. But I use her as much as Runge does. When he's with Vishnia, he's not with me.'

'It doesn't have to be that bad,' murmured Beck.

'Remind me,' spat Ilse.

'I thought I had.'

'Oh, darling. You have.' She began to press against him again. He kissed her gently on the mouth. She broke away and giggled. 'I've just remembered, I came to ask you if you wanted to share a secret?'

'Another one?'

'Come with me.'

As they were about to open the bedroom door, Beck thought he heard light footsteps hurrying away but when they emerged the corridor was empty. Beck put it down to a guilty conscience.

In the kitchen, Vishnia gave Ilse a searching look. *Twice in one day: whatever next?* she seemed to be saying.

Ilse first made sure that the drinkers in the larger *Stube* had full glasses before she led the two of them into Runge's office and closed the door. As she turned on the Bakelite wireless, the sound of the actress Zarah Lander singing 'I know there'll be a Miracle' filled the room.

'I loved her in that film *Die Grosse Liebe* but the coward fled back to Sweden after a bomb fell near her Berlin home this month,' said Ilse. 'What sort of person would do that? If you take so much out of a country, you must give something back.'

Ilse turned down the volume and put her ear close to the set as she slowly turned the dial.

'Vishnia and I sometimes listen to American jazz from Switzerland when we know it's safe. Shall we dance with you, *Hauptmann* Beck?' She performed an elaborate curtsy in front of him.

'My leg.'

'Of course. I'm sorry.' For a moment he thought she was going to kiss him right in front of Vishnia, but she drew back, putting her finger to her lips. 'Listen.'

Through the mush and crackle of static came the faint strains of 'Lili Bolero'. It faded and Ilse frowned. 'The weather sometimes makes reception difficult here. The mountains do not help.'

'. . . *News from London* . . .' Ilse made minute adjustments as the announcer, speaking immaculate German, began. 'British and New Zealand forces continue to make a steady advance towards Tripoli with the *Deutsche Afrika Korps* fighting continuous rearguard actions. More than five thousand German and Italian troops have surrendered in the past few days. As the RAF and the Royal Navy tighten their hold over the Mediterranean, German supplies of fuel and ammunition are running out . . .'

Both women were looking at him to see how he took the news of his former comrades. He composed himself to appear suitably concerned.

'. . . On the Eastern Front, the Red Army . . .' *Bang.* Something metallic crashed to the floor in the scullery. Ilse, leaped at the wireless and twisted the dial to a German station. She flung open the door. Out in the corridor, Hänschen was disappearing round the corner.

'He was spying on us,' she breathed. 'The little swine was spying on us.'

Vishnia put an index finger in her mouth and bit until her teeth left a coronet of white indentations on her knuckle.

Purefoy had belatedly reached the conclusion that he should have given Operation Nightshade to Nye to draw his sting. It was too late for that now – but not too late to bring Nye into the fold. Better have him inside the tent pissing out than outside pissing in.

'I've been meaning to ask you how you'd feel about your section taking over Special Projects and Austria. It would make more sense to lump them with Germany. Think you could handle it all?' Purefoy signalled to an elderly club servant for more drinks.

'Absolutely.' Nye nodded in agreement. 'It's what I've been suggesting for some time.'

'Splendid!' Purefoy smoothed his moustache. 'Between you and me, Cricklemarsh won't survive the debacle of Operation Nightshade. He's just not up to this sort of work. He can't cut the mustard.'

The false sincerity, oozing from him, was matched by Nye's mask of friendship.

Nye was still bristling at having been publicly humiliated by Annie but his pride did not allow him to mention the incident to his superior. He took comfort in the fact that the American girl's aggression suggested that she and her boss were cracking under the strain, losing the plot just when it mattered most.

A servant, wearing a black morning coat green with age, appeared at his shoulder.

'A phone call for you, colonel.'

'Thank you. Excuse me.' Purefoy followed the man through the tall double doors and down the broad stairway to the cramped telephone booth behind the porter's desk. He squeezed inside, ducking to avoid the naked light bulb bumping against his hair.

'Colonel Purefoy? We've heard from our man.'

'Sorry?' It was a poor line.

'It's good news. He's gained a means of access to the secure area.'

Purefoy recognized the distorted voice as Cricklemarsh's. 'That doesn't change anything,' he said irritably.

'But it does. He's found a way in. And it's possible he's going to meet Wolf in person. Think of all the options that opens up.'

'What are you talking about?'

Cricklemarsh tutted in exasperation. 'He hopes to meet the leader. Do you understand?'

Cricklemarsh's irate tone rankled. This coming from the man whose foolishness was jeopardizing Purefoy's future! Damn him!

'Of course I understand,' he barked. 'But nothing has changed. Midnight tomorrow and then that's it. Don't bother me again.'

Purefoy strode back to the library, furious.

'That was the final straw,' he told Nye. 'Tomorrow, start to pick up the pieces. Get Lusty out by tomorrow night if you can or make sure he has no links to Baker Street if you can't. Make the best out of a bad job, eh?'

'Monika? Monika?'

'In here.' Her voice brooded with a surly indifference.

Jäger took off his greatcoat and automatically straightened the oil painting of the Lorelei that hung in the hall next to a hunting tapestry. The radiator was pulsing out heat as usual. Monika was curled up in a corner of the sofa, a cheap novel in her hands; Wagner's *Tannhäuser* was doing battle with weather interference on the wireless.

'So you've decided to come home at last.'

Jäger produced a jar of cherries in kirsch from his overnight bag. 'A present from Berlin.'

Monika glanced incuriously at the cherries and continued to pretend to read.

'Have you heard anything from Alix?' Jäger carried the jar into the well-stocked kitchen.

'No. I wasn't expecting to.'

Jäger helped himself to a bottle of beer. He wished he could open a window to let in some fresh air but he knew Monika would object.

'Drinking again.'

He did not bother tell her it was the first drink of his eighteen-hour day.

'I met an old friend in Berlin yesterday,' he began.

'So?'

'You remember Heinrich Müller?'

'Gestapo Müller?' He had her interest now.

'He told me there was a new White Rose recruit in Aachen.'

'Oh, my God! My God!' Monika's hand flew to her throat. 'Why would he tell you that?'

'He owes me.' Jäger took another swallow, feeling the beer wash away the day's dust from inside his throat. 'You're going to have to go to Aachen and warn Alix that she's being watched and mustn't do anything stupid. There's a train at ten in the morning, changing at Frankfurt.'

'They're watching her,' repeated Monika weakly. She moved towards the telephone like a sleepwalker. It was not just her only child's life that was in danger. The Gestapo would take its revenge on the whole family. For the misdoings of just one family member, it was common for parents, brothers, sisters, even children, to be rounded up and sent to a concentration camp. And the Gestapo was viciously cruel. The first the wife of White Rose leader Christoph Probst had known of her husband's execution was when she received a bill for three thousand *Reichsmark* for wear and tear to the guillotine.

Monika paused with her hand on the telephone. 'Wait a minute! You saw Müller in Berlin *yesterday*. You've been back in Munich all day. Why didn't you tell me this sooner?'

'I didn't get back to Dachau until midnight. I was up before dawn and I haven't stopped working since. This is the first chance I've had to talk to you.'

'The first chance!' Monika's voice rose in shrill indignation. 'You knew the Gestapo were watching our daughter and you did nothing about it for God knows how many hours just because you were busy.'

'I could hardly tell you on the phone . . .'

'You could have found two minutes to drop in. Is your job more precious than your own daughter?'

She picked up the receiver and gave the operator her sister's number in Aachen. After a long delay, she was put through.

'Hanna? It's Monika. Can I speak to Alix? . . . Gone? This is a terrible line . . . She left? What do you mean, she's left? She's only just got there. . . .'

The colour drained out of Monika's cheeks. She turned to Jäger. 'She's gone from Hanna's. She's moved in with some students she met at the university . . .'

Cricklemarsh climbed into the back of the Humber limousine, redolent with mellow cigar smoke and old leather. 'Thank you for seeing me, sir.'

'I keep my word. Years ago, you warned me about German tank rearmament while the British government insisted it wasn't happening. If people had only listened to me then, we would not be where we are today. I'm sorry we have to talk in such a rush but I'm due for supper with the American ambassador and then I must catch the midnight sleeper north.'

A policeman saluted as the car glided out into the wide thoroughfare and past the Cenotaph into the unlit streets of London.

'I'm very grateful, sir.'

'Now to the point. Why did you want to see me?'

Cricklemarsh swivelled to face the darkened bulk of the Prime Minister. 'Have you heard of Operation Nightshade, sir?'

'No,' replied Churchill immediately. 'Should I?'

'It's an operation to assassinate Hitler.

'The devil it is!'

'And you've not heard of it?'

'I have said so.' The cigar glowed.

'Almost two months ago I was tasked with putting together an operation to kill the Führer. We have an agent in Berchtesgaden as we speak.'

'Do we, by God!' Churchill let down a shelf to reveal a tantalus of decanters and glasses. He poured two brandies and passed one to Cricklemarsh. 'It never does to arrive at these functions completely sober. There's an strong teetotal strain running through American diplomacy just now. So tell me about Operation Nightshade.'

Cricklemarsh described the details and how his own assistant had volunteered. He had been dropped into southern Germany a week ago. At first things went wrong because their information was false, but just as things had started moving their way, Cricklemarsh had been ordered to scrap the entire mission. Was there a reason for this change of heart? Didn't it make more sense now to let the operation go ahead?

Churchill smoked in silence for a few moments as they drove up Regent Street towards Oxford Circus.

'This concept was indeed raised obliquely and informally some time ago. I opined then that I would like to see Hitler dead but I insisted that the assassination must appear to originate from the German side. We could not be responsible for the inevitable acts of reprisal that would cost the lives of thousands of innocent people. Hearing no more of it, I assumed that the idea, like so many others, had fallen on stony ground.'

'Not three hours ago our man radioed to say he was getting very near to Hitler. Surely it'd be criminal to abort the operation just as it's coming to fruition.'

'How close exactly are you to achieving your aim?'

Cricklemarsh hesitated. 'I honestly can't say. Neither can I guarantee the operation will succeed. But I believe we can't give up now. The prize is too great.'

'I might agree. But after midnight tomorrow your man's escape route will be blocked?'

'That is correct, sir.'

'It sounds as though someone wanted to present me with a *fait accompli*,' growled Churchill. 'But once things started to go wrong, they decided to wash their hands of it; to pretend it never happened, even at the cost of a brave man's life.' The Prime Minister drifted off into his own thoughts again, occasionally sipping away at the brandy and puffing on his cigar. Just as Cricklemarsh started to worry his presence had been forgotten, Churchill murmured, 'The Americans aren't going to like it.'

'Sorry?' The car drove into Regents Park.

'Punishment of war criminals by proper judicial process is an Allied war aim,' explained Churchill. 'A War Crimes Commission has already been set up to begin collecting and sifting evidence. The Americans want Hitler alive to put on public trial. I, however, am happy to see the Nazi bugger dead – and the sooner the better. If you remove the head from a sick and malignant body, all you are left with is putrefaction. It's all right for the Americans to seek the moral high ground after the war. I'm more concerned with winning it.'

'Indeed, sir.'

'And as the Americans have not yet formally notified His Majesty's Government of their desires in this, there is nothing to prevent me supporting an attempt to kill Hitler. In fact, I would delight in his death. I consider him evil incarnate.'

Cricklemarsh slowly understood that he was being given Churchill's blessing. The car slowed down. Ahead he could see a knot of policemen on the pavement outside a grand house.

Churchill waved his cigar. 'I must warn you, though, that as soon as the American government makes public its desire to keep the man alive for a show trial, then, for the sake of the Alliance, I must concur with them. An announcement is due soon but, one hopes not for the next few days. By then this operation must be resolved, one way or the other.'

A policeman stepped forward and opened the door as the limousine drew to a halt.

'Good hunting,' said Churchill, shaking Cricklemarsh's hand.

'Thank you, sir. Thank you very much.'

'I'll see that they leave you alone to finish the job – and that the border meanwhile stays open. But remember what I just said: as soon as the Americans come out publicly, I will not be able to help you.'

Brendan Bracken came up from a second car and watched the retreating figure of Cricklemarsh with open curiosity.

'Don't let appearances deceive you,' murmured Churchill. 'One of the bravest men I know. Served as one of my company commanders in the Royal Scots Fusiliers in 1916. Should have got the VC. Damned shame he didn't.'

15

Sunday, 28 March

A shell-pink dawn was breaking in Munich's eastern sky as Jäger arrived at the Ettstraße police headquarters. He had been summoned from his bed while it was still dark. He had had less than five hours' sleep, but that was not unusual. Finding *Standartenführer* Esser already there waiting for him, in his best uniform, was. Esser grasped his sleeve and led him to one side.

'What's the problem?' demanded Jäger, irritable at being denied a cup of coffee.

'The Gestapo are convinced the Englishman has come specifically to kill Hitler,' whispered Esser.

'Makes sense.' Jäger lit a cheroot. 'What made the Gestapo come up with this idea overnight?'

'Hmm.' Esser cleared his throat. 'They didn't.'

'What!'

'I was informed yesterday afternoon.' Esser winced at the thunder-clouds gathering over Jäger's bushy eyebrows .

'So why the hell didn't you tell me?'

'Operational security,' bleated Esser. 'It was highly classified. Essential personnel only.'

'Oh, good God! So why tell me now?'

'We've been ordered to the *Kommandozentrale der RSD/Staatspolizei* on Obersalzberg.'

'I've got things to do here.' Jäger turned away in disgust. 'Bunting has to jog his memory about the mystery officer – or maybe I'll get the Gestapo to jog it for him. You go off and play policemen. I'm staying here.'

'*Sturmbannführer*, this is a direct order from Albrechtstraße.'

'So? I'm not regarded as "essential personnel".'

Esser had never hated anyone as much as he hated Jäger now. He held out the teleprinter signal from Kaltenbrunner's office for his inspection. 'Look, you are *named*. You have to come with me.'

Jäger used the journey to pretend to sleep. In fact, he was running over the row he and Monika had had a few hours previously, and wondered whether he really was being unfair or if she was being selfish.

'I can't go to Aachen just like that,' she had objected.

Jäger could think of no reason why she could not go, apart from the fact that she disliked having her routine upset.

'You have to find Alix and make sure she's safe.'

'You're the great detective. *You* go and find her. I wouldn't have a clue where to start.'

'She'll have had to register her new address at the town hall. Anyway, she's probably left a forwarding address with Hanna. You didn't even ask about that, did you?'

'Next time, you speak to her.'

Jäger knew from bitter experience that confrontation would drive them in increasingly unpleasant circles.

'I would go to see her, I promise, but I can't leave this investigation. It's too important.'

'They all are,' she replied sourly.

'I don't normally get flown to Berlin to brief the head of the *Reich*'s Security Service, do I?'

There was no answer to that. Instead, Monika gave a long-suffering sigh.

Jäger pressed on. 'If I went off to Aachen tomorrow, the Gestapo would want to know what I was doing there – and I don't see Müller getting me out of that one. Please, Monika, I don't ask much.'

'You don't give much,' she shot back.

'Please, for Alix's sake.'

A pause, then, 'All right.'

It was said resentfully and Jäger knew that she despised him more than ever.

Owing to Esser's nervousness, they arrived at Berchtesgaden with three-quarters of an hour to spare. The storm of the previous day had passed, leaving the sky a deep, satisfying blue with fresh snow glistening on the surrounding peaks. Still trying to placate Jäger, Esser proposed breakfast. Jäger, whose stomach had been rumbling since they'd left Munich, agreed.

An old coaching inn, its ochre walls bedecked with swastikas, attracted their eye. White smoke drifted in a gentle plume from a chimney while a thin serving girl shook a tablecloth outside the open door. She watched the police car come to a stop before running back into the inn. Jäger was already hoping to find *Münchner Weisswurst* – the white sausage eaten by Bavarians only before lunch. He knew that people in the country ate better than those in the towns since the peasants hung onto what they produced in spite of threats from the Party. Bartering was the norm out here. *He who has one thing, has everything.*

The smell of coffee drew the two policemen into a small *Stube* on one side of a long passageway. Next to a green-tiled stove, in one corner, a solitary Panzer captain was finishing his breakfast.

He looked startled as they entered. '*Grüß Gott*,' he said.

'*Grüß Gott*,' replied Jäger.

'*Heil Hitler*,' barked Esser.

Jäger gave the officer the once-over he gave everyone he encountered. Mid- to late twenties, fair hair, regular features, medium build. A walking stick rested against the bench. Iron Cross, first class, the cuff of the DAK, silver wound stripe and, unusually, a tank-destroyer badge. As the captain went to smear crab-apple jelly on a slice of black bread, Jäger noticed that the middle two fingers on his left hand were missing.

A handsome blonde woman hurried in, wiping her hands on her

white apron. Certainly they could have breakfast. She could offer them pressed meat, cheese, brawn, home-made preserves, but only rye bread.

'Any chance of an egg?' queried Jäger.

The woman chuckled at the notion. The very idea! No, she had no eggs.

'Forgive me, but I don't suppose you have any *Münchner Weisswurst*?'

She thought she might have, and Jäger cheered up.

'Is there anything else, *Hauptmann*?' She turned to the officer.

At the back of Jäger's mind, small bells began to jingle. He'd seen both the woman and the officer before – but in a different context. Together, too. He scowled with the effort of recalling where and when. The memory was elusive, slipping away like a dream lost on waking. He told himself it was not important, otherwise he would have remembered.

The officer was folding a napkin. 'Have you seen Hänschen this morning?' he asked the woman.

'No. Have you?'

'No.'

Something had passed between them, sensed Jäger. Some unspoken message. The officer was troubled. He ran his right hand up over his forehead, pushing back a flap of hair.

'Perhaps he had errands to run before going to school.' The officer limped to the door. 'Good day, gentlemen, enjoy the scenery.'

'Thank you,' said Jäger, again wondering where he had seen this man before. Then a slice of *Münchner Weisswurst* appeared before him and Jäger ceased to care.

The ground floor of the Hotel zum Türken was still painted in cream, the upper stories clad in dark wood with rustic balconies bedecked in red and greens. *It must have looked a picture when it actually was a hotel,* thought Jäger. But he could understand why the place had been taken over by Hitler's bodyguard; it sat less than two hundred metres above and to the right of the Berghof. It was inconceivable that the public could be allowed this close to the Führer's mountain home. Now the hotel housed the commander of Hitler's bodyguard, the local SD and the officer in charge of the *Nebelkompanie*, whose smoke-making devices could cloak the mountain in minutes at the approach of enemy bombers.

Jäger had never set foot on Obersalzberg before. Since 1934 the mountain had been closed to the public, apart from organized pilgrimages to worship the Führer, and even they had been stopped in 1938. The two policemen were made to show their identities at three different checkpoints on the road up from Berchtesgaden before they could enter the *Führersperrgebiet* – the innermost security zone where pairs of guards patrolled with Schmeisser machine pistols over their shoulders and German shepherd dogs straining at their leashes.

Once inside the old hotel, Jäger and Esser were led to a sunny room where *Standartenführer* Helmut von Hummel, head of Hitler's personal bodyguard, was waiting. Jäger was not given time to appreciate the view. Von Hummel, fussy and dogmatic, instantly demanded an up-to-date report. Jäger gave a brief outline of developments since Hamm's murder. He had a question of his own, in turn.

'Has anything at all suspicious taken place either in Berchtesgaden or on Obersalzberg in the past few days?'

'No,' replied von Hummel, firmly.

'No intruders? No one caught loitering outside the perimeter?'

An aide-de-camp sniggered. 'We had a guard who—'

'We do not talk about that.'

'About what?' demanded Jäger.

He never received a reply. The doors were flung open and a stocky, belligerent man in Nazi uniform strode in at the head of a lengthy entourage. Everyone leaped to their feet.

'So. What do you have for me?'

'*Reichsleiter* Bormann, these are the *Kripo* officers leading the hunt for the killer of Officer Hamm,' announced von Hummel. 'As you know, the murderer is believed to be the British agent we're seeking.'

'What does this agent look like?' snarled Bormann, coming up to stare closely into Esser's face.

'We don't know yet, *Reichsleiter*,' Esser stuttered, while standing rigidly to attention. 'We still have four men to eliminate from our inquiries. The Englishman could be any one of them.'

'Or none of them,' shouted Bormann. Having successfully terrorized Esser, he switched his attention to Jäger.

'Hamm's body was found between the parachute drop zone and the railway station,' explained Jäger evenly. 'The time of the murder suggests the agent was aiming to catch the early train into Munich. Because it was a Saturday, the train didn't contain its regular weekday passengers. Consequently, it's proving harder to trace everyone on board.'

'We are doing our very best, *Reichsleiter*,' fawned Esser.

That was a mistake, Jäger recognized instantly. By all accounts, Bormann was a pig. Even among the uncouth bullies who made up a large part of the higher ranks of the Nazi Party, Bormann stood out for his sheer coarseness and lack of intelligence. He was a bully who preyed on the weakness of others. A subordinate by nature, he treated those under him as if he was dealing with oxen. No wonder von Hummel had deflected the man's questions towards them.

'Your best!' stormed Bormann. 'Fuck your best! Your best is a pile of horse shit. I don't want your best, I want results. I want this man caught. You'll find your balls in a Gestapo vice with a broom handle up your arse if you fuck up. Just go and catch him.'

Jäger thought Esser was going to faint.

'You.' Bormann swung back towards Jäger, his face thrust forward so it was only inches away from the detective's. 'Tell me how far *you*'ve got.'

'We have descriptions of four, maybe five, passengers who we have yet to trace. The agent may be one of those.'

'Who are they?'

'One is a wounded army officer who stood up as if to offer his seat to a Polish woman—'

'What!'

Flecks of spittle, products of Bormann's anger, landed on Jäger's cheeks and forehead. He barely stopped himself wiping them off.

'We believe the same man later helped the authorities catch a student terrorist at Munich railway station.'

'For fuck's sake. Contact every *Wehrmacht* unit within two hundred kilometres.'

'We have, *Reichsleiter*. We are also checking medical units for one hundred kilometres around.'

'What did this officer look like?'

'Witnesses' accounts differ, *Reichsleiter*.' Even in normal times, witnesses could seldom agree, but nowadays most people stared at the floor or glued their eyes to a newspaper.

'Give your witnesses to the Gestapo. They'll help them remember. The Führer's life is at stake here. Nothing, but nothing, must be allowed to stand in the way of his safety. You want to make an omelette, you crack eggs.' Bormann thumped his fist on the table, sending maps flying. Aides hurried to pick them off the floor.

'Then there's a possible foreign worker, unshaven, nervous-looking, who was observed slipping away at Munich station while the terrorist was being captured . . .'

'He's your man,' bellowed Bormann. 'I'll bet a *Pfennig* to a hundred *Reichsmark*. Find him and you've got the hit man.'

'My thoughts exactly, *Reichsleiter*,' agreed Esser.

Jäger curbed his tongue. In his view, the foreign worker was the least favourite suspect.

'And there's also a Party member.' Jäger quickly rephrased his description. 'At least, a man, aged thirty to thirty-five, in Party uniform, possibly with the rank of *Arbeitsleiter* and carrying a large parcel wrapped in newspaper. Fourthly, we have a *Luftwaffe* man who jumped on the train at the last moment and got off before the main Munich station, probably at Hackerbrücke. We are questioning all AA units. Meanwhile there is also mention of a bespectacled Party member but he may be the same man as the one with the parcel . . .'

'It's the foreign worker,' decided Bormann. 'Take my word for it. Find him and you've found your killer. It's obvious, isn't it? Von Hummel, what have you done about finding an agent posing among the foreign workers on Obersalzberg?'

The SS commander snapped to attention. 'Most of the three thousand foreigners working on local building projects have been here for many months. The forty who have arrived in the past ten days are already being interrogated. Another two hundred who arrived in the last month have been expelled to work elsewhere.'

'I trust their absence will not affect any of my current projects.'

'We are transferring the same number of Belgians from a Munich munitions factory,' von Hummel reassured him. 'At the same time, four hundred extra members of the *SS Leibstandarte* are arriving from Berlin this afternoon. Guards will be doubled around the mountain and tripled in the *Führersperrgebiet*.'

Bormann grunted. 'I shall report this to our Führer. Find the foreign worker and you'll find the agent. Fail and you'll find the guillotine waiting for you.'

It was hard to believe that Cricklemarsh had taken time off for a haircut but he had gone off to his barber in St James's puffing on his pipe and looking very pleased with life. Annie buffed her nails and wondered what lay behind this unusual good humour. It had been impossible to persuade him to go home at nights – now he was sauntering out of the office in mid-morning.

She hoped he had slept better than she had, torn between worry for Lusty and fury at Purefoy's decision. Sleep had come slowly, like drifting face down in a shallow sea, translucent green with the occasional flash of sunlight penetrating the periphery of her vision. She had floated over an underwater shelf till the sea turned dark and deep without bottom. She was searching for someone . . . Lusty's face, in a sickly, greenish-white hue, rose towards her. He had no eyes and a gaping, empty maw for a mouth. She could not see a body, just that face, which grew larger and larger in front of her, putrescent white and dead.

Annie awoke to find the bed sheet wringing with her sweat. It took her a long time to get to sleep again.

The memory of her dreams made her go and pick up the photograph of Lusty from the mantelpiece and place it in front of her. She was still looking at it when Nye entered her office. He paused, grinning superciliously at the unattended transmitter.

'What do you want?' she asked coldly, slipping the picture into her drawer.

'I've come for the Operation Nightshade files.'

Annie snorted. 'Oh, yeh?'

'I'm terminating the operation.'

'The hell you are!'

'Special Projects is being put under my section. You can clear your desk.'

'I don't know what you're talking about,' said Annie, wishing Cricklemarsh hadn't chosen now of all times to go for a haircut.

'Don't lie to me.'

Colour flamed in Annie's cheeks. 'I wouldn't demean myself by lying to the likes of you.' Her voice rang with contempt.

'Where's Cricklemarsh?' Nye peered into the inner office.

'He's out.' Annie slammed the door, locked it and dropped the key into her breast pocket.

'I want the Operation Nightshade file and Lusty's personal file,' repeated Nye.

'Go to hell.' Annie resumed her place behind her desk and continued buffing her nails.

'Colonel Purefoy has authorized me to take over your department . . .'

Just then, Annie would have swapped her future in SOE for one good punch. Nye must have read her thoughts for he backed away out of reach. 'Until I hear from Colonel Purefoy or see some form of authority, you're getting sweet Fanny Adams.'

'I'll be back.'

Fuming, Nye strode to Purefoy's office to get a written order. On the way, he bumped into the colonel himself striding importantly along the corridor.

'Can't stop. On my way to see Brigadier Gilbert. Something urgent's come up.'

Nye scurried after him. 'Have you spoken to Cricklemarsh yet, sir?'

'Not had time. I'll do it as soon as I get back. Big powwow to attend.'

Purefoy left Nye standing impotently as he marched on, arms

swinging as if he was on the parade ground. Gilbert's secretary had sounded unusually terse on the phone. A variety of crisis situations ran through the colonel's mind. Whatever was up, he was ready for it. Bristling with efficiency, Purefoy marched into the large office – and stopped dead as he cannoned into an ice wall of hostility.

Gilbert was sitting behind his desk, a basilisk scowl on his face. His eyes were shuttered with anger and if looks could kill, Purefoy would already have been on a mortuary slab.

'I've just had an interesting conversation with Downing Street about Operation Nightshade,' he began in a bleak and wintry voice.

Purefoy swallowed. 'Yes, sir?'

'Good God, man! Not only do the Germans know about the operation, but Number Ten does as well!'

Purefoy assumed this was an attempt at a joke and smiled weakly. That was a mistake.

'I'm glad you find it amusing.' Gilbert's tone hardened from frosty to absolutely glacial. 'I trust that the Australians will share your sense of humour.'

'Australians?'

'You're going to Darwin to liaise with the Australians in the Pacific. There's a troopship leaving tomorrow at 0600. Make sure you're on it.'

'But . . . sir!'

'I do not enjoy being lectured by politicians on how to run a military operation. Especially an operation that never had any formal basis and was supposedly deniable. Security on Operation Nightshade has been a farce, a bloody farce, dammit . . .'

Gilbert was working himself up into a fury. Operation Nightshade had always been a high-risk operation, both as originally mooted and – even more so – the way he had turned it for his own ends. The very last thing he needed was for anyone in higher authority to take an interest. He could not risk an official investigation that might ask some awkward questions about why he had deliberately run the operation into shoal waters. He had to remove Purefoy immediately. And there was nowhere further away than Australia.

The Gestapo learning about Nightshade was perfect – but for their own political masters in Whitehall to find out was a disaster! The very thought made his blood run cold. And it was all Purefoy's fault. *Bloody arsehole.*

'. . . You couldn't be trusted to run a whelk stall.'

Purefoy had gone pale, still scuffing his moustache with his fingers in short, jerky movements like a nervous mouse cleaning its whiskers.

'I've no idea how Number Ten could have found out,' he stammered. 'I'm certain it didn't come from my department.'

'Then who *did* it come from? The Gestapo? Of *course* it's come from your bloody department. Now get out.'

Gilbert picked up the phone and was demanding to be put through to Major Nye even before Purefoy had reached the door. He was walking at the pace of a funeral march, his world in tatters, dazed as if a heavy artillery shell had exploded next to him. He could not believe this was happening to him. He could still not believe it when, a short time later, he stood outside on the pavement – his travel orders in his hand.

Nye wasted no time moving into Purefoy's office. Tonight he would celebrate – but first he was going to deal with that uppity American cow. He was going to enjoy this. Today was a day of comings and goings and Annette bloody Cunningham was just about to be booted out on her backside.

The plain, round-faced woman rocked the baby in her arms and peered wistfully through her spectacles at the snowy peaks towering above them.

'Sometimes I look at the Dürreckberg and the Pflughörndl up there and I think they are like me and Heini – always destined to be apart.'

Beck made a sympathetic noise and avoided Ilse's eye. She had suggested that he might like to accompany her on a short drive to deliver a parcel of baby clothes to a friend of hers. As they'd pulled up outside a stone-and-wood house in Schneewinkel-Lehen, Ilse had sprung her next surprise.

'Be very careful what you say in front of Häschen.'

'Häschen!' echoed Beck. 'You mean Bunny?'

'That's his pet name for her.'

'Whose?'

'Heinrich Himmler.'

'What!'

'Her real name's Hedwig Potthast. She was once his secretary.' Ilse grinned at the open-mouthed amazement on Beck's face. 'You'll swallow flies like that.'

Beck followed Ilse towards the door, still reeling. Ilse's high spirits were making her particularly mischievous. *Every day I see her afresh,* he thought. *Every day she captivates and entrances me.* You couldn't get bored with Ilse – not in this happy mood.

All *Fräulein* Potthast seemed able to talk about was her thirteen-month-old son Helge. It was clear that he had become her whole life.

'He's teething at the moment so he's a little grumpy, aren't you, my sweetheart? But he's so good usually. He's trying hard to walk but he scoots around on that fat bottom of his, don't you, my angel? Ye-es. You should see him performing the Hitler salute. He throws his chubby little arm out. *Sieg Heil. Sieg Heil.* Come on, bumikins, you can do it.'

The swaddled creature in her arms raised one arm – more in self-defence than as a salute, reckoned Beck. He wanted to pinch himself at the thought that this vapid woman was the mistress of Himmler, the most feared and hated man in Germany.

Fräulein Potthast allowed Ilse to hold her baby for all of thirty seconds – clearly the greatest compliment she could bestow – before her nerve cracked and she took the child back.

'Bormann's wife sends Häschen baby clothes as well but she only does it to spite Magda Himmler,' explained Ilse as they walked back to the car.

'Häschen's so ordinary,' complained Beck. 'I can see that Eva Braun's no intellectual giant but she does have a certain spark to her.'

'Have you ever actually set eyes on Himmler?'

'Only photographs – but how could any woman . . .?'

'Power,' replied Ilse succinctly. 'Power is a great aphrodisiac. It turns many women on. Now wave her goodbye.'

Fräulein Potthast had walked around the side of the house to stand next to the crucifix on one wall. She lifted her son's arm in farewell.

'That crucifix must be new,' muttered Ilse as she pulled away. 'The Nazis tried to replace all crucifixes, excluding those in churches, with pictures of Hitler but we Bavarians wouldn't put up with it. Hitler is not our God, whatever the Party tries to make out.'

'But basically you approve of the Führer.' Beck found the inconsistencies in Ilse's political thinking hard to follow.

'He has restored Germany's pride and won back our lands,' declared Ilse, stoutly. 'It's just a shame he's surrounded by the scum at the top of the Nazi Party.'

'But you disapprove of what he's done to the Jews?'

'I can't think he knows about it.'

'Oh, come on . . .'

'People could keep things from him. I don't know.' Ilse was irritated by the direction of the discussion, conscious of the paradoxes in her stance. 'What about you? What did you soldiers in North Africa think?'

'That we were glad we weren't in Russia, mainly.'

'No. About the Nazis. After all, you're fighting for them.'

'No, we're not. You fight for yourself first, your comrades second and then for your battalion. The country comes a long way down the list – and the Nazi Party isn't even on it.'

Ilse was intrigued. 'But you must have been fighting for your country.'

'It doesn't work like that. You can't see very far in battle, so your loyalty's to your mates – those near you. Men will die for each other, yes, but the concept of dying for the Fatherland is too vague. Soldiers who try being patriotic are soon told to put a sock in it.'

'What about soldiers who are also Nazi Party members?'

'They're not popular – not in the *Wehrmacht*. They tend to stick together and are shunned by the others. It'll be different in SS divisions. But they're not popular at home either, it seems.'

'Party officials are leeches who should be at the front. But we're being too serious. You may kiss my cheek if you wish.'

Beck leaned over to touch her soft skin with his lips. She smelt like warm biscuits and he wanted to nibble her.

Ilse gave a laugh. He was beginning to recognize that sound. It meant she had remembered a funny story.

'Did I tell you about the Nazi teacher who set his class an essay on the subject: "Would Goethe's Werther have committed suicide if he had been a member of the Hitler Youth?" A woman colleague thought she would go one better, so she asked her class, "Would Schiller's Maid of Orleans have remained a virgin if she had been a member of the *Bund Deutscher Mädel*?" '

Beck covered her hand, which was resting on the gear stick, with his own left hand. As soon as he did so, he felt awkward about touching her with his mutilated fingers. He lifted his hand quickly away.

'No, keep holding my hand,' she said in a little girl's voice.

Annie picked up the rumours about Purefoy's dismissal within minutes. A quick call to Penelope confirmed them as facts even as Annie heard Nye's triumphant footsteps approaching along the passage outside. Hell! Where was Cricklemarsh when she most needed him?

'You're fired,' Nye barked without preamble. 'Give me the key to your boss's office and clear your desk. I want you out of this building in ten minutes.'

Sullenly, Annie handed Nye the key.

'What's going to happen to Lieutenant Lusty?' she asked.

'The escape route over the border will be closed at midnight. After that, it's entirely up to him how he gets out. I only hope he's got the guts to bite on his pill – it's quicker than dying at the hands of the Gestapo.'

Annie pursed her lips, vowing that she would do Nye an injury before she left this office. Very slowly, she began opening each desk drawer. She'd be damned if she left Nye any of her Brazilian coffee, or the precious sugar. Nye meanwhile was struggling to open the door to the inner office. The key had jammed halfway and Nye was failing to free it. Annie heard voices. A second later she recognized the loud bray of Brigadier Gilbert. Nye heard him, too. He abandoned his efforts to unlock the door and straightened his uniform.

'Nineteen-sixteen, was it? I never knew it was *he* who put you up for your first gong. Ah, Annie, good morning. And Major Nye. Good.'

Gilbert was a picture of affability. Having arranged for Cricklemarsh to be steered to his office as soon as he entered the building, it had taken only moments to establish that not only had he and Churchill served together in the last war but that Cricklemarsh had helped Churchill in his campaign against appeasement. Gilbert was inwardly seething that Cricklemarsh had gone over his head and wrecked his secret plans, but there was nothing he could do at the moment.

'Major Nye, you're probably unaware that there's been a change of direction with Operation Nightshade,' he began smoothly.

Nye was trying to conceal his horror at the friendship between Gilbert and Cricklemarsh. The brigadier even had his hand resting on the other man's shoulder, for heaven's sake.

'Sir?'

'This operation must be given every opportunity to succeed. I'd be grateful if you would ensure that our *Abwehrpolizei* officer knows that the border must be kept open for as long as possible.'

'Yes, sir.' Nye was aware Annie was looking at him as a mistle thrush might regard a snail before cracking it open.

'Major Cricklemarsh has been in charge of the operation since its conception. Any change in supervision now would be detrimental. I'm sure you have more than enough on your plate, acquainting yourself with the running of the European department.'

'Yes, sir.'

Gilbert turned towards Cricklemarsh with a friendly smile on his face. 'I don't believe I've ever been up here before. Annie, is there any chance of one of your famous cups of coffee? By the way, I saw your uncle at the club last night. The admiral was in splendid form, telling us about a round of golf with Eisenhower. Had us all in fits.'

You old bastard, Cricklemarsh, thought Annie. *You suckered the lot of them.* As she moved past to get to the coffeepot, she surreptitiously squeezed his hand.

'Why's this door locked?' demanded Gilbert, pushing at it.

'Security reasons, sir,' replied Annie quickly. 'There's a knack to opening it. You have to be very gentle. It won't work if you force it.'

As Ilse and Beck pulled up outside the Red Ox inn, she announced, 'If Bunny can have one, so can I.'

'Sorry?'

'We used to have a crucifix in the small *Stube* but Runge made me take it down.'

Ilse disappeared upstairs to return a minute later holding a small, exquisitely carved wooden crucifix. Beck grimaced at the sinuous, twisted body of the Christ figure; the contorted agony of the face.

'The Christ must always be seen to suffer more than the people,' explained Ilse. 'In the cities, Christ can be plump and comfortable but out in the country, life is harder so the Christ has to suffer more so that his sacrifice is the greater.'

She was hanging the crucifix on a nail just as Vishnia came in. The Ukrainian girl's face opened in a beam of pleasure. She bobbed in front of the crucifix, crossed herself and produced a cloth to begin gently polishing the dark wood. Her presence made the linnets send up a medley of notes. Their song was shattered by a sudden shriek from Hänschen.

'You can't bring that in here.'

It was the first time Ilse or Beck had seen the boy since the previous night when he had spied on them.

'Why aren't you in school?' demanded Ilse.

'You can't have that in here,' he repeated. 'We follow Horst Wessel, not Christ. The Church can rot. The swastika alone brings salvation on earth.'

Vishnia crossed herself. Ilse exploded. 'Who's been filling your head with such sacrilegious rubbish? Get to your room. And stay there until you've apologized; otherwise you can starve to death.'

Beck sensed that he was being watched. He turned round. The Gestapo man was standing at the doorway, watching the row with an expressionless face.

Diels clicked his heels. *'Heil Hitler.'*

'Heil Hitler,' echoed Hänschen.

'Grüß Gott,' murmured Ilse. Beck gave a stiff military bow.

Hänschen crossed the room to the Hitler corner, scuffing his sleeve on the tables and continually glancing at Diels.

'You've been out, *Frau* Runge. Where did you go?'

'I took some baby clothes to a friend in Schneewinkel.'

'I see.' Diels slowly unbuttoned his long leather coat, letting tension build in the room. 'Where were you last night? Around ten o'clock.'

Ilse was frowning but Beck composed his face in what he hoped was the expression of someone concerned but curious. Vishnia remained unnaturally still.

'We were all listening to the wireless in the kitchen.'

'What sort of wireless?'

'A People's Receiver, *Volksempfänger* 301.'

'Why not listen in the *Stube*? You've a wireless here.' Diels indicated the Bakelite set on a shelf.

'We didn't want to disturb the men drinking in here with our light music.'

Diels swung around to face Vishnia. 'Why are you shaking? Why are you so frightened?'

Vishnia was knotting the duster between her fingers, desperately trying to conceal the fact that her hands were trembling.

'Don't you think any foreign girl worker would be scared, being questioned by the *Geheime Staatspolizei*?' intervened Beck.

'Only if they've something to hide,' drawled Diels.

'And what do we have to hide?' enquired Ilse, crossing her arms.

She knew. Hänschen had informed on them. When she got her hands on the little brute, she was going to beat him black and blue – then send him back to his miserable parents under the bombs in Lübeck. And pray one landed on the little sneak. But first they had to persuade the Gestapo that they were innocent.

'You were listening to an enemy broadcast from London, weren't you?' Diels was talking to Vishnia, not raising his voice but larding it with menace. Vishnia's eyes widened; she was transfixed like a rabbit before a stoat. It seemed inevitable that she would nod in agreement; inevitable that she would confess.

'This is ridiculous.' Beck had to break the spell. He pulled out a handkerchief. 'Here, Vishnia, wipe your eyes. There's no need to cry. You've done nothing wrong.' He moved to position himself between her and the Gestapo man.

Ilse was watching Hänschen intently. He was barely able to conceal his delight at their discomfort.

'Someone's been telling lies around here.' She rounded on the boy. 'And that was you, Hänschen, wasn't it?'

'I will decide who's telling lies,' barked Diels, angry that he had lost control of the situation. Ilse ignored him and continued her attack on the boy, who was reddening under her glare.

'You wicked boy. That's it. You're going back to your parents immediately. I'm not having you under my roof another day.' She spun round towards Diels, arms out in reasonable supplication. 'Surely you can't take a child's word against ours?'

'Hitler's children are invariably more reliable than their parents, we find,' said Diels.

A door slammed and Runge lumbered into the room. His scowl deepened when he saw the confrontation.

'What's going on here? Vishnia, fetch me a beer. *Hauptsturmführer* Diels, do you want one, too?'

'Thank you, but I'm here on official business.'

'Yeh, yeh, but you can still have a beer. Fetch two glasses – and hurry.'

The servant left the room. Ilse spoke quickly. 'Your nephew here has accused us of listening to enemy broadcasts, which is treason.'

'Is this true, Hänschen?'

'Yes, Uncle Gottlob. All three of them were listening to the wireless.'

Runge gave an imperceptible shrug of acceptance – but instantly he started having second thoughts. He didn't care at all what happened to Vishnia. He'd be perfectly glad to be rid of Beck and a spell in a concentration camp wouldn't do Ilse any harm but . . . Three people illegally listening to an enemy broadcast on *his* property. His wife, his servant and his guest. His wireless. People's Courts could be as capricious as the law was all embracing. Maybe they'd decide he was an accomplice. He could end up in a *KZ*, himself, lose the Red Ox and his other businesses. Whatever happened, he'd certainly be tarnished. No, he dared not take the risk.

Beck seized the opportunity of the innkeeper's silence. 'Both *Frau* Runge and I have chastised this boy in the past few days. He's trying to get his own back.'

'And he's going to be chastised again soon, in no uncertain terms,' muttered Ilse, grimly.

She would not even remotely admit that Hänschen's story might be true. There was no guilt in her, no contrition, only the desire to punish the boy for lying. Beck remembered how glibly she had lied when Runge had questioned her about her trip to Munich, when he'd thought she'd been having an affair. She was a natural. He wondered if she'd ever lied to him.

'I am bound to believe my wife before my nephew,' announced Runge stiffly. It clearly took him an effort to make that admission. 'She is always honest and honourable. Hänschen has been known to . . . have a colourful imagination, sometimes.'

'I don't, uncle. You know I don't,' blurted out Hänschen, close to tears.

'I could take the Ukrainian girl away for questioning,' said Diels.

'What good would that do?' asked Runge. 'She'll end up confessing to whatever you want her to.' Beck thought he sensed a plea to leave well alone. 'Hänschen, you've been telling lies again!' He grabbed the boy's ear and twisted it savagely.

Hänschen howled in agony. 'I've not, uncle. I've not.'

'What time were they supposed to be listening to this enemy broadcast?'

'Ten o'clock last night.'

'As you know, Streicher's speech ended around nine-thirty so I was home myself just after ten. There was nothing going on here when I got back, I can promise you.'

'If you say so, *Herr* Runge.'

Diels appeared to let the matter drop but his sheer lack of expression and the absence of any inflection in his voice made Beck's stomach churn. It was impossible to know what he was really thinking. Here was a man who would seem to be agreeing with you in the morning and return with an armed guard to arrest you in the afternoon.

'Uncle . . .' the boy whimpered.

'You bloody ungrateful little troublemaker. Get to your room at once. I haven't finished with you yet.' Runge hurled Hänschen across the room, aiming a kick at him.

The weeping boy darted through the door, just missing Vishnia who was carrying a tray with two glasses of beer on it and a letter addressed to Ilse.

Ilse started reading. Then she gasped, her hand flying to her throat. 'It's from Evi – oh, my God! Captain Beck, the Führer himself wants to see you tonight at the Berghof. He's keen to meet a front-line officer and hear his experiences. I'm invited, too.' Her eyes glowed with excitement. 'Our Führer also sends his regards to *Herr* Runge whom he recalls from the early days of the struggle.'

Runge preened. 'The Führer never forgets.'

Ilse said a silent thank-you to Evi for adding those sentences – and then panicked. 'My hair looks dreadful! What am I going to wear? Your uniform, captain. Vishnia will need to clean and press it.'

Beck had gone cold. He remembered the radio transmitter still lying under his bed. He had forgotten to return it to its usual hiding place. For all he knew, bloody Hänschen was going through his room at that very minute.

'Excuse me.'

His fears were unfounded but nonetheless he let himself into his room with his heart pounding and his mind racing. To actually meet the Führer was incredible! To try to kill Hitler at the meeting would be suicide and Beck did not want to die. Still, some good must come out of it, if he kept his eyes and ears open. He had to warn London. His time was running out, but he had to risk an extra day or two. To be this close . . . it was just a question of finding the opportunity. It had to come.

Down in the *Stube,* Diels hid his feelings about Runge's support for his wife. He himself was in a difficult position. The *Wehrmacht* got very angry if one of their own was interrogated too rigorously. And *Frau* Runge was not an average *Hausfrau* who could be bullied into confession. She had put down her marker about *Fräulein* Potthast who had the ear – and the rest of the body – of Himmler himself. She was also a friend of *Fräulein* Braun. That left only the Ukrainian girl. And, as Runge had said, she would confess to being the Queen of England, if they wanted her to.

For the moment, he was prepared to ignore the boy's information, even though he secretly believed him. That would put Gottlob Runge in his debt.

Hauptmann Beck troubled him, though. There was something about the man that just was not right. Diels had already put in inquiries to 21st Panzer, to the hospital in Italy and to the Cologne police, but no one had yet replied. The nightly bombing raids made communications with Italy difficult. Cologne had been flattened and the *Wehrmacht* were never in a hurry to answer any query from the Gestapo.

'Did you find anything?' he demanded of Runge.

'What?'

'Did you find anything in Beck's bedroom? Have you searched his belongings?'

'Yes. There was nothing. I'll look again when he's at the Berghof tonight.'

'Make sure you do,' said Diels, grimly.

There was no easy way to do this. Annie took a deep breath and swept into Cricklemarsh's office. He was standing in front of the montage of Obersalzberg. His welcoming smile changed as he saw the look on her face.

'Are you all right?' he asked.

'I'm afraid there's bad news, sir. Your son Ken's plane's crashed into the sea. He's in hospital at Scapa Flow.'

Cricklemarsh closed his eyes for a moment as if in pain. 'Is it serious?'

'It's not good. He was brought in with hypothermia and exposure. I've got friends trying to find out what happened. I'm sorry.' The phone rang on Annie's desk in the outer office. 'That could be . . .'

She hurried out. Cricklemarsh took off his glasses and rubbed his eyes with the heels of both hands.

Please don't let Ken die. Please, God, don't let Ken die. He couldn't remember when he'd last prayed. He picked up the recent photograph of Ken: a good-looking young man standing proudly in front of an antiquated aeroplane, smiling self-consciously and not knowing what to do with the hand holding a cigarette. *Don't let him die.* Cricklemarsh hated war, the waste of young men's lives. The last time round, they'd said it was the war to end wars. Peace had lasted a scant twenty years.

He was still staring at the photograph when Annie returned, clutching a piece of paper.

'Ken didn't return from a flying exercise yesterday. He was found drifting semi-conscious in a life-raft by a Walrus search-and-rescue plane. They reckon he must have been in the water for about five hours. The Walrus took him directly to Scapa Flow but he's unconscious so no one really knows what happened.'

Annie did not mention that Ken had been found miles off course and an initial inquiry was already blaming pilot error.

'What happened to his observer?'

Annie hesitated. 'He hasn't been found.'

Cricklemarsh's face creased with pain. 'What's Ken's prognosis?'

'Fifty-fifty. He received a knock on the head and he was in the water a long time but he's young and strong. There's a Royal Navy flight to Scapa at 1400 hours. I'll get you on it.'

By God, she *would* get him on it. She'd use every connection, pull every string, call in every debt and get overdrawn in the favour bank but she'd get Cricklemarsh up there to see his son.

'No. I can't leave here. Not now.'

'But he's your son!'

'I can't leave the operation. I can't abandon Lusty in Germany.' Cricklemarsh looked pleadingly to Annie for understanding. *I can't leave one man for the other,* he was saying. *You know I can't.*

'I could relay any incoming messages to you from here. We'll set up a radio link . . .'

'Annie . . .'

Unwillingly, Annie nodded agreement. The concept of duty had been drummmed into her all her life by her strict Bostonian father and by her mother who had wanted to return to England immediately at the outbreak of war to *do her bit* for King and Country. It had taken the arguments of the British ambassador in Rio to convince her mother that she would do more for the war effort by staying there and staging a one-woman social and diplomatic offensive on behalf of the Allies, from inside the American embassy – including pressing for America's inclusion in the fighting. Yes, Annie knew all about duty.

When she left, Cricklemarsh sat down behind his desk and set the photograph of Ken with his Stringbag before him. Then he took off his glasses and again closed his eyes in prayer.

16

Claude Ismay waited for Nye in the pub for more than ten minutes. That annoyed him intensely. Ismay always made a point of arriving late so that the other person would have already bought the drinks. He regarded Nye's tardiness as an act of the uttermost rudeness. Ismay hung around until he accidentally let the barmaid catch his eye and he was forced to order half a pint of mild. At that moment Nye hurried in, looking very pleased with himself.

'Evening, Ismay. Whisky, please. Large one.'

Looking as though he had been stuck with a hatpin, Ismay ordered the drink.

'Congratulations,' he managed to say.

'Thanks. It's been on the cards for some time,' lied Nye. 'I can't stay long. I'm just getting up to speed on the French operations. You know what it's like with a war to win.'

There was a new strength of purpose and sense of confidence about Nye that Ismay found very unsettling.

'You've plenty of time, dear boy. Rome wasn't built in a day.'

Nye took a first sip of Scotch and said nothing. He did not know why he had ever agreed to meet Ismay. There was nothing he wanted or needed from him, although it was always possible that Ismay possessed a snippet of gossip or information that might come in useful. A veritable snapper-up of unconsidered trifles was Ismay – and Nye respected him for it. It was about the only thing about Ismay that he *did* respect. The man's parsimony annoyed him as much as his inflated sense of self-importance.

'I gather Purefoy is still in shock.' Ismay stretched his long neck. 'He was seen wandering through in a daze.'

'Really?' His predecessor's psychological health was of no concern to Nye.

'Of course, now you can scrap that troublesome little operation of his.'

'Which one do you mean?'

Ismay leaned forward so that his mouth was almost touching the other's ear. Nye could smell the cloying sweetness of his hair oil. 'Nightshade,' he breathed.

'Why should I scrap it?' demanded Nye briskly. 'I've always wanted to control it and at last I am. In fact, it's going remarkably well.'

'Oh!' Ismay was beginning to sense which way the wind was blowing.

'It could change the course of the war.'

Ismay's eyebrows twitched. 'I'm surprised. The Americans seem to think they're going to put Hitler on trial for war crimes.'

'That's not official State Department policy, is it?'

'But if it ever becomes—'

'But it won't. Anyway, it's a damned silly idea to give a demagogue like Hitler a soapbox to spout his views from. Bloody thing would turn into a farce.'

'Maybe.' Ismay pursed his lips. 'But that's what they want.'

Nye was aware he had better things to do. 'I really must dash.'

'No problem,' smiled Ismay, chewing on ashes. 'Um . . . what about that weekend at my place in the Cotswolds?'

Irritation flickered across Nye's face. 'Sorry, old boy. Too busy right now, you understand. I'll give you a call.'

Ismay stood rooted to the spot, as he watched Nye halt near the doorway to receive congratulations from other colleagues. Nye hadn't offered him a drink in return nor even apologized for being late. Ismay did not like being taken for granted.

The expression on his long face curdled as he considered Nye's short memory. *Foolish boy!* As if everything could be weighed out and sold so simply. He would have to be taught a lesson. And his first lesson would be the demise of Operation Nightshade. As Ismay understood matters, the proposal to put Hitler on trial was sitting on a desk in the State Department just waiting to be circulated to the Allied leaders before being declared an official war aim. It shouldn't be too difficult to speed up its progress – to expedite its exposition, as the Americans would grandiloquently express it. He'd have a word with Kim in Washington as soon as he got back to his office.

No drink. No gratitude. No operation. Ismay began to sharpen his talons.

Beck was in for a surprise when he came downstairs to hand over his greatcoat to be cleaned. Runge and Diels were sharing a drink in one corner, their heads close together, but sitting by himself at another table was an army officer nursing a beer and a bowl of Erbsen soup. On his left cuff were the distinctive palm trees of the Afrika Korps.

Beck was ready to ignore the newcomer when Diels called out, '*Hauptmann* Beck, here's a comrade of yours.'

The officer rose and made a stiff bow. 'Meinder, 21st Panzer. Fifth Panzer Regiment.'

Hell! He'd be expected to pass the time of day with an officer from his own supposed division. And with Diels listening.

'Beck. 21st Panzer. 3rd Motorized Reconnaissance Battalion. You were behind us at Halfaya Pass . . .'

Meinder sat down. His thin face looked as though it had been eroded by a sandstorm until it was raw and spare of flesh.

'And we moved through your lines on the southern flank at Tobruk. In fact, I believe I remember you. You briefed us at a divisional planning conference at the White Mosque.'

The real Beck had never said anything about briefing the division. The pretend Beck felt a ball of lead forming in his stomach. Diels was watching with interest. Beck took a gamble.

'I remember the White Mosque on that yellow hillside just outside El Alamein. At Sidi Abd el Rahman, wasn't it? But I'm afraid you have the advantage of me.'

'You gave a short lecture to squadron commanders on the new ambush tactics the New Zealanders were using to draw our Panzers onto their anti-tank guns. There's no reason, of course, why you should remember me.'

There was something wrong with Meinder's eyes, Beck thought. The man wasn't looking at him at all. In fact, his eyes were staring into the distance.

Beck decided to play for time. Was he supposed to know this man? 'Were you at the Fuka?'

'That's where I got this. We took a freak hit off a British two-pounder. It ricocheted off the turret armour but the flash pressure cost me my sight – and my hearing for a while.' Meinder felt around for the bread on the table in front of him.

'I'm sorry. The two-pounder was always better than the short 50mm. But please don't let me interrupt your meal.'

'It's good to talk to an old comrade. What happened to you?'

Beck had started to explain when Ilse called out for him. '*Hauptmann* Beck. Where's your greatcoat? What are you doing?'

Beck made his excuses and hurried out. Meinder resumed eating slowly until Diels slid into the seat across from him.

'May I buy you a beer?' he asked. 'It's the least one can do for a soldier who has paid such a price for the Fatherland. I overheard you saying you knew *Hauptmann* Beck in Africa.'

'I didn't actually know him.' Meinder fumbled for his beer mug. 'I just saw him once.'

'Can you describe him?'

Meinder paused with the mug touching his lips. 'Who are you?'

'Gestapo.'

Meinder froze.

'Forgive my inquisitiveness,' Diels reassured him silkily. 'I was curious how much you can remember about appearances once you lose your sight.'

'My memory is still intact,' said Meinder gruffly. 'He's about one metre seventy-five or so, fair hair. Nothing special about him.'

'Did he have three fingers on his left hand?'

Meinder drank deeply, put down his mug and located his spoon. He pulled the soup bowl closer to him. 'He was briefing thirty divisional officers in a hot, crowded tent. All we wanted to do was get out of there and get some air. I have no idea how many fingers he has.'

'What about his voice? Does it sound the same?' Diels persisted gently. 'Yes, Vishnia, another beer for the captain.'

Meinder hesitated. 'No. I thought it was deeper then.' He shrugged. 'But my hearing has been affected. Sometimes things get distorted. Why these questions?'

'I'm just interested. Do you think you could tell by talking to somebody if they've genuinely fought in North Africa?'

'Of course. We who were there shared experiences we'll never forget. If you weren't there, you couldn't invent them.'

Diels nodded as if satisfied – then he had to remind himself that Meinder couldn't see his actions. 'You're staying locally, aren't you?'

'I'm billeted in the old sanatorium on the Kranzbichl road.'

'Tomorrow, you must come back here and have a longer chat with your old comrade,' said Diels. 'I'll pick you up.'

'You're very friendly with the Swiss border police, *Herr Major*.'

Voss nearly jumped. He had not heard Schnitzler creep up behind him. The sergeant managed to make his statement sound like an accusation.

'One has to stay on good terms with our Swiss neighbours if we're to serve the *Reich* to the best of our abilities,' Voss heard himself say. He was so on edge around Schnitzler that his words emerged distorted and artificially formal. He just had to get through the next two days without cracking.

At midnight on Tuesday, the tyranny of the telephone would end. God, Voss hated that bloody phone! There it sat on his desk, black and malevolent, shrilling ten times a day. Each time it rang his heart stopped. Even worse was the fear that Schnitzler would get to the corridor extension before Voss could answer. Come Tuesday midnight and it could ring for all it was worth for all he cared. Not that he would be there a single minute after twelve. He was planning a night of celebration with Heidi. He had some catching-up to do. And some naughty but nice sadistic tricks to repay her with.

'Big Josef is trying to attract your attention, *Herr Major*.'

Voss frowned. What could Big Josef want now? Voss did not want to set foot outside his office. He knew what would happen – as soon as his back was turned, the agent would phone and Schnitzler would answer. Why didn't the bloody sergeant just go home? He had been on duty since six this morning.

'You don't need to stay any longer, *Feldwebel*,' said Voss, stiffly. 'Your attendance to your duty does you credit but we all have to rest sometime.'

Voss rammed his cap on his head and strode on past the barbed wire and the striped pole to join Big Josef in the middle of the bridge. They turned sideways to look over the river so that no one could read their lips. Voss was aware of Schnitzler watching them from the barrier.

'You're not going to like this.'

'What?' Something knotted inside Voss's stomach.

'The operation's been extended for an extra two days – until Thursday.'

'No.' Voss put his face in his hands. The waters looked very tempting. He could so easily end it all.

'You're being watched.'

Voss did not care. He knew he could not stand the strain of four more days. He hated Big Josef for telling him the bad news, Schnitzler for watching him – but most of all the unknown Englishman for making him continue to suffer on his bed of nails.

Beck leaned on the windowsill to collect himself and watched the sun sinking like a rich yellow yolk behind the mountains to the west. It was a small mercy that Meinder was blind but Beck knew he could not hope to survive an exchange of Afrika Korps anecdotes and experiences. He'd be exposed within five minutes. He had to stay out of the way.

Beck made himself put the apprehension out of his mind and composed his signal as Vishnia brought up his clean uniform and newly polished boots. Just before six o'clock he locked his bedroom door and turned on the set. Beck allowed himself to enjoy a deep sense of satisfaction as he transmitted the news that he was about to achieve the impossible. He was about to breach the innermost security zone and enter the Berghof to meet the man he had been sent to kill.

As he was hiding the set away, the radio detector van crossed the old bridge over the Ache at Markt Schellenberg, five miles up the valley, heading for Berchtesgaden. Its crew had worked out that the British agent was sending from in or near the town. They would establish their base at the first inn they came to.

Jäger was a professional police officer who believed results came from methodical hard work. The visits to Berlin and Obersalzberg had been distractions as far as he was concerned. It was time to get back to business. Immediately after the interview with Bormann, he made two phone calls. The first was to Dachau to order a further search of the surrounding fields and the second was to Munich, ordering Wulzinger to go and take charge until he arrived. In the car, he tried to explain his latest thinking to Esser, still gibbering from Bormann's brutal savaging.

'We've overlooked something,' began Jäger and chuckled to himself as Esser went rigid with fear at the prospect of having to confess a failure to Bormann.

We know the Englishman came here with a job to do. To kill the Führer. But where's his weapon? Where's his means of communication? Put yourself in the Englishman's shoes. We've found only his parachute and his jumpsuit. He buried those where he landed. He didn't conceal them well because he was anxious to get away. But once he was safe, once he'd put some distance between himself and the compromised area, then he'd hide his weapon and transmitter properly. He couldn't risk travelling with them until he'd spied out the land. He would have taken care and trouble to hide them thoroughly. And he must have done so between burying the parachute and killing Hamm because he then moves into a built-up area on his way to the station. We should therefore be searching between the drop and the murder site. Whatever the agent buried might still be there. It is a long shot but worth trying.

They halted at Rosenheim to check how the search was progressing. Greim had not moved from Dachau police station, whining that he could not spare men for a wild goose chase. Jäger handed the phone to Esser. No one bullies like a coward.

Was Greim aware that both the Führer's right-hand man and the head of the *Reich*'s state security had ordered that this investigation be given the highest priority, the very highest priority? And yet he, Greim, did not think he could spare the men for it. Did he want to tell *Reichsleiter* Bormann that himself, or perhaps he would rather talk to SS *Obergruppenführer* Kaltenbrunner? Esser could give Greim both their telephone numbers.

By the time Jäger and Esser arrived, local SS, off-duty *Ordnungspolizei*, SA volunteers, even Dachau's firemen were combing the fields and countryside for evidence of a fresh digging. The disturbed earth by the three elms was found ten minutes later. Whatever had been buried there had been recovered.

'Who owns this land?' asked Jäger.

'Old Thorna,' replied Greim. 'He farms all the land this side of town. You've already interviewed him. He's the one who won't pay for his Polish worker to go to the dentist.'

Jäger and Wulzinger pulled up in the yard of the long, low, red-roofed farmhouse nestling below the brow of a hill. Jäger's interest was immediately caught by the barn perched on the crest. 'That's where Stan the Pole sleeps,' grumbled Old Thorna, muttering through the white whiskers on his stubborn, weather-beaten face. That was the only information he gave them. He was a simple farmer and, as he had already told them, he had never seen anyone drop from the skies, nor did he have a clue who had killed officer Hamm. If they wanted to speak to Stan the Pole, they were welcome. He himself could never get any sense out of the man.

They found the Pole deepening a drainage ditch at one edge of the farmyard next to a mound of pig shit. When he saw them coming, he stopped digging, climbed out and began pushing a barrowful of mud towards them. As he approached, they saw he had wrapped a dirty scarf around his grotesquely swollen face.

The promise of the fine morning had given way to a cold, dull afternoon. White clouds were piled on top of each other to the west and a chill wind had risen, piercing Jäger's black greatcoat. The Pole, in just a cast-off suit jacket of Thorna's, must have been perishing.

'Take him into the barn,' ordered Jäger. 'There's something I want to look at.'

He turned up his greatcoat collar and braced himself against the wind to peer down on the area where they had recovered the parachute. In the distance, Dachau clung to its hill, its onion-domed church rising above the sharply pitched rooftops. With his eye, he followed the lane from the foot of the hill, past where they had found the fresh digging and on to the crossroads settlement where Hamm had been killed. And it all lay on old Thorna's land.

At the far end of the barn was a shelf, six feet off the ground, covered in straw and old horse blankets, that served as the Pole's home. Wulzinger lit a storm lamp and searched through the man's few meagre possessions. When Jäger returned, the Pole was sitting quietly on a wooden crate, nursing his swollen cheek in his hand. He had sad, watery eyes, a red rash along his scant hairline and he looked very sorry for himself.

'You lied to us earlier,' said Jäger simply. 'In fact, you lied to us twice. Now, we can do this the easy way or the hard way. It's up to you.'

'I don't know what you mean,' muttered Stan through the tattered scarf.

Wulzinger dragged the Pole to his feet, cuffed his hands behind his back and ripped off the scarf. He slapped Stan's swollen cheek three times before pressing with his thumb into the infected gum. The Pole screamed.

'You told us you hadn't seen anything. What's this?' Jäger held up the short spade with a retractable handle the Pole had been using to dig the ditch.

'I found it. It's handy around the farm.'

Wulzinger grasped the Pole's head under his arm and screwed his knuckles into his throbbing face. Stan howled again with the pain that pierced his whole jaw like an electric drill.

'All right. I saw the man come down on a parachute,' he whimpered.

'When was this?'

'The night before the policeman was killed. I couldn't sleep because of my tooth.' Snot trickled over the Pole's top lip. 'He landed behind the hedge at the bottom of the hill.'

'Then you must have seen him walk away. You know you did,' coaxed Jäger. 'It's not worth the pain, is it?' His face was very close to the Pole's, peering deep into his eyes in the amber light. 'What was he wearing?'

'A uniform. An army uniform. There was a three-quarters moon. I couldn't make out anything when he landed but when he walked away, I could see he had on a cap and a greatcoat like yours.'

'Black?'

'I think it was field grey. It's hard to tell colours in the moonlight.'

'Officer or ordinary soldier?'

The Pole hesitated. 'I think he was an officer.'

'Why do you think that?'

'I don't know. Maybe the cap.'

'What was he carrying?'

'I think he had a case and a sort of rucksack. It was difficult with the shadows, and I only saw him for a moment.' The Pole ran his tongue over his distended gums. He longed to be able to cradle his cheek again. He tried to rub his cheek against his shoulder and failed. 'Please take the handcuffs off. I won't run away. I need to hold my cheek to ease the pain.'

'In a minute,' said Jäger. 'But you saw the same man again.'

'Did I?'

The Pole screamed as Wulzinger dug his finger into his face.

'I don't know if it was him. Honest. Three, four days later, I was furrowing over on Long Mound when I saw a Nazi Party VW car driven by an army officer. I knew he was an officer because he wore breeches and boots. I can't be certain it was the same man.'

'What did he do?'

'Please let me hold my face.' The Pole rocked back and forth in his agony.

'In a minute. What did he *do*?' persisted Jäger.

'He dug up a sack. Then he put it in the car and drove away. I was a bit curious so I went down to have a look. That's when I found the little spade.'

'You're sure about the car?'

'Yes. I could make out the red "V" emblem.'

'What time of day?'

'Early afternoon. Please let me put something on my face.'

Jäger was lost in thought. This didn't make sense. How could the English agent have got his hands on a Party car and petrol so quickly? Unless he had accomplices. Unless there was a resistance cell already in place to receive him. But if he *did* have confederates, why hadn't they formed a reception party to meet him and whisk him away? Then he would never have had to kill Hamm. If there really was a cell, it would make the hit man's task that much easier. Jäger had discounted the notion simply because of the stranglehold the Gestapo, the SD and the Party had on the German people. This was going to put the cat among the Gestapo's pigeons.

On the other hand, the fact that the English agent was disguised as a German officer confirmed his theory that they were looking for the same man who had tried to give up his seat on the train, to an *Untermensch*.

'Please, please, my face,' pleaded the Pole.

'Take him away.'

'But you promised you'd take off the handcuffs,'he sobbed.

'You're not the only one who can tell lies,' replied Jäger evenly.

Hitler took Beck's hand. Beck found the Führer's grip soft and damp.

'You know, captain, I can always tell who are my friends and who are my enemies by looking into their eyes.'

'I am your servant and desire only to be your friend, my Führer.' Beck heard a distant voice say.

Hitler held him with his stare: his eyes were large, light blue, almost sky blue, glistening with fanaticism, yet at the same time dead and immobile.

'Good.' Beck had passed the Führer's scrutiny. 'So, you are convalescing here. A wise choice. Obersalzberg is very special to me. Here, and here alone, can I breathe freely and feel truly alive.'

While Beck was thinking how to respond, Hitler changed tack. 'So tell me, what is our most effective weapon in the Western Desert?'

'We have two, my Führer. Field Marshal Rommel and our 88mm guns. Both are the best of their kind in Africa.'

Hitler was clearly pleased with the answer and Beck allowed himself to relax slightly. The time since they left the Red Ox had seemed unreal. When the driver and escort with *Adolf Hitler* inscribed on their cuffs had arrived to collect them, Ilse had been ready and waiting for half an hour. As they approached the Berghof, they had passed through successive security gates in high, barbed wire fences until they were finally allowed into the innermost *Führersperrgebiet*. At each halt, their papers, invitations and passes had been rigorously inspected even though they were passengers in a Berghof car. At the door, Beck's pistol had been taken away and he had been given a receipt for it.

They waited with an adjutant in the marble-pillared Gothic reception hall until Eva Braun came skipping down the sweeping stairs from the private quarters on the first floor, wearing a bottle-green frock embroidered with small white flowers. She had a simple gold chain around her neck and her fingers were free of rings. She gave Ilse an affectionate kiss on the cheek, then shook hands warmly with Beck.

'The Führer knows you're here,' she said, linking arms with Ilse. 'Let's go into the salon. There's a good moon tonight so we can see across to the Untersberg.'

She led them into a vast room with a coffered ceiling. The space was lit by two huge candelabra and sparsely furnished with such outsized pieces of furniture that for a second Beck's overwrought mind told him he must have arrived in Brobdingnag. The sideboard was ten feet high and eighteen feet long. The massive clock was topped by a fierce bronze eagle. The glass-fronted case for china would have comfortably held half the British Museum's ceramics collection. A twenty-feet-long table stood in front of a gigantic picture window. Eva turned off the lights and pulled the cord to open the curtains.

'Look, you can just make out Mussolini,' she laughed as their eyes adjusted. Across the valley, the mountain crest resembled the prominent forehead and profile of the Italian dictator, silhouetted against an indigo sky. Berchtesgaden and the valley floor lay in darkness apart from the glimmer of vehicle headlights crawling along the road by the river.

Eva showed them to a sunken sitting area with a log fire, ordered tea and began chatting to Ilse as though they had not seen each other for weeks. Beck took advantage of her prattle to inspect the room. Rich tapestries among oil paintings of nudes and landscapes adorned the white walls, a huge vase of fresh flowers sat on the grand piano near the double doors while more flowers set off a bronze bust of Richard Wagner.

'The weather's due to be fine tomorrow so I've finally persuaded the chief to take an afternoon walk to the Mooslangerkopf tea house,' announced Eva.

'I hope it does him good,' said Beck.

'You gave me the idea, captain. That used to be his favourite walk, and no one could persuade him to go anywhere else. It used to drive Bormann mad. He'd built all these paved paths but the chief always stuck to this one route. It'll be the first time he's been there since the war began.'

Beck was still fighting to keep the excitement out of his eyes when Eva bounced to her feet. Hitler himself was approaching. He wore a simple grey tunic and black trousers. Half a dozen other men in a variety of uniforms trailed in behind him. Beck was shocked at how ill Hitler looked. His left hand trembled visibly, his back was bent and he was stooped like a kindly uncle, an image enhanced by the flecks of red in his cheeks. His movements were jerky and over-emphatic.

'*Heil Hitler*,' Beck rapped out sharply.

Hitler flapped up his right hand in response and then clasped it in his left as if unwilling to let the other man see it shaking.

'Chief, you remember *Frau* Runge?' Eva prompted.

Hitler took Ilse's hand and bent over to kiss it in an old-fashioned gesture. 'Of course I do. I always say you make the finest *Linzertorte* in the whole *Reich*.'

'You're very kind, my Führer.' Ilse blushed, dropping her eyes.

'And this is *Hauptmann* Beck . . .'

'So you like the 88mm, do you?' echoed Hitler a while later. 'Better than the Panzer Mark IV?'

'The Mark IV is the best tank in Africa, my Führer.'

'Better than anything the British or the Americans can offer?'

'Yes, my Führer. The British Crusader, even up-gunned from the two-pounder to the six-pounder, is thin-skinned and is always breaking down on them. Their Valentines and the Matildas are much slower than the Mark IV. The American Grants are all right but they only have a limited traverse.'

'The 88mm gun can penetrate 8.3 centimetres of armour at 2,000 metres,' quoted Hitler, showing off his memory of detail. 'Did you know that?'

'No, my Führer, I just know it's a very good gun.'

'So we have the best general, the best tank and the best piece of artillery. Why are we not advancing anywhere in North Africa?'

Shit, what a question! Beck struggled desperately to come up with a diplomatic reply. 'The enemy has many more men, my Führer. They have unlimited ammunition and fuel.'

'Rommel seems to have enough fuel to retreat,' snapped Hitler. 'Why doesn't he use it to attack instead?'

Beck opened his mouth to begin on a perilous defence of Rommel but then realized Hitler was not inviting an answer. He recalled Ilse's earlier briefing.

'A word of . . . advice. You don't have conversations with him, in the sense of an exchange of views. If he asks you a question, you'll be expected to answer but don't question him and do not, whatever happens, disagree with him.'

Now he understood.

'. . . The generals are soft. Even the soldiers are soft. The fighting man of the last great war was much tougher. Think of what we had to go through at Verdun and on the Somme. They couldn't take that today. They'd just run away. The General Staff are always wanting to retreat and the soldiers are happy to take their lead.'

Hitler swung away from Beck to direct his scorn at the Staff general-major in his train. The officer blanched.

'The General Staff aren't to be trusted. They are far too willing to give up ground hard won with German blood. Left to their own devices, those cowards would never have dared start the war. They continually advised me against it, saying our armed forces were too weak. But who's been proved right – in France and Belgium, in Greece and Crete?' Bubbles of spittle appeared at the corners of Hitler's mouth. His face turned purple with rage as he waved his arms like a mad semaphore. 'They're not only notorious cowards but they're liars. Our General Staff is schooled in lying and falsehood. They give me false figures, false information. They betray me, betray Germany. They perpetually want me to authorize cowardly retreats but I'll never do so. We shall never take a step backwards. We need strong nerve and resolution as never before. I alone possess that nerve and that resolution. I alone am capable of making the decisions that govern our very existence. No other man in my place could do what I have achieved – no one would have nerves strong enough.'

Beck now knew why Hitler was nicknamed the Carpet Eater. But as Hitler finally subsided from this outburst, Beck was struck at the way everyone just stood and listened in awe, hanging on every word. No one dared to interrupt even when what Hitler said did not make sense.

Murmuring quietly, Eva Braun took Hitler's arm. Having persuaded him to sit down, she huddled next to him, holding his hand. He signalled for his official entourage to leave, then stared brooding into the fire.

After a minute's silence, he turned towards Eva. 'At least you are loyal to me, *Tchapperl*. One day, and it may not be so far away, all I will have left is you and my dog Blondi.'

Beck picked up on Hitler's use of the word *'Tchapperl'* – a Bavarian expression for 'pet' that had slightly contemptuous undertones.

'Nonsense, chief. Every German loves you, while your enemies fear you.' Eva swung towards Ilse as a thought hit her. 'I didn't tell you. The English have parachuted a man into the Fatherland with orders to assassinate the Führer. What a sneaky, underhand thing to do.'

Eva's indignation seemed to amuse Hitler. 'War is like that. Not everyone's as good-natured as you, my pet.'

Hitler might have first appeared to be paying her a compliment but as he drifted into another monologue, Beck realized that "good-natured" was a euphemism for something more pejorative.

'Any highly intelligent man should always have a primitive, stupid woman,' explained the Führer. 'Imagine if I had a woman around me who interfered with my work. I can never marry. They'd want to make my son my successor but the chances of him being as capable are so slim. Remember Goethe's son who was such a complete wastrel. No, I certainly don't want any witty and intelligent woman around me.'

Beck blushed inwardly for Eva. He imagined she'd feel embarrassed but she sat placidly content, listening to the Führer as though he was deciding what to have for supper. Maybe she was rather stupid after all, he considered – then he rejected the idea. Eva Braun was no intellectual but she had too much energy and zest for her life to be dull. Perhaps she had deliberately cast herself in this role to please Hitler.

There was no doubt that, in spite of his periodic ranting, Hitler could cast a spell. When he began lecturing them on how man was forged through battle, the words were commonplace, the arguments banal but they rang with a sense of truth – at the time. Later that night, when Beck reran them in his memory, they echoed with the hollow ring of base metal.

'Man has become great through struggle. Whatever goal man has reached is the result of his originality, together with his brutality. Struggle is the father of all things.'

An adjutant entered and coughed politely. Hitler stopped speaking abruptly.

'My Führer, there is a telephone call from the *Reichsführer* Himmler in Berlin. He says it is urgent.'

Hitler stood. The others rose with him.

'*Frau* Runge, it is always a pleasure to see you here in the Berghof. Your presence graces our house.' He spoke with such charm that Ilse coloured as she made a small curtsy. '*Hauptmann* Beck, it is refreshing to meet a soldier who has fought in the front line, as I once did.'

'Thank you, my Führer.'

When Hitler had left, Beck felt himself deflate like a balloon. His shirt was sticking to his back. Eva was again talking about her projected walk tomorrow.

'There's such a brilliant view towards Salzburg. You can even see the castle in the distance.' She paused, smiling. 'Now here's an idea, Ilse. You know how the Führer praised your *Linzertorte*. Why don't you make one for him specially for tomorrow? Could you do that? He can enjoy it at the tea house. It'll be like the old days.'

'I . . . I don't have all the ingredients,' stuttered Ilse, caught between feeling flattered and being scared of the challenge.

'The housekeeper here's sure to have everything you need. I'll send the stuff down to you first thing in the morning. Please?'

'All right.' Ilse gave in. 'As long as I can have the ingredients.'

'You're a true friend,' beamed Eva. 'Why don't *you* take it straight to the tea house? We could meet there. I'll organize a pass for you. You too, Captain Beck, if you wish.'

Just as they were preparing to say farewell, Hitler reappeared to sit with them. Occasionally, he asked Beck about some facet of the desert campaign. Each time, Beck's answers set him off on long monologues about the perfidy and cowardice of the General Staff, or how he himself had known they should have built more tanks at the expense of fighter planes. Ilse had been right: it was impossible to hold a conversation with Hitler. Once, when he was lecturing them on the difficulty of conducting a battle with inadequate, misleading and frequently out-of-date information, Beck, forgetting himself, chipped in about the 'Fog of War'.

Hitler immediately picked up on it. 'On the Somme, we could not see beyond our trenches. Frequently we had to try to make out things through clouds of poisonous gas while wearing our masks. It was my task as a battalion runner to find my way to the rear lines or to neighbouring units in the middle of bombardments, gas attacks – at night or in rain. Enduring the fog of war equipped me with unique clarity of vision.'

'Yes, my Führer.'

'Did you yourself ever experience such problems, *Hauptmann* Beck?' asked Eva Braun dutifully.

'We were once attacked in a sandstorm,' replied Beck. 'It was the most disorientating experience I've ever known. It was impossible for us to tell friend from foe.'

'That is exactly how I rule Germany now – as if living in a sandstorm.' Hitler began on another lengthy discourse as the others listened respectfully and despite his initial excitement Beck fought to stifle a yawn, overcome by the banality of evil.

On their way home Ilse let her fingers walk across the seat to feel for Beck's hand. As far as the driver could see they were sitting a respectable distance apart, but in the darkness Ilse clasped Beck's hand in her own.

'Fancy him coming back just to talk to us. We're really honoured,' said Ilse softly.

'Indeed.' Beck was still finding it difficult to believe what had happened that evening.

Ilse stroked Beck's fingers. 'You stirred the Führer's imagination with your "fog of war", but I still don't understand. Surely you can see the enemy to shoot at.'

'Not always.'

'Tell me.'

It was his one real experience of desert warfare, not culled from the memory of the man he was pretending to be. The intelligence officer McKillican had come up with the idea.

'The 51st Highland Division are having a spot of bother along the main road to Misurta,' he had said. 'Jerry's making it hot for their advance units. It's no big deal, just something they do once in a while to stop us feeling

we're winning the war too easily. You might be able to pick up a prisoner hot off the battlefield. If you want, I'll even drive you up there.'

'You just fancy an outing,' Lusty accused. McKillican grinned.

An hour and a half later they were passing a battery of eighteen-pounders dug into a low wadi with salt marshes strung out to their right. An MP directed them to the tented headquarters of the Cameroons battalion and from there it was a two-mile drive over shale and rock to the advance company, dug in on the reverse slope of a low rise.

'It was a fine day, almost cloudless. Then I saw a low wall of what I first thought was cloud on the horizon,' Beck recalled. 'Others had seen it as well. There was a strange air of foreboding. Men began muttering and looking to their weapons. A team of gunners, stripped to the waist, began taking the breech and nozzle covers off their battery of mediums. I was visiting another unit and I couldn't leave. Everyone had a job to do except me and that made it worse.'

'So what did you do?'

'I just watched this wall get closer and closer and higher and higher. It was unreal. It grew until it hung like a crimson curtain across the sinking sun. Then from the swirling storm came yellow flashes. The enemy were attacking under cover of the storm . . .'

Lusty and McKillican took cover in a slit trench. It grew hotter as the maelstrom of dust and grit approached. A sergeant ran up and shouted in McKillican's ear. He jumped up to follow, gesturing for Lusty to stay where he was.

'. . . It was like being in the middle of a roaring furnace. You couldn't see ten metres. I pulled my scarf over my nose and mouth and tucked my chin into my knees to make myself as small as possible. I remember the flames of the guns as the enemy advanced. There was the clank and rattle of tank tracks. Shells were exploding all around . . .'

Lusty pressed himself deeper into the trench. He caught snatches of harsh commands blown away on the wind. In the neighbouring trench someone was shouting bearings into a field telephone.

'Soon I could make out shadowy figures running across my front.'

'Why didn't you shoot at them?'

'I couldn't tell if they were ours or theirs – and anyway, I wouldn't do much good with a pistol, would I?'

A machine gun opened up behind him and mortars started landing just ahead adding to the din.

'. . . Then a tank loomed out of the storm dead ahead of me. I saw the sparks where machine-gun bullets were bouncing off it . . .'

A tank with black crosses on its sides reared up out of the swirling debris. Just as it seemed about to crush Lusty, it slewed over on one track, sending a shower of stones rattling off his helmet as he cowered close to the earth.

'. . . I thought I was for it, then the tank turned to one side and vanished back into the sandstorm . . .'

Lusty heard his own laboured breathing through the hot, damp scarf. Baking grains of dust blasted his skin, filling his eyebrows and hair.

'. . . I kept my head down and after a while the storm died away and we beat off the enemy attack . . .'

The air all around shimmered in the heat, a myriad of particles refracting the dying rays of the sun.

'. . . I'll never forget the sky that evening. We watched the retreating tanks, small black shapes that headed into the setting sun, as if seeking shelter there. I've never seen a sun like it. It was massive and such a deep, rich crimson. Its rays struck the undersides of long, white clouds so each appeared to have a golden lining. We were mesmerized. It was as though there was an altar in the sky and we were profaning it by our fighting. Even the gunners stopped firing. The shadows got longer and longer and the drab desert was transformed under this sky of deepening blue and gold. I remember I felt sad and very unimportant.'

'You're being very poetical.' Ilse squeezed his hand.

'I was very scared.'

Just then they pulled up at the Red Ox. Parked outside was a grey van, bristling with aerials.

17

Cricklemarsh watched indifferently as a pigeon landed on the window ledge. It had something in its beak that looked like a crab apple, although goodness knew where it could have got it at this time of year. The pigeon tilted back its head, then, after two false starts, swallowed it whole. The outline of the apple slid down the pigeon's throat. Its beady eyes bulging, it puffed out its chest feathers and tottered backwards until it stood swaying from leg to leg right on the edge. Then it shook its head, cooed loudly and took off.

This tiny episode cheered Cricklemarsh up. He needed some cheering. It occurred to him that it was one of Sod's Laws of Nature that nothing ever went totally right – although things sometimes seemed to go totally wrong.

It was incredible that Lusty could be going to meet Hitler in person. Indeed, he should have already met him by now. Yet Nightshade's apparent success was being overshadowed by Cricklemarsh's concern for his son. What was that poem Lusty so frequently quoted? *'In balance with this life, this death.'* How apt.

He had earlier rebuffed Annie's repeated offer of a flight. It had been tempting but he could not leave his desk, even though there was little he could do to affect the operation. It was a point of principle, a matter of honour. Bloody-minded stubbornness, Annie had called it.

She erupted into the room, smiling broadly.

'It's good news. I've just been talking to the hospital. Ken's regained consciousness. They're hoping he's turned the corner.'

Cricklemarsh exhaled hugely. He had not realized there was such a tight band around his chest until it slackened in that moment.

'It's a long way yet, but, fingers crossed, he's going to make it.'

'He's young and fit,' said Cricklemarsh like a mantra.

'And he's stubborn, like you. The hospital says young Ken is showing a huge will to live.'

'All young people do, don't they? Don't you yourself? You think the light will last for ever.'

'Apparently the doctors were seriously concerned about an infection in a wound to his head. They're treating him with a new miracle drug called penicillin.'

Cricklemarsh realized he had not been told about the head wound. What else was Annie not telling him? 'I've not heard if it,' he confessed.

'They don't give it to everyone.'

'Your doing?'

Annie kept her head down, busying herself with shuffling files on Lusty's desk.

'Thank you, Annie.'

'So, at last things are working out for us,' she said quickly.

'Don't tempt fate, Annie. Don't say things like that.'

'Anyway, on that high note, I'm off to enjoy dinner with my dotty aunt Flora. She's very sweet but totally scatty. What are *you* going to do?'

'I'll stay here in case Lusty signals again. There might be something I can do to help him from this end. It's always a comfort to an agent in a hostile land to have someone friendly to talk to in London, even if it's only in dots and dashes.'

'I'll see you tomorrow,' said Annie.

But she never would.

Down in the entrance hall Annie saw Penelope Hardinge queuing ahead of her to pass through the security desk. As they walked out of the building together, Annie recounted the good news about Ken Cricklemarsh.

'That's not the only good news, is it?' Penelope laughed. 'Everyone's really excited by the recent developments in Nightshade. What with the PM's approval and your man's invitation to the Berghof, you're hot stuff, you lot.'

'Oh, really?' exclaimed Annie, in what she hoped passed for a semblance of modesty.

'Don't take this the wrong way, but everyone's been surprised that your department was given that job, if you understand.'

They turned left to walk towards the Tube station. The streets in the early Sunday evening were largely empty apart from older couples in their best clothes, making their way to church.

'I did wonder about that,' confessed Annie. 'I tried asking Cricklemarsh once, but he's too close to the operation. I think he was so grateful to have something serious to do that he didn't question it. After all, it's easy to get swept along on a wave of enthusiasm, but when you stand back and think, you're right, it didn't make a lot of sense.'

To be honest, she told herself, when you stood back, it didn't make any sense at all. As far as Purefoy or Gilbert knew, Cricklemarsh had never before run an operation in an occupied country. To them, he was just an unwelcome academic foisted on them. Nye's German department had far more experience, expertise and resources. *So why us?*

'Don't knock it.' Penny adjusted the strap of her shoulder bag. 'It seems to have worked.'

But Annie kept wondering why they had been chosen. She knew about looking gift horses in the mouth, but what if it was the mouth of the Trojan Horse? Something wasn't right – but it was too late now.

Ilse sat in front of her mirror, wearing her slip, and brushed her long hair until it crackled. She smiled at the thought that, like Rapunzel, she'd let down her hair and a gallant knight had climbed her lonely tower and rescued her from the ogre. She regarded herself in the mirror. That wasn't really her looking back, she mused. The usual Ilse had the inward gaze of someone used to keeping her thoughts to herself. The Ilse who now smiled at her glowed with a zest for life and an open curiosity. Ilse liked what she saw, approved the broad forehead, good cheekbones and parted lips. She winked at the mirror. A beautiful woman, with a devilish glint in her eye, winked back. She put out her tongue and a little pink tongue peeped back at her. Ilse suppressed a giggle. This was silly, beautifully silly.

Christian, you've made me silly.

The silly girl in the mirror tied her hair into a bow under her chin like the ribbons of a bonnet and tilted her head. This was fun. Ilse measured off a thick sheaf and held it under her nose. She give a Hitler salute, then bit her lip to stop herself from laughing out loud.

Christian had been magnificent tonight: charming, modest and humorous. Besotted as Ilse was, it seemed to her that even the Führer had been captivated by him.

Ilse pulled her hair into a shape like a little Dutch girl with wings above her ears. She wished she could remember more of the Leader's words but they were elusive to recall. She resumed brushing her hair and began to think of Beck's firm, scarred body. They hadn't made love today. In fact, they hadn't made love for twenty-four hours. She ached for him. It was so difficult keeping her hands off him. She yearned to touch him; to feel the smoothness of his skin, to inhale his smell, warm and fresh.

Ilse closed her eyes. She put out her tongue and ever so gently ran its tip from the knuckle of her right forefinger to the first joint, floating on the tiny, fine hairs, believing this was Christian's face. Suddenly, she experienced a terrible pang. What was going to happen to her once he'd gone? She would wait for him, wait until the war was over. Then they'd go away. Her father would understand, and who knew what the world would be like after the war.

Ilse's movements slowed until they were imperceptible. She held her breath and in that instant she knew that she was carrying Christian's child. She slid her hands over her breasts to her belly. No doctor could tell yet – but *she* knew. She had conceived Christian's child. She felt so small, so insignificant, like a snowflake in a Russian winter. For some reason she saw herself soaring above Europe, above the battlefields of Russia where millions of men in brown and field grey writhed and fell. She feared for her son. How did she know their child was going to be a boy? She just did. And she feared all the more. This war could not go on for ever. Surely, it must end before he was old enough to fight, old enough to get killed. *My baby.*

Ilse undressed and put on her thick woollen nightdress that reached to her ankles. In bed, she lay with her hands over her belly and felt warm and drowsy and happy.

She awoke to the stench of stale beer, feeling Runge pressing his stubby hardness into her back.

Beck looked in disbelief at the radio detection van parked outside the inn. From talking to the bespectacled lieutenant in charge he had learned that, incredible though it sounded, someone in the area had been transmitting under the very nose of the Führer. He shouldn't be difficult to catch, the lieutenant had said. Already there were other RD vans in Salzburg and in Bad Reichenhall and a fourth was on its way. The next time the rogue transmitter went on air, they'd have him.

Beck knew he could never send again. He would have liked to tell Cricklemarsh of his plans but it was impossible. He intended to kill Hitler next afternoon as the Führer walked to the tea house. This time tomorrow night Beck would be safe in Switzerland. It would soon be time to transform himself into a major of the 394th Mountain Regiment based near Feldkirch.

In his room, he extracted a tightly folded silk road map of Germany from the heel of his boot. His escape route lay along the *Autobahn* before turning off along minor roads through Bad Tölz, avoiding any large towns until he reached Kempten and dropped south to the Bodensee and Bregenz and then to the border at Feldkirch.

In the right heel was a Gestapo silver identity disc, a simple medallion that gave unlimited access and powers of arrest to its holder. There was an eagle and swastika on one side and the words *Geheime Staatspolizei* and a four-figure number on the other. This was Beck's ultimate fall-back. If all else failed, he would produce this and bluff like hell.

Tomorrow's task was pressing on him; making it difficult to sleep. He fetched the rifle from its hiding place in the junk room and set about cleaning and reassembling it in one final practice. After all his time on the range, the rifle was part of him. He knew its peculiarities like the back of his hand. It was inclined to shoot low and to the left but he and Taffy had corrected the sights so he could split a walnut at four hundred yards.

He screwed the barrel into the receiver group, which he then fitted to the stock assembly, divided into two to make it easier to carry. He tried not to think what would happen after the attempted hit. The Gestapo would take the Red Ox apart piece by piece. They'd do the same to everyone associated with the place. He was signing the death warrants of everyone he'd met since he'd arrived. It was a terrible weight to bear. He couldn't afford to think about it – but he could not help himself from brooding. He slotted the rifle butt to the stock. What if he warned Vishnia in advance? What would she do? Where could she hide in a hostile *Reich* that extended from the English Channel to the Russian Urals?

He inserted the trigger guard and magazine. And Ilse? He wasn't to have known that she would fall in love with him. If he allowed himself, it would be so easy to fall in love with her in return. He made himself weigh the lives of Ilse, Vishnia and the others against the millions of lives lost through Hitler's evil. If he could end this war, the small sacrifice, even of his own life, would be repaid so many times.

Beck made himself concentrate on the task in hand. He pushed the bolt and bolt carrier into its holding and attached the telescopic sight. Now the rifle was complete. Tomorrow he would squint through the sights at Hitler's passing torso and squeeze the trigger. Tomorrow.

Lines echoed in his head. *Tomorrow and tomorrow, and tomorrow, Creeps in his petty pace from day to day, To the last syllable of recorded time.* Wasn't that Macbeth on learning of the death of his wife?

He dismantled the rifle and decided to keep it in the bottom of the wardrobe for the night.

Next, he laid out a dull brown sheet he had stolen from the inn's linen cupboard earlier. *Improvise to survive.* He cut one hole in the middle of it and two smaller ones for his arms, trimming the cloth so it reached to his knees. Now he had a camouflaged poncho that would blend in with the pine needles covering the forest floor.

His eyes were tired by now. He would sleep but it would not be an easy rest. He knew he would have the same dream he'd experienced every night since he'd landed in Germany. In the dream, he was in a concrete pillbox that he knew dated from the last war. He should have been looking out of the slit towards a rolling green plain, except he wasn't. He was looking instead at the rust stains on the ferrous concrete on the side of the embrasure. He knew that if he twisted his head slightly he would see fields and the countryside, a cloudless sky – but his gaze would not shift from the concrete.

In another dimension of his dream, the gap was stepped inwards, becoming smaller and smaller – a design intended to give the defenders maximum field of vision while minimizing the effect of a hostile blast. But in this case the tunnelling seemed to go on for ever, getting ever narrower but never actually closing. Beck wondered, since he believed he had the power to edit his dreams, why he allowed himself to suffer this claustrophobic image night after night.

Good old Kim, you could always rely on him. Since their days together in Cambridge, Ismay had known that if you wanted something done, Kim was your man.

Claude Ismay's signal to him had been brief and only partially misleading. *In company's interest that US intentions Hitlerwise made public soonest.*

It was Ismay's good fortune that the signal arrived just before a scheduled meeting between SIS's American liaison and the State Department's intelligence adviser Peterson McAuley. Dr McAuley, a former Yale professor of international law, was the high advocate of a moral foreign policy. He was pleasantly surprised at SIS's request to have the US position made public. It would strengthen the hand of those battling against the skulduggery of the thuggish SOE and his own dubious OSS colleagues. The announcement was duly slipped into the Secretary of State's speech to War Bonds workers in San Francisco that same evening.

Ismay was ecstatic. He'd never dreamed he'd achieve such a perfect result so speedily. All that remained was to tell Nye personally before he heard it from elsewhere. So much of the pleasure in wrecking the man's operation would be in watching his face when he heard the news. Revenge, believed Ismay, was like British justice: it not only had to be done, it had to be seen to be done. Sometimes, indeed, it had to be seen to be believed.

He found Nye still celebrating in the SOE mess. He was in an excellent mood. The latest news was incredible. Lusty was actually meeting the Führer personally. It was only a matter of days, even hours, before Hitler was dead. Nye had been so delighted that he had passed on the news to Brigadier Gilbert.

Now he winced as he spotted Ismay standing in the doorway.

Ismay noted Nye's fleeting disdain and mentally danced a jig of glee. Wasn't *Schadenfreude* a splendid word? Delight in the misfortune of others. From *Schaden* meaning 'hurt' and *Freude*, 'joy'. Trust the Germans to invent such a delicious word. This would teach that jumped-up little squirt to cast him off so arrogantly.

Nye half turned away from him. Ismay cruised through the knot of uniforms like a shark through a reef, sinuous and deadly.

'I need a private word,' he murmured in Nye's ear, taking his arm in an unexpectedly strong grasp. 'I'm sorry to have to spoil your party but I'm afraid I'm the bearer of bad news.'

'Yes?' snapped Nye.

'There's something you should know.' Ismay smiled sweetly. 'The Americans are going public on their intention of putting Hitler on trial at three a.m. London time.'

'Hell!' Nye swore so loudly that men nearby stopped talking and peered curiously in his direction. Nye had been drinking heavily, Ismay could tell. His eyes were glassy and his face was flushed. 'Did you have anything to do with this?'

'Don't shoot the messenger, old boy. Only trying to help.'

'Hell's bells and damnation. But I've told the whole top floor that it looks like our chap might succeed.'

'Better hope he doesn't, old chap. That would *really* upset our American cousins.' Ismay failed to prevent triumph seeping into his voice.

'This *is* your doing, isn't it?'

'I'm flattered you think I have the power to influence American foreign policy.'

Nye was at a loss, trying to work out in his befuddled mind what he should do next.

Ismay turned the knife. 'We're standing down the friendly border guard as we speak . . .'

'You what!'

'He was ours, remember, before he was yours. We had to act quickly. You know how sensitive the Foreign Office is.'

Nye glared at him helplessly, speechlessly.

'Must dash. Fear I don't have time for a drink. So busy, you know.' Ismay echoed Nye's own words in mockery.

'No. No.' Ilse could not pretend to sleep any longer. Runge was struggling to pull her long nightdress up over her knees. She rocked away from him across the bed, tucking her protection tightly around her legs.

'I'm your husband,' growled Runge. 'It's your duty.'

Ilse recoiled, as always, from the overpowering stench of beer and tobacco smoke. He smelt like some fetid animal, reeking with lust and the sourness of sweat. Her eyes were wide open now but the bedroom around her, with its blackout curtain, resembled a heavy, velvet darkness that threatened to suffocate her.

'Then respect me as your wife should be respected.'

'*Respect* you? You fucking tart!' The words came thick and laboured. Runge tugged again at her nightdress. For a few seconds they fought silently, then Runge lashed out with his fist. Ilse tossed herself aside so the blow smacked into her ear. As she instinctively raised her hands to her face, Runge tore the nightdress up around her waist and began muttering a terrifying litany.

'They're all laughing at me. They're mocking me because they reckon you're being shagged by that bloody soldier. Well, you're *going* to get shagged. But *I'll* be the one shagging you.'

He rammed his knee between her legs to force them open, pressing down on her throat with his left forearm. Ilse choked, grasped one of his sausage-like fingers and wrenched it savagely backwards. Runge yelped and snatched at her hair.

She clenched every muscle against the humiliation of the defilement about to happen to her. She'd fought against him like this in the past but it had made no difference. When she'd scratched his face, he had once blacked her eye. Then he'd split her lip and taken her while she'd bled into the pillow, swallowing her own blood.

She would escape. In her mind, she swore she would escape. This would be the last time.

Ilse let herself go limp.

He was trying to enter her.

'Help me, you cow.'

She raised her knees.

This would be the last time.

Never again. Not now with my baby growing inside me.

She would sleep with a knife under her pillow – and plunge it into his sweaty, heaving back. Plunge it into him as he plunged into her. Never again would he defile her. Never again would he threaten her unborn child. Never.

'Are you sure you're eating enough, Annie? You're looking even thinner to me.'

'It's just the cut of the jacket, Aunt Flora.'

'That's all right, then.' Her aunt smiled apologetically. 'This fish isn't very fresh, is it? If it's the best Brown's can do, then God help the rest of London. Another glass of wine to improve the taste?'

They were sitting at a table for two positioned beside a pillar in the hotel restaurant. Each of the four Doric columns in the room was flanked by jardinières containing ferns and aspidistras that formed partial screens, breaking up its huge expanse.

'I had a letter from your mother yesterday. There's a possibility that your father might be posted to London in the summer, some sort of liaison with Eisenhower's staff. It seems Randolf's keen to be near the centre of things and, of course, Emily can't wait to get back. She was enquiring about taking over the flat in Half Moon Street.'

'That's good,' smiled Annie, 'I'm overdue a letter from her, so no doubt she'll tell me all then. How is Half Moon Street?'

'Rather run-down, I'm afraid. It's so difficult to maintain somewhere in London in wartime, especially since I'm spending most of my time in Devon.' Aunt Flora inspected the piece of haddock on the end of her fork, pulled a resigned face and popped it in her mouth. 'Did I tell you I got a frightful ticking-off from the local WRVS dragon-in-chief?'

'No.'

'She accused me of wasting valuable food because I carved some vegetables into classical sculptures. I was really proud of my David. Not the Michelangelo, the Donatello – you know, the one with the strange-shaped thing. You can't get the musculature with a turnip but I was pleased with the body planes.' She paused for the wine waiter to pour two more glasses of Meursault. 'Two of the land girls on Trevelyan's place are pregnant. And, it's rumoured, one of the London evacuee girls – and she's just fourteen. I don't know what it is about the war that makes everyone feel they have to behave like rabbits.'

Annie grinned fondly at her aunt. Her mother's younger sister had always been the arty one of the family. Vague and impractical, she had been allowed to attend art college and enjoy Bohemian life in Paris until the family had decided it was time she was roped into the corral of respectability and married her off to a decent and humorous lieutenant commander who was happy to indulge her eccentricities.

'You're spineless. That's what you are. Spineless.'

Annie became aware of fierce, bitter reproaches hissing out on the other side of the pillar.

'Apparently they're convinced they can't get preggers if they do it standing up,' her aunt went on blithely. 'I told one of them that was rubbish. You had to do it upside down. I got some funny looks the next morning . . .'

'Yes, I will have another glass. I'll have another bottle if I want one. You're letting them walk over you again.'

There was a low murmur from an unseen male dining companion.

'No young men on the go at present? That's unlike you, Annie. Or maybe, just *one* young man.'

'You always did know me too well.'

Flora gave a sympathetic smile. 'Do you want to talk about it?'

'I can't'

'Yes, you can *do something about it. Nightshade is yours. So kill it off.'*

An electric jolt shot through Annie. She strove to tune into the conversation on the other side of the pillar.

'Marjorie. Please keep your voice down. The PM has approved.'

Annie recognized the voice of Brigadier Gilbert.

'Don't you tell me to be quiet. It's easy to order me about, isn't it? I'm only your wife. Tell those jumped-up nobodies instead, the ones who think they run the show.' The woman's voice was jagged with scorn and contempt.

'That woman sounds tipsy to me, whoever she is,' whispered Aunt Flora, as they started on a fruit salad of apples and prunes.

Marjorie must have noticed other diners looking in her direction for her voice dropped in volume while carrying the same poisonous venom. Annie had to turn her head so she could hear better.

'Did I tell you I've started a life drawing group in the village?' volunteered her aunt. 'Some of those Italian prisoners of war have really wonderful bodies. You should see the old biddies! Half of them think it's disgusting, the other half can't wait for Tuesday evenings. There's one chap, Antonio . . . well.'

'I'll get the final credit for the operation succeeding . . .'

'You'll get the credit, will you? And how much more will your superiors get? You start something, then haven't the guts to see it through. Just tell the Gestapo who the assassin is. They'll soon find him.'

'There's no time for that now.'

'That's what you said before. If you'd only done it then, they'd have caught him by now. You just don't have the guts to see anything through.'

There was a deeper murmur.

'What do you mean, you didn't expect he was going to do so well? It was no good just hoping *the operation would fail, you should have made bloody well sure . . . No, you didn't. Oh, you did a few things, but, as usual, it was so half-hearted.'*

'Annie, are you all right, my dear?'

'Sorry, Aunt.' Annie dropped her voice. 'I'm trying to listen to that couple behind the pillar. One of them works in Baker Street. No, don't look,' she said quickly as Aunt Flora craned her neck.

Annie was trying to make sense of what she had overheard. She did not understand the conversation but she knew that she had to report it to Cricklemarsh immediately. He would know what to do. He'd still be up in their garret office, waiting patiently in case Lusty transmitted.

'Office gossip?'

'Not really.'

'You know, they say that eavesdroppers never hear well of themselves. Shall we pass on the coffee?' Aunt Flora raised her hand to summon the bill. 'I've loads of Emily's Brazilian back in Half Moon Street, and some good pre-war liqueurs. Be a shame not to get stuck into them.'

'I can't, Aunt Flora, as much as I'd love to. I've got to get back to the office.' Annie watched a waiter approach the other table. There was a brief murmured conversation and Brigadier Gilbert rose to follow him out of the room.

'My treat.' Her aunt Flora laid down several banknotes and waiters pulled back their chairs. As she crossed the dining room, Annie could not resist one glance back. Mrs Gilbert was staring directly towards her. Annie felt a shiver run down her spine.

The Swiss Customs office was overheated, dusty and smelled of boiled eggs. Big Josef regarded Voss warily as the German poured himself another glass of aquavit. He was as taut as a drum and kept looking around in a distracted manner. It was clear the last few days had pushed him to the brink.

'So what do you have to tell me that can't wait until tomorrow?'

'Good news. The operation's off.'

'You're joking!'

'No. It's off as from this minute.'

'Why can't they make their minds up instead of fucking us around? Extended one minute and off the next.'

'Maybe their left hand doesn't know what the right hand's doing. It was a different man who phoned this time. He was adamant that the operation was off.'

'So that's it, is it?' Voss's surge of relief mutated into anger. 'All this waiting . . . What about the spare clothes I've got hidden? What about the documents and train tickets?'

'Destroy them.' Big Josef hoped that Voss would have the sense not to try to wear the clothes himself or sell the documents for a few marks. 'There is one thing . . .'

Voss stopped reaching for the bottle again and glowered suspiciously. 'Yeh?'

'The agent might still try to make contact. My instructions are that he must *not* make it across the border and he must *not* be taken alive. Set up a rendezvous and kill him.'

'What!'

'If he gets in touch, shoot him. It's simple. He'll be carrying false papers, attempting to cross the border illegally. You suspect something's wrong, you go to arrest him, he pulls his gun, you shoot first.'

'Did you know who lived here during the last war?' Aunt Flora stood on the pavement outside a dark, red-brick terrace house in Half Moon Street, fumbling in her handbag for her key. 'Robert Ross. He was Oscar Wilde's friend and executor. If only these walls could talk, eh! What do you think they'd say?'

'Ducky!'

Aunt Flora laughed. 'That's better. I thought you were getting bored with your old aunt.'

'I'm sorry.' Annie became conscious that she hadn't said a word in the short walk here. 'I'm still thinking about what I overheard. It's really preying on my mind.'

'Is it important?'

'I think so, but I mustn't . . .'

'I understand. Are you sure you won't come in? No? All right. How will you get back to Baker Street?'

'I'll walk up to the Ritz and get a taxi.'

But after a few steps, Annie changed her mind. It was little more than a mile to the office. She might as well walk. There was low cloud but the night was surprisingly light and the white-painted kerbstones helped. So she grasped the strap of her shoulder bag and set off purposefully up Half Moon Street, past its shuttered and darkened houses, into Curzon Street. Four Polish sailors walked abreast, arms linked, down the centre of the road. Ahead of Annie strolled a huge American GI with a diminutive girl who clattered along on high heels and still did not come up to his armpit. Annie turned into Queen Street. Near the end, she heard the unmistakable sound of the diesel engine of a taxi behind her. She turned quickly, arm half raised, only to drop it again when she saw the cab's dim 'engaged' light. The street behind was empty apart from a single woman on the other side, walking in the same direction. The sound of a wireless came from a basement.

The dark canyons grew increasingly deserted. London was going to bed early. Annie was surprised how easily she lost her bearings. She found herself passing a blacked-out pub, with its buzz of conversation and smell of sweet beer and cheap tobacco.

She knew the area well enough, but now one street looked much like another, their opulent town houses, of London brick or grey stone, all shuttered and closed. She had not been paying as much attention as she should have been, she realized. Instead, she kept repeating that conversation over and over, trying to get it word-perfect to tell Cricklemarsh.

'Just tell the Gestapo who the assassin is. They'll soon find him.'

'There's no time for that now.'

'That's what you said before. If you'd only done it then, they'd have caught him by now. You just don't have the guts to see anything through.'

She made herself concentrate. Berkeley Square, stripped of its railings and with American troops bivouacked on its grass, lay to her right. If she kept heading north she'd come to Oxford Street.

Annie began to get the uneasy feeling that someone was following her. She put it down to her her overheated imagination. At the corner of Chesterfield Hill she stopped, as if unsure which way to turn. Someone moved into the deeper shadows behind her.

She hurried on. A dark mass lurched out of a shop doorway.

Annie stifled a scream, her hand flying to her throat. The shape split into a drunken, courting couple. They giggled, threw their arms around each other and staggered back into the doorway.

'Yes, you can *do something about it. Nightshade is yours. So kill it off.'*

What did it all mean? A sliver of moon emerged from behind the clouds, throwing intricate gables into relief against the night sky.

'Goodnight, miss.' The reassuring bulk of a policeman loomed past, touching his helmet.

'Goodnight, officer.'

Too late, Annie realized she should have asked him to accompany her. She dismissed the idea as pathetic. But – but she still had this sense that someone was following her. She could feel eyes on her. The hairs on the back of her neck began to prickle.

She looked around again. The policeman had vanished. His place had been taken by a middle-aged couple. Annie made out the man's top hat. His wife wore a long frock. There were two soldiers, smoking, their cigarette tips glowing, also a woman and a lone man in some sort of uniform, his cap pulled low over his face.

'What do you mean, you didn't expect he was going to do so well? It was no good just hoping *the operation would fail, you should have made bloody well sure.'*

Annie was hurrying so much that she was beginning to get a stitch. She put her hand to her side and made herself slow down as she past the wreckage of two bombed houses, now no more than a pile of bricks and rubble. The streets were pushing her to her right. The lone man was still there, still following her.

She found she was at the beginning of Mount Row, a narrow cut-through at the back of Grosvenor Square. It would take her to South

Audley Street, and then it was a straight line, across Oxford Street to the safety of Baker Street.

Annie slipped into shadow and darted into the narrow passage. Ten yards on, she pressed herself into a niche in a wall, feeling her heart pounding. Had the man spotted which way she'd gone?

He strode slowly past the entrance. Annie did not dare move. Everything was still apart from the clacking of a woman's shoes hurrying along a nearby pavement.

'Just tell the Gestapo who the assassin is. They'll soon find him.'

They'd find Robin Lusty, and kill him? Not if she could help it.

'It was no good hoping the operation would fail, you should have made bloody well sure . . .'

Suddenly Annie understood. Anger surged inside her as she set off, hurrying across Carlos Place and into Adams Row. As she passed a shop doorway, she saw someone waiting, hiding in there. She started to turn. A flash of bright light exploded inside her head. She staggered, gasping at the searing pain that split her skull. Then a deeper blackness enveloped her.

'Where have you been?' Gilbert scowled at his wife as she emerged through the revolving door from the street back into the hotel foyer. 'I go to the phone and you disappear for twenty minutes.'

'I need a drink.' Marjorie Gilbert clenching her outsize handbag, hurried past him.

'But where've you been? I came back to find the table empty. The waiters didn't know where you'd gone; the maître d'hotel didn't have a clue. I thought you must have been taken ill and that you were in the lavatory. They sent someone to look but—'

'Oh, don't go on,' snapped Marjorie. A waiter held open the door to the bar and she flounced through.

In the discreetly lit bar, she collapsed into an armchair and demanded brandy. Gilbert regarded with her growing impatience.

'Well, you might like to know what that phone call was about,' he began. 'According to that fool Nye the Americans are turning moral on us.'

'What?' She grabbed for the brandy as soon as the waiter placed her balloon glass on the small table at her side.

'They are about to publicly announce, as an official Allied war aim, their intention of putting Hitler on trial for war crimes.'

'So where does that leave Operation Nightshade?'

'That's it. It's over, finished. SIS have already pulled out their tame border guard. Lusty's on his own.'

'But this Lusty's still in Germany, as far as they know?'

'Yes.'

'But this works in our favour. Get me another brandy.'

'Does it?' He raised an arm.

'Really, Adrian, why are you so slow? This is the best thing that could happen. If this Lusty succeeds in killing Hitler, or even if he tries and fails, it's going to make the British government look very silly. A case of the Allies' right hand not knowing what the left is doing. The Foreign Office will be furious. If Lusty gets as far as the Swiss border he'll be arrested. I'd bet a penny to a pound the Nazis will put *him* on trial. It'd be a great propaganda coup for them. Heads are bound to roll in Baker Street after such a debacle. You win every way.'

'Yes, looking at it like that, I suppose I do.' He waited until the waiter delivered her second drink. 'But you still haven't explained where you've been.'

'Adrian, it doesn't matter. It was just something I had to do.'

18

Monday, 29 March

Beck woke while it was still dark. At first he pulled the duvet up to his chin and burrowed down, the way he used to do at his grandmother's home in Dresden. He kneaded the goose feathers and pretended he was back in his small bedroom there with its model aircraft and the aroma of baking ham rising from the kitchen behind the shop. The last time he had seen the shop, it was boarded up and there were piles of broken glass from the front window lying in the gutter. He touched the scar on his forehead. With the memory of *Kristallnacht* came a renewed bitterness at the murder of his *Oma*, his gentle, stooped German grandmother, beaten to death by Hitler's thugs.

Vengeance is mine; I will repay, saith the Lord.

In his mind, he saw Hitler walking along the woodland path in his field-grey greatcoat. He could almost hear the shot, see Hitler stagger, clutching at a neat bullet hole in his breast.

Dawn was breaking. A new day. Maybe his last day. The last day of his life. Maybe almost the last day, too, for Ilse and Vishnia. But certainly the last day for the Führer of the Third Reich.

Beck felt too restless to stay in bed any longer. He needed to move, to expend some of the nervous energy pent up inside him. Hearing noises coming from the kitchen, he guessed it was Vishnia going about her early-morning chores and remembered that he would need a boiled egg to transfer the date stamp.

As soon as he dressed, he transferred the rubber-coated suicide pill to his top pocket. Later he would wedge it in his mouth.

'Boo!'

Vishnia was scrubbing the old blackened range, sleeves rolled up above her skinny elbows. She jumped.

'I'm sorry. I didn't mean to frighten you.'

Vishnia smiled to show she had forgiven him and pointed to a basin of white eggs, lifting her eyebrows in interrogation.

'Yes, please. Hard-boiled. I'm going out for a walk so I'll take one with me.'

Vishnia put the egg in a pan, then returned to cleaning the range, every so often peeping in his direction as he waited. After seven minutes she handed the egg to him, wrapped in a small cloth. When Beck kissed her forehead in gratitude, Vishnia clapped her hands together, a delighted sparkle in her eye.

Outside, in the crisp morning air, Beck's eyes were drawn to Obersalzberg. In his walk, he halted at the wall overlooking the river Ache. Out of sight and down to his left was the rickety bridge he had crossed in the darkness. It seemed a long time ago. He made out the guard stationed on the other side of the river and realized how lucky he had been not to have been caught. In a sheltered dip, a wild rose was coming into blossom, ridiculously early. Beck picked two white roses for Vishnia and Ilse and headed back.

The radio detection team outside the Red Ox were fussing over their instruments in the back of the van, preparing to move off to higher ground locally.

'Any luck?' Beck asked the bespectacled lieutenant.

The officer shook his head. 'Not a peep from this end but there's been a series of strange messages coming out of London overnight. Someone's sending the same group time and time again. Whoever it is, he's not a radio operator, not a proper one, if you understand. He knows what he's doing but he's very slow and rusty. Can't make any sense of it.'

Beck wondered briefly if it was something to do with him. Too late now to do anything about it. He wouldn't be able to receive from London at this time in the morning, anyway. The die was cast – for better or for worse.

*

Cricklemarsh rested his aching hand and watched the creeping grey light with despair. His mouth was dry and he felt a growing sickness in the pit of his stomach. It had been a long and fruitless night and with every minute atmospheric conditions were worsening. The likelihood of Lusty receiving his transmissions was growing slimmer. He would not stop trying, even though, realistically, he knew there was no reason why Lusty should be listening now anyway. But if there was the still slightest chance, Cricklemarsh would pursue it. He refused to give up, refused to abandon his friend.

One more time he tapped out Lusty's call sign and the code word indicating immediate flight followed by the code word warning him to ignore the border crossing and make his own way into Switzerland. Then he waited . . . as he had been waiting ever since Major Nye had gone crashing out of the garret office, slamming the door behind him.

Nye had stormed in hours earlier and had instantly dismissed the duty radio operator.

'What are you doing?' demanded Cricklemarsh.

'Nightshade's over. The bloody Yanks are about to declare that Hitler must be put on trial as a war criminal. Everyone's washing their hands of your operation.'

Nye had just been made to look a fool in the eyes of his superior officers – and that hurt. He had been outmanoeuvred by Ismay. He could not vent his humilation on Ismay nor Gilbert but he could do so with impunity on Cricklemarsh. He had just phoned Gilbert who'd been having dinner at Brown's and had had his head bitten off.

'You can't just end the operation like that,' protested Cricklemarsh.

'You just watch me.' Nye's dark face was bloated with drunken anger.

'At least give me time to pull him out.'

'SIS have already closed the border. The director-general has spoken to Number Ten and everyone agrees that this operation has never taken place. If the Gestapo didn't know about our involvement, it would be different, but since they do we can have no more contact with Lusty.'

'Leave the radio operator here on listening watch,' pleaded Cricklemarsh. 'If Lusty tries to raise us, we can still warn him.'

'The Gestapo's RD vans must be on top of him by now. If we establish communications, we'll giving the Nazis the evidence they need to embarrass us with the Americans.'

'But we can't just cut him adrift.'

'Don't you understand plain English? This operation has never taken place. I only hope Lusty has the guts to use his suicide pill.'

Cricklemarsh could not believe his ears. 'Surely, if he manages to get back to Switzerland . . .'

'That's up to him. But if he pulls that trigger, he's a dead man.'

As soon as Nye left, Cricklemarsh locked the door and struggled to relearn old skills. All through the night, at ten-minute intervals, he sent out his message. He recalled his promise to Annie that he would bring Lusty back safe whatever it took. He had given his word. Cricklemarsh flexed his fingers and began tapping out his message again.

Party member Walter Bunting folded his arms tightly and blinked like an unhappy owl behind his thick spectacles. The big man, Wulzinger, was standing close behind him, so close that it made Bunting's skin creep.

'Forgive me, I *have* been trying. I promise you.'

Jäger let the silence build until the little man shuffled his feet under its weight. Jäger rose slowly and, with a rasp of a match, lit a black cheroot. He imbued even this minor action with infinite menace.

'But I *have*. I really have.'

Jäger believed him. A runt like Bunting would go through flames to ingratiate himself with the SS. Why did memory always play tricks on people?

'Let's go through it again. We have all day – since your superiors know that you're helping us in a matter of national importance.'

Appeal to his vanity, Jäger reminded himself. *Don't terrify him; make him feel part of a team.* Wulzinger had suggested hypnotizing the little clerk. It was a good idea – but where did you find a hypnotist in wartime Munich?

'We'll re-enact the scene, shall we? Pretend you're sitting on the train. Put your briefcase on your lap. You said you were reading a report?'

'Yes, on increasing pig production in Bavaria.'

'Fine. So the officer is sitting diagonally opposite you. The carriage is crowded. Close your eyes. Can you see the officer? In your mind's eye, can you see him?'

'Yes.' Bunting nodded desperately.

'Describe him.'

Bunting hesitated. 'There's nothing out of the ordinary . . . he's reading a paper. His walking stick is propped to one side.'

'All right. It's Allach station. The Polish woman gets on.'

'Can't you find the Polish woman?' Bunting whined.

'We're trying,' replied Jäger in a tone that warned Bunting it was none of his business.

Bunting flinched. 'The Polish woman – she gets on. The officer looks up and starts to rise for her.' He screwed up his eyes in the effort of remembering. 'He realizes he's committing a faux pas and sits down quickly. He lifts his paper up before his face. It's clear that he's embarrassed.'

'How's it clear if the paper's in front of his face?'

'Soon afterwards, he gathered the paper in one hand . . .' Bunting spoke slowly, dredging the facts from his memory. '. . . He raised a hand to his forehead as if to brush away the sweat from under his cap band.'

'Which hand was that?'

Bunting imitated the action. 'Left hand. He pushed his cap back a bit. I told you he had fair hair, yes? Then he raised his paper in front of his face again. I got off at Neuhausen and he was still there.'

Bloody useless! Bunting's latest account contained fewer details than his original. Jäger fought to master his impatience. He had to carry on probing for the one vital detail that Bunting had hinted at so elusively in their first interview.

'There was something,' he had said. *'Something different.'*

'Some mark? A distinguishing feature?'

'I don't know.'

'It'll come to you – and when it does, call me.'

But it hadn't come.

'Something different, you said before,' prompted Jäger.

'I know. But I can't remember what.'

'All right.' Jäger smiled reassuringly. 'We'll take a different tack. You say he had a stick with him. Did he have an artificial leg?'

'No,' snorted Bunting.

'It's not as silly as it sounds,' explained Jäger. 'Sometimes we overlook the obvious in our search for the small details. Did he have both his arms?'

'Yes.'

'Both hands?'

'He wore gloves. Black leather gloves.'

'That just leaves his face,' observed Wulzinger sourly. 'Did he wear glasses?'

'No. Definitely not.'

'His nose all right, was it?' Wulzinger thrust his head close to the civil servant's face. 'No duelling scars on his cheeks?'

'No,' he whimpered.

'Both eyes?'

'Yes . . . Aaaahhh.' Bunting raised his left hand in a series of jerks towards his forehead. He brushed away imaginary hair with the back of it. Relief suffused his face. 'That's it. The scar on his forehead!'

Jäger held his breath.

'He had a white scar on his forehead. Just there.' Bunting indicated a spot about an inch below his hairline. 'It was like a crescent moon. I saw it when he lifted his cap. See, I *knew* there was something else.'

He was so pleased with himself that Wulzinger wanted to hit him.

Jäger was frowning in concentration. He screwed up his eyes against the smoke that drifted up from the now-forgotten cheroot. He had seen a scar like that recently. But where?

He started cursing his own memory.

Ilse loved baking. She found it relaxing and satisfying. The homely smells reminded her of her own mother and her kitchen with its warm cinnamon and vanilla. All the ingredients for the *Linzertorte* had arrived, together with a note from Eva that the Führer's party would be leaving for the Mooslangerkopf tea house around two o'clock. If Ilse – and Captain Beck – wished, they could go there directly. Eva had enclosed passes and promised to alert the guard commander. Security was very tight at the moment because of the threat of the English gunman.

Ilse sifted flour, cloves and cinnamon together before adding almonds, sugar, lemon peel and boiled-egg yolks. She hadn't seen lemon peel or almonds since 1939. She hummed to herself as she worked, beating in butter, raw eggs and vanilla. She stirred until the final trace of memory of last night's sexual assault had faded back into the insignificance of an all-too-common occurrence. Being raped by Runge was not such a traumatic event, merely a distasteful five minutes she could usually pretend had not happened. It took place at least once a fortnight, usually when he'd got drunk and she had failed to direct his lechery towards Vishnia.

But last night had been different. No worse – but different. Maybe it was because now she had someone special to share her body with. *Never again,* she swore – and she meant it.

But such repugnant rutting belonged to the darkness. Now it was a brilliant morning with a vibrant blue sky and the snow, white and glistening, covering the peaks. She put the dough away in the larder, to allow it to become firm, and carried on baking.

When Beck entered the kitchen, she was crooning a popular Berlin song from the Twenties in a throaty alto. *Das gibts nur einmal. Das kehrt nicht wieder. Das ist zu schön um wahr zu sein.* It happens only once. It will not come again. It's too beautiful to be true.

Beck had already presented Vishnia with her rose in the corridor. He had surprised her and moved swiftly on, so he did not see the look of adoration that followed him, nor the way she pressed the rose to her lips. No one had ever given Vishnia a flower before, not even a wild white rose.

Beck stood in the doorway to the kitchen, letting Ilse finish her song.

'For you,' he said, holding out the other flower.

Ilse blushed. 'Thank you. It's out very early.'

'It bloomed especially for you.'

'Fool.' She kissed him softly on his cheek and wrapped her arms around him with a ferocious longing. Then, as if to stem the torrent of emotion rushing through her, she pushed him quickly away. 'You can stay if you sit quietly and let me get on with my baking.'

'Yes, miss.' He sat on a stool by the window, admiring her sureness of touch as she bustled from larder to worktop to oven, seeming to be doing two things at once yet never hurried or flustered. When she opened the tin of raspberry jam, Beck could not resist trawling his finger through it. He was rewarded with a sharp tap on his knuckles with a wooden spoon. She scowled in mock anger. It was the play of lovers.

'Stop it. You know, this is for the Führer.'

'He won't mind sharing his jam with a serving officer.'

Ilse remembered Eva's note. 'There's a pass for you if you want to come with me to the Mooslangerkopf. We'll have to leave a little early to get through the extra security checks.'

'Right.' The pass provided another string to his bow – even an escape route if it all went wrong. He slipped it into his pocket.

Ilse lined a shallow baking tray with dough and spread the jam over the top. She began cutting more dough into long, half-inch-wide strips, and laid three across the jam. She swivelled the tin round to lay another three strips so they that formed Xs.

'Ah, cream!'

'Gerroff.'

The pair dived for the jug of single cream Beck had spotted under a weighted cloth. Ilse beat him to it and held it out of his reach.

'You can lick the jug when I'm finished.' She poured most of the cream into a copper basin and broke in a whole egg, beating lightly before brushing the mixture over the pastry.

'How many eggs have you used in that?' Beck enquired.

'Five.'

'All right for some.'

'Yes,' replied Ilse in a neutral tone. As if to make amends she passed him the cream jug.

'Well, go on, put it in the oven.'

'It shows how much you know, then. It needs to stand for a good half an hour first. That's the secret of a really successful *Linzertorte.*'

She loosened the band tying back her hair and shook it free. It fell in front of her eyes and she winked at Beck from behind her curtain of hair.

'My lovely rose doesn't like the heat of the kitchen. It's already beginning to wilt.' Ilse held it in front of her face and softly plucked a petal. 'It's such a lovely day. Shall we go out for a walk while the pastry sets?'

The sun was still hiding behind the grey mass of the Hoher Göll and they could feel the crispness of the air bite into the backs of their throats as they stood close together, looking down on the waters of the Ache. Tiny particles of moisture danced and sparkled in the air, a fleeting, elusive kaleidoscope of rainbow colours. Ilse pretended to try to hold some in her fist, and giggled at her own silliness.

'I always like mornings,' she exclaimed. 'It's the start of something new. Who knows what the day will bring? There's always hope in the morning.'

'Don't you like evenings too?'

'No. They're depressing. I find summer evenings especially sad. The day's over but it won't admit it. It clings to the light. It doesn't let in the dark as it should but lingers until it's almost too late for the night. Greedy daylight.'

'You're being too hard on evenings,' protested Beck.

'It's the end of something. It's a signal for sleep, short-term death. It's so predictable. The sun always dies to the west and . . . darkness . . . reigns.' Her words died away. She repeated, as if to herself, 'To the west.'

Beck was watching her, an indulgent smile on his face.

She was thinking about him, her hero from the African desert. In her mind she was replaying the scene he had described on the way back from the Berghof last night, of the enemy tanks retreating into the sinking sun.

Suddenly, with a shock, he read her mind.

Ilse was staring at him in terrified disbelief, her eyes wide like saucers. She knew. She knew.

'It's you, isn't it?' she whispered. 'It's *you*'

'What is? What's me?' He leaned towards her.

Ilse backed away, her breath coming quickly. Her life had just broken in two. All she held up as decent and loving had been exposed as base and false.

She saw in his face that she had guessed correctly. She had remembered his poetic account of desert warfare. The image of the squat black shapes of the tanks retreating into the deep rich crimson ball of the sun had stayed with her. Ilse had liked the picture, had painted it in her own head. But there was something very wrong with that image.

'The tanks you talked about were going in the wrong direction.' She folded her arms across her chest protectively, grasping her forearms so fiercely that her nails dug into her flesh. The sick ache inside her blotted out the pain. 'You said you beat off the enemy attack and they retreated into the evening sun – but that means they were heading west. The British are advancing from Egypt, from the east. The Afrika Korps is holding the ground to the west. The tanks were going home to the German Afrika Korps.'

Beck's face was an open book and Ilse watched its pages turning behind his eyes – the dreadful dawning of how he had betrayed himself.

'Who *are* you?' Time seemed to be standing still for them.

'You know who I am.'

'I don't. The person I knew is a fraud, an impostor.' Her voice climbed in hysteria. 'I loved you. I loved you. Oh, my God. What have I done?'

Ilse took Beck's deception as a fact. She did not allow him to deny it. She brooked no arguments.

'You've come to kill the Führer.' Ilse stared at the white rose in her hand. Was that some gesture on his part? Was he testing her? She held up the flower. 'Is this deliberate?'

'I picked it for you.'

'You don't know, do you? The White Rose is *the* symbol of a resistance movement. Its leaders Hans Scholl and his sister Sophie distributed anti-Nazi leaflets – the only people in the whole of Germany so brave or so foolish . . .'

'What happened to them?'

'*Ihr Geist lebt weiter*. Their spirit lives on.'

Beck seized on the moment. 'And you secretly support them. You don't really believe in what the Nazis are doing. You know you don't. Just look at the way you're hiding Hugo Guttmann and his wife.'

'But I'm not aiming to kill anyone,' she shot back. 'Who exactly *are* you?'

'I'm a British officer who mother was half German. I grew up in Dresden.' He tried again to persuade her. 'Ilse, you already hate what the Nazis are doing to the Jews. You know they're thugs, ruling Germany for their own ends. If I succeed, it will shorten the war. I'll save thousands of lives.'

'The Nazi Party and the Führer are not the same . . .' she began firmly.

'But everything they do is done in the Führer's name.' He *had* to win her over, to keep her silent.

'He can't know everything. They keep things from him.'

'Ilse.' Beck reached out to hold her shoulders and turned her to face him. Mistrust and suspicion glared out of her eyes. 'That man is the fountainhead of evil.'

'No.' She broke free. '*You* are the enemy.' She covered her face with her hands. 'Oh God! Why you? Why you?'

Her tears began to flow as the sun, the treacherous sun, rose above the Hoher Göll and Ilse shielded her eyes from its rays. She did not resist his attempts to dab at her tears with his handkerchief.

'I am a good German,' Ilse was insisting, almost to herself. 'I cannot let you do this.'

'You said you loved me.'

'But I am also a German. Would you let some enemy agent kill Churchill? No, you wouldn't!'

'You will denounce me?' Beck held his breath.

Her shoulders slumped. 'How can I?' she asked in a small voice.

'Ilse . . .'

'You used me.' Resentment was growing in her battered and tortured mind. 'You've been using me to get close to the Führer. You never wanted me at all. You just used me.'

'That's not true. Ilse, please, believe me, that's not true.' He really did not know if it was true or not, did not know whether he loved her or not. But he could not lie to her.

'Isn't it?'

'I've never met anyone like you before.'

'Tell me your real name.'

'Lusty. Robin Lusty.'

'Robin Lusty.' Ilse bent her head as she played with a button on his greatcoat. 'No, I think of you as Christian Beck. I prefer you as a Christian. Is there a real Captain Beck?'

'He was taken prisoner in North Africa.'

Ilse at last flung her head back to look up straight into his face. She had come to a decision. 'You will have to leave here – leave today. Now, straight away. Promise me.'

'I've a job to do, Ilse.'

'No. No, Christian. Promise me.' Ilse was pleading with him, clasping his hands in hers. 'I will not betray you but you must go immediately. Get out of Germany. Can you do that?'

He nodded. 'By tonight I'll be in Switzerland.'

It was not a lie. Tonight he *would* be in Switzerland.

They came for Cricklemarsh just after eight o'clock. The morning was like the first day of spring and London felt as if it had woken up from its grubby winter sleep. Swathes of daffodils were blooming in the park and air was fresh and invigorating. People sensed the change. The bright sunshine gave a sense of well-being, put a spring in the step.

In his garret office Cricklemarsh was not aware of the day outside.

The transmissions had been intercepted. Though the frequency was one assigned to SOE, the professional listeners had become concerned at the sheer regularity of the message. Every ten minutes all through the night – and always executed by the same slow, heavy hand. They contacted SOE's regular radio station at Poundon who in turn had phoned the night duty officer at Baker Street. Not knowing that Nightshade had been aborted, he explained that there was an ongoing operation using an independent transmitter inside the building. Poundon did not mention the frequency of the transmissions and, in retrospect, the duty officer was puzzled at the inquiry, because he knew the operation had been running for over a week and there must have been other transmissions earlier.

It was only when Rupert Nye, arriving early at his new post, studied the overnight log that he realized Cricklemarsh was flagrantly disobeying orders. Brigadier Gilbert, arriving soon after, ordered Cricklemarsh's immediate arrest.

When Nye led the two MPs into the garret, Cricklemarsh was still bent over the RT set, tapping out Lusty's call sign.

Cricklemarsh turned slowly to face him. Nye's jaw dropped. Cricklemarsh had aged ten years in ten hours. There were salt-and-pepper bristles on his unshaven grey face. His tie was undone and his shirt was open. The room was heavy with stale pipe-smoke and the smell of an unwashed man.

But it was his eyes, glassy, bloodshot and defeated, that most caught Nye's attention. Cricklemarsh stared uncomprehendingly as Nye placed him under arrest. He was hauled to his feet by the MPs and shuffled between them out of the office, a broken man.

His phone rang less than a minute later. The Royal Navy chaplain needed no encouragement to hang up sooner rather than later. This was the one part of his job he hated. He could now send a telegram with a clear conscience, to inform the next of kin that sub lieutenant Kenneth Cricklemarsh had died at 0635 of a rare penicillin reaction.

Beck looked at his watch. Almost time to return to the inn so that Ilse would think he was catching the train to Bad Reichenhall. Once she had set off for Obersalzberg he would change his identity and check his equipment. Then he would leave the inn – as he had promised.

He had been unable to persuade her. Ilse insisted that her loyalty lay with her country, right or wrong. 'I am a good German,' she had repeated time and time again. A *good* German.

Back at the inn, Beck found Ilse had changed into a smart azure frock. The cakes she had baked lay covered by a cloth on the old coffer by the door. He hazarded a rueful smile and, as a token of his good faith, handed back his Obersalzberg pass.

'I've checked and there's a train at fourteen-fifteen,' he said. The bill for his stay was amazing reasonable. He placed an extra sheaf of *Reichsmark* on the plate. 'This is for Vishnia, in case I don't see her.'

They were not looking at each other, as if refusing to admit what had passed between them, what they meant to each other. Beck was at the foot of the stairs when Ilse finally yielded.

'Maybe when the war is over, you'll come back to me,' she whispered, so quietly that Beck did not know if he had imagined it.

'When the war is over, yes.' He continued climbing the stairs.

'Don't look so sad,' she said, unwilling to let him go. She assumed he looked depressed because he had failed in his mission. She did not know he was already grieving for her.

'I must go and pack.'

She nodded. The strong woman who was also a good German.

Up in his room Beck cursed and cursed again, every foul word he knew and a few he'd just invented. A few hours ago he'd believed himself ready to kill Ilse if she was likely to denounce him. Now he only wanted to save her life.

I'm no good at deception of this sort, he told himself. Cricklemarsh had not coached him in the art of betraying a lover. He had not warned that you might meet someone who would make you question your loyalty, who would demand a share of your loyalty.

Still cursing, he made himself get on with the task in hand. He removed the rucksack containing the rifle from the wardrobe. The handle of his walking stick unscrewed clockwise to reveal the hollowed-out core. He slipped the barrel inside and tightened the handle till the join in the rosewood was invisible.

He shelled the boiled egg and rolled it over the correct date on his page of heavily printed dates before transferring *29 März 1943* to his travel orders. When he heard a car drive up, he watched from behind the curtain as Ilse, helped by an SS orderly, laid her three cakes carefully on the rear seat. As she slid in beside them her pale face peered up at his window. The Mercedes-Benz pulled away and Beck felt sadly alone.

He was still staring out of the window, unpicking the Afrika Korps emblem from his cuff, when Runge strutted into sight. Beck frowned. Last night Runge had spoken of spending today at local Party headquarters. He had been picked up by a comrade after breakfast. What was he doing back here? His presence would make it difficult to steal the car. Beck was considering whether he would need to kill or imprison Runge when the innkeeper bellowed up the stairs.

'Captain Beck? Are you there?'

Beck went to the top of the stairs. 'Yes.'

'*Hauptsturmführer* Diels is on the phone. He wanted to check you're in before he brings your Afrika Korps comrade round for a drink and a talk.'

Jäger had been racking his brains ever since he'd interviewed the clerk Bunting.

'It's bloody ironic,' he told Wulzinger for the tenth time. 'I can coax a sodding little runt like Bunting into remembering something but I can't manage it myself. I know I've seen a scar like that just recently but, for the love of God, I can't think where.'

'Maybe on one of the prisoners,' suggested Wulzinger. 'Or on a mug shot?'

'Could be, but . . .' Jäger tilted back in his chair and tried to visualize all the photographs he had viewed in the last few days.

He was finding it difficult to concentrate. He had not yet heard from Monika who should have arrived in Aachen yesterday evening. Even if Alix had not left her new address with Monika's sister, it should only have been the work of minutes to discover it at the town hall. Families all over Germany were being split up and reunited because of the bombing so local officials were under orders to keep their residential lists well up to date.

Jäger decided that if he had not heard from his wife by late afternoon, he'd have to start making inquiries through official channels. He was loath to do it because Esser might demand to know why. The thought of that little popinjay ferreting into Jäger's family affairs infuriated him.

He was still leaning back, feet up on the desk, his eyes closed, a cheroot dangling from his mouth, when Esser himself marched in to learn of that morning's progress.

'*Sturmbannführer!* What are you doing with your feet up in the middle of the day?'

'Thinking,' replied Jäger, squinting up at his superior through the curling smoke. 'Or, rather, I was until you disturbed me.' He closed his eyes again. 'Oh, this is impossible!' Jäger swung his legs onto the floor. 'My memory's going. I still can't remember where I've seen that Afrika Korps officer and the blonde woman from the inn before.' Realization dawned in his face. 'Yes, I can.' He stabbed the air with his cheroot. 'They were in a Party car together when we set up that roadblock.'

'The one when we pulled that black marketeer,' agreed Wulzinger.

'*He*'s the one,' breathed Jäger. '*He*'s the one with the scar.'

'Who?' Esser did not understand. 'The black marketeer?'

'Yesterday morning, we had breakfast. In that inn, the . . . Red Ox. There was a Panzer captain . . . He was sitting by the stove, eating bread and jam. And he had two fingers missing on his left hand.'

'Oh, yes.' Esser vaguely recalled such a man.

'At one point he ran a hand through his hair and . . . that's when I saw the scar, like a crescent moon.'

'But he had two fingers missing,' repeated Esser.

Bunting was brought in from the waiting room where he had been kept kicking his heels. Yes, he was still convinced about the scar.

'Was there anything special about his hands?'

'Not as far as I noticed,' replied Bunting. 'He was wearing black leather gloves, as I told you.'

Jäger picked up the phone and demanded to be put through to the Red Ox inn in Berchtesgaden.

Runge swore. He resented being disturbed in his meal. He was sitting by himself in the kitchen, a large mug of beer alongside a plate of cold *Leberwurst* and pickles. Ilse was not there and it would be a waste of time getting Vishnia to answer the phone. Stuff it, it would only be

Meissner bleating on about needing supplies of this or that. Runge cut off another thick slice of sausage, speared it with the point of his jackknife and shoved it in his mouth. He grunted in satisfaction when the phone stopped and resumed reading his *Völkischer Beobachter*. A minute later the phone rang again. This time it did not stop. Runge wiped his hands on his breeches, and picked it up.

'Yes?'

'Red Ox?'

'Who is it? What do you want?'

'*Kriminalpolizei. Sturmbannführer* Jäger in Munich for you.'

'It's a bad line. Say that again,' bellowed Runge.

'*Kriminalpolizei. Sturmbannführer* Jäger in Munich for you.'

'*Kripo*. Munich!' Runge choked on his sausage. There was a silence punctuated by a series of clicks. Suddenly there was a new voice.

'This is Jäger, who's that?'

'I'm Gottlob Runge. I own the inn.'

'Good. There was a Panzer captain staying with you yesterday. Is he still there?'

'Yes, he's still here.'

'How long has he been there?'

Runge did a quick calculation. 'Ten days.'

'He has two fingers missing on his left hand?'

'Yes. He wears a glove with stuffed fingers.'

'Does he?' Jäger sounded interested.

'*Hauptsturmführer* Diels of the local Gestapo told me to search his room the other day. Is there anything wrong?'

Jäger ignored the question and signalled to Wulzinger, who was listening on an extension, to call Diels. 'What's the officer's name?'

'Captain Christian Beck, or so he says.'

'Where's he now?'

'I think he's up in his room.'

'Hold the line.' Jäger waited until Wulzinger got through to Berchtesgaden Gestapo.

'Diels left his office about five minutes ago,' reported Wulzinger.

'Ask them about Runge,' whispered Jäger.

'*Alte Kämpfer*. Dyed-in-the-wool Nazi,' Wulzinger repeated when he'd got the information.

'Beck's our man, I'm sure of it,' said Jäger, his hand still over the mouthpiece of the telephone.

Wulzinger swore. 'Shit. I've been cut off.'

Air-raid sirens began to wail for an American daytime raid. Jäger had little time left before the telephone operators fled to their shelters or bombs fractured the lines.

Runge was speaking again. '*Hauptsturmführer* Diels phoned me a short time ago to say he was bringing along an Afrika Korps officer to talk to Beck.'

'Good. Listen. As soon as Diels arrives, get him to phone police headquarters, Munich and ask for me, Jäger. Got that?'

'Yes, Diels must phone police headquarters.'

'If Beck tries to leave the inn before Diels arrives, stop him at all costs. Do you understand?'

'Ah, yes. Stop Beck from leaving at all costs.' Runge swallowed nervously.

'Tell Diels to arrest Beck if he can't reach me. Beck is an English agent who's already killed one man.'

'An English agent!' repeated Runge. The line went dead. 'Hello. Hello. Operator. I've been cut off. Reconnect me to *Kripo* headquarters in Munich. This is an emergency. What! . . . An air raid! . . . Shit and damnation!'

Runge slammed down the receiver, his eyes flickering to the ceiling, towards the killer lurking upstairs. He poured himself a brandy from the bottle in his desk drawer, then pulled out another drawer and weighed a heavy old Mauser in his fist. With his head bent intently over the pistol, he missed a shadow that flew past the door. Nor did he hear the gossamer steps of Vishnia as she hurried to Beck's room.

Beck sat on his bed, doing up the straps of his rucksack. At a rustle in the corridor, Beck paused. The next moment there was a frantic scrabbling and scratching at his door – a high-pitched whimpering like some small, wounded animal, terrified out of its mind. Beck opened the door. Vishnia rushed into the room. Trembling with fear, she pawed at Beck, then raised her fist to one ear and made circular motions with her other hand.

'Hush. He won't hurt you.' Beck caught hold of her flailing arms.

Vishnia was white as paper and Beck wondered what sexual humiliation that bastard Runge had forced her to this time. Her face kept working away in a soundless scream of frustration.

'You'll be all right. I'll look after you.'

Vishnia wrenched herself free of his grasp and darted to the door. She pulled Beck's greatcoat off its hook and thrust it towards him. She put a finger to her lips, then pointed at him before drawing a wide circle in the air over her head. Beck frowned.

'Is it about me?' he asked gently. 'Vishnia, I wish you could talk.'

Her eyes contracted in pain, then she rallied. She nodded vigorously and continued with sharp birdlike gestures of mime and description. A hat. A coat, a long coat. A telephone. In triumph, she reached up and lifted a flap of his hair to touch his scar.

'I'm sorry, I'm sorry,' he kept whispering as Vishnia grew ever more frantic. She was weeping now, biting her lower lip, pleading with her eyes, making strange noises deep in her throat.

Why didn't he understand? She stamped her foot in frustration and pretended to pull a trigger. His eyes betrayed his anxiety but he still believed *she* was seeking shelter. Why couldn't he understand that she was trying to protect him! Vishnia rocked back and forth, eyes bulging.

Beck noticed for the first time her small, fine bones. In another time, in another place, Vishnia would possess a tantalizing elfin beauty.

Still her mouth worked away. She was turning red, coughing and gagging as if trying to expel a demon deep inside her.

'Gestapo.' The word came as a tiny whisper. A sibilant breath of chill wind across a desolate moor.

Vishnia gulped down air. 'You go. Gestapo come.'

She tried to drag him towards the door. Still he would not move.

'Try, Vishnia. Please. Try, for me.'

Vishnia *was* trying! Trying as she had not tried since that terrible day. She had thought she would never be able to speak again – never until the day she died.

Every sound she uttered took an effort greater than he would ever know. She began slowly bringing out the words like fine gems, unpolished but in their rarity beyond price.

'Police phone . . . about scar . . . Runge try keep you here . . . Gestapo coming . . . Runge has gun . . .' Vishnia scrunched up her thin body and rocked again with emotion. 'Go.'

Vishnia led Beck down the back stairs and unlocked the door. He clutched his rucksack and his walking stick, though he no longer pretended to limp. The doors to the garage, one of a clutch of outbuildings that had grown up around the inn over many years, were firmly locked. Inside were the Volkswagen and the hoard of petrol. The keys to both the garage and the car hung in the kitchen, where Runge was keeping watch.

'I fetch keys . . . yes?'

'Yes, please, Vishnia.'

She started off down the long passageway. After a few paces, she stopped and returned.

'You British spy?' she whispered.

'Yes.'

'Come to kill Hitler?' Her eyes gleamed brightly. 'Good.'

Beck slid around a corner, unbuttoned his holster and drew his Walter P38, feeling the floating pin that told him there was a round ready in the chamber. He thumbed off the safety catch and replaced the gun. He did not rebutton the holster.

19

'What do you want?' snapped Runge as Vishnia pushed opened the kitchen door.

A half-empty bottle of brandy sat on the desk beside him and a heavy pre-World War One Mauser automatic rested in his lap. It was all right for that policeman to order him to stop the British agent leaving at all costs – he was safely in Munich. From Runge's swivel chair, he could see the foot of the staircase through the partly open office and kitchen doors. Anyone coming down the stairs could not as easily see him. There was a back way from Beck's room but it was always locked. If Beck came down, looking as though he was leaving, Runge planned to creep to the passage and shoot him in the back before he reached the front door.

That bloody foreign peasant was bustling around with a bucket and a mop, making so much noise that he would not be able to hear Beck on the stairs.

'Shut up, you bitch, and get out of here.'

Vishnia risked a quick glance at him and ignored his command.

'Get out,' Runge repeated, snarling. That bloody Ukrainian slut was infuriating him. He could not concentrate when she kept moving around. He noticed Vishnia watching him out of the corner of her eye. What was she up to? She was watching and waiting for something. He rubbed the back of his hand over his mouth and poured himself another glass of brandy. When he looked up again, she was heading into the passage. She carefully left the door ajar, as she had found it. Runge heard the slap of her shoes' thin soles scurrying away over the flagstones as if she was in a hurry.

*

The garage had been converted from old stables back in the Twenties to cater for the new type of tourists with their automobiles. It could house six cars comfortably but the Volkswagen sat alone in the dim light filtering through the high, narrow windows. The rest of the space was filled by ever-growing clutter – the frame of a motorbike and sidecar without wheels, a bench seat from some grand tourer, a rusting mangle, sheets of corrugated iron leaning against one wall, three double-handed saws hanging from pegs on the wall above the top of an oval table. In one corner, an iron bedstead could just be seen behind a stack of discarded tyres, and right at the back, hidden beneath a thick tarpaulin, was a stack of jerrycans containing enough petrol to reach Moscow.

Vishnia silently passed Beck the car keys and stood aside.

'Good girl.' Beck unlocked the car door and placed his rucksack and walking stick on the back seat. A pair of Ilse's gloves and a lace handkerchief lay on the dashboard. Her scent penetrated through the heavy odour of Runge's tobacco. He switched on the ignition and watched the petrol gauge rise to show one-third full.

Beck pulled off the tarpaulin – and remembered his radio in the junk room upstairs. It was the first time he had thought of it since Vishnia had warned him. He dared not leave it behind. The inn would be searched from top to bottom and the radio was as good as leaving an SOE calling card. So much for the assassination appearing to be the work of a disillusioned German.

'Vishnia, I've left my radio transmitter behind,' he admitted. 'It will incriminate you.' He knew she was already dead – but he did not say so.

'I go.'

He described its hiding place.

'I find . . . You hurry.'

Runge sat holding the heavy Mauser in both hands, aiming through the gap in the door. The waiting was getting on his nerves but his initial fear of coping alone with a trained killer had worn off under the effects of the brandy. A growing part of Runge now *wanted* Beck to come down the stairs so that he could kill him and claim the credit. He poured himself another glass. Where was Vishnia now? Her earlier activities had left him irritated. She had been scurrying around with a mop and pail but then she had left, leaving both items behind. There was something different about the girl. For the first time, she had actually looked at him. Normally, she stared at the ground in his presence but this time he had caught her furtively watching him. Perhaps she was in league with the spy! The thought made him rise slowly to his feet, glass in one hand, pistol in the other.

Bitch of Hell!

Slowly, step by fearful step, Runge walked out of the office into the kitchen. He eyed the huge coppers, the blackened range, the tower of saucepans, the chipped sink, the ladles hanging neatly in a row. Everything appeared normal. The only sound was the ticking from the big old wall clock. And next to the clock was the brass hook where, ten minutes before, the keys to the garage and the car had been hanging.

Bitch of Hell!

Vishnia ran lightly up the back stairs, her heart pounding. The corridor was in darkness except for a paler rectangle of light at the far end, marking the top of the front stairs. The junk room was half a flight further up, off a narrow dead-end passageway. Its door was unlocked and she slowly opened it. Between the listing linen chest and the parrot's cage, she found the sturdy attaché case wedged behind a rolled-up mattress. Vishnia needed both hands to heave it free. The effort dislodged an ancient tapestry, which slipped to the ground in a cloud of dust. She paused, listening to the inn creak and settle in the middle of the day, before setting off briskly to return to the garage with her prize.

Beck was filling the VW with petrol when the garage door began to open. He could not turn round easily. The rusty metal funnel was too big and he needed all his concentration to hold the can's spout in position while tilting it.

He knew someone was in the doorway. He was slowly lifting his eyes when there was a shrill, unearthly scream from Vishnia.

Beck spun around to find Runge holding a huge Mauser pistol at arm's length in front of him, his mottled red face glistening with sweat.

Runge jerked his head towards the source of the scream even as his finger increased the pressure on the trigger. Behind him, Vishnia grasped the transmitter case by its handle and put all her strength into heaving it up and forward so that it swung in a wide arc.

Thirty-two pounds of transmitter smashed into the side of Runge's face. The impact sent him reeling across the garage. He tripped over a toolbox and crashed heavily into a wall, the pistol dropping from his fingers.

Beck sprinted for the gun.

Vishnia was ahead of him.

Runge was on his hands and knees, blood trickling from the corner of his mouth; a splinter of pink-and-white bone protruding from his pulped cheek. He pushed out shattered teeth from his broken mouth with his tongue and groaned.

Vishnia bent over the tool box. Beck snatched up the Mauser.

The girl straightened up with a heavy foot-long screwdriver in her hand. As Runge twisted his head to look up, Vishnia dropped on her knees beside him. She raised the screwdriver in both hands, high above her head. For a second, Beck had a vision of a sacrifice. Runge, the beast on all fours: Vishnia, the priestess. The screwdriver flashed. Runge tried to jerk aside. The blade ripped through the front of his throat. Crimson bubbles of blood gurgled from the torn flesh, dripping onto the oily floor in large splashes. Red on black, the colours he had followed so devotedly all his life.

'Die,' whispered Vishnia, as fragile and as indestructible as thistle-down.

Runge's body sagged and rolled onto its side, his neck resting over a drain. His fingers reached up. He tried to call out but Vishnia's blade had severed his vocal cords. He managed only to croak out the coming of his death.

The smile that lifted the corners of Vishnia's mouth would have chilled the heart of a ghost. Malice, pleasure, menace – and utterly, utterly without pity. She raised the screwdriver again. Her smile did not falter as she skewered Runge's throat to the grating.

She was still smiling as she rocked back on her haunches.

Hänschen had enjoyed the morning's excursion. He and his troop of *Hitler Jungvolk* had been practising field exercises, firing live ammunition from outdated rifles at targets representing Russian soldiers. It had set his imagination racing. He was at the head of the honour guard of *12 SS Panzer, Hitler-Jugend.* He marched alongside the river, shrilling out loud orders, goose-stepping proudly as he led the imaginary parade. In his mind, the Führer himself was taking the salute. Hänschen began to hum the Horst Wessel Song, kicked his legs even higher, left arm held stiffly across his chest, his right arm extended rigidly in the Hitler salute. Hung around his neck was the Knights Cross, the *Ritterkreuz* with diamonds, awarded for countless feats of bravery against the subhuman Russians.

He noticed there were more guards than usual patrolling along the road. He longed to have a rifle like theirs. Hänschen recalled the sense of power as he'd pulled the trigger earlier. He wished he was fifteen so he could join the Hitler Youth and help man the anti-aircraft defences ranged around Munich. He abandoned the Hitler Salute and aimed instead at imaginary enemy aircraft overhead. He was still firing his imaginary automatic cannon when he spotted his Uncle Gottlob's car turning to cross the Kilianmühle bridge. He would get a lift home the rest of the way if he could only attract his uncle's attention.

He started running but halted abruptly when he saw that Captain Beck was driving. What was *he* doing in uncle's car? And turning now into a country lane that just looped past a few farms before rejoining the main road further down the valley? The car slowed and stopped. Hänschen ducked behind a tree. He was curious and still smarting from the humiliation of his attempted denunciation of Aunt Ilse and Captain Beck yesterday. But he would get even with them. They'd see.

So what was Captain Beck up to?

As Hänschen watched, the officer got out, looked all around, and reached into the back of the car, first for his walking stick, then for a small rucksack. He pulled something small, like a sweet, from his top pocket and transferred it to his mouth. It appeared to get caught in his teeth for Beck had to use a finger to probe and push. Throwing his greatcoat in the car, Beck locked the vehicle and strode off up a farm track. It took the boy a full ten seconds to work out what looked different: Beck was walking without a limp. It made him more curious.

Once Beck was safely out of sight, Hänschen ran across the bridge. Beck was already close to the farm and Hänschen had to jogtrot to keep up. It crossed his mind that the man was heading for the hamlet of Stanger but instead Beck turned off on a rutted track leading into the pine forest. As the ground rose sharply, the track narrowed into a path and then vanished completely. The trees pressed in on all sides. Beck was setting such a cracking pace that Hänschen was soon out of breath, with a stitch in his side, but he forced himself to keep slipping from tree to tree, always holding Beck in view.

When Beck suddenly stopped and knelt down, Hänschen ducked too. When he next looked up, Beck had vanished. Hänschen ran forward to the edge of a broad clearing where a high fence marked the perimeter of the forbidden zone. He looked to his right and to his left but Beck was nowhere to be seen. Tears of anger and frustration welled in the boy's eyes. Then, ahead, on the other side of the wire, a branch moved.

Two guards were approaching from the left, patrolling at a measured pace, rifles slung over their shoulders. Hänschen dropped flat. He found he was staring straight at a gap beneath the fence. Once the guards had gone, he squirmed through. Beck must also have been hiding for now he emerged from cover and began striding up the densely wooded slope. After a moment, Hänschen set off in pursuit.

Hauptsturmführer Diels steered Meinder to a seat in the deserted *Gaststube* and called out for service. Meinder sat bolt upright, his hands resting on the stick between his knees, ill at ease in the presence of the Gestapo but helpless against Diels's persistence. During the short drive, Diels had already questioned Meinder on mutual acquaintances whom he might have in common with Beck.

When Diels shouted again for service, the Ukrainian servant girl came hurrying out, wiping her hands on a cloth. The linnets twittered a welcome to her.

'Two beers.' The inn was exceptionally quiet. None of the normal background sounds from the kitchen or from the office. 'Where's *Herr* Runge?'

Vishnia held an imaginary telephone to her ear, then mimed Runge driving a car.

'No matter. Just tell *Hauptmann* Beck that his comrade is here.'

Vishnia pretended to be pulling on an overcoat before letting her fingers walk across the bar.

'He's gone for a walk,' exclaimed Diels angrily. 'Didn't he know we were coming?'

Vishnia shrugged and moved her hands together to signify a short walk.

'Maybe Runge had to leave before he had the chance to tell Beck,' suggested Meinder, not at all sorry that the Gestapo man could not listen to them converse.

'Where's he gone?' demanded Diels.

Vishnia shrugged and wiped froth off a beer mug with a spatula.

Diels was furious. His inquiries about this man Beck to Italy, Africa and Cologne were still incomplete. Cologne police confirmed that there had been a Beck family who had all perished in the Thousand Bomber Raid. They had a son in North Africa. That had not taken his inquiries forward a centimetre. When he complained about the *Wehrmacht*'s lack of cooperation, he was told most of 21st Panzer's records had been lost in an air attack. The hospital in Italy had finally called – just to say they could not find any records of a Captain Beck but they were still looking. They too had been bombed. Diels was still backing his hunch. There was something not quite right about Captain Beck.

Vishnia carried the two beers to the table and went back behind the bar. If Diels had not been so angry, he might have noticed that Vishnia kept her hands out of sight beneath the counter. The big old Mauser was heavy for her frail wrists but she could hold and aim it with two hands. Beck had shown her how to take off the safety catch. All she had to do was pull the trigger.

Ilse could not sit still. She had laid out the *Linzertorte* on the round table dominating the main, circular room of the Mooslangerkopf tea house and tried to compose herself as she waited for the Führer and his party to arrive. Unable to relax, she flopped in a soft chair and struggled to read a magazine but her eyes wandered aimlessly over the pages. She put down the magazine and began rearranging the burning logs in the fireplace. Finally, she made herself go out to the promontory, where she stood gripping the rails as though testing the strength of the wood. Behind her, a thin cord of blue smoke rose into the clear, still air.

Leutnant von Renn, the young *SS Leibstandarte* officer in charge of the guard, could have been chosen as the epitome of the Nazi ideal. With his white-blond hair and straight Nordic features he could have stepped straight out of the racial purity posters. Because von Renn worshipped Hitler, he interpreted Ilse's agitation as the natural nervousness of someone about to meet their god face to face.

'The view is spectacular, isn't it?' he asked, making an effort to put her at her ease.

Far below, the waters of the Ache raced between conical wooded hills towards Salzburg and its archbishop's castle, a shimmering spot in the distance. Directly ahead was the stark mass of the Untersberg where Charlemagne supposedly slept. Down in the valley, she could even make out the ochre walls of the Red Ox. Ilse had occasionally accompanied Eva on walks up here before the war, when Hitler had been away in Berlin. Then she had marvelled at the panorama but today it made as much impression on her as a raindrop on a window pane. She liked the metaphor. She was like a pane of glass, she told herself: cold, impermeable, and brittle.

Her head seemed to be spinning, a dynamo whirring incessantly but getting her nowhere – racing in neutral. She worried and wondered if she had done the right thing. Ten past two: Beck would be getting on the train now. He had lied to her, used her, made love to her – and yet she could not feel angry with him. After the war . . . would they ever meet again after the war? She had not denounced him but she had not helped him. She had done nothing. Or had she?

Ilse was a good German. Her love for her country was indisputable – but even if she agreed with Beck that the Nazis were evil, did that give him the right to kill Germany's leader? Was one act of evil permissible to end a greater evil? Could she even believe the Führer to be evil? Her head ached as she was forced to confront questions she had done her utmost to ignore for so long.

Ilse put a hand to her forehead and massaged her brow. Out of this dark maelstrom of conflicting thoughts and emotions, she was certain only of one thing. She had at last found a man she loved. She said a silent prayer for him. *God speed. Go well, my love. Go well.*

A shot rang out, and Ilse bit back the scream rising in her throat.

Beck unscrewed the top of his walking stick and tipped it so that the barrel of the rifle slid into his hand. From the rucksack, he removed the two parts of the stock, the rifle's working parts and the telescopic sight. He assembled the rifle, lastly fitting the magazine holding five rounds, each weighed to a grain. One, or two at the most of these were for Hitler. The others might come in useful to dispose of any guards who picked up Beck's trail.

Beck pulled the brown sheet over his head, fumbling to find the armholes before smearing his face with dirt. In the car was a clothes brush, damp cloth and towel to clean himself up with on his return. His senses were in overdrive, nerves tingling as he fought to hold the body-juddering adrenalin under control. Instinctively, his tongue traced the outline of the suicide tablet, now firmly wedged in the gap between his upper molars.

The hidden dell was somewhere ahead of him. To the left lay occasional meadows set among the trees. He knew he must be careful not to blunder out into the open or go too close to the wood's edge where he might be seen by watching eyes.

It was time to begin putting into practice the stalking skills taught by his Welsh sergeant friend Taffy, all those weeks ago. *Silhouette.* Blend in with your surroundings. Never stand out against the light. *Shape.* Guards look out for a familiar shape like a man's body or a rifle. He fixed some twigs to the barrel with a specially hoarded elastic band while the poncho sheet broke up his own body shape. *Shine.* His watch was in his pocket and he had already rubbed dirt on the rifle barrel. *Shadow.* No worries there. *Movement.* Any small movement can betray you, even just working the action of your rifle. He'd have to chance it. Once he reached the secret dell he would lie up and make his final preparations.

Beck had changed his plans. The day was so fine that Hitler would inevitably stand outside the tea house to gaze over his favourite view. There was a spot towards the top of the glade that gave a clear line of sight to the Mooslangerkopf. The range was closer to five hundred metres than four hundred but cancelling out the problem of the extra distance was the advantage of having a stationary target.

Beck was moving cautiously uphill, keeping parallel to an alpine pasture, when he heard the snap of a twig. Someone was behind and below him. Beck dropped flat behind a fir tree. Some way beneath him, in the gloom of the forest, he made out the pale orb of a face appearing and disappearing. As it moved into a patch of light, Beck recognized Hänschen. The boy must have felt Beck's eyes upon him for he looked directly up at Beck and met his stare. Hänschen's nerve broke. He spun around and took off, running hell for leather diagonally down across the slope, following the same animal track that Beck had crossed a few minutes ago. At one point, Hänschen tumbled head over heels and disappeared for a moment before scrambling to his feet and haring off again, crashing wildly through the forest, his arms flailing to keep his balance. Beck saw that he would come out in the meadow close to where a path emerged from the forest opposite. The path crossed the open space before it doubled back in a hairpin bend to disappear back into the trees beside a rustic wooden bench.

Shit! Two SS guards had appeared. As Beck watched, they sat down on the bench. One fished in his top pocket and produced two cigarettes.

Beck considered his options. He would never catch the boy in time. To shoot Hänschen meant aborting the mission. Once he had fired the shot, he would have to flee instantly before the SS could seal off the mountain.

But what if he didn't kill him? Beck realized the boy must have followed him so that he knew about the car.

Beck had no option. He had to kill Hänschen.

Beck lifted the rifle to his shoulder and braced himself against a tree. He had once saved Hänschen's life. Now he would reclaim it. He made himself breathe easily, fixing both eyes on the point where the boy would emerge into the open.

There he was now. A dark figure flitting just inside the tree line. If he had known the guards were there, he had only to call out and Beck would be as good as dead. Beck worked the bolt and noted how surprisingly clearly the black of Hänschen's shirt stood out in the gloom of the close-packed trees. Hänschen stopped. He too had seen the guards. He began running towards them. Beck took up the first pressure on the trigger.

The cross-hairs began to track behind the speeding boy. Smoothly, they caught up with him. The guards jerked round towards Hänschen and a microsecond later Beck heard the boy cry out. As the cross-hairs moved ahead of the target, Beck exhaled and increased his pressure on the trigger.

The noise of the gunshot sent the birds rising into the air. The first round picked Hänschen up and flung him back against a sharp, jagged branch. The second removed half his face.

The booming shots echoed over the forest slopes until there was silence again and the only sound was that of the birds cawing and screeching in protest.

At the first shot the guards around the tea house had tensed, hard-eyed. At the second, they clicked back the bolts on their rifles and two men went crashing down through the trees to investigate.

'Did you hear where they came from?' demanded von Renn.

'Towards Spornhof, I think,' replied Ilse, one hand instinctively clutching her throat.

'Don't be alarmed. Gunshots aren't that unusual on Obersalzberg, especially when *Reichsmarshall* Göring's in residence. Don't worry. Nothing will be allowed to harm the Führer.'

The phone started to ring inside the teahouse and the lieutenant ran to answer it as Ilse gripped the wooden rail. All around her everything, including time, seemed to be moving in slow motion. She had the sensation of both watching and taking part in some grainy old news film.

The lieutenant, still clutching the phone, put his head out of the door to yell to his sergeant. 'The Führer set off from the Berghof ten minutes ago. Take four men up the path to meet his party.'

A few minutes later a red-faced guard panted up the steps. Von Renn ordered him inside the tea house to make his report. Ilse drifted away in her own melancholy thoughts. She sensed the shots had something to do with Beck. Two shots? Maybe he had been discovered. Maybe he had fired and someone had shot back. He could be lying dead on a carpet of dried pine needles. *A soft bed for my love.*

Her thoughts were disturbed by the shrill ringing of the phone. She moved closer to the tea house to listen.

Von Renn was standing to attention, holding the phone just inside the door. 'The intruder was a boy, *Reichsleiter*. A *Pimpf* . . . He burst out of the wood, against the sun. The guards were warned to be especially vigilant because of the assassination alert. The boy should not have been there . . . No, both shots hit him . . .' The lieutenant visibly relaxed, his shoulders dropping in relief. 'Yes, *Reichsleiter*, excellent shooting ... Absolutely. The boy was trespassing. The guards were merely obeying your orders to shoot first and ask questions later. Thank you. I'll pass on your commendation. No, *Reichsleiter*, I've no idea what the boy was doing there. No doubt the Gestapo will want to ask his parents a few questions ...'

Ilse wandered back onto the viewing promontory in a dream. It was dawning on her that Beck was not involved; that he had not been killed. He was still alive. And with that came the dull and certain knowledge deep inside her that he was out there, somewhere on the mountain. She sensed his presence firmly enough to know her intuition was correct. She put her hand over her stomach, which felt as flat as it had always been. Again intuition: his baby was in there. She was certain about that, too.

Von Renn came out, mopping his brow.

'What happened?' asked Ilse.

'Some youngster trespassing,' he replied, almost apologetically. 'Perhaps it was a prank or maybe he just wanted a glimpse of the Führer. It was irresponsible and he's paid for it. But it couldn't have come at a worse time, with all the guard dogs chained up.'

'Why's that?'

'One of them almost killed *Fräulein* Braun's little black dog last year. Since then they've been locked up when either the Fräulein's dogs or the Führer's dog Blondi are let out.'

Beck, twenty feet up a pine tree on the edge of the glade, watched through the telescopic sight as Ilse smiled at the lieutenant, an embodiment of Nazi perfection. He let the cross-hairs drift onto the man's chest. It would be like shooting fish in a barrel. There was no wind and he had a firm firing position wedged in the branches. Ilse looked back down the slope and her gaze began coursing over the treetops as if searching for something, or someone. She wrapped her arms around herself and rocked gently as if she was cold. Did she know yet that Hänschen had been killed? The guards had been trigger-happy but, with luck, finding the intruder had been only a small boy should have allayed their fears.

Ilse had stopped scanning the woods. She was looking directly towards him, as though she could see right through the canopy of trees, straight into his soul. Beck shivered.

Esser fussed and fidgeted, picking up a phone and putting it down again, swearing that he'd have all the cowardly operators sent to a *KZ* before the day was out.

'The lines could be down,' suggested Jäger, drawing heavily on a cheroot. He was as anxious and frustrated as Esser but he refused to show it. Wulzinger sat in the corner of their office, pretending to read a newspaper, keeping well away from the tension growing between his superiors.

Esser began drumming his fingers on the edge of the desk, beating out one rhythm after another.

'You could use the teleprinter to speak to Berchtesgaden Gestapo,' suggested Jäger. Anything to stop this bloody man getting on his nerves any more.

'The damn thing's not working. A mechanic's trying to fix it.'

Jäger's phone rang. He snatched it up before Esser could reach it. There was a woman's voice, faint and scratchy and sounding far, far away.

'Hello, hello.'

'Monika, is that you?'

'Yes. I've found her.'

'What the hell are you doing? Get off that line!' Esser erupted in anger. 'You haven't got time for personal calls.'

Jäger swivelled in his chair so that his back was towards Esser.

'And?'

'I've told her everything. It came as a shock to her. She won't be so foolish in the future. She's moved back in with Hanna.'

Other phones began ringing on the *Kripo* floor as, outside, the all-clear siren sent up its continuous high note.

Esser was turning purple with rage, his eyeballs bulging from their sockets.

'I'm staying here for a while,' Monika continued.

'Okay.'

'You don't need me. Alix does.'

'I said, okay.'

'If you ever sort things out, you know where to find me.'

The line went dead.

'Shit!'

Esser was beside himself with fury. 'I'll break you for this. How dare you put your own family before the Führer and the Fatherland? I won't forget this.'

'Neither will I,' said Jäger drily. He tapped the bar on the phone for the operator. 'Get me the Red Ox inn in Berchtesgaden.'

'The Führer's still coming here?' asked Ilse.

'Yes.' Von Renn hesitated. '*Reichsleiter* Bormann does not want the Führer to know that anyone's been shot.' He peered keenly at Ilse. 'Excuse me, *Frau* Runge, but are you all right? You look as though you've seen a ghost.'

'Forgive me. The shooting's upset me . . .'

Ilse knew what he was really thinking. Hitler hated to be near anyone who was ill or sick. Von Renn was clearly debating whether it was his duty to shield his Führer from this woman who looked as if she might faint at any second.

'Are you sure you feel strong enough to meet the Führer?' he pressed.

Ilse did not hear him. Beck must be closer now. She felt his presence more strongly. He had told her that there was a train to Bad Reichenhall at quarter past two. She recalled his words exactly. He had not said he would necessarily catch it.

I know you're here and I know where to find you. I know exactly where you're hiding.

'*Frau* Runge?'

Ilse came out of her reverie to find von Renn scowling at her. 'Perhaps I'd better go,' she murmured.

'I'll offer your apologies,' he said, a little too eagerly. 'One of my men will escort you to the car.'

'That's kind of you, but *Fräulein* Braun and I were walking this mountain while you were still in military academy. I know my way and I'm sure your men would be better staying here at the service of the Führer.' She complimented herself on such a pretty speech. 'That is, unless there are other intruders on the mountain?'

'You have my word you'll be safe, *Frau* Runge.' The young lieutenant drew himself up. 'Extra guards are even now being posted around the perimeter to ensure the Führer's safety and to discover how the boy got in.'

'Excuse me, sir.' A corporal slammed to attention. 'The Führer is due here in less than ten minutes.'

'I'd better go,' murmured Ilse. 'Give my apologies to *Fräulein* Braun. Tell her I'll phone her later when I'm feeling better. I hope they enjoy the cakes.'

In Runge's office at the Red Ox, the phone began ringing, a shrill, insistent sound. Diels looked at Vishnia but she ignored it. The ringing did not stop and it began to irritate him.

'Why doesn't someone answer it?' he muttered to Meinder.

The ringing stopped, only to start up again straight away. It was really getting on his nerves. The Ukrainian girl stayed behind the bar counter, pretending to polish glasses. Diels's antennae started twitching. Something was wrong. It was unusual for there to be no one else here – and that bloody phone was unremitting. Someone was trying very hard to get through.

He rose and the Ukrainian girl started. For a moment he thought she might attempt to stop him going through to the back. He felt her eyes on him as he picked up the phone.

'Red Ox inn.'

'Jäger. Munich *Kriminalpolizei*. I want to speak to Diels, the Gestapo man.'

'This is Diels speaking.'

'Didn't you get my message to call me?'

Diels bristled. Gestapo men were not used to being spoken to by coppers in such a way. 'What message?'

'Regarding the officer staying at the inn . . .'

'No.'

'We've discovered he's a British agent, sent to kill the Führer.'

'What!'

'Where is he now?'

'I don't know. There's no one here.'

'Shit. Runge was supposed to alert you.'

Diels felt for his pistol in his shoulder holster. 'He's not here. There's no one here.'

'I'll alert the *Kommandozentrale* on Obersalzberg.'

'No,' said Diels, sharply. 'I'll do that from here.'

'I can do it myself.'

'That will not be necessary,' said Diels coldly. 'The protection of the Führer is the responsibility of the Gestapo. No doubt you will be thanked for your efforts in due course.'

Jäger understood. Others wanted to reap the glory of his discovery. 'Okay, but get on with it.' The line went dead.

Diels put down the phone, a small smile of satisfaction on his normally expressionless face. He turned to see the Ukrainian girl standing in the doorway. She was struggling to hold an old-fashioned Mauser automatic, massive in her frail hands.

The first *boom* hurt her ears and almost made her drop the gun in shock. The shot sent Diels staggering back against the desk. He slid down to the floor in a sitting position.

Vishnia took three uncertain steps until she was almost touching his body. Then she fired again and again.

The air was thick with smoke and cordite and her ears were ringing. Dimly, she heard Meinder calling out from the *Stube*.

Vishnia would deny the Nazis their final triumph. She stepped over Diels's corpse to sit at Runge's desk. She reversed the heavy pistol, resting its handle on the surface. She hooked her thumb through the trigger guard and bent to take the hot, smoking metal in her mouth. In her other hand, Vishnia held the locket of her mother's hair.

*

Ilse looked down on her secret glade with a bottomless sadness. She felt a yearning for safe times, long past. Her life was about to change for ever. Beck was *here*. She knew he was. The stream gurgled and cascaded over the black rocks into the pool below. At the water's edge, two yellow wagtails bobbed. Out of the corner of her eye, she saw a high branch in a fir tree bend, then straighten. She crept lightly forward over the soft pine needles. Twenty feet above her, she made out a dark shape.

'How did you get up there with your bad leg?'

Beck almost jumped out of his skin. He whirled around, the rifle pointing at Ilse.

'I said, how did you get up there?' repeated Ilse softly.

'How did you find me?' His voice betrayed his nervousness.

'I knew where to look. I haven't told anyone. Come down.'

Beck did not reply.

'The Führer's not coming. He turned back when he heard the shots. You're wasting time. You must get away.'

Beck swore under his breath. That bloody kid had spoiled everything. It made sense that Hitler had turned back. He was paranoid about his security. The news that even a child could penetrate the security of mountain fortress would send him scurrying back to his burrow. *Shit!* So near and yet so far. Just three and a quarter pounds of trigger pressure and Hitler would have been dead. Reluctantly, Beck began to climb down, taking infinite care not to shake the branches, until he stood in front of her.

Ilse reached forward and removed a twig from his hair in an unconsciously intimate gesture. Then she slapped his face so hard that Beck rocked. 'That's for lying to me. You said you were catching the train.'

Beck rubbed his cheek. 'I thought you were supposed to be in the tea house. What are you doing here?'

'There was no point staying there any longer,' she said glibly. 'I came to warn you. The guards are inspecting the perimeter fence to find where the intruder got in . . .'

Beck noted that she did not know that Hänschen had been the intruder. He did not enlighten her.

'They might find the hole – if you came in that way.' His eyes told her that he had. 'And they're about to release the dogs to flush out anyone else who's on the mountain – as soon as Eva's pets are safely inside. You must run immediately.'

She was right. The minutes were ticking away. Hänschen would be traced back to the Red Ox. There, investigators would discover Runge's body and then all hell would break loose. With Hitler safely back in the Berghof, there was nothing to be gained staying here. Time to fly. *He who fights and runs away, lives to fight another day.*

Ilse was regarding him gravely, her face latticed by shadows.

Beck turned for one last glimpse of the Mooslangerkopf, the place where he could have changed the course of history. From their position, two yards inside the forest, he could clearly make out the promontory and the red-brick tea house with the smoke rising slowly like an Indian rope trick.

A group of people was standing by the rails: men in uniform and one woman. A short man in an officer's cap and a field-grey overcoat was pointing down the valley towards Salzburg. Beck whipped the rifle to his shoulder and peered through the telescopic sight.

Hitler!

The bitch had lied to him. There was still time to kill the Führer. Beck's lips narrowed. He wedged himself against a tree, feeling again the sticky resin on his hands.

'No! No!' Ilse pushed the rifle aside.

'Get out of my way.'

'Please, Christian. Please.' Her voice shook with desperation.

'You lied to me.' The sight swung onto the group.

Ilse grasped the barrel.

'I wanted to save you. Don't sacrifice yourself.' She closed her tear-welling eyes for a moment. 'You're going to have to kill me, Christian. Kill me too. And how are you going to do that? Shoot me? A shot will alert the guards. Stab me? You haven't got a knife. Will you strangle me with your bare hands? Is that what you'll do, Christian?' She was chanting the words in a breathless, jagged monotone. 'Will you gobble me up like the Wolf? I'll be *Rotkäppchen*, shall I? You'll gobble me up. You'll consume your own child if you do.'

'What!'

If Ilse had been a man, Beck could have killed her in seconds. As it was, he was helpless against a woman, especially the one he loved.

'I'm having your baby.'

'You can't know that.' The group was breaking up, shuffling, re-forming. The one he thought was Hitler had moved to the left now. The shot was becoming more difficult.

'A mother's intuition.' Ilse saw the disbelief on Beck's face. 'I wouldn't lie about our child.'

Beck saw she was serious. But . . . but . . . just because Ilse believed it, was it true? And did it matter?

Of course it mattered. Ilse was returning to the inn to face torture and certain death. The Gestapo would take their revenge on her. How long would they keep her alive while she prayed for release?

Hitler was turning round. He had taken one, two steps away from the railings. Eva Braun was standing in front of him.

'I love you, Christian.'

He could not kill Ilse. He could not let her return. He could not leave her.

'I'll love you until I die. Go. Save yourself.'

Only Hitler's upper body remained visible. In a second he would disappear completely.

Beck gave a sad smile, one half of him in the past, the other in the future. Lines of verse echoed through his head.

> I balanced all, brought all to mind,
> The years to come seemed waste of breath,
> A waste of breath the years behind
> In balance with this life, this death.

He became aware that Ilse had extended her hand towards him; a slim, pale hand extended in benediction. The blessing of a Good German.

All around them, the woods fell silent.

Hitler was in profile, looking back towards his native Austria.

Their hands touched. 'Run.'

'Run?'
'Run. Away. Together.'
'Together?'
'Together.'

Aftermath

Beck and Ilse drove safely to Rosenheim where they stole another Party-owned VW. Now he was with Ilse, Beck ignored the crossing at Feldkirch. Instead, by mid-evening, they had reached Bregenz on the Bodensee. Stopped by a suspicious patrol just two kilometres from the border, Beck used his silver identity disc to brusquely order them not to poke their noses into the Gestapo's affairs. The soldiers were only too happy to oblige. Finally, Beck and Ilse crossed the border on foot. Initially, they were treated as pariahs by British intelligence in Berne before being given a safe house in the remote Mattertal where they were married by the local pastor in September. Ilse gave birth to their son on Christmas Eve 1943. When France was liberated, they were sent to Britain where they saw out the remainder of the war on the Isle of Man. In 1946 they and their son emigrated to Canada. Ilse never set foot on German soil again.

Dr Meissner was arrested and tortured to death in the cellars of the Wittelsbacher Palais, the Gestapo headquarters in Munich, sometime in April 1943.

Hugo Guttmann died in the Mauthausen concentration camp near Linz on 22 November 1944.

His wife Myra died of typhoid in Ravensbrück in the first week of February 1945.

*

On 20 July 1944, Count Claus von Stauffenberg placed a bomb in a briefcase under the table less than twelve feet from Hitler in the conference room in the Wolf's Lair – and left the room. When another officer moved the briefcase, Hitler escaped the explosion with nothing more than minor cuts and singed hair. Months of vengeance followed. The principal conspirators were hanged with chicken wire.

Admiral Canaris and Hans Oster continued to shield anti-Nazis and further the fledgling resistance wherever possible. They were arrested following the assassination attempt on Hitler in 1944 and executed in the Flossenbürg concentration camp in April 1945, just before the Americans arrived.

SS *Obergruppenführer* Ernst Kaltenbrunner was put on trial at Nuremberg. He protested he was being used as a scapegoat for the crimes of his predecessor Reinhard Heydrich. He was hanged.

Heinrich 'Gestapo' Muller vanished off the face of the earth at the end of the war. He had used his position to painstakingly remove every picture of himself from public archives and newspapers. To this day, no one knows what he looked like – or what happened to him.

SOE again considered killing Hitler in 1944 when British fear of American disapproval had lessened. This time, the plan was codenamed Operation Foxley. Surprisingly, the plan for one or two snipers disguised as members of a German mountain regiment to kill Hitler while on Obersalzberg was based on Private Pabst's story – which somehow survived the shredding that followed Operation Nightshade. As late as March 1945, SOE recruited Captain E. H. Bennett, a military attaché in Washington, as their chosen marksman. An alternative plan involved an SAS team parachuting onto the mountain and attacking Hitler's armoured Mercedes-Benz using a Piat bazooka as he drove back up from the tea house to the Berghof. By the time the plans were finalized, the end of the war was in sight and they were redundant.

Eva Braun married Hitler late on the evening of 28 April 1945 in his bunker under the burning remains of Berlin. Not twelve hours later, pale but composed, she said goodbye to the few friends still left. Wearing a dark blue polka-dot dress, her favourite brown Italian-made shoes and a platinum watch studded with diamonds, she embraced the women and smiled at the men, who each kissed her hand. Then she and Hitler withdrew to a small room, twelve feet by nine. They sat together on a couch. Eva bit into a phial of potassium cyanide. She was found with her head resting on Hitler's shoulder. In dying, she had flung out an arm and overturned a vase of flowers on the table in front of her. In death she looked at peace. Hitler shot himself in the right temple with his 7.65mm Walther pistol. Their bodies were subsequently doused with petrol and burned in the garden above the bunker.

Gilbert never made director-general; nor was his acting rank of brigadier ever substantiated. He reverted to lieutenant colonel when SOE was dissolved in indecent haste at the end of the war and saw out his service in a War Office backwater. He had realized as soon as he heard of the attack on Annie Cunningham where his wife had been for those missing twenty minutes. They never mentioned it in their increasingly bitter and loveless relationship – proof, as their dwindling circle of friends said, that hell was indeed other people.

The SA systematically ransacked the Red Ox. The surviving shell of the building was hit in the daylight raid by RAF Lancasters on Obersalzberg on 25 April 1945. Its remains were razed to the ground in the late 1940s. No trace remains today.

Another Time; Another Land

The pretty young girl held open the outer door of the porch with one hand and looked at the perspiring man in front of her.

'I'm sorry. If you want to talk about the moon mission, you'll have to go through NASA. My father's not allowed—'

'No, I've come to see *Mrs* Greenslake. You must be her daughter.'

'Why do you say that?'

The man brought out a photograph and handed it to the girl. 'I phoned earlier. My name's Fred Blunt, from the *Sunday Times* in London.'

'Mom didn't mention anything, but she does forget . . .' The girl's voice tailed off as she examined the faded black-and-white photograph of a beautiful young woman flanked by two army officers. Even though the woman was in uniform, nothing could disguise the sheer love of life pulsing off her. 'Gee, is this mom?'

'You're very much like her.'

'I wish!'

'*Is* your mother at home?'

'Yeh. She's asleep. She usually has a nap in the afternoon. I guess you'd better come in. My name's Miranda, by the way.'

'Hello.'

Miranda showed him the way into the cool sitting room filled with large chintz-covered pieces of furniture. 'You haven't come all the way out to Florida just to see mom?'

'No. It's a fortunate coincidence. I'm here to write a piece on the attempt to put a man on the moon but Penelope Frobisher said your mother lived in Florida. She gave me this photograph. Do you know Mrs Frobisher?'

'Sure. Classy English lady. She and mom used to be best friends in the dark ages.' Miranda performed a perfect forward roll over the back of an armchair to end up sitting pertly upright. She grinned in delight at her trick. 'So why do you want to see mom?'

'I'm researching a book on a secret British wartime organisation called Special Operations Executive and I came across a tantalizing reference to a plot to assassinate Hitler . . .'

'And mom's involved! Wow!'

'Well, I don't know. It's not easy to find out. Many people are dead; others are unwilling to talk and most of the records are still closed. Then, of course, many files were deliberately destroyed when SOE was broken up so suddenly at the end of the war.'

'So you're a detective?'

'No. I'm a journalist who writes books. Mrs Frobisher said your mother spent the best part of two years recovering from being attacked in the blackout in London.'

'Yes, I heard about that. She came back to the States in 1945 and that was when she met my dad. He was a test pilot then. He looks after her well. Who're the other guys in the photo?'

'The elder man is an Oxford don called Geoffrey Cricklemarsh. He passed away last year before I could speak to him. Sadly, after both his sons and his wife died back in the war, he became a recluse in the deepest groves of academe. Lived a very solitary college existence.'

'And who's the young, good-looking one?'

A sound made Blunt look towards the hall. An elegant woman stood in the doorway. Blunt recognized her instantly: the same high cheekbones, the same full mouth. Only the hair was different. Instead of falling darkly onto her shoulders as in the photograph, it was cut short – and it was pure white.

Miranda ran to her mother and gave her a hug. 'Mom, what are you doing up so soon?'

'I heard voices. I'm fine, I've had a rest. Now, what about some grape juice, eh?'

'Sure.'

Blunt rose to shake hands. 'We spoke on the phone yesterday.'

Mrs Greenslake brushed her fingers through her hair. 'I'm sorry. My memory is not my strong suit. Please forgive me.'

'I've brought a photograph from wartime London to show you. I was wondering if it might ring any bells.' He held out the picture.

'Wait. I need my glasses.' Mrs Greenslake moved towards a large Welsh dresser and began searching along the shelves.

'I was explaining to your daughter that I'm researching a book on SOE. Penelope Frobisher says she vaguely remembers you were involved in a small department with some scheme to assassinate Hitler.'

'Oh.' Annie Greenslake found her horn-rimmed glasses. She held out her hand for the photograph. 'Is that me? God, I look young.'

'It was twenty-six years ago,' replied Blunt. 'Can you remember anything about the men with you?'

Annie Greenslake screwed up her face in concentration. 'Yes,' she said finally. 'That older one with the pipe had a funny name. He came to see me in hospital. Crickslade, Crickhowell . . .'

'Cricklemarsh.'

'Yes, that's it. Whatever happened to him?'

'I'm afraid he died recently. What about the young man? It's possible he was your assassin. Penelope Frobisher thinks you were sweet on him.'

Annie squinted at the boyish, open face of the young man. She shook her head regretfully. 'I lost my memory, you see. There's almost a year of my life missing. I'm sorry but I don't ever remember seeing him before. What's his name?'

'I wish I knew.'